TURN THE DIAL FOR DEATH

Jeremy Vine is a journalist and broadcaster who reaches an audience of millions per week. He hosts a daily breakfast show on Channel 5 and a peak lunchtime slot on BBC Radio 2, presenting news, views, interviews and popular guests on Britain's most listened-to radio news programme. He has previously hosted *Eggheads* and *Points of View* among others.

He lives in London with his wife, two daughters and two cats. In his spare time, he rides a penny farthing.

- @theJeremyVine
- @thejeremyvine
- @TheJeremyVine

Also by Jeremy Vine

The Diver and the Lover

The Sidmouth Murder Mysteries
Murder on Line One

Non-Fiction

It's All News to Me
Your Call: What My Listeners Say and Why We Should Take Notice

Jeremy Vine

TURN THE DIAL FOR DEATH

HarperCollins*Publishers*

HarperCollins*Publishers* Ltd
1 London Bridge Street
London SE1 9GF

www.harpercollins.co.uk

HarperCollins*Publishers*
Macken House, 39/40 Mayor Street Upper
Dublin 1, D01 C9W8, Ireland

First published by HarperCollins*Publishers* Ltd 2026

1

Copyright © Jeremy Vine 2026

Jeremy Vine asserts the moral right to be identified as the author of this work.

A catalogue record for this book is available from the British Library.

ISBN: 978-0-00-870710-1 (HB)
ISBN: 978-0-00-870711-8 (TPB)

This novel is entirely a work of fiction. The names, characters and incidents portrayed in it are the work of the author's imagination. Any resemblance to actual persons, living or dead, events or localities is entirely coincidental.

Typeset in Sabon LT Pro by HarperCollins*Publishers* India

Printed and bound in the UK using 100% Renewable Electricity at CPI Group (UK) Ltd

All rights reserved. No part of this publication may be reproduced, stored in a retrieval system, or transmitted, in any form or by any means, electronic, mechanical, photocopying, recording or otherwise, without the prior written permission of the publishers.

Without limiting the exclusive rights of any author, contributor or the publisher of this publication, any unauthorised use of this publication to train generative artificial intelligence (AI) technologies is expressly prohibited. HarperCollins also exercise their rights under Article 4(3) of the Digital Single Market Directive 2019/790 and expressly reserve this publication from the text and data mining exception.

*To my lovely mum, Diana S. Vine
Born in 1939, baffled by 2025, but still the
greatest company on a Sunday afternoon*

I know death hath ten thousand several doors
For men to take their exits; and 'tis found
They go on such strange geometrical hinges,
You may open them both ways: any way, for heaven-sake.

― *The Duchess of Malfi*
Written by John Webster, 1612

CHAPTER ONE

In the weeks to come, the surname of the tall man and his daughter would be spelled incorrectly by almost every newspaper and website that covered the story. It was spelled wrongly now, and the girl's father had to correct the man with the strange sandy-coloured hairpiece who was bending over his flight book.

'There's no "e" in it, sadly.'

'So we are C-o-o-m-s, sir?'

'No. Keep the "b", so C-o-o-m-b-s.'

For heaven's sake! He was always having to spell it out. Call centres were particularly bad. That ghastly American rapper had not helped – he was Sean Combs. So now Andrew Coombs got Cooms, Coomes, Coombes, and Combs as well. Even Combes! How could anyone be Combes?

Clara, in a sing-song voice, tried to help. 'Double-o, then "m-b-s". Thank you!' Well, she was ten. Andrew Coombs ruffled his daughter's hair. 'I'm sure the nice man has got it, love.'

'And can I fly the plane for fun, like you promised?' said the young girl.

'She's joking,' said Andrew quickly. He ruffled her hair harder, accidentally catching the ribbon, trying to convey the message: *Don't say that, darling; not in front of the chap who runs the airfield. I'm a new customer.*

'That's not allowed, young lady.' The other man straightened up with an audible clicking of vertebrae and looked out of the window. He was wearing a pilot's jacket with service ribbons arranged in a line above the left breast pocket. He stared at the expanse of grass, mown down the middle in narrow strips to show pilots where to taxi. Beyond the strip, six single-propeller planes were parked side by side. Their noses faced the thick forest on the furthest edge of the apron, as if daring each other to take off in a slashing arc through the greenery. 'We're rather proud of this place. Devon's finest tiniest. And you notice something? No fence around the strip. We trust our locals here. Not like London.'

Andrew would not defend the capital city, even though it had been good to him. 'Yup. In London those planes would get smashed up in a minute.'

'Or be stabbed,' added the other man enthusiastically.

'Thank you very much, Mr . . .' He saw a name badge and read the name out loud, just as the man with the hairpiece said it too. 'Gracey.'

Gracey addressed Clara. 'Your daddy only just learnt to fly, didn't he?'

'My first flight,' said Andrew Coombs, answering over her shoulder in case Clara said the wrong thing again. 'I did the thirty hours and now I'm cleared for take-off. Fresh in my hand, look.'

'Still warm,' said Gracey, taking the flying licence with Andrew's photo. It said his age: forty-three. Andrew felt like an obvious banker, and knew that by paying his £1,200 fee up front without hesitation, he had nailed himself. He saw Gracey thinking: *A banker with an expensive hobby who is probably raising an expensive daughter, judging by the pink ribbons in her hair.* 'As you'll know, sir, we are a private airfield, all grass, short runways, so no Civil Aviation Authority inspections. Unlicensed but safe is how I like to see it. You mind me asking where you learnt your flying? Normally people take their first solo flight at an airfield they're known at.'

'Outer London. We moved down here before I could properly get my flying going. The wife wanted a decent view. There are no views in Pimlico.'

'So you took off?' Gracey laughed, enjoying his pun. 'Oh, it's beautiful down here. Proper country.'

'We're on the coast at Instow, and you love your new school, Clara darling, don't you?'

The little girl wiggled a nose full of freckles.

'She doesn't look so sure!'

'Daddy,' said Clara, 'I want to fly now.'

'Righto, young lady. Yours will be the Ikarus. Single engine. That one in the middle.'

He pointed. They followed his gaze. The middle one of six was meaningless, but Andrew knew the plane because he had done half his lessons with that model. They were in the airfield office, a stained-wood cabin on stilts which everyone jokingly called 'the ATC', for air traffic control, of which of course there was none.

Half an hour later, Andrew and Clara Coombs felt the ground beneath them give way as they took to the skies in the two-seater fixed-wing single-engine Ikarus C42 FB. In the ATC, Joshua Gracey looked on, pressing his trusty binoculars to his face. Something was worrying him, but he could not put a finger on what it was.

Andrew Coombs shouted, 'Can you hear me?' The engine was loud, so they wore caps with earpieces and wraparound microphones.

'We are going into the clouds!' said Clara. The October sun was suddenly dazzling. 'It's so small, this plane!'

'Just us two! Hey daughter, you can have control when we get up high, if you like!' shouted Andrew, laughing.

'And Daddy,' said Clara, 'I saw a starfish!'

He eased back the throttle, not sure he had heard her right. He pointed at the compact instrument panel, feeling his nerves abate as he recognized each control. 'These are for the ailerons, which roll us this way and that.' He showed her, tapping the control from the left and right. The plane banked twice, more than he was expecting. Clara screamed.

'And we call this the elevator – what do you think it does?'

'Up!'

'Up and down, yes, and this is the rudder.'

'Rudder goes left and right,' said his daughter.

'What's that about a starfish?'

'On the ground, a long way down, behind us. In the forest. Never mind!'

He must have misheard. They flew for another hour. The airfield was east of Chittlehamholt. They had flown ten miles north, above miles of lush green, until the houses arrived below them in singles, pairs, then clusters and lines, and then it was the ugly greys of Barnstaple. Easily he found the mouth of the River Taw. They took the river line west, heading south where it started to give into the Bristol Channel. They moved above and below the cloud cover, swapping warmth for a view of the landscape when he needed to find their way. Appledore and Bideford were below, and he swooped the Ikarus low to show Clara the work a group of enthusiasts were doing to restore the old train station at Bideford; not that the trains would ever run there again.

Now it was the River Torridge they were following, narrower and criss-crossed with heavy bridges. 'Heading back,' he said eventually, in his voice a pang of regret but also triumph. He was more confident than he expected.

He heard himself explaining the workings of the aircraft to Clara, and he could almost hear his daughter not listening. 'Roll, pitch and yaw are the three key words.'

'What about speed?' she asked.

'Well, yes, okay,' he said. 'Speed is this handle, the throttle.' He knew it was more complicated – the throttle was a way of controlling altitude too. 'You want to take it?'

They were blanketed by cloud now, and the cabin had cooled. He had the sudden sense of how mad this was, the art of flying – who ever thought you could suspend two armchairs three thousand feet in the air inside a tiny metal box, just by using an engine and some cute levers and buttons? *Don't look down*, he told himself. As they broke back through the cloud, he placed her hand on the throttle.

'If I speed up, I can show you the starfish.'

'Nothing sudden. Here, just a push to make it slower.' He eased off the trim – his instructor had called trim the 'cheap man's autopilot', because it enabled you to maintain a set altitude without constantly adjusting the yoke – but when he took the trim off, the yoke was harder to move than he expected, and the plane dropped fifty feet with its tail down.

Clara screamed and took her hand off the throttle.

'That's okay, love, all is fine.'

She calmed quickly and then, as they approached the airfield via the forested area along its northern edge, his daughter said: 'Look! There's the starfish!'

This time he knew he had not misheard. He looked. She was right. It was the strangest thing. A starfish lying on the forest floor . . . but if it was a starfish, it was six feet wide. No, that large white object below them was not a starfish.

'What the . . . holy . . .' he began.

He was not experienced enough to do what he wanted to do – slow the plane and take it down in a single motion, a combination of yaw and yoke, pointing the nose up with a sudden stab to lower the throttle. He did not know the plane, but he tried it. She thought he had cut the engine by accident, and instinctively reached for the throttle, thinking she was helping by pushing it to maximum. The plane was suddenly upside down and she was screaming.

Andrew Coombs felt himself blacking out, with no sense of where the sky and where the ground were. He looked furiously out of the canopy and saw trees. He saw, in a single instant, like the snapping of an old camera shutter, that the starfish his daughter had seen was a human form. There was a body on the forest floor dressed all in white; as the plane fell, it was as if the father and daughter were being dragged towards it.

The sound of an aircraft throttling, stalling, falling – if an aircraft can be heard falling in an empty forest – was the last noise on earth to reach the ears of Jonathan Wrigley. Wearing his white linen suit, he lay on the forest floor, arms outstretched, legs akimbo. Moving in and out of consciousness for what could have been minutes or hours, he knew he could not survive. The noise of the plane reached his ears and he opened his eyes. He strained one last time for life, but it was like using a length of cotton to stop a truck pulling away. The crossbow bolt had been fired so close to him that it must have gone straight through his body, straight through the centre of his heart. He had felt his torso flood with adrenaline, enough to kill him on its own. And then the blood came, internal of course, a body drowning in its own rivers.

He wondered who would find him. That plane – could they see him? Could they see the red rose growing on his chest; would they try to get help?

He was conscious for only another second. Somewhere the plane engine cut and he felt his face move into an expression of utter calm. Then the truck in his body pulled out with a roar and he was dead.

If the world had frozen at the exact moment of Dr Jonathan Wrigley's violent death near Chittlehamholt Airfield, the Ikarus two-seater would have been silent in the air, upside down, directly above him. But of greater relevance to the subsequent police investigation was the position of Thor.

The superhero had been tied to the ceiling of a cave by his arch-nemesis Gorr the God-Butcher. Each time Thor resists, Gorr ties him tighter with heavy gags and bonds he conjures from the air. The confrontation came one hour and nineteen minutes into *Thor: Love and Thunder*.

The relevance of Thor's position to Dr Wrigley's death was that at the exact instant Andrew and Clara Coombs hung in the air above Jonathan Wrigley, and Jonathan breathed his last, his wife Wendy was watching the scene in Gorr's cave – in a cinema in Barnstaple.

Her unshakeable alibi, as solid as the sinews on Thor's forearms, would be very important for two reasons. Firstly, the life insurance payable in the event of Dr Wrigley's death was just shy of seven hundred thousand pounds.

Secondly, his wife had bought the crossbow.

EIGHTEEN MONTHS LATER

CHAPTER TWO

Edward Temmis knew for certain that his boss did not want him to go into the room on the other side of that door. He raised his gaze from the polished brass handle to the two patches of sweat under the arms of the older man in front of him, spreading in the fabric of his shirt like colonial nations on a Victorian map. Pearls of moisture speckled his temples.

They both looked down at the brass knob again. Like a gunslinger, Edward reached for the cold metal first.

'Hey!' barked Douglas Aspinall.

Ever since his arrival in the southwest of England to run the troubled radio station on which Edward had his evening show, Aspinall had come over as the hair-trigger type. 'A heart attack waiting for a final ice cream', one of the DJs had unkindly called him. There were stories (surely untrue) that he had once jumped out of his car during a road-rage incident in London holding a fireman's axe. True, he was capable of a certain teeth-clamped charm. Once in a while he would smile, as if he was chewing the end off a cigar.

The London-based chief executive of the entire radio group had apparently known Douglas Aspinall at Leeds University. He had been prevailed on to come out of early retirement and be the acting boss at Sidmouth, the smallest of the sixteen stations. Edward had often wondered: who took that amount of low-level panic into retirement? If you were boarding a plane and saw Aspinall in the pilot's seat, on edge as he always was, you would turn around and head straight back to the airport bar.

The events before Douglas Aspinall's arrival were never spoken of by the staff in anything other than hushed tones. His predecessor Agnes Chan had presided over a series of disasters – or, as the official line went, 'decided on a career break to spend time with her growing family.' The list of shocks the station had suffered was so long and so lurid – including an industrial-scale fraud and two violent murders – that three-quarters of the staff from the period were gone. A small mercy was that some of the worst publicity had been avoided. Time had given the story the quality of legend. Among the few at the station who had experienced the events directly, there was rarely any direct reference to them. Most used just a two-word phrase: 'The Case'.

Now, as both men tussled for control of the door handle, for a second the controller became a Wild West character too – the squinting left eye and, across the top of his domed head, a crest of grey hairs, standing on end, dancing as if in protest at the body they were attached to. A foot taller, a big man, Edward looked down at him. Douglas might have been a collection of ill-fitting limbs bought in a jumble sale and badly slotted into place.

Both of them held the doorknob now. They looked down at the nest of fingers, alarmed at the physical contact. They froze.

'Don't go in there until you've listened to what I have to say.' Edward whispered. 'Why not, though?'

'What's happened to your voice?'

'I think I might be losing it. I felt an infection coming on this morning.'

'Jesus, Edward. An infection? Aren't you on air later?' Aspinall shrugged. 'We'll cross that bridge when . . .' He drew a quick breath, interrupting himself. 'Okay, listen up. This is meet-and-greet. Our audiences love meeting the . . . stars.' (Had he paused for a microsecond before the last word, worrying about exaggeration?) 'But unfortunately, we've been blown out by the others.'

Edward wanted to laugh but knew he must not. He was the oldest five-days-a-week presenter, but was still nearly twenty years junior to his average listener, whom he always pictured as a sixty-six-year-young grandmother. As her own exit loomed, Agnes Chan had savagely binned the last cohort of DJs who were over sixty. The Farmers, as they were nicknamed, had been vile and sometimes even racist towards her. Her putsch against the last three became known as The Night of the Long Combines – but, once she had quit herself, the rump of the station had to soak up the resulting audience fury.

Douglas Aspinall's response on arrival had not been what was expected. Instead of shoring up the schedule with new pensioner-presenters, he had rapidly brought in fresh faces in their twenties, including the station's first black and Asian DJs – respectively Miriam Tamla and a man called DJ Satan Fiendy, which had been misprinted as 'Stan Friendly' in the *East Devon Gazette*. It made the audience even crosser. The figures sank for months.

Adding to Aspinall's stress, the new generation were tricky to handle, as evidenced when a delegation went to see him to register a protest over RTR-92's new slogan. The young DJs said putting the words 'SLOW ENOUGH FOR DEVON' on the side of buses made the station look dull and would kill their social media. Aspinall responded by jumping out of his office chair and shouting, 'Dull? There was a murder here, for God's sake! How exciting do you want it to be?' Two of them reported him for bullying.

Then, out of nowhere, a small audience uptick occurred. Aspinall held celebration drinks for the new presenters but forgot to invite Edward. The evening was ruined before it started anyway. The *Gazette* published a column by Vic Turnbull, one of the ousted presenters, who called the slight rise in listeners 'dead cat bounce'. Turnbull, aged sixty-seven, had been removed from his morning show by Agnes and now appeared every week in the paper with a writing style as thick and salted as old gruel. 'Even a dead pet will move upward a teeny bit,' he wrote, 'if you drop it from high enough.' Edward received a passing mention, which rang alarm bells. 'I guarantee Edward Temmis, now the radio station's geriatric, won't even get to fifty before they do what they did to me – cart him to the abattoir and make him into questionable pasties.'

Turnbull's ugly turn of phrase highlighted a truth. As the most senior presenter, Edward had become the tribune of the very section of the audience that felt excluded and angry. The really furious ones were a lot older than him, but that was not the point. They had rioted – well, politely protested – when, at one point, Agnes Chan tried to depose Edward himself. They celebrated when she reversed her decision and reinstated him. 'We are getting our station back,' said an online post in a listeners' forum. He printed it and proudly used a magnet to stick it to his fridge door.

His new show was the same as the old one, just with a different producer and a fresh name: *The Temmis Session*. A local comedian had done a whole routine about it. 'They have chosen the one name you cannot say while drunk or on medication.' The small bounce in listening figures did not hide the pensioner anger. On the same listener forum Edward saw a post he resisted the temptation to print out:

RTR SCHEDULE
6pm–9pm: LOUD RACKET,
9pm–midnight: INTELLGENCE AT LAST.
MDGA

He discovered that MDGA stood for 'Make Devon Great Again'. He knew the oldies would stand up for him, but also that Aspinall resented their influence over his schedule.

'Talk to me, Edward, please, before you even think of turning that handle.'

'I was told to get down here by your office! An urgent call. "Go to the village hall in Harpford at four thirty because Douglas needs reinforcements". It was Chrissie,' added Edward, a reference to the controller's secretary that he immediately regretted.

'Well, of course it was Chrissie, and I will have words with her later. We can't put you out there on your own.'

'But the young ones haven't turned up!'

'No. Gen Z didn't make it. Better things to do than fulfil a work commitment,' he said bitterly. 'But of course I'm not allowed to say that, because it would be bullying.'

There was stirring on the other side of the door, and someone seemed to be blowing a whistle. 'We know you're out there!' came a croaking shout, followed by laughter.

Douglas withdrew his hand and shoved it deep into his jacket pocket, a signal that he trusted Edward not to go into the room just yet. He snapped his teeth together, forcing a grin. 'I've had a peek through the curtain. In English history, what did they call the century after the middle ages?'

'No idea. The Tudors?'

'Right, that's who we've got out there. That lot were middle-aged about a hundred years ago. And they are . . . tricky, Edward, okay? You understand? Tricky and cross with us, with me. The sodding Tudors.' He filled his lungs with air as if preparing for a regretful sigh. 'Not cross with you. I thought we'd get at least a few young couples. You know, the newer listeners we've brought in . . .'

The sigh came. It smelt of king prawns. Edward wondered if the fabled 'audience rise' might be Vic Turnbull's dead cat or even a rounding error. Hoarsely, voice a fading whisper, Edward said: 'What do you want me to do? I just came because I was told to.'

'Right. Listen up. As regards The Case,' said Douglas Aspinall, voice sunk to a similar whisper, 'obviously not a word on that because we can't concede liability and there's just the slimmest chance someone out there knows how to use a smartphone and you get recorded. *Capisce?* And also, regarding station direction . . .' Douglas reached again for the door handle, but this time he began to turn it. 'Keep saying that we are playing great music with presenters young and old. Use the word "inclusive" a lot. Talk about the sea.'

'Okay.'

'Look here, I didn't come out of retirement to be taken down by a posse of people in reinforced underpants.'

Thinking that no one said 'Look here' any more, Edward shook his head indignantly. 'I'm sorry if that's what you think of our audience. Why don't you come in with me? Just tell them I've lost my voice. Or if you like, I can go home.'

Another shout from the other side of the door.

'I can't come in with you because then we get the pantomime. I'll get booed and hissed. I'm Paula Vennells in all this. They're the subpostmasters. Go. You're on. You're the . . . the star.' Again, a staggering of the sentence; the infinitesimal pause before each word.

He added: 'Remember – inclusive.'

As his hand turned on the brass knob and the door opened for Edward, the controller faded away like a ghost. The door gave way onto a stage, which was not what Edward had expected. A stage he was now standing on. The sunlight outside was blocked by short, heavy curtains drawn across the fanlights in the upper part of the walls. He saw rows and rows of faces, and heard the polite applause as he moved towards them and a single spotlight which found his face.

*

'Firstly, I am sorry about the terrible state of my voice,' Edward Temmis began, 'and the younger presenters, who haven't made it.' The sentence came out wrong and caused laughter he was not expecting. He felt a little dizzy. 'I'm just a cog in this. I'm a tiny cog. I have a miniature role.'

The audience was hushed, trying to hear. In the silence he whispered, 'Is there a microphone? Could someone turn off this big light that's on me? And put on the hall lights again, or draw back the curtains? Please?'

He heard a man's voice mutter, 'Who's the diva?'

When the lamps came on, he looked at all the faces. He should not have been surprised to see Kim's mum Barbara here. The two were so close. The exchange of information was constant – the latest was that Barbara had a new boyfriend, who was a specialist in military re-enactments. Kim had joked that they spent the first month together just re-enacting Barbara's first marriage.

The older woman was a short, enthusiastic divorcee with two new hips and two old dogs. The world might have decided Barbara was fit only for retirement and daytime TV, but she had a lively brain, a good social life, and nothing got past her.

In Harpford Hall were also a number of faces he might see at his local church come Christmas. This was a sea of grey, and he felt sudden pride that these were his people; these were the ones who gathered around their radios for his show every night, who had paid their taxes and just wanted a little respect. They were his Republican Guard.

For some reason, Edward Temmis felt a stab of depression. He adjusted his hearing aid. He was less than half the man they thought he was. They wanted him to be Frank Sinatra. In reality he was Frank Spencer. He was not even a father any more. He was just a greying guy on a short-term contract living alone in a house that was falling off a cliff, doing a show-off job to prove the bullies at school they were wrong. What had he ever done?

Solved one murder. That was it.

A heavy velvet curtain in the wall above him was being jerked back. Through a fanlight came a broken beam of late afternoon sunlight. It fell directly onto three of the women in the middle of the hall. One reached immediately for sunglasses, the sort you saw in black-and-white pictures of cinema audiences watching early 3D films.

Pushing his voice to the limit, he said, 'This was billed as meet-and-greet the presenters, and I know there were four of our exciting young names on the bill, including' – he knew he must not mess this up – 'Satan, Honor, Tamla, and of course the brilliant Tessa K. They send their apologies. Satan especially is very sorry. I was drafted at the last moment. It's a great privilege to be here with you.'

He added, thinking of Aspinall's eager words: 'Inclusive. We are an inclusive station, sitting here by the open sea, the big sea, and it's great you all feel included still.' He should not have added the last word.

Edward decided to stare at Barbara for reassurance. She was nodding and smiling.

'I love the radio more than I can say. The pioneers – I once met Tony Blackburn. Wogan of course. And how we miss Annie Nightingale, and the chap who did the golf.'

'Did you meet Terry Wogan?' someone shouted.

'No,' Edward said, feeling his throat hurt and his voice getting fainter and fainter. A man with an untidy beard was dragging a microphone on a stand down the middle aisle. 'However, I once met someone who worked with Terry, for many years, in a lift.'

Again, he had misspoken. He was off his game. He saw the looks of puzzlement – some thinking 'Why was Terry Wogan working in a lift?' while others were perhaps unable to hear him at all. His voice was close to giving up and he could not elaborate.

'The microphone will help me here. Sorry everyone.' The base of the stand came at him first, the three prongs launched from below the stage by the man with the beard, like Neptune hurling a trident from the ocean.

He did his best, whispering for ten minutes about why he loved the radio and why he loved RTR-92. 'I am inspired by the sea,' he said. He remembered to use Aspinall's line: 'We are playing great music with presenters young and old.' Then, out of ammunition, he asked for questions. A line of four people jumped to their feet in the back row.

It was an odd movement – four of them, sitting next to each other, all jumping up at once.

Without asking to be called, the tallest one, a beak-nosed man with a long neck who wore a bright red golfing jumper, said: 'We respect you so much, Mr Temmis. But we need to know what is happening in the matter of our compensation.'

'I'm sorry,' said Edward, 'for what?'

But he already knew.

'My wife and I lost fifteen arsing grand in that scam no one talks about,' said the beaky man aggressively. 'I personally think we should bloody go public. It's time.' Beside him were three women. The middle one wore an anorak of such violent orange it seemed to be acting as a light.

The three women started speaking all at once. Numbers tumbled out, stories of pain and humiliation. *The Case.* He desperately wanted to make it better, to heal the pain of those who had been scammed. Although the perpetrator was now behind bars and the victims had got some money back, the rest of the money was gone; unrecoverable. The victims held the station in part responsible. And the station simply did not have that kind of cash.

Edward tried to say, 'I can't comment, I'm not allowed to.' He was helped by a man at the front – younger than the others, possibly in his late forties, maybe escorting his mother – snapping over his shoulder at the red jumper, 'This is neither the time nor the place.' Someone else shouted: 'No publicity!' But still the four stood there at the back, with the long-necked man in red saying, again and again: 'Fifteen arsing grand.'

He was so focused on the four that he failed to see Barbara Sinker had climbed onto the stage. He towered over his lover's mother. 'How did you get up here?' he tried to ask, but his voice had gone completely now.

Barbara raised her voice, almost theatrically. 'Can I say, Edward, how much we appreciate you being here?'

Applause, at last.

'And how much we understand the care you give us, the oldies?'

Warmer applause.

'Now . . .' she raised her voice a little and pointed. 'You four, don't just go on and on. I was a victim too. I don't blame this man.'

There was now even warmer applause, interrupting Barbara's next sentence.

'Perhaps, given . . . perhaps given the vocal difficulties Mr Temmis is having, I could help relay a message of some kind?'

Edward smiled apologetically. Ideally he did not want Barbara on the stage with him, but her support was probably what he needed. He wore a genial frown. He bowed his head and mouthed, 'Okay.'

'Great,' said Barbara. 'What can you tell the four at the back to help deal with it all, at least for this afternoon?' She laughed. 'So they can pipe down.'

'I promise we care,' Edward said in a whisper, pushing his voice. He adjusted his hearing aid, more from habit than anything. 'I really do promise.'

'May I have the microphone?' Barbara asked. 'You're not infectious, are you?'

He detached it from the stand and handed it to her. 'He says, "I promise we care,"' Barbara repeated. '"I really do promise", he said.'

'It's just that . . . in the radio station's vault, there isn't any money to refund you with,' Edward went on, looking from the audience to Barbara. 'They just have tomorrow sorted and that's it. But . . . we will have your back.'

What was he saying? It was a terrible word salad, bits of phrases, sticky-taped together, which basically meant the radio station would not compensate its listeners. He was only telling the audience what Douglas Aspinall wanted him to say. Yet it sounded hollow, and Edward suddenly knew what politicians felt like.

His hearing aid whistled as Barbara repeated the words. Strangely, they were greeted by a whoop from the four at the rear of the room, and soon the whole hall was cheering loudly.

Barbara looked delighted at the response and joined in, clapping and waving as if she had won a prize. The long-necked man and his three companions gave each other hugs and thumbs-ups and sat down. Edward blinked in amazement at how receptive the audience were. Perhaps The Case could rest at last.

But then the door at the back of the stage sprang open. Douglas Aspinall strode in, like a man trying to catch a bus without breaking into a run. His arm was outstretched – was he going to shake Barbara's hand? No, he wanted the microphone. The older man caught Barbara's elbow and ushered her off the stage. He turned to Edward, putting his back to the audience, face like thunder.

As the applause died down, Aspinall hissed at the presenter. 'Well, that was a total fucking disaster. Satan would have been better. Please get off the stage *now*, Edward, and I'll pick up the pieces, you absolute walloper.'

Edward felt his knees turn to jelly. A silence descended on the room. The audience had detected something was very wrong. Edward backed away towards the door at the rear of the stage, but Barbara must have heard Aspinall's words, or at least his tone. She had now climbed back up the steps at the side of the stage. As the station controller turned to the audience, she was in his face. The two were almost the same height and squaring up.

'If the words came out wrong, then that's on me.'

'Wrong? You two characters have probably just bankrupted my station!' hissed Aspinall.

Completely confused, Edward checked his movement, not wanting to leave the stage as directed. 'I'm sure it's not as bad as that,' he said. His voice was so weak he barely heard it himself.

Douglas made a diagonal move and came closer to Edward, like a chess piece in the hands of a player trying to avoid checkmate. 'She promised to pay them back! With what? And the stuff about us having to borrow – who, what, how? You are on borrowed time, matey, you and that soft-scoop show of yours.'

The words were hissed like darts from a blowpipe, each syllable arriving in an aerosol of spittle. Thrown, Edward did nothing but stand, arms at his sides, feeling like a schoolboy on detention. Leaning forward keenly, the audience could still not hear the conversation. Douglas turned to face them all and raised his voice.

'I don't want to cause any confusion. What my presenter has just promised didn't . . . it wasn't sanctioned.'

The man in the red jumper was on his feet again, yelling now. 'I LOST FIFTEEN ARSING GRAND!'

Barbara moved to the front of the stage, snatching the microphone from Aspinall. When she spoke into it, her voice had strength and clarity.

'Let's not spoil the afternoon. We are here because we love the station and we love Edward!'

The audience were too discombobulated to clap. But there was a murmur of approval.

'I don't think we need this now,' said Aspinall, but as he reached to take the microphone back from Barbara, she started a hymn. '"Then sings my soul, my Saviour God to Thee—"'

'"How great Thou art, how great Thou art,"' the rest of the audience joined in.

As Edward quietly made for the door at the back of the stage, the singing continued. Douglas Aspinall was shouting. Barbara was physically holding him off, shielding the microphone. The beaked-nose man was belting out the song louder than anyone. Beside him, the three women had linked hands. It was chaos.

Touching his throat, feeling the soreness behind the skin, Edward caught a final glimpse of the controller as he left. He had the strangest thought – there was no such thing as a radio station controller, especially not here in Sidmouth. His place of work was constantly, completely, delightfully out of control. And that was why he loved it.

CHAPTER THREE

In the car park Edward used a vape, a new habit. Aniseed. Standing there alone, he drew the flavoured steam down tentatively. It stung his throat, but he kept drawing on it. He reached for his hearing aid and found he had accidentally turned it off while he was on the stage. He could not work out what had happened in the hall just then, why Aspinall had been so enraged. The nicotine calmed him, but he also felt a little strength return to his voice and began trying to stretch it by humming. Might he even make his show tonight?

The presenter would always push to be on, would always be . . . *present*. That was the whole point of presenters. The microphone light went on, and they were there. A presenter would literally need to lose both legs to miss an appointment in the studio. A loss of voice was almost worse than a loss of legs.

He allowed himself a hoarse chuckle, then saw a woman approaching with a purposeful bustle that made him resentful. She was going to invade his space.

'Mr Temmis?'

'It's me,' he offered. 'I still don't know what went on in there.'

'Save that voice of yours. I'm new to the area,' said the lady.

She was immaculately dressed, with smooth skin and manicured nails. 'I'm a bit lost myself.'

His throat hurt, so he replied with a nod.

'Don't you answer. You're not on the radio tonight with that croaky voice?'

That was a useful prompt. He held up his index finger, as if to say 'Wait', and sent the text to his producer.

> Sore throat but I think I can make it.

The reply came straight back.

> Aspinall already told us no chnce. Don't worry. Hope you're well enugh to enjoy the weekend. Esther Thmpson already on way in. Melody

To save him using his voice, Edward showed the phone screen to the woman.

'Sweet, their concern,' she said kindly. 'Does vaping help the throat?'

Was the stranger lecturing him? 'I think I'm on the mend.'

'You'll get there. I do think there are a lot of chemicals in the modern world that exacerbate things. Personally, I stay away from lipsticks and mascaras. Blusher only. I always think—'

A screech of tyres at the other end of the car park interrupted her. It was Aspinall's car, wheels spinning, which had lurched out of its place and roared into the small gateway that emerged onto the road.

'The anger in that man,' the woman said. As it shot forward, the car broke a flowerpot, clipped by the back wheel. 'Your boss, yes? I was in the hall. I just think the old lady translated you badly, that was all.'

He tilted his head quizzically. The woman's voice was posh but with a trace of Midlands, maybe somewhere near Birmingham.

She went on: 'I heard it all because I was at the front. You said, "In the radio station's vault there is no money" – and somehow she made that into, "It's the radio station's fault there is no money." When you said, "We have tomorrow," it came out as, "We have to borrow."'

'Sweet Jesus.'

'You did say you'd pay them back.'

'I did not.' It was dawning on him, what had happened. He pushed his voice. The explanation was important. 'I just said, "We'll have your back." That's all I said. Not—'

It was too much. He looked at the woman. She had her hand over her mouth, in polite surprise or to suppress a giggle. She seemed unusually young to have emerged from the Harpford Village Hall audience. She was in her forties, like him, with a close auburn bob and a rayon jumper cinched at the waist. The outline suggested sport or healthy eating or both. Her skin was clear, her forehead free of lines. The tightness across her cheekbones gave her eyes the compact, radial intensity of a bird's. He had the instantaneous thought that the woman had had cosmetic work done. Botox, in Devon! Holding her spine unnaturally straight, on six-inch heels, she looked tall, even compared to him. When she smiled, he saw tiny bumps on her teeth that were applied to keep a dental mould in place, although the plastic liner was not there at the moment (vanity, because she was at a social event?). She wore classy earrings, small gold seashells. The warmth in her voice suggested great kindness, as though she was the sort who would stop to help a person who fell over in the street.

Yet she was also a little too perfect to be truly beautiful. Devon was a county of farms and coastal paths, the land of people who worked outdoors, the only place in the UK outside the Scottish Highlands where there was a degree-level course in dry stone walling. A person got used to seeing muddy boots and weathered skin, and, frankly, to hearing people break wind in supermarkets. This woman looked as if she had spent her life in a spa. She was the bone-china cup you were scared of holding in case it broke.

But what struck Edward most forcefully was an uncertainty about her demeanour, as if she was a supremely confident person who was suddenly having to deal with uncertainty. She dipped her head slightly as she spoke, like a bird at water.

'Were you part of – part of the . . .' He tailed off, choosing his words carefully. 'Were you part of The Case?'

'I know nothing about any case,' she replied. 'I've only just moved down here.' She looked embarrassed. 'I had to leave North Devon. It was a source of great sadness to me.'

At that moment, there was a round of applause and a cheer from inside the hall.

Had to leave North Devon. The phrase pinballed around Edward's head. 'Why?' he croaked.

'I was married to a wonderful man; we lived in North Devon for many years and we were so happy there. And then he died suddenly and I had to leave.' She fidgeted in her purse. The sun was high in the sky, and Edward wanted to move into shade. 'I'll be honest with you, it broke my heart. I loved where we lived, the sense of community we had there. I had so many friends . . .' She tailed off, looking down. Edward followed her gaze: her fingers were white where they pinched the edge of her purse. 'So I moved, and my neighbour, who doesn't know who I am, thank God – she suggested coming here today as a little outing. She says if I'm to live down here in Sidmouth, I should listen to your show. And then she said you were known for your investigating.'

He looked at her, stopped by the sentence.

'Investigating?'

'Like – you're a kind of secret sleuth. It's just . . . it seems to be something people know about you. That's what she said.' Her voice dropped. 'I hadn't wanted to offend you.'

'You haven't.'

'You see,' she said, 'people who loved me, or at least truly liked me, the people who ran the local charity, the people at church who went to see the old ones in the area and who I willingly volunteered with, the people at the whist club, at the school . . .'

She tailed off. All he had heard was 'people', as if everyone had banded together against her. 'No one will look at me. Not even the places I volunteered for. I have lost my position.'

Position. That, thought Edward, was such an interesting word. A century ago, it would have meant an actual job. She was using it differently, for something less tangible, but it carried the same load. Her status in North Devon had been as real as a payslip or an office chair. She had been sacked from the life she had had. The sacking – by all those 'people', that crowd of silent faces gelled into a giant moon – had exiled her.

'So,' she said, 'I wanted you to investigate something for me.'

Edward tried to laugh but his voice seemed to have gone completely now, his throat strained. *A sleuth?* If he had known the woman better, he might have leant towards her to speak into her ear to make himself heard, but instead he circled his index finger in the area of his Adam's apple and shook his head.

'Don't worry,' she said. 'Not the time. But let me give you my card. You might know the name.'

He looked. The card said WENDY WRIGLEY. In the lower corner was a Gmail address and a mobile number. Not knowing the name was a little embarrassing for Edward. He prided himself on being aware of local authors, local singers, especially folk artists who played at the Sidmouth Folk Festival. Was she a celebrity of some sort?

Edward turned the card over and pulled a pen from his jacket.

Cupping the card in the palm of his hand he wrote:

What do u want me to investigate?

When he showed the card to Wendy Wrigley, she chuckled as if at a private joke.

And then she replied softly, as if passing on a secret. 'Oh, that's easy Edward. I want you to investigate me.'

CHAPTER FOUR

The tyre was hissing. Kim Sinker wondered if she had time to fix it. She was fifteen minutes early; she was always fifteen minutes early. She had parked, felt the potholes in the road and then heard the grinding sound by the front left wheel. The sun was bouncing off the red roof, warming and blinding her, and she reached for her sunglasses as she moved towards the boot.

Popping the latch, she remembered. There was no spare tyre on her Porsche Carrera. The manufacturer had long since phased out spare tyres, 'to improve fuel efficiency'. Instead, the second-hand car had come with a tube of gunk, a jack and a compressor. It was her second red Porsche. The first had been a brand-new electric and she suffered too much with range-anxiety to keep it. When she traded it in for the 2004 Carrera, the dealer had mentioned that punctures were so rare she would not miss the spare: 'You just lift, seal, reinflate.'

She looked away from the tyre and up at the top floor of the property. From one flat to another. It was the last she would show that week, and was much more than a regular apartment – this was a rare penthouse in Sidmouth.

The lane was one road back from one of the finest seafronts

in Devon and the large block of private flats overlooked the cricket green.

The property was one she had always wanted to show. The flats had first been sold the instant they were completed. But she would have been at college when those sales went through, back in the early 2000s. Most residents tended to leave the place in a box. Their families often found a way of keeping the flat when the will was actioned. Sons, daughters and grandchildren all fell in love with their mum and dad's view of the sea, the brightness of the air. Being an estate agent, Kim would have liked 100 per cent inheritance tax and zero stamp duty. The more sales, the more turnover. No one should be allowed to stay in a place for forty years. But only death and divorce got them out of a spot like this. She laughed at the radical thoughts she allowed herself when she had a moment to reflect – positively North Korean.

Kim had parked diagonally. She would have to find out if the council had an action plan on the potholes; a single one could kill a sale.

She contemplated the flat tyre. She was not going to play the role of damsel-in-distress and call Edward. He was practical in his own way, but sometimes seemed to get lost inside his own head. She loved him for his warmth and humour, and the way laughter could roll from him like water from a stream, suggesting an infinite supply. Moments of sadness were understandable. She loved him for it all.

The picture of Edward in her mind spread warmth across her body. She had sold him that crazy property above Ladram Bay and the affair had begun then and there – just as crazy. Her using him rather than the other way around. Then he had lost his young son and disappeared from her life. Just before her own divorce, events had brought them back together.

She never expected him to be capable of the love he had shown her. She only saw the fire of her first marriage as she left it, like a driver watching a motorway pile-up in her rear-view mirror. Divorce from a violent husband was like a rebirth. But Edward, this six-foot-something, sideburned, badly dressed man in permanent need of a haircut, who moved at times – in his oversized shoes – as if he felt he had no right to fill a hole in the air: he had been torn, not reborn, by his son's death. Somehow he had willed himself to move beyond it. His love for her was a miracle.

Her phone was ringing, and she saw the name on her screen. As if her thoughts had drawn him. When she picked up, she heard a croak.

'Nightmare.'

'What? Who is this doing heavy breathing at me?'

'It's your boyfriend with no voice. I can't even do my show tonight,' rasped Edward at the other end. 'I think I now have five minutes of voice thanks to a pastille.'

'You poor thing.'

'Listen, I was at an event for listeners and your mum was there.'

'Why was it a nightmare?'

'She decided to translate for me because of my voice. And I gather she got a few things upside-down.'

'Like what?'

'Apparently I promised the radio station would compensate victims of The Case. I've just had a call from Aspinall; he was ultra-aggressive, but also laughing at me, which was worse. He said if I wanted the scam victims compensated, he would divert "your own modest salary, Edward" straight to them, or, better yet, I could find a way to turn my show into a ratings driver. Which he said was unlikely, as "your bloody show has fewer scoops than theatre interval ice cream". He was exceptionally rude.'

'Well, that's unfair. You're not there to break stories, you're there to talk about what's happening already.'

'He called me "The Official NFC".'

'What does that even mean?'

'"Next for the chop". Then he really started raging. He said if my show ever broke a story, it would probably collapse.'

'Bastard. Workplace bullying.'

'It all happened at Harpford Hall. I was speaking and I couldn't make myself heard. Your mum's translations were a bit wayward, to say the least, and—'

'Don't. I can't bear it.'

'Now Aspinall's furious. He says compensating the victims of the scam would be half a million quid. I didn't even say we would.' He coughed. 'Where are you? I wanted to talk to you about something.'

'What?'

'Something good, big. I don't want to get into it on the phone.'

'That's lucky because I can barely hear you, sweetie.' Kim kicked the flat tyre. 'I'm at Thirdfield Terrace with a puncture. Showing a gorgeous penthouse which I've lusted over for years.'

She turned to the cricket field. The green would need careful handling when it came to selling a property. 'The gentle sound of leather on willow in the summer' is what you had to say. Not: 'Long winter nights listening to teenage kids pissed on Strongbow snogging each other's faces off.'

Still, early May was the perfect moment to show the place. They'd surely been at the lawn with nail clippers, all those old buffers in scuffed flannels. The sun's rays touched the sea and scattered, lines of white razored in the deep green.

'This place,' she said, 'honestly. You should see it, Edward. It has everything.'

'Let me sort out your tyre while you're showing the flat,' said Edward. He landed on the same pun. 'You do their flat, I'll do yours.'

'Very good, but—'

'Really. I'll come over. It's something I don't need a voice for. Hey – do you know a Wendy Wrigley? The Birmingham crossbow—'

The line dropped for a moment, and her attention was taken by a middle-aged man with a stick walking up the terrace towards her. Was this her client? The name had been double-barrelled, so it could well be.

'Did you say crossbow, Edward? Hello? The line—'

'Yes. A woman came up to me this afternoon, and—'

Kim yelped as someone behind her tapped her shoulder. She whirled around to face the stranger, a young man in his late twenties, smirking, flat-foreheaded, with shiny blond hair swept backwards and outwards like a mane. 'Wait, baby, I think my client's here.'

The stranger repeated her words: '*Wait baby.*' Then he roared with laughter, as if he had just played the most incredible prank.

He was smartly dressed but oddly proportioned, with extra weight around his waist and nowhere else, making his body oval. His legs were locked straight, feet planted apart in red brogues as if he was squaring up for a fight he knew he would win. Kim had the thought that the manly stance was hollow – was he imitating an abusive father or school bully who had done him some long-remembered harm? The young man laughed again, a single loud yelp this time.

'I'll call you back shortly,' Kim said to Edward, then disconnected the call without waiting for an answer. She was a little disconcerted. This man must have sidled into position behind her, in his sharp suit and buffed shoes, despite the gravel underfoot and the fact that the only way around to this side of the road would have been via the cricket green. But rather than shake her hand or say his name, he turned. 'Ruhi, mate!' he shouted in a London accent. 'Over 'ere!'

A woman who might have been a model appeared between a line of five cars parked at the edge of the green. The contrast between the two could not have been greater. She was walking – almost floating – in their direction. She was tall and wore a dress so diaphanous that Kim thought she could see black underwear through it, or maybe no underwear at all. When Ruhi drew closer to them, somehow navigating the cricket green in heels, Kim was dazzled by her high-cheekboned beauty. Could she smell expensive perfume, carried on the breeze? The other woman would tower over them both when she reached them. The wind caught her dress and lifted it at the hem.

'You're cold,' said Kim, dazed.

'Goose pimples,' said the woman, arriving with the grace of a royal. There was only one imperfection that Kim could see – her long, narrow nose was a little askew. 'Didn't expect the seafront to be like this.' She sounded disappointed already. 'I'm Ruhi, this is Tank, and you must be Sinker the estate agent?'

'Kim, please.'

'Sinker!' exclaimed the man.

The classy-looking middle-aged gent with the walking stick was long gone. What a shame: these two were her clients instead. Kim scrolled through her mental Rolodex. She had never had an initial customer interaction like this before. It was not very . . . *Devon*. If the lady was wearing no underwear, as she suspected, they were in uncharted territory.

The client name in her phone calendar was Thomas Slater-Glynne. Back in the day, a double-barrelled surname said old money; she could expect a silver fox in tweed with a gentle handshake and proper manners. But these days, even the chap barking prices on the fruit-and-veg stall in Exmouth had a hyphenated surname, so a Slater-Glynne could be anyone. Was this fellow called 'Tank' the Thomas she was expecting?

Oh. Of course he was. She got the joke – Thomas, Tank. The young man must have seen the penny drop because he shoved his hands deep into his pockets and flapped his elbows like wings. 'Yep, I'm "Tank" to the lady.'

Ruhi, the six-foot tower of dark beauty, spoke. 'I watched Thomas the Tank Engine growing up in Kerala. He and I need codenames because we work together and nobody knows.'

'I call her Fire,' said Tank. 'Because, you know. She works for me.'

Fire and Tank. For God's sake. Kim didn't 'know' and did not want to know. 'You've come down from London?' she asked.

'How did you guess? American Bank, all on the QT,' said Tank. 'Cash purchase for our shag cabin.'

Kim felt her shoulders slump. *Oh, Jesus Christ, bloody London bankers with the hots, spare me.* She had a few days off next week to do some home decorating. She had plans for the kitchen and the lounge and she had a plan for how she would do it that felt . . . right. So this was her last customer meeting for a while. Did it have to be this pair? Could she not have a Tweed/Silver Fox customer instead? She shot a glance at Ruhi, believing the woman must be more classy than this, seeing her delicate fingers studded with gems, wanting her at least to show exasperation – or maybe an acknowledgement that this grubby man was punching well above his weight – but she was smiling serenely, apparently smitten.

The pair turned their gazes slowly to the sun-drenched frontage of the apartment block with *Shall we get on with it?* expressions. Okay, they were colleagues having a secret affair and could lash out a million on a penthouse flat. Amazing that sheer money could lure such a stunning woman, an elongated Nicole Scherzinger, to a milk-haired Weeble.

Kim told herself not to care. She was in a good mood and this would not ruin it.

She looked at her watch on the way in, tried to think of her footsteps as elapsing seconds that were drawing her closer to the weekend and the week off. Ruhi moved past her – through her, almost – into the hallway. There were letters on the mat. Instinctively Kim dropped to her haunches to move them. Her face was so close to the man's red shoes she saw her reflection in the toecaps.

Bristling, she moved the letters to the radiator shelf. She was slender herself, but was conscious of how much less glamorous she was compared to the other woman. Fire would not squat for anyone.

'Communal areas always give buyers a bad first impression,' said Kim, 'because they can seem impersonal. But at least this one is tidy.' Then she thought, *Maybe I'll kill this sale. I don't want to deal with these people.* So she added, 'Well, I thought it was going to be tidier than this. Disappointing, really.'

The trio climbed the stairs. The carpet was a pastel green – Kim would call it thick pistachio – and the paint on the walls was an off-white emulsion which must have been refreshed recently because there were no scratches or other marks.

'No lift?' asked Tank.

'You don't need a lift. You're not an old man,' said Ruhi, ascending the stairs as if she was made of air.

Tank laughed coarsely in Kim's direction. 'I have already proved that to her in so many ways.' Why did he need to constantly signal that they were having perpetual sex?

'Nearly there,' said Kim on the fourth. A white banister led the way. But suddenly a stranger blocked them.

The woman's white hair was bunched at the top of her head and slightly wet, as if she had sprung from the bath to confront them. She wore a felt-green dress with a matching belt which pinched at a frame that suggested skin and bone. Her eyes were black and shone like drops of crude oil.

'Visiting, you three?' she asked keenly.

'Hopefully buying,' said Tank crassly.

'I chair the residents' association, and usually we would expect the courtesy of advance—'

'I'm so sorry,' Kim broke in. 'I'm the agent. I haven't shown anything in this block before. I didn't know—'

The other woman had not finished. 'My name is Beryl Woodward. As I say, Residents' Association Chair*man*.' The very last syllable was stressed.

Tank pushed his hand out. He was reaching for a handshake, but the motion was aggressive. 'We may not buy! Depends on 'ow you treat us, so watch out!'

'And will it be a second home?' asked Ms Woodward stiffly, still not shifting.

'No, gawd!' cried Tank. 'Course not!'

'You're very young to be moving down here from . . . London, is it?'

'She works for me,' he said for the second time. 'We made a lot of money in investments,' said Tank. 'I mean *a lot*.'

'It's a lovely spot to retire to,' said Beryl Woodward, tempting Tank to say that wasn't what they were doing. Her eyes narrowed. Kim was starting to like her. *Go on*, she thought, *one more question and you can frighten them off.* But the wise old lady just offered half a smile, stepped backwards and let them pass. 'Another two floors, and then I think you might like the view.'

Kim kicked herself as the trio continued their journey up the stairs. 'Chair*man*, Chair*man*, Chair*man*,' Tank chanted. All she would have had to say to Beryl was 'second home', and the Residents' Association would have picketed the apartment and probably organized a sit-in rather than let it go to these two. She was fully on Beryl's side. She did not want Tank and Fire to buy the place either – to see this cherished piece of real estate become a 'shag cabin' – but something stopped her from torpedoing her own business.

The top floor was split in half, giving the entire space over to just two apartments. Here the landing carpet was shagpile white and their feet sank into it. Kim fidgeted for a second and then took the bankers left towards a door marked *Larksmoor South*.

The empty space was huge. The main room had a kitchenette in the corner, generous space for dining and seating and high rafters. Sun drenched every inch of the interior. The floor was pock-marked timber, weathered just right. Kim moved across the space to pull the blinds but could not find the controls. Her eyes would not adjust to this much sunlight. She could barely see Tank and Ruhi, who had stayed in shade near the entrance.

The windows stretched all the way along one side, and the corner gave a view of the Clock Café and Jacob's Ladder, which led down to the beach. Kim gasped at the light and the view – the windows were floor to ceiling, nine feet tall – and rummaged blindly for her sunglasses.

As she searched her handbag, she heard Tank's voice.

'We'll take it.'

'Wait,' said Ruhi.

Where were those damned glasses? She couldn't see. The light made her sneeze. 'Don't you want to make an offer first, just to—'

'A million is our offer.' That was Tank.

'Wait,' said Ruhi again.

'I'm afraid there's so much light in here, I'm having trouble seeing,' said Kim. 'I'm just going to . . . I'm sorry, I . . .'

Her eyes were physically hurting with the light. She found her way to a side room that might have been a study.

'Do you need to see us to hear what we're saying? A million.' That was Tank's voice.

At that moment Kim heard a sharp report, like a single clap. What were they doing, smacking a magazine at a wasp? She found her sunglasses and moved back into the open-plan area.

The other two were silent, staring at her.

It was a slap. The report had been hand on cheek. Had Tank just slapped his girlfriend? Kim goldfished, uncertain how to respond. Why would he hit her?

Ruhi and Tank had found sunglasses already and put them on. Their spectacles seemed to be a matching pair, the sort you get as fairground prizes, pink with Edna Everage wings on the upper corners. The match only made the statuesque woman and the squat man look even more unsuitable for each other.

Standing away from the window, no longer blinded, but still heated by the oven-warmth of the huge window pane, Kim felt a shiver. She stared at the two.

What was she missing? Why would Thomas have suddenly slapped Ruhi?

Then she saw the mark.

But it was not on the woman's cheek.

It was the man who had been slapped. Kim was speechless.

She found her voice at last. 'I couldn't hear – did you make an offer?'

Tank was quiet. Ruhi spoke. 'A million.'

'She's the one with the money,' he said, as if quietened.

The vast empty room was like a swimming pool full of light and she was drowning in it. *A million?*

A million pounds, a completely improbable duo, a moment of violence . . . what was going on here? Kim felt genuinely scared for a second. She removed her sunglasses and pushed them back into her handbag, because it was better to be blinded than to see this couple for who they were.

CHAPTER FIVE

'It was really nasty. I had to get out.'

Barbara Sinker was silent at the other end of the phone, so her daughter felt the need to say it again.

'What would it be, Mum? She hits him even though she works for him?'

'Maybe he works for her.'

'He suggested they were having some sort of secret affair.'

'If it's secret, why would he say that?'

Kim thought for a second. 'Maybe everything they told me was a lie.'

'She actually slapped him with you in the same room?'

'I had nipped out for a second. It was so bright in that place I couldn't see. I felt dizzy with all that light. I popped out, got my sunglasses, heard the smack, thought they were after a wasp or a fly, then I saw the mark on his cheek.'

'If you want a guess from me,' said her mother, 'it could be crime.'

'Crime?'

Kim had looked carefully to make sure the couple had gone. She was still creeped out by the way the man had sneaked up behind her at the start. Now she had to offload. The penthouse was behind her, glittering in the sun. Fire and Tank, or whatever their bloody names were, had gone their separate ways as soon as she had locked the front door behind them.

'That was another sign,' she told her mother. 'They were so, like . . . professional with each other. Almost cold. That was a business meeting and they weren't lovers.' Kimberley had turned left onto the promenade now, her phone conducting heat into her ear. 'What sort of crime gives you a million quid to burn?'

'I don't know. Parking?'

Kim laughed so loudly that a child in a pram, part of a family passing her on the promenade in optimistic summer outfits, burst into tears. She gestured an apology at the disconcerted father. Kim's mother saw all parking charges as theft, so by extension a massive criminal enterprise must involve car parks. She changed the subject.

'I gather you saw Edward earlier, Mum.'

'Oh I did. I did indeed. A very odd radio station event where we were supposed to meet the presenters, but he was the only one who had the decency to come, and the poor thing had no voice.'

'He said you helped him get his message across—'

'Yes, I certainly did. When I wasn't fending off that wretched man he works for.' Barbara's reply was defensive. As if daring her daughter to ask for more. 'Where are you, darling?'

'My car has a flat tyre. I'm walking down the promenade. I'm passing Muffles, to be precise.'

'Oh, Muffles.' Barbara's voice said: *I love that store.* To Kim, Muffles was a place for baggy fleeces and unisex cardigans, not to mention elasticated denims; she would be as likely to visit Muffles as Alcatraz. In fact, come to think of it, less likely – she had toured Alcatraz once.

'Mum,' she teased, 'do you think Muffles is the thing you love more than anything else in the world?'

'Not more than Edward.'

'Oi! That's my boyfriend. You can only love him from a distance.'

'Well, that's what I do,' said Barbara. 'My favourite radio presenter.'

'Hands off, Mum.'

'There are no hands, only ears.'

'Well, I'm glad you love him more than Muffl—' A quick knocking on the window to her left brought Kim to a halt. She turned to face the café she was passing.

There was a face pushed up against the window, stretched and warped by the glass between them like a work of modernist art, only one bright blue eye showing. It was a familiar face: a youthful expression enhanced by some of the clearest skin Kim had ever seen, with strawberry blonde hair combed into an unfamiliar thick fringe. In a split-second, Kim's alarm was replaced by the glow of recognition.

'Old friend!' she cried.

The face broke into a tentative smile, as if Stevie Mason was hurt by the brief moment Kim had not recognized her. For Kim the feeling was different – a stranger might see Stevie as a collection of scars, but recognition wiped all of that away. She just saw her friend.

Kim said into her phone: 'Can I call you back, Mum? Just seen a mate.' An instant later she was at the bar stool next to Stevie's. She placed her handbag on the counter at the window and looked at the younger woman.

'My my,' Kim said. 'What a treat to see you after all these months, wonderful girl. A tonic.'

Events had thrown the two women together more than a year earlier. Stevie's late grandmother had been a victim in The Case. Stevie went to Edward for help; he had needed Kim for his investigation. The three had bonded, especially after Stevie's face was burned with acid. When the case was closed, she had faded away.

Now, she stared at Stevie, studying her face. The burn across the hairline would usually be most noticeable to a stranger, because the hair had not grown back and Stevie had previously made no effort to hide it. Today it was hidden by a thick fringe. Her face looked wider, the cheeks puffed like a squirrel storing nuts for winter, but the most distinctive feature was the eyepatch that covered the left eye.

'You're staring, Jesus Christ Kim, you're fucking staring, and forgive my blasphemies, God help me, get tae fuck.'

The volley of obscenities made Kim laugh. A combination of saloon bar sweariness and high church godliness peppered almost everything Stevie said: a mix of her early years in Glasgow, the Tourette's, and now her buttoned-up vicarage life all made Stevie Stevie. Kim laughed at the reminder of those double barrels the young woman always fired. 'Here you are, Stevie, effing and jeffing and then asking God for help.'

'I cannae help it, you're looking at me like you've never seen my face before.'

'It's the new fringe, my love! I've never seen you with one before; almost as if you're covering yourse—' Kim broke off, cringing inside.

Stevie said, 'Sorry if my face shocked you. I'm on some steroids. Makes my cheeks puff like a nutty squirrel. The healing is soooooo slow,' she added. 'Roddy wanted me to try to cover it.'

'Roddy?' said Kim, eyebrows lifting.

Stevie looked down. What was that, discomfort? 'He's here in a minute. My fiancé.' Stevie adjusted her eyepatch then lifted her head up, proudly.

'Wow! I didn't know! Congratulations, you superstar! Love came knocking!'

'Well, that's one word for it.' Stevie shook her head and loosened a hairband, allowing a thicket of rich, blonde curls to tumble across her shoulders. Kim could see the discomfort more clearly now, and she wondered if it was caused by the fact that there must be a wedding planned, and evidently neither she nor Edward were invited.

'He was supposed to be here twenty minutes ago.'

'Can I stay to meet him?' asked Kim excitedly.

'If he actually comes.'

'What does he do?'

'Estate agent.'

Kim's jaw dropped.

'Kidding you. Nothing to do with flats and mortgages. Well, in a way he is. Bailiff. He's late.'

'Bailiff, meaning he goes in and gets people's TVs—'

'When they owe money. Don't get prim and proper about it. Usually it's justified, I suppose.'

Kim had never met a bailiff. She always assumed they were conflicted about their work, and she was hoping Stevie would say something along those lines.

'So do you like the fringe then?' Stevie asked, changing the subject. 'Roddy says he likes everything except my face so I'm trying to change it.'

Kim's lips parted but no words came out. They were both facing the sea through the big front window, and Kim saw the faintest reflection of her own gaping mouth.

'It's nothing, just a joke he makes,' said Stevie.

'But you are a beautiful person in every way, a beautiful soul.'

'A beautiful burned crisp.'

'No! Getting better,' Kim tried. She turned away from the window, back to Stevie. 'Can you not see what I see? A trailblazer, a total original? The aci . . .' Kim did not want to say the word 'acid' so she quickly substituted, 'the accident won't change any of that, silly. How's your eye been?'

'Gradually light comes through the pupil. It's still very blurred. They don't want it taking in light for more than a couple of hours a day. I still need hospital every three or four weeks.' Stevie's hand moved. Her thumb slid under the lowest edge of the patch and she lifted it off the pitted skin.

Kim bit her lip, seeing the almost-sightless right eye. The healthy iris on the other side was bright blue. But from the right eyelid, burn scars fanned out like jagged loudspeaker lines in a cartoon. The iris was darker, with the vagueness of milk. A feathered border between iris and pupil suggested an artist's eraser applied to a crisp pen-and-ink sketch; nothing was quite where it should be.

'What are you doing, kiddo?'

The male voice matched a new reflection in the glass and they both turned. The young man was stout, muscled, with a nest of brown hair slicked back from his brow. He wore a black tracksuit with white lines which ran from his shoulders to the cuff, and the top was unzipped to his solar plexus. Below the top was a white T-shirt. Kim's gaze alighted on a small red stain in the T-shirt, no bigger than a penny. He wore sunglasses, which looked like a prescription pair because, behind the shaded lenses, his almost-invisible eyes bulged. The effect was disconcerting, like seeing a stranger's eyes in the dark beyond a window.

'Meeting a friend.'

Kim had not heard this tone in Stevie's voice before, as if she was choosing each word carefully.

Roddy said, 'Pleased, I'm sure.'

Kim shook the outstretched hand, which took hers briefly in such a powerful grip she almost gasped in surprise. It was a bailiff's hand, she thought, one that had removed a lot of baby toys and computers. On the wrist was an emoji, '100' written in a red slant.

'Sorry I'm on time,' he joked.

Kim wanted Stevie to reply, *You're not, you're late, and my friend knows you're late*, but she was amazed how quietened Stevie had suddenly become.

'Were you showing her your eye? I told you that's not a good idea. Scare the kiddies.'

Kim felt her hackles rising. Surely a fiancé would want to build Stevie's confidence, not undermine it? But then she remembered her own marriage, and how she had stayed there, never feeling the water temperature rising, like a frog in a saucepan. Before she could open her mouth to retort on Stevie's behalf, he spoke again.

'I know I'm a bit late but we had to do a house. Another gas bill arrears. Front door in and we took the carpets.' He thumbed at a van down the street. 'Logging them is ridiculous. They're worth nothing. Need burning. Same with the children's coats.'

'It's just a temporary job,' said Stevie quietly.

'What's your line?' asked Roddy, jerking his chin towards Kim. It was a strange expression to use, almost 1970s, and Kim looked at the deep troughs in his face again. This twenty-five-year-old had done fifty years of living already. He had the parched skin of a smoker and even his frown had wrinkles.

'Estate agent,' Kim replied.

'Good money. You put 'em in, we take 'em out.'

Stevie put in, 'It's not always about the money, Roddy—'

'It's not, but it sort of is.'

Kim tried to help. 'It's not about money for me. I just love my customers.'

'Says the lady with the bright red Porsche.'

How had Roddy clocked which car she drove, especially since the Porsche was currently stranded elsewhere? Perhaps Stevie had mentioned it; or perhaps Roddy had seen the car in Sidmouth and thought he would like to confiscate it at some point after so many dirty rugs and children's coats? Did he measure the asset value of everyone he met?

'Roddy says I can have it off on the wedding day if I want to, the patch.'

'Have it off on the wedding day!' repeated Roddy, pleased with his seizing of the innuendo. 'Only a few weeks to go now, babe!' he said with a leer at Stevie, then he walked to the counter to get a drink, whistling under his breath, having not offered a refill to either woman.

Kim wanted to ask, *Is he kind to you?* Her abusive marriage had made her spot red flags everywhere. But she had not seen Stevie for a year and did not feel it was her place to point out danger with Stevie's wedding day so close.

'What's that tattoo – the number "100" inked on his wrist?'

'He's getting it taken off.'

'But what does it mean? I've seen it or heard about it. "One hundred" in red?'

'Means nothing,' Stevie deadpanned.

Kim sensed hazard in the conversation and fell silent. She saw a smattering of rain above the sea, moving backwards and forwards like water from a garden sprinkler. The sun was still bright. 'I was just talking to Edward; he'll be so thrilled to hear I bumped into you.'

'The radio god!' Stevie blurted, laughing as if in relief. 'How is he?'

'He's having a difficult day. He had to speak in public with no voice,' said Kim. 'Actually,' she went on, struck by a thought, 'we were cut off when he started telling me about this lady he'd met. Crossbow lady, he said. Name wasn't familiar.'

'Can you remember it?'

Kim put her head in her hands. 'You and your true crime, Stevie.' The young woman was a repository for murder stories she had seen online and on TV. 'Now let me think. The name was – hmm, chewing gum. Spearmint. No, Wrigley.'

'Crossbow, you said?' said Stevie.

'Yes, he said "crossbow" and "Wrigley". Came from Birmingham.'

Stevie set down her tea and toyed with the remains of a cookie on her plate. 'Hmm. Birmingham? I thought North Devon.'

'Honestly,' Kim said, 'I might have got it all wrong.'

'I did hear of a case involving a crossbow. Not around here, for sure.'

'Like I say, the line went.'

'Ah! I have it! The case I heard about was a doctor in North Devon. And the wife,' said Stevie with sudden certainty. 'Wendy Wrigley gets away with a crossbow murder.'

'That's it! I'm sure that was it. Wendy Wrigley.'

'I'll tell you the story because I remember it. But listen, she killed her husband and she got away with it. We need to tell Edward to stay away from that dangerous bitch.'

'Which bitch?' asked Roddy, who had arrived behind them silently, holding the mug while he popped five artificial sweeteners into his tea.

CHAPTER SIX

Edward stood by the red Porsche in the blazing sunlight.

He had wanted to go back home to bed, because now his throat was bitingly sore and he had lost his voice completely. But he could not leave Kim stranded, as he pictured it. He saw himself momentarily as the handsome knight, riding to the scene and dismounting from . . . okay, his 50cc moped. He had keys for the car, but he had opened every door, as well as the boot, and found no spare tyre.

The last place to look was underneath the Porsche chassis. Was a spare somehow bolted to the underside? There was so little room there.

He dropped to his haunches and opened the right pannier on the bike. He found the tatty plastic sheet he covered the moped with at night. Edward placed it on the ground and lay back on it, facing the brilliant blue sky. There was a whisper of rain for a moment. Somewhere above him, a lone cloud must have emptied itself like a pissed concert-goer on a sunny day at Glastonbury.

On his back, Edward used his heels to slide his body under the car. Soon he was squished against the underside of the Porsche, almost scratching his nose on the metalwork. A pothole in the road helped a little, giving his body an inch more space.

'No tyre here either.' As he lay there, he heard footsteps alongside the car, above his head.

His feet were projecting from under the front number plate. Edward tilted his head, pushing it back into the gravel. He could only see the ankle of a man's suit trousers, polished red brogues, and a woman's slim calves, the skin a deep tan or maybe Asian, the feet propped in a towering heel.

The woman's voice said, 'Fuck's sake.'

The man said, 'I got carried away is all.'

'We'll buy it, I guess,' said the woman. Then: 'Did Vinnie say the parachute was through?'

He said something Edward failed to hear, there were more footsteps on gravel, and then the two were gone.

As soon as he got out from under the car, his phone rang. 'Where are you?'

'Where you left your car.'

'You'll never guess who I met in – sorry, what, my car? Why?'

'Thought I'd change the tyre for you.'

'Oh, my beautiful fool. There's no spare on a Porsche.'

'Who have you met?' asked Edward, trying to spare his own blushes.

'Come to Nine Chairs and you'll find out.' Everyone knew Nine Chairs. The place had been called 'Twenty-Two Chairs', until legislation insisted that any establishment with ten seats or more must provide a customer toilet.

He arrived fifteen minutes later, inching through the door as a wide-set young man in a black tracksuit shouldered his way out.

'Edward!' exclaimed Stevie, getting up as though to hug him, but he held a hand out in warning.

'No no, please don't, I might be infectious.'

'You should see a doctor,' Kim tutted. This took them into medical territory, and Stevie described her slow recovery from the burns and hospital visits.

'But you look as right as rain to me!' said Edward hoarsely.

Stevie shot back: 'Come off it, sunny Jim.'

Her turns of phrase were so distinctive, so very *Stevie*, that they all burst out laughing together. Stevie added, seriously: 'I've just counted the chairs in here. Nineteen. WTF, actually,' which made Kim and Edward laugh again.

Kim said: 'Don't ever change, lovely girl. Not for anyone, not even Roddy.'

'Roddy?' asked Edward.

Stevie froze. 'Don't be chilly on it, Kim. He takes a little getting used to, that's all. I'm going to get him out of his tracksuit on the day.'

'Whose tracksuit? What day? What have I missed?'

Increasing his confusion, Kim seemed unwilling to engage. Stevie asked Edward, 'Are you still the most famous person in Sidmouth?'

'I'm not even the most famous person in this café,' said Edward, surprising himself by adding: 'I think I'm getting sacked soon.'

'What?' asked Stevie.

'Problems with the boss. He says my show doesn't have any stories.'

'That could be a problem if it's a news show.'

'Wrong thing to say, Stevie,' said Kim in a stage whisper. 'Anyway. Edward darling. You were whispering something down the phone about your crossbow lady.'

Edward nodded, then shrugged as if to say it might be something and nothing.

'Well, Stevie knows who this lady is,' said Kim.

Stevie said, 'Have been googling while you walked over. I know this case. But I think you might have missed it because you had quite a lot of . . . very difficult, fucking difficult, bloody shite basically in your life at that time. Oh, and I lost my grandmother too, so for me the Wrigley case was . . . argh, what word am I looking for . . .?'

'Peripheral?' suggested Kim.

'Lost in the wash,' Stevie preferred. Her voice was strong, the accent broad Glasgow. 'Anyway, memory refreshed. Shall I fill you in? Because I really don't think you should be seeing this lady. Not even getting close to a waft of her expensive perfume.'

Stevie kept them in suspense, insisting on fetching a drink for Edward before explaining. Kim looked at Edward while Stevie was away from their window seats. He could not read Kim's expression. Their stools were in a straight line facing the window, with Stevie's, now empty, placed between them.

'Nice to see her,' mouthed Edward, thumbing at Stevie's back as she queued at the till. Kim pursed her lips and rocked her head, moving a hand out in front of her, palm down, and tipping it left and right. 'You're not so keen?' asked Edward, misreading.

'God, no, I love her to bits. But I'm worried,' whispered Kim. 'She's getting married to a chap called Roddy. I don't think he respects her. He left a minute before you arrived and he asked to borrow money and she gave him her last twenty and then he got cross that she didn't have any more and—'

'Wait. Are you crying?'

'He had a tattoo saying "one hundred" – what's that?'

'Oh, I read about it, I think that's—'

She cut in. 'Cover for me.' He saw Stevie returning.

'What is it?' Stevie asked a second later. 'Did you say something to upset her, because if you did I'll tip this milkshake over you.'

'No,' said Edward, unable to laugh. 'She has hay fever.'

'It's strawberry. Lots of pips all over you.'

'Pips don't make me guilty.'

Stevie set their drinks down. She sat between them, sucking loudly on the milkshake, facing out of the café to the street. The other two turned inwards towards her.

'Can I just say . . .' Edward began.

'No, you can't,' said Stevie, 'because you've got no voice.'

'Only that – the three of us . . .' His voice gave up. He formed a heart with his hands.

'He loves us,' said Kim, her eyes clear of tears now.

'I know what heart-hands mean,' said Stevie, 'but thank you for explaining, old lady.' Kim laughed. Stevie continued: 'Listen up, team. The key person is a GP called Jonathan Wrigley. He was out walking, and he was shot with a crossbow.'

Edward held up his hand. 'Where?' he mouthed.

'Through the heart.'

Edward shook his head.

'Oh, you mean "where-where"? In a wood by Chittlehamholt Airfield. Where he was out walking.'

'That's definitely Devon,' whispered Edward. He shook his head and pulled a face that said, if it happened in Devon in the last ten years – a GP shot dead with a crossbow – he would definitely know about it. But Kim reached across and put her hand on his knee.

'Matty,' she said. 'That's why you've got no memory of the time.'

Edward felt his heart sag, like a washing line suddenly overloaded with a wet rug and about to snap. He inhaled sharply, waiting for the feeling to pass. The three of them were silent for a moment. The death of Edward's boy at the age of eleven would have been around that time. Edward had been signed off work for more than a year. The period was a blank. He nodded. Kim squeezed his knee gently.

Stevie continued. 'It was a long way from here. The other side of Devon. The doctor lived in a village somewhere. He was out walking. He was shot. The weirdest thing is, a bloke in a plane saw him lying there.'

'A plane?' asked Kim. 'Like, a commercial flight?'

'A light aircraft. He landed and reported it straightaway, so they timed the death really precisely. The reason I said you need to stay away from Wendy is that everyone thinks she did it. Can you believe I'm getting married, Edward?'

The change of subject was the equivalent of a hairpin bend in a racing car, and it left Edward breathless.

Edward tried to say, 'Who to—?' but no words came out.

'Where's your hearing aid?' Stevie asked. 'I've just saw you're not wearing it. Have ye been healed?'

By now, unable to speak at all, Edward wrote on a napkin: *Battery went.*

'Typical guy,' Stevie said to Kim. 'If he can't speak, why would he need to hear anything?' That made Kim roar with laughter. Edward smiled bleakly, feeling like the old guy, and shook his head at the unfairness. The hearing aid was in his pocket. He could still hear with his right ear, and he pointed at it now, making a thumbs up. He wrote on the napkin: *Who's the lucky guy?*

'Roddy. He has prospects, too.'

'We are both so excited for you, Stevie,' said Kim. She waited a beat, to see whether more needed to be said about Roddy. Then she added: 'That's probably why Wendy moved down here. The finger-pointing.'

Edward wrote a single word on a napkin. *Alibi?*

'She was in a cinema watching some Marvel film and there's no way she could have done it herself,' answered Stevie. 'That's the mystery. They didn't have problems in their relationship—'

'That's even more suspicious,' put in Kim.

'She bought the crossbow.'

'What?' Edward mouthed, eyes wide.

'Yep,' said Stevie.

Again, Edward wrote on the napkin: *Where was the crossbow?*

'Could you write faster as my birthday is in August?' Stevie said. Edward laughed. She replied, 'Missing. She had a crossbow, for God's sake, and it was gone from the house! So everyone assumed she used it to kill him. Basically she did it. Case closed. Stay well away. She'll probably murder you next.'

Stevie wanted to be done with the explanations, Edward could tell. He remembered Wendy Wrigley's immaculate appearance and now, in retrospect, saw her as she was – below the clear surface, a roaring ocean of silent distress. Her exterior was impeccable, as if Wendy Wrigley had used Photoshop to blanch her own sadness. The spotless jumper hid a bleeding heart. The lady was in trauma and he had not seen it. She was no killer.

Kim said, 'Wait. Do I remember she wasn't seen to mourn enough? Not reacting in the right way when your husband dies, that's a crime these days.'

Stevie, as ever ahead on the detail, said: 'There was a headline: "Mystery of Smirking Widow". The papers took against her. The police made it clear they were sure it was her, they even said they were not looking—'

'"For any other suspects in connection with the murder".' Kim completed the sentence, remembering now. 'Brutal.'

'Pardon my French,' said Stevie, 'but she fucking deserved it.'

Edward pushed his voice. 'If she was in the cinema when it happened, it can't have been her.'

Stevie looked out of the window, as if summoning facts from the sea. 'The inquest could have gone for murder, but they couldn't rule out an accident or even suicide. Total mystery. So it was an open verdict.'

Edward thought it all through, for a moment distracted from his throat. A madman attacks a local doctor with a crossbow, apparently the one his wife owns. That made no sense. A different crossbow, then? But if so, why did hers go missing? If he shot himself with a crossbow, the weapon could not have gone missing after his death. Did she tell someone else to kill her husband and create a too-obvious alibi, going to the cinema like that? If Wendy's crossbow was a red herring and it was nothing to do with Wendy or a madman, then you had to work out why a third party would want the doctor dead so badly.

He came back to his certainty: *She didn't do it.* Why would a killer, who has got away with it, bring him in to investigate?

'He's writing again. Take your time, Edward,' said Kim.

Edward needed more space, so he had taken Stevie's napkin, then slid it back towards the other two.

Want to talk to her.

Stevie rolled her good eye. 'Come on. What's to investigate?'

Edward stared at Stevie. He was aware of Kim's gaze on him. Kim said, 'I think he wants to ask some more questions when his voice comes back.'

Stevie said, 'You're thinking we should bring her in?'

Now Kim and Edward both snorted with laughter. 'Stevie! "Bring her in"! We aren't the police!' cried Kim. 'Edward, love, what are you writing now?'

'He thinks he's fucking Columbo,' said Stevie.

'If he's fucking Columbo that would be a major scandal in Sidmouth.'

'Not like that!' protested Stevie.

'This is what happens when you pipe down, Ed. We get to tease you.' Kim was tender for a second. Stevie chimed in, 'Ignore us, sir. We love you.' The younger woman took the napkin. Edward pointed at the words, which had scratched small holes in the tissue, as if he was getting crosser when he wrote them.

I want to see where his body was found
And talk to her again

And then: *Delighted to hear your marriage news Stevie.*

When Kim saw the last sentence, she shot him a glance he could not comprehend.

Stevie upped and left a minute later, pulling a cowboy hat from a stool where neither Edward nor Kim had noticed it and pushing it hard onto her head. When she was gone, Edward tapped on his phone, brought up a webpage and showed it to Kim.

> URBAN SLANG: The 💯 emoji is commonly associated with misogyny and incel groups. It purports to mean that 80 per cent of women are only attracted to 20 per cent of men.

'Oh God,' said Kim as she read it. 'Edward darling, is this really happening? Stevie is marrying an incel bailiff and we can't do anything about it?'

'Bailiffs do a necessary job, I guess.'

'He was boasting about burning children's coats earlier!'

'Do we intervene somehow?'

'You think Stevie would let us say anything this close to the wedding?' Kim asked desperately.

Edward signalled at his throat. His voice was a whisper and he did not want to push the words out.

'Well that's convenient,' said Kim, only half-joking.

CHAPTER SEVEN

Kim spread her wedding dress on the thin polythene sheet she had stretched across the bed. It was the classic turn-of-the-century design. The cream satin sheath fitted her body like a child's glove squeezed onto an adult hand. Along the arms was the lace detailing she had taken a fortnight to settle on. The neckline was bateau – at least, that's what she had asked for. 'Bat—? Oh yes, I see, *boat neck* is what we call it,' the sales assistant in Sidmouth had replied firmly. Okay – a satin *boat neck* with lace arms. Fussy floral appliqués had been sewn on, but only half a dozen, because she had straightaway realized they were not right for her.

Now she took the first paint pot that came to hand, a sage green eggshell she had bought for the hallway. A screwdriver allowed her to prise the lid off. Carefully, she laid the lid upside-down on the polythene sheet.

Then Kim dipped a brand-new paintbrush into it and flicked great gloops of sticky green all over the wedding satin.

The wedding dress massacre had not been in her plan for the day. Kim had woken to the alarm, ready to set about a list of tasks. She scanned her phone quickly before leaving the bed.

The AA had patched up her punctured tyre – although a dealer would need to replace it soon. The mobile confirmed it was a Saturday and, yes, WEEK OFF was her only diary event. Sitting up with a pillow propping her, Kim emailed the office.

> Let me know if we get a firm offer on Thirdfield Terrace from Slater-Glynne. Not sure we want to progress it. Call me anytime to update, am just wallpapering at home.

Yesterday had been hectic. That stressful property viewing, that hideous couple, the flat tyre. Stevie and Edward in the coffee shop. From there she jumped selfishly to thoughts of her own defunct marriage. She did not want to lie in bed remembering the violent oaf of a cop who tied her up (in every way but literally) for a decade, arresting people in the day whose crimes were far less serious than the ones he committed after sundown against his own wife. She knew she could not have his kids and now guessed it was too late to have anyone's.

She had jumped out of bed in her knickers, as if running away from the memory.

And that was when her mind went to the wedding dress. She knew where it was because her move to the flat had been so recent. She found it vacuum-packed at the bottom of a deep drawer. When she had opened the bag, air rushed in, as if the dress was gasping for life. 'No, honey,' she whispered, 'your time has gone.' That was when she resolved to paint the house in it. How else to show that her miracle in satin was worth less these days than charity shop overalls?

She had told the office 'wallpapering', but it was more. She was like Armstrong on the moon – putting a flag down to mark her new life on this bare planet. Kim's divorce apartment was on the western edge of Sidmouth, right beside the golf club, a spot she had chosen partly because it was only fifteen minutes from there to her mother's home in Colaton Raleigh. Oh, and she could never live more than half an hour's walk from the Clock Tower Café!

The first globs of green emulsion meant the die was cast. They sank into the cream material like cancer on the skin. What was 'sage green' anyway? Was there a range of greens, from sage through to unperceptive, and at the end of the line, what – Idiot Green? Twat Green? Her mind went to Edward. Her beautiful big fool. Twat was rude, wasn't it? She could still say it to herself. Her beautiful big twat. That really did sound rude. Edward had wanted to ask her – hang on, wasn't it 'something, something important'?

She hoped to God it was not . . . not that. Surely he was not the shade of green that proposes marriage because it's a quiet Friday? If so, he was lucky he had lost his voice. Neither of them needed another marriage. She flicked more paint at the dress. Then some wallpaper glue, so viscous it landed with a slap. Her answer to Edward.

Before beginning the decorating, Kim hesitated. She would go for her daily run first. She wrapped the paintbrushes in clingfilm and grabbed her Lycra. Enjoying the snug pinch of the newly washed material on her legs and torso, Kim picked up her phone and reread Edward's WhatsApp message, sent late last night.

> Eeeeuuuurgh this blimmin throat thing. What is it when it's serious? Streptococcololoulus or was that a Roman emperor? No way can I do my show tonight, tomorrow etc. Or even speak to you my lover! Got LOTS to talk about too. Can you ask Wendy Wrigley three questions for me? 07700 900178 is her ☎

There we go again. 'LOTS to talk about'? Kim wondered if she should call Edward, but it was early and it was Saturday, and how would he even speak with Strepto-whatever? She pulled the front door closed behind her and stepped lightly down the carpeted stairs of the apartment block so as not to disturb the neighbours.

Arriving in the outdoor air, she was on the balls of her feet immediately, jogging with the wind in her hair, mini-backpack strapped tight, new trainers still bright white, body braced against the sharpness of the seven-thirty breeze from the sea. Her running bra was pinching. She worked her thumb under the left cup as she ran and found a twist in the support strap.

She loved the speed and randomness of her thinking when she ran. But then, padding along the almost empty promenade, running east with the sea to her right, she stopped.

Three questions?

Quickly typing as her body reacted against the sudden halt, she messaged Edward back.

> Three questions for Wendy? What are we – the police now?

She ran for another hundred yards, past Muffles and Nine Chairs, past the old pizza parlour, and then, before she reached the tallest building on the seafront where Edward's radio station was located, she felt the phone vibrate beside her skin.

> Be my voice

Curses, she thought, this exchange could stop her running. She carried on for another fifty yards but could not resist the reply:

> Male grandiosity or what 😂

Then, as she sat in the rotted bus shelter facing the sea, they were away with a texted conversation.

> Are you planning on having no voice for several years?

> Right now it feels like I may never speak again, I can't even swallow.

She sent a series of eye-roll emojis and Edward replied:

> Don't you even want to know my three questions?

To which she, feeling pleased with herself, wrote:

> Why did you do it, when did you do it, how did you do it?

before laughing into the air, snapping her phone shut, tucking it back into her bra and continuing to run. Edward could talk to the boob, she wasn't listening.

Kim ran the length of the promenade, loving the way the morning sun brought out the early summer holidaymakers in their pessimistic cagoules. At the end of the seafront, where the beach pebbles became huge rocks and a sheer red cliff face cut a line between land and sea, she patted the wall of the lifeboat station (a daily ritual, for luck) and then turned 180 degrees, put on a sprint, and covered the length of the seafront in seven minutes. The last was a brutal climb to Connaught Gardens. It was just before eight now and, through misted glass, she saw the coffee machine steaming and young servers getting cakes ready in the

Clock Tower Café. She stood outside, breathless, running on the spot, until one of them caught her eye and took pity.

'Come on in, madam. We'll unlock early for you. Suzy's in today doing the accounts and Lewis is in the kitchen with Georgie. They always tell us to make sure everyone gets a welcome here, and the largest piece of cake. Coffee's not hot yet, but we'll do one as soon as we can.'

'And this is why we all love you! Just something savoury when you can.'

'Banana bread?'

'One of my five a day. Perfect.' She did not want to be a nuisance. She tucked herself away and went back to the WhatsApp exchange with Edward. She copied the mobile number from it. She was just too curious not to call.

Wendy Wrigley said her name as she picked up, as you might in the days of landlines. There was something classy about that. Stately home manners.

'Hello, Mrs Wrigley? You don't know me, but I'm a friend of Edward Temmis the radio presenter. I think you approached him.'

'Yes?' The voice at the other end was cautious. 'Yes, I met him. I didn't know he'd told people about—'

'Don't worry. We are . . . partners in crime, as it were.' The wrong word. 'We investigate together.' She was all in now, deep in a farmer's-sized consignment of the warm brown stuff. 'He's a bit embarrassed. He can't call you because his voice has gone.'

Wendy Wrigley's response was a little warmer now that she could be confident this must genuinely be Edward's associate. 'The poor man! His voice was fading at this wretched radio event I went to.'

'He wants to chat, but right now he can't. He asked me to put a couple of questions to you. Well, three questions.'

'Only three! Where are you?'

'Oh, I'm not really around. I'm out running.'

'Can I come to you?'

There goes my run, thought Kim. But there were worse things. Meeting a new person in Sidmouth was always worth the trouble. And she sensed this lady would be interesting. 'I'm at the Clock Tower Café.'

'I know it.'

'Then you're a local,' said Kim.

Wendy Wrigley arrived within fifteen minutes. She and Kim were the only two customers. The new arrival moved quickly, catching Kim's eye, discreetly nodding, then ordering mint tea at the counter, voice hesitant, as if she was worried about being recognized. Wendy came back from the counter with a milkless tea, bag still in.

'You must live close, Wendy.'

'Yes.' She brought out a small mirror. 'Oh dear. I'm afraid I find myself crying a bit in the morning.'

The honesty almost took Kim's breath away.

'It's so nice to be with someone who wants to be with me,' Wendy went on. 'I have had somewhat of a . . . a fall from grace. I feel I must be repellent in some way. Sidmouth was where my husband grew up and we had many happy years here,' Wendy went on, 'so I thought I could start again here. I can feel it going wrong already. People suspicious of me. In Sidmouth I feel closer to Jonathan, if you know what I—'

'Oh, I do,' said Kim, amazed at her openness.

'You said three questions, but you can ask as many as you want. The police must have asked me a thousand. And I was grieving, but also trying to contain my grief, and I think perhaps it made me look, I don't know—'

'Unsympathetic?'

'To them, yes.'

'They thought you did it.'

'They still do. It's the bane of my life,' she said bitterly. 'To lose the man you love and then be accused of . . .'

She had narrow features, with piercing eyes, and tears welled in them again. The skin on her face was taut and free of make-up. It was chilly outside, and the widow wore an army green gilet which, as she unzipped it, showed a slender physique with firm contours. If she were not cut to ribbons by her grief, Kim thought, she would look sharp of dress and mind.

Kim suddenly said, 'I think we've met before.'

Wendy replied, 'No, no.'

'How can you be sure?'

'You probably saw my picture in the papers. And – to my extreme embarrassment – I was onscreen a little as a teenager, in a soap.'

'Oh! Which one?'

'*Gibba's Farm.*'

'Yes!' said Kim, warming to the woman hugely.

'Nothing stranger than being a little recognizable from twenty years ago.'

'You didn't go on to acting?'

'I was so rubbish at it. The whole of my life I've been told I'm just too honest for my own good. I would come on set happy, they would tell me to play upset, and I would just look slightly less joyful. I made my life with dear Jonathan, and we had two perfect children, now grown-up, and it was all so wonderful, and then it was destroyed. I've tried to be strong for them.' Wendy sipped her mint tea. 'Like I say, ask me anything.'

Kim wondered what Edward's three questions would have been, but she knew hers could be better.

'Your husband died as a result of being shot by someone with a crossbow—'

'Not me.'

'I know, I've seen all the reports,' said Kim. 'You were at a cinema watching *Thor*.'

'To be precise – *Thor: Love and Thunder*.'

'Had you ever seen a Marvel film before?'

'First question, and it's a good one. No, I had not.'

'Is that suspicious?' asked Kim. 'You were in a cinema watching a film you weren't interested in, which meant you couldn't be on the scene?'

'My husband bought me the ticket. He loved Marvel films. Wanted me to share the joy.'

'Do you mind if I write that down?'

'Kim, do you promise you aren't police? Ordinary people don't write stuff down.'

'I have to tell Edward, that's all.'

'The sleuth.'

Kim prickled. 'There are three of us, and we only solved one crime, but I think he'd like to help you. He's very . . . sympathetic.'

'Good for a radio presenter.'

Kim reached into her top and pulled out her smartphone.

'That's a good place to keep it,' said Wendy.

Kim said, 'The first time it buzzed in there I thought I was having a heart attack.' She opened a Notes file and typed.

'So you got to the cinema in Barnstaple, and while you are in there, your husband is – is sadly killed—'

'You can just say "killed", Kim.'

'—with your crossbow. Why did you have a crossbow?'

'I honestly think the crossbow we owned is just a distraction. Okay, he was killed with one. And yes, we had one, and it was missing. But crossbow bolts are not like bullets. They don't have barrel-marks that trace them back to the weapon.'

'The bolt went through his heart.'

'It did. It really did. Every day I wonder who could have done that, and then I imagine him flat out on the forest floor, knowing he was dying.'

'Do you mind me asking why you had a crossbow?' Kim tried again.

'It wasn't mine. I bought it for Jonathan. He was wondering out loud about getting one because we had rabbits by the dozen on our land. But he was getting a lot of fatigue, working so hard. Long story short, crossbow for Christmas and then it mostly stays in its box. The police called it mine because it was my purchase.'

'So where did it go?'

'You didn't hear? Some magnet fishers pulled it out of a river halfway between our house and where the body was found. Months later, this was. We lived in a little village called Zeal Monachorum. Jon's dead body was found fifteen miles from Zeal, next to the private airfield.' She added, thoughtfully: 'I was amazed Edward didn't know of me.'

'He was dealing with a personal tragedy when your husband died.'

'Oh, how sad.' Said with real feeling. 'I understand. How could I not?'

Kim noted the found crossbow in her Notes, and Wendy spoke again before she could ask her next question.

'The police have been absolute bastards,' said Wendy, as if wanting Kim to take every word down. 'They've been over every phone, every computer, been through every drawer, even turned out a drawer of socks, looked at every website I've ever visited, I guess just wanting to find out that I'd googled HOW TO KILL A HUSBAND, or texted a contract killer or had a secret lover. If I had got someone else to do it, they would have found messages, surely? Or deletions? In the end I almost wanted them to. But there was nothing! Nothing! I was in the *cinema*!'

Kim looked up from her phone to see the face opposite her crumpled with sadness. She had noted some of the words, but not the emotion. 'Edward had three questions, but he didn't get as far as telling me them – oh, wait.' She saw an unread text.

> Just ask if she can take me to where doc died

Kim showed Wendy the screen.

'Of course I can. I want that. But I haven't been there. He will need to find the exact spot. And it will be hard for me, so I may cry.'

'Are you sure you can do it?'

'I'll do it if he can clear my name.'

'Did your husband have any enemies?'

'None I can think of. He'd got a bit unfocused at work and made a couple of mistakes, and he was thinking of winding down or stopping. It being a rural surgery, he would end up doing a bit of stitching and sewing, you know, and take bloods, and he even did some vet work as a favour. But he told me he wasn't so good at it lately. He lost interest in his hobbies – he loved making fireworks, for example.'

'How unusual!'

'He would always be explaining his "recipes". You get the different ingredients and mix them all together and bang.'

'Literally.'

'It wasn't my thing. But like I say, he was losing interest. I figured, he was hitting his fifties, that's all.'

'That's not old. Did your husband have mates?'

'Oh, a couple of great friends here in Sidmouth from university days. Twin guys who were both medics, the Hursts. Also a vicar called Zircher, pronounced like "Circus". Jon was quite close to the lady who did the admin at the surgery, Jocelyn. Just tremendously good, kind people who have made so many sacrifices for patients and parishioners. There were a few others. A tight friendship group, you might say. The murder just destroyed them all.'

'And definitely no enemies?'

'Look, doctors sometimes misdiagnose. They might miss a cancer, call it a stomach ache, get blamed. There are probably some of those on his books.'

'Gosh. Could Edward meet his friends?'

'The Hursts? The others? Anything that might move this on. I need you to help me. Hey, do you mind if I head on now? Talking about it wipes me out. And I think those ladies have recognized me.'

Sure enough, while Kim and Wendy had been talking, the café had opened. A pair of elderly ladies had stopped with their teas, whispered urgently to each other, and then took two seats on the same side of an empty table diagonally opposite Wendy and Kim. The only reason for taking a position where they both faced the inside of the café, not each other, was surely so they could keep an eye on Sidmouth's most suspicious widow.

They stared through thick spectacles, eyes unblinking and magnified by the lenses, like owls fixed on prey.

CHAPTER EIGHT

While ill, Edward had scoured websites which mentioned Jonathan Wrigley's death. He discovered the first TV report on YouTube, filed by a regional reporter in Bideford. DEAD BODY FOUND IN FOREST CLEARING was the caption. The businessman who had seen Dr Wrigley from the air looked ruffled in the interview, as if his tie had been torn off: 'It was my daughter's first flight, we were coming in to land, and she kept saying "starfish". I am an inexperienced pilot, and it was all I could do to hold her steady.' The aircraft or the daughter? The man was named onscreen as Andrew Cooms.

Once Edward had seen through the misspelling, it was easy to find him through LinkedIn. Kim's portrait of Wendy – so downcast, so poorly treated – had reminded Edward of how he had been after Matty's death. He was unable to do his show; the radio station had dumped him. The decision had subsequently been reversed after a small riot by angry pensioners, but he still smarted from the unfairness. Wendy's story made him smart again.

Edward rang Coombs, who sounded warmer on the phone than he did in the YouTube clip. Edward said he was a radio presenter in East Devon. 'I'm sorry I haven't heard of you,' the banker said. 'I gave the whole story to the police, and also the telly person, really. The TV didn't use it all. I spoke to them for twenty minutes, and they just used twenty seconds of me saying we might not get over it.'

'It must have been truly awful,' said Edward with feeling. His voice was hoarse now, and he apologized for it. The conversation felt like *The Temmis Session* – he the presenter, Coombs the caller, Edward wanting as much story as possible without seeming to pry. 'You landed and reported the body straightaway?'

'Of course! I wasn't sure he was dead at first. Certainly not murder. I wondered about a practical joke or what, yoga? He might even have been sleeping, for Christ's sake! But not like that.' This sounded like Andrew Coombs talking to himself, talking through the horror. 'We couldn't see the wound from up there. Shot in the chest? Who fires a crossbow bolt into a doctor's chest, a man with no enemies, they say? He might not have been found if we hadn't seen what we saw. But we could hardly miss it, the bright white suit.' He paused. 'I didn't say it on camera, obviously, but Clara and I were both having a go at controlling the plane and . . . You're not recording me, are you?'

'Of course not!' Edward coughed.

'You sound a bit unwell, if I may say so.'

'Just getting clear of a throat thing.' Edward breathed in. 'I just wanted to work out where exactly his body was found.'

'Really? Why?'

And now the truth came out. 'I have to be honest. The wife of the doctor himself asked me to look at the evidence for her. I am not a—'

Edward stopped. The line had gone dead.

He had paused the TV report on his laptop and screenshotted the frame showing the forest location, then used the most basic tools on his laptop to sharpen the image, then printed it out. He looked for a long time at the superimposed red cross. He must visit the scene with Wendy Wrigley. He had heard it said by Columbo or, maybe, years ago, read the words spoken by a character from an Agatha Christie: *The scene speaks to you.* If Wendy Wrigley was serious (and the banker hanging up the phone just then was yet another reminder of why she wanted exoneration), she would come with him and look at the place her husband was found. And then, while they looked, he could make progress and work out what had happened.

After seeing Wendy Wrigley at the Clock Tower Café, Kim changed her running route. Normally she would be home by now, but she ran a further two-and-a-bit miles to Ladram Bay, the site of the house she had sold Edward, when he was just a customer. She had made a joke about 'the one property no one will even look at', and then he goes and makes an offer. Coastal erosion had left it on the cliff edge. It was supposed to go into the sea in a hundred years, and one day half the garden had disappeared.

Unsaleable? Edward had proved there was no such thing. She wasn't sure how he could bear to live there, but the loss of his son might have something to do with it – which poet had written, 'after the first death, there is no other'? Edward had a superpower now. He could sleep soundly on a clifftop. She would not remind herself that the day she showed him around the house was only the second time they had met, and the first time they made love. So bloody unprofessional.

She knocked at his door, noting that it seemed more askew in its black-painted frame, suggesting the ground might be moving again. Before she could have another thought, a piece of paper was sliding out of the letterbox towards her.

I'm not talking to you

'Wait – what?' Kim protested at the front door. 'I need a glass of water apart from anything else. Are you cross with me?'

A pause. A faint sound of folding on the other side of the door, and then another scrap of paper emerged like postage in reverse, Edward's messages disobeying the one-way system which governed all letterboxes. This one was scrunched up as it came through the door from inside. She pulled the corners apart and read.

Did you ask my questions? I bet not

'Are you Sherlock Holmes today? Sorry but I wasn't feeling secretarial,' she said. 'I forgot your questions and asked my own.'

The door opened. He was standing there – smiling! – with an old notepad in his hand. Then he raised a knee, balancing with difficulty, and found the last blank page to write on.

A&E told me not to talk.

'Mama told me not to come. But I'm here anyway. Apologies for my Sherlock Holmes remark, but yes, I did ask her my own questions. If we are going to set up as a detective agency, I can't be your number two. In the movies, the number two always gets killed first.'

She went to kiss him, but he pulled back. He managed the slightest whisper. 'Infectious.'

'Yuk.'

Then he beckoned her through to the living room, which opened out onto the crumbling garden and the sea beyond.

'Well, this conversation is going to be a bit one-sided,' Kim remarked gently. 'Poor you.' She pulled out her phone and, finding the Notes app, ran Edward through the nuts and bolts of her conversation with Wendy Wrigley. She had written 'acrobats' and she could not remember why. 'Oh, a friend, a vicar with a name like Circus. Maybe he'll have an idea. And there were doctors, twins.'

'Should we talk to them?' he whispered.

'I don't know. It seems like he might have been a bit paranoid, or depressed, or unwell. Making mistakes at work, that kind of thing. She had a good explanation for watching her first Marvel film – he bought the ticket.'

Edward was silent.

'So he's shot in a forest, the crossbow is gone, she's in a cinema.'

Edward nodded at Kim's summing-up. 'Did you say paranoid?'

She craned in to hear the question. 'Could he have been a drug user? I would be if I was a doctor. The crossbow is the weird thing.'

Edward tilted his head quizzically.

'Well, she bought it for him "to kill rabbits", which sounds quite North Devon, but it was missing after the murder.'

He wrote on the scrap of paper he balanced on his knee. The marks were legible, but only just.

He kills self, someone finds body and nicks crossbow

'Why was he wearing a white suit near an airfield?' asked Kim. She shrugged. 'Sorry, it just occurred to me.'

Insurance payout?

'I didn't ask. There won't be one if she's a suspect.'

Grimacing, he wrote: *Murder fo sho.*

It was not looking good for Wendy Wrigley. He pulled an iPad from the wall socket where it was charging and detached the Apple pencil from the side. The screen shone. He scribbled quickly and handed the tablet to her.

Been trying to work out where doc died

'Near an airfield. That's all she said.'

Spoke to pilot who saw him

'Did he help?'

Edward pursed his lips and tilted his head sideways, as if to say no, not really. He typed again.

Would like to go see
'She said she'll go with you.'

Edward looked at Kim. She noticed, as if for the first time, the slate green of his eyes below his ragged fringe. The pupils were dilated but the outer ring of hard colour shone like gemstones. She felt a thrill in her stomach which she knew was love. She would never love him more than she did now, so why did she insist on being apart? She wanted him in her life, but she needed space. She hated herself for that contradiction.

'Do you care enough to get into this?'

He took the Apple Pencil again.

Hate injustice

'Wow,' she said. 'No messing. Well, our Wendy hasn't been to the place where her husband died, so I guess it's down to us to find it . . .' She was about to search for a news cutting on her phone when a message alert flared on the screen with the subject header *Thirdfield/Slater-Glynne*.

'Oh, cripes,' she blurted. Edward looked concerned. 'Office rubbish,' she shrugged. 'Two weird people wanting a beautiful flat. Came yesterday. Just not sure I want them on the books. The most beautiful Indian lady you've ever seen, and a squat blond guy with red shoes. Fishiest couple ever.' She felt she was talking too much. 'What's that?'

Kim was pointing at a picture on the TV, which looked to be a DVD image on pause. Lines of electronic snow rolled down the screen.

He did a moment's theatre, a flash of the hand by his forehead, halfway between nervous tic and military salute.

'Is that your Columbo impression?'

An embarrassed shrug.

'You were watching Columbo. You are an idiot. A wonderful idiot. Idiot green.' He looked puzzled, because she said that just for herself. 'Shade of paint. Ignore me. Please get your voice back soon.'

Turn the Dial for Death

His response was to pass her a piece of A4 showing a map with a cross on it.

'What's this?'

He whispered, 'Where the body was found.'

ONE WEEK LATER

CHAPTER NINE

Stevie, getting married in eight days, was walking along the line of shops that led back from the seafront. It was nearly two o'clock on a Friday. The pavement was narrow and getting more crowded now that they were halfway through May. Unkindly nicknamed 'God's waiting room' in winter months, Sidmouth was starting to get its annual invasion of young families. In high summer the town would be packed to the rafters – every restaurant table taken, every ice-cream van serving a queue.

Stevie heard the motorbike coming from behind. It was evidently travelling to the right of the crawling cars and, without looking, she knew there was barely the space. She caught sight of a little girl, walking alongside her mum, doing what children always did with her – staring at her eyepatch and the burns on her face. She wanted to pull a sudden horror-movie gurn, like Donald Sutherland in the last moment of *Invasion of the Body Snatchers*. The motorbike revved, making the child jump, taking her attention.

Stevie kept her gaze forwards, navigating the bustle. She was conscious of the noise of the motorbike engine as she passed. She remembered the first part of the number plate: NPH.

*

The plates were false. The bike was fast. It turned right by the lifeboat station. The corner was sharp. The bike rider alternately braked and revved, powerfully, as if trying to dig the rear tyre into the road. The bike half-turned and the back wheel, suddenly reconnecting with the tarmac, jumped from the road like a rocket.

The 1800cc Yamaha was airborne when it ploughed through the front of Toppings Pizza Parlour. The smashing of the sunburnt glass was like an explosion. Inside, families were eating late lunches. Several had small children. At one table, a mum and dad sat either side of a baby in a high chair. On its side, with a deafening scrape, the motorbike slashed a gouge in the floor and broke down the far wall, revealing a piped toilet cistern which promptly burst like a fountain. The motorbiker's chin had caught on the wooden frame of the frontage, snapping his neck. He lay on his side with his arms and legs crooked, spread on the floor like a swastika. There was silence, then shouting and screaming. Every parent reached for their child. Every adult counted the heads at their table: again, again, again. One mother, seeing her toddler had slipped off his chair and was walking towards the steaming Yamaha, raced to get him.

People on the street now made their own noise. Yelling in shock while drawing closer. The sounds came together — a man yelling as he spread his palm blindly across a shard of glass in the shopfront, the motorbike engine burping and sputtering, cistern water cascading onto the floor. The pizza restaurant staff were shouting. At the back the chef yelled, 'Shut the oven down!' This caused a second wave of panic. Could they smell leaking petrol from the bike? Two of the pizza staff headed forwards to unbuckle children from high chairs; the other three ran through the back door in a panic.

Sirens. More screaming. Smoke, fuel. A man inside the

restaurant – a young dad – asked, 'What was in that pannier?' The storage box had cracked open and spilled a second box, which itself had opened and sent tiny yellow balls, the size of garden peas, rolling across the floor. One of the children broke free from her mum, picked one up and threw it. The parents were shouting at each other now, trying to move through the door and into the street, but the crowd was hemming them in. 'Let them out!' A policeman at last. 'Let them out or I'll use my taser, I swear to God!' More sirens. More chaos. And then the fire started.

Detective Sergeant Jordan Callintree arrived at the scene on foot. He was off-duty, fetching groceries for the family at the Morrison's on Fore Street. The cop was thin-shouldered, tall and skinny at the waist. Clean-shaven, with no obvious chin, Callintree's hollow eyes shone with intelligence. He dumped his groceries and ran. Later he would be certain he had heard the roar of the motorbike and the smashing of the storefront glass while paying for his food and drink. He was sure he looked at his watch and saw it was two p.m. on the dot.

By the time DS Callintree arrived outside Toppings, the crowd had spilled into the road. There was smoke belching from the top of the broken shopfront. His immediate concern was whether anyone was trapped inside. Shouting 'Police! Police!' he cleared a path in front of him. At moments like this he wished he had more heft to his body and more depth to his voice. A middle-aged constable with twice the girth and a grey-streaked beard was waving a truncheon left and right, trying to move the crowd away from the frontage. There was a fire at the back of the shop.

'Is that motorbike fuel I can smell?' Callintree asked the constable, flashing his warrant card.

'You bet.'

'Appliances?'

'On their way.'

'Need to clear this crowd. No one inside? Injuries?'

'Just the rider. A miracle,' said the constable. 'The bike sliced through the middle. The rider is inside.'

'Jesus! Really?'

'Below the shopfront. I thought I should wait.'

'What – there's a guy on the floor?' Jordan Callintree shouted again to move people. 'You should all be getting back! We have fuel and fire! Move your kids away!' His words were repeated verbatim by the other officer, who turned back to shepherd the crowd.

Callintree jumped through the open storefront. As he moved forwards, the crowd had lurched back, as if suddenly pushed by a wave of panic. He looked down at the body of the biker. Coughing in the smoke, his mouth tasted like acid and his tongue burned. He could tell, staring down at the body, that the man was almost certainly dead. His face was swollen, yellowed already. But if there was any chance of life, he must move him before the fire caught hold. Flames had spilled over the edge of the pizza oven and were licking at the ceiling. A line of fire, like a fuse, led to the huge motorbike fuel tank. He could not wait. He had to lift the man, but he must lift him without wrenching his head, which was inside a crash helmet which he could not remove.

The crowd were now on the other side of the street. What if he asked for help and the place exploded? He would be blamed. As he waited for what must have been only a fraction of a second, he felt a presence beside him and looked up. A young woman with an eyepatch and scarring on her face was beside him. 'I've done first aid,' she said.

They both coughed in the smoke. Jordan Callintree could barely speak. 'You shouldn't be here, but I need to try to move him before that bike blows.'

'Happy to fucking try. Not as if I have a face to lose. He's dead, isn't he?'

'Think so,' replied the police officer. 'You shouldn't be here,' he said again.

Stevie Mason did not reply. She saw what he could not see. The flames were spreading behind them. The ceiling was on fire. Heroic copper this man might well be, but he was going to get himself killed, maybe both of them. She held her hands underneath the man's crash helmet, determined to transfer no movement whatsoever into the neck as the body was dragged.

'You're a very brave young woman,' shouted the police officer. His raised voice was thin in the roaring air and she could barely hear him. She wondered if she had seen him before. They had the rider halfway through the door now, dragged over broken glass. She did not need to reply. He would not hear her over the noise – the noise! Two fire engines were arriving, klaxons sounding to move the last stragglers from the crowd. The firefighters paid no attention at all to the young woman and the wafer-thin off-duty police officer wrestling with the prostrate motorbiker on the pavement. They had a job to do, and they turned on their hoses with an explosion of water.

CHAPTER TEN

For the rest of the day, the promenade was cordoned off. Edward headed into the radio station early, knowing they would cover the story on his Friday phone-in at nine, maybe spend the first two hours on it – he had already seen an account of the crash on the local *Coast Live* website, which made much of how near the bike had been to 'wiping out four entire families'. The rider had not been named by police.

Edward's antibiotics had kicked in quickly and his voice had almost returned to normal, so he was back to work, speeding in on his moped. When Edward's phone buzzed, he was on the outskirts of Pinn Village. He stopped, cut the engine, and answered in a single action.

'Mr Temmis?'

'DC Jordan Callintree, hello.'

'I forgot you had my number. And,' he cleared his throat, 'it's DS now.' It was a while since they had last spoken, after Jordan had been key in solving the hit-and-run that had killed Edward's son, Matty. Edward thought the young police officer's voice sounded more distant, more formal than he remembered. 'Have you got a minute?'

'I have,' Edward replied. 'I'm guessing it's you that's busy right now.'

'Yep. It's that. Obviously it's the crash . . . I'm calling in connection with that. I need to contact someone you know.'

Edward had the sudden inkling that this was about the crossbow woman, but Callintree quickly swept the thought out of his mind.

'The crash in the pizza place,' the police officer said stiffly. 'I was there. Motorbiker dead, as you'll have heard. Getting him clear of the fire – a young woman helped me out. Now, I think you know the woman. During my investigation last year—'

'Of course.' *The Case.*

'She was the person you tried to help, Mr Temmis, am I right? She got some terrible injuries on her face.'

'Stevie Mason. Is she in trouble?'

'No! Well . . .' The hesitation was telling. 'A witness statement would be helpful. Are you presenting your show tonight?'

'On my way in now.'

'And this won't go on it, what I'm about to tell you?'

This was difficult. But Edward respected Jordan Callintree more than any other acquaintance in the town. Young and junior at the time, the gangly police officer had been the only one to doggedly refuse to drop the investigation into Matty's death. While radio presenters skimmed facts and stories, Callintree had the good officer's desire to dig deep. Edward believed they respected each other, not that they would ever say it out loud.

'I'm going to take your silence as agreement, Mr Temmis.'

'Edward.'

'The motorbike rider doesn't check out.'

'I'm not following you.'

'There's a lot I can't say.' The policeman seemed to swallow before continuing. 'False plates.'

'Really?'

'And that fact alone means we need to do more comprehensive follow-up, to rule out . . .'

The sentence tailed off. Edward waited. But there was no more. *To rule out what?*

'I should have taken Miss Mason's name and number, but police officers suffer shock too.'

'I'm so sorry. Let me send you her contact card as soon as I get off the call.'

'Not a word on the air, please.'

'About what?'

'False plates.'

'I won't mention that on the air,' Edward promised. 'God knows there's plenty else to say. But what do false plates mean? That he's trying to avoid getting done on the speed cameras?'

At the other end, the police officer gave no answer.

'If you need to trace people, we can help with that,' said Edward a little desperately. 'We could do an appeal for you. That's something radio is very good at.'

There was silence at the other end, so long that Edward finally had to break it.

'Hello?'

'Mr Temmis, I might take you up on that.'

After the throat infection, this was Edward's first day feeling like himself again. He felt the keenness of youth as he flashed his pass at RTR-92's security guard, Jojo. The man stood, stiffened his back and saluted, a joke they shared. 'Hope you're on the mend,' said Jojo. Then his face turned serious. 'That crash today—'

'I know, right?' said Edward. 'And so close to us.'

He took the lift to the fourth floor, where the studios were. Waiting to meet him was his producer, Melody. She was slender and nervous, with Bugs Bunny teeth and uneven shoulders.

She wore willowy dresses which channelled Kate Bush on a moor somewhere. Her thick black hair was normally bunched tightly, pulling the skin taut on her cheekbones – he had heard that called the Tiverton Facelift. The only disruption to the sense of a slightly fragile twenty-two-year-old was the small dagger inked at the base of her neck. She had been at Oxford University, and her accent was posh Devon. Edward had unfairly decided a relative had wangled her the job before she had even realized she had an interest in radio.

'This story . . .' she started, wide-eyed.

Melody's hair was tumbling now, as if the crash at Toppings had shocked it out of bed. He wondered if she had come in especially early herself – saw unusual lipstick and guessed at a date abruptly cut short.

'Toppings. Incredible.'

Melody said, 'Before I forget, Mr Aspinall rang.'

'What does he want?'

'He'd heard about it, of course, asked if we can "bring the show out of hibernation" and broadcast from the promenade.'

Insulted, Edward was about to say, 'That's crazy, the line will just cut out the whole time,' and then remembered that he was the official NFC: he had to get scoops or he would be out of a job. What if he could make this story his own, make his show appointment to-listen? He might just recover from the shambles at Harpford Hall.

'Great idea, Melody, let's do it!'

'We can't get it running till tomorrow; will it still be a story then?'

Edward was tempted to say he didn't have a show on Saturdays, but he was beginning to feel the heady possibility of professional revival. 'Could be, or could be the start,' he said, deciding that the confidence with Jordan Callintree excluded Melody, and he should say no more. He opted to add only: 'There may be more to it than just a crash.'

She let the comment go, tipping her head left and right as if she had a crick in her neck. 'It's only a few hours ago, I guess, so it's hard to judge.' Now they were in the production office and he was swishing through pages of local news on his smartphone. 'Like you, I rushed in,' he heard her say.

'Well done you.' His phrase sounded like an old man's congratulation. He was not her boss. Still, she glowed when she heard the words. 'All I see online is a "Miracle Escape for Pizza Families" story,' he murmured, 'and he's being described as "Tragic Toppings Biker" in the headlines. There's no name.'

She said, 'Is there a question for the phone-in?'

'We should just ask, "Were you there?" Find out who saw it. Give the latest. Or' – he thought of Aspinall's anger and the way the village hall meeting had revealed how precarious his position was – 'scoops. We should get scoops.'

'You want me to go to Taste?'

And there it was.

The complete absence of understanding that what they were doing was journalism, and they were supposed to be discovering things. Taste was the ice-cream shop on Old Fore Street. He wanted to cry. Their jobs might depend on Melody understanding this.

'I don't mean *scoops* of raspberry ripple. I mean news scoops. Exclusives.'

'What if there aren't any?'

'News,' he announced gravely, 'is what someone else wants to hide. All the rest is advertising. I can't remember who said that.' He was thinking about Callintree's call. Had he promised to be silent about Stevie's presence, or just the false number plate? He decided only the latter. 'You know, I might have a witness to it.'

'Really?' Melody had been looking down at her smartphone. Her finger froze on the screen.

'A . . . source rang. Said a friend of mine was there. Also, the police want to find the families who were in the restaurant. We should check for an official statement.'

Edward could not get through to Callintree, but when he rang the Devon Police press office, they did indeed have a statement to give him. He read it out on the air, as sombre as a 1960s newsreader:

'Local police are appealing for witnesses who might have seen the fatal crash earlier today. A motorbike rider smashed through the front window of Toppings, the pizza parlour on Sidmouth waterfront. It's believed at least five families were dining inside. One group has been traced, but there are others who haven't yet spoken to the police. We appreciate this has been a very stressful day but we urge you to tell us if you were in the restaurant so we can speak to you about the incident.'

'Wonder why they need to follow up?' Melody asked into his headphones when the first adverts came on. She was in the control room, behind three panes of glass.

Edward was only half-listening. He stared at his phone, waiting for a reply from Stevie Mason. Then he was swept away by the listener calls. They poured in. There were a dozen in the first hour – Trevor in Plymouth saying restaurants beside main roads should have protective railings; Dot in Haccombe asking what we knew about the poor dead person on the bike and whether he had family ('I don't think we know anything at all, not even a name,' said Edward); a listener coincidentally also named Edward calling from Yelland village to suggest prayerful thanks for the sparing of life; the same message from a vicar in Torridge, and an angry call from Pinki, a young environmentalist in Ringmore, who said: 'We were asking for this tragedy ever since we put roads along seafronts.' (Edward thought: *Okay, Monday's show – the question – Ban roads next to seafronts?*)

There were so many callers. A fatal accident involving young children in an almost miraculous escape, right in the middle of Sidmouth on a May Friday... Penelope in Langtree rang to say,

'As the Germans said after the Second World War, so we must ourselves pronounce, "*Nie Wieder*". Which means never again.' She pronounced it 'Knees Wider'. But it was hard to work out what had caused the crash, and even harder to see what you could do to prevent such a thing recurring, so by eleven o'clock, when the topic would change for the last hour of the show, Edward had the feeling that he had explored a blizzard of reaction without getting even an inch closer to the reality of what had happened, and by next week there would be nothing more to say.

During the news at eleven, his phone sparked into life.

'Stevie.'

'I was out, wedding prep, fuck, exhausting.'

'Did the cop get you?'

'What cop?'

'Oh.' Was Edward allowed to be the first to speak to her? 'DS Jordan Callintree. Intelligent, you can trust him. You helped him at the pizza house.'

'Am I under suspicion or something?'

'The opposite! I gave him your number. The news is ending in a minute. I think it's just formalities with—' He saw the clock. 'Wait. Can we speak on air about it?'

'I don't know, I'm a bit in shock still.'

'I know this is a big favour, but I've got a boss who basically says my show is going to be closed unless it starts being interesting. He wants us to break things.'

'And you want to break me?'

'Not like that, but yes, have you on, like an exclusive sort of thing.'

'Shite, really? Broadcast me? I don't know, my parents will go potty if they hear what I did.'

'We can use a pseudonym.'

A pause, then: 'Use Rebecca.'

He managed to get her patched through just as the news

ended. As his programme jingle played, he said through the phone talkback: 'Stevie listen, *no swearing*, okay?'

Then he introduced her. Melody, in the control suite on the other side of the glass, had been caught cold by the sudden introduction of a guest she knew nothing about. He scrawled on a sheet of paper and held it up: FRIEND STEVIE WAS AT PIZZA.

Now he was introducing her. 'I won't give her real name,' he said, 'but I gather this person was at the scene of the accident. We will call her Rebecca.'

'Yes.'

'Could you tell us more?'

'About what?'

'The fire, the other families in there?'

And then she was away. The voice – still that undertow of Glasgow accent; the rasp, almost as if the throat had been scarred like her face. She dropped words like stones, rounded, separate, each one pertinent.

'I came in via the entrance on The Backs. I didn't see the bike crash. I just heard the terrible noise from the other side. The promenade side. I had a job there once, so I knew the back door was always open. I thought maybe – I don't know what I thought. I opened it and I was looking out into the street. I saw the biker. The motorbike, bloody hell—'

'Just please, the language, if you can, Rebecca, we have boring rules about that.'

'Sorry, Mr Temmis. I don't know what the noise made me think, but whatever it was did not prepare me.'

'Some people would have turned around and just got out.'

'Not me,' she said. Only Stevie could say such a thing without sounding like she was blowing her own trumpet. 'Also – I saw the policeman. Didn't know he was police. Thought I recognized him but wasn't sure. He was with the biker. The families were climbing out of the window. I passed the crumpled bike on my right and then I clocked the fire . . .'

Her description took in every detail. Edward closed his microphone, knowing she would speak for five minutes before another question was needed. It was like watching a movie, hearing her voice paint the picture. He turned to see Melody, entranced like him. They stared vacantly at each other through the glass as Stevie described the children being bundled out by parents, the smell of the smoke, the efforts to remove the body of the biker. He wondered at Stevie's heroism and couldn't help but think that if he had been close when the fire and smoke erupted from the pizzeria, he would have turned and run.

When he left the radio station at midnight, the security guard handed him an envelope.

'Strange one this,' she said. The woman was new, and in the dim of the reception he could barely make out her face. 'There was a knock on the main doors, Mr Temmis, and when I got there, this was slipped under. They could have come in, but they must have slid away into the night.'

He took the envelope, studying his name on the outside: E. TEMMIS. It was written in thick pencil and the handwriting was like a child's. He pocketed the note and thought no more of it as he left the building and stepped into the warm night air.

CHAPTER ELEVEN

'. . . and then Stevie slipped away. Didn't even expect thanks.'

'Jesus,' said Kim, listening to Edward repeat their friend's words verbatim. 'Impressive. As my dad would say, quiet gumption. And Stevie's never been quiet.' It was one in the morning. He was at Kim's flat. The lights were low. A candle flickered on the coffee table between them. He often came over on Friday and stayed for the weekend. 'Poor Stevie. And her wedding in a week!'

'Lucky none of the customers died. There were kids in there.'

'So lucky.' She was handing him a second glass of red wine, and Edward thought the last two words might have been for him, served with the wine, as in: *Lucky you, having me, punching.* Or was that just his insecure self, the cat's paw that kept clawing at the curtain of his confidence?

They were silent for a minute, thinking about the fire. Kim said, 'Glad you've got your voice back.'

Edward smiled, put the wine to his lips, paused before sipping and looked around the room. 'Hmm.'

'What does "hmm" mean? You don't like my new paint and wallpaper? You take to your sickbed, and I spend the whole time in my wedding dress.' She fetched it and held it up.

'Jesus, what have you done? It looks like . . . something out of Eurovision.'

'I just wanted to wreck it, I guess.' The satin was smeared and flecked with orange, green, dark red, and a mass of thick blue. 'Eggshell front and back.'

'Why would you do that?' he asked.

'Painting over bad memories.'

He stared at the dress. 'A week ago I was all geared up. I was going to ask you if you wanted to come live with me. You remember you had your flat tyre and I wanted to ask you something important?'

'Look at the dress, Edward.'

'I'm looking.'

'What does it say to you, darling?'

'I wasn't proposing marriage.' He felt genuinely hurt. 'So do you have an answer to the question I never asked?'

'I do.' She sat opposite him, looking at him intently, knowing her eyes would glint in the light of the candle.

'Watch out saying "I do" like that, you might be misunderstood.'

'Misunderstand that dress if you can.' She pointed, though she hardly needed to. She turned back to him, face dark with the pain of memory. 'To get this straight. I've only just got out of a horrible marriage, and yes I love you, Edward, I completely fucking adore you, and I want you wrapped around me every night like a great big bear, but I've set myself up here. I'm just trying to simplify my life first. Understand?'

Now it was his turn. 'I do.'

'Ha!' she laughed. 'If we've both said "I do", maybe we *are* married.'

'It wasn't marriage I was after.' He thought of Tara, his first wife, with her new children and husband, leaving him a million miles behind. 'I knew I shouldn't ask when you told me you were spending the week decorating your—'

'My divorce shack.'

'—your post-marital living quarters.'

'"Quarters" is the right word. Quarters are what I feel my life has been cut into. I need to put the parts back together. I need some stability.'

'I was trying to offer that!'

'In your house on the edge of a cliff?'

'Fair point. I would like to point out that the estate agent who sold me the house has yet to face justice.'

She smiled.

He said, 'I just love you so much.'

'Sweet boy. Reciprocated. What's that?'

He was pulling the letter from his jacket. 'I forgot this. Handed in at the radio station.' He ripped the envelope open. Inside was a single sheet of lined paper torn from a spiral notepad.

'Well?'

'Makes no sense' He held it up, the words facing Kim.

'What on earth—?'

'"Temmis, we are warning you, stop with your questions",' he recited, seeing the words back-to-front through the paper.

'All in capitals, black marker pen.'

'Someone's angry.'

She said, 'Bit difficult to stop asking questions in your job.'

'This is what we had before social media. Letters slid under doors. So much better.' Edward wanted to make light of it. He changed the subject. 'Are you looking forward to being back at work on Monday?'

'I've almost been back at work this week,' she said ruefully. 'In the sense that the office kept ringing me about a couple who wanted to buy a flat and I don't want to sell it to them.'

'You haven't quite got the hang of this estate agent thing, have you?'

'You know you can get a sense that something is off? A tall Asian lady in heels and this wobbling weeble of a guy, slicked back, red shoes and tubby in the waist. Wanting to pay cash for the beautiful penthouse on Thirdfield Terrace which I've lusted after. And it didn't smell right.'

'Red shoes and high heels?'

She stared at him. 'I'm not making it up.'

He scratched his head. Stared at the carpet, trying to remember something that suddenly seemed important. 'When I was trying to find your spare tyre, I looked everywhere and I ended up underneath it.'

'Lovely man,' she whispered.

'And when I was underneath it, searching for a tyre that didn't exist because Porsches are worse than Morris Minors, two people started talking right next to me. Man and woman. I saw their feet. That was your Asian lady, and that was your man. Red brogues.'

'They returned to the scene? What were they saying?'

'She sounded angry with him.'

'She actually struck him, almost in front of me, can you believe that? Slapped him! When we were in the flat!'

'I remember exactly what she said. "Did Vinnie say the parachute was through?" God knows what that meant. Parachute? Were they going paragliding or something? There's quite a bit of that in Sidmouth.'

'Did Vinnie . . . say . . . the parachute . . . was through.' Kim turned the phrase over as she repeated it slowly. 'Through what? What does a parachute go through?'

'A letterbox?'

She roared with laughter, surprising him.

'Can you refuse to sell it to them?'

'We can just be useless,' she said, her attention snapping

back to the present. 'We're quite good at that.' The business was Kim's, and she occasionally complained about two of the youngest staff members. 'I'll pass them onto our Gen Z secretariat, tell them to do it quickly, and they'll still be waiting for the Acceptance of Offer letter in December.'

'Rude.'

'About Gen Z? I don't mean to be. They have to clean up the planet, after all.'

'Poor bastards,' he said.

When he awoke on Saturday morning, Kim was rolling her body across his.

'This is not amorous,' she said. 'I'm trying to stop your phone going. Twice now.'

Bleary-eyed, he grabbed it and cancelled the alert. Then he saw it was from a name he knew.

Wendy Wrigley had typed:

> I'm outside your house.

And then, ten minutes later:

> I'll stay in case you've overslept.

And finally, as if in frustration:

> The forest!

CHAPTER TWELVE

Just before she awoke on Saturday morning, Andrea Lopez had had a strange dream about her daughter's hands. They were like the work of an artist, she had always thought that: delicate and perfect. But in the dream they came to her in a vision that was not always comfortable. Making the silhouette of a dove, then a horror movie claw. Shadows on the wall. First a rabbit, then reaching out for help, fingers outstretched.

She opened her eyes to a thick headache. She turned to kiss her husband's shoulder, then rolled heavily to see the bedside clock. Okay, the weekend. But still. Lie-ins? No chance. A normal waking time was before six, with their child not yet five years old. She wondered if that was how it worked. The two-year-old got you up at two, the five-year-old at five, and then by the time they were teenagers they were having to be poked and prodded awake in the afternoon.

But no Nina yet. Not this morning. What was it, seven already? Perhaps she was giving them a break after what happened yesterday. In a minute their little darling would busy herself into the room as if she had never slept. She would shake her curls and drop her fists on the edge of the duvet and claim the emergency of a lost dinosaur or a broken handle on a toy saucepan.

Andrea shut her eyes, opened them again. The clock said eight thirty. Wait . . . how could it be that late?

The young parents had moved to Sidmouth for a better life soon after Nina was born. They had had four rounds of IVF and three miscarriages and were both emotionally exhausted. After years in a flat in Exeter, where property was madly expensive, they cashed in for a semi with a garden. A mile back from the seafront, their house even had room for a dining table. Now parents, they were almost obscenely happy. They had put down roots quickly, finding friends in the local Labour Party branch. Gabriel had even started giving Spanish night classes at Sidmouth Tech, a side hustle to his job as a planning inspector. And now Nina would have a sister. Her ever-curious Nina would have a sibling to poke and prod.

Andrea felt the baby in her womb as she blinked at the time. The blinking brought the clock into focus but also the events of, what, less than eighteen hours ago?

It was incredible. The whole thing. She placed her right palm on the bump below her breasts. Her husband spoke quietly.

'Are you awake?'

'I'm thinking about it.'

'I couldn't sleep,' he said. 'Thank God. Sweet Jesus, our Nina. Protected by angels.' His voice was muffled by the pillow, but Andrea thought she could hear his throat narrow, tears coming. 'Today I will go to church to thank Him. That motorbike could have—'

'Sweet, don't,' she cut in. She had glimpsed the dead motorbiker. Nina had not seen him. But she had been out of her mother's sight for an instant in the chaos.

'I was glancing around so rapidly,' her husband said. 'Sweet Jesus we thank you for saving our precious daughter.'

'Why is she not out of bed?' asked Andrea.

'Exhausted, I guess.' Gabriel's voice was clearer. Andrea could tell without looking that he had propped himself up, and imagined him on an elbow behind her, the thick black hair tousled (not a single grey yet!), moustache wayward with a slept-on-my-face look. 'I should go see.'

The little girl's bed was new, and she had slept better after a bout of night terrors on the smaller mattress. But still, thought Andrea, eight thirty was *very* late for her. She was suddenly filled with a terrible sense of foreboding.

'Where is Nina?' Despite the cumbersome shape of her midriff with Nina's sister due in ten weeks, she sat up quickly on the edge of the bed, back straight.

'Honey . . .' Her husband was lying back down, and his arm reached instinctively to stop her, catching her nightshirt.

'Something is wrong,' she told Gabriel sharply. 'Let me go.'

As she wrapped the dressing gown around her she thought she saw her whole life as a movie, playing out in a second: the Madrid childhood with angry parents, dad leaving for a child of a lover, her alone with *mami*, losing her virginity at sixteen, finding her facility for spoken language, flowering at university, the brush with cancer, dad's early death, meeting Gabriel, the traditional marriage, the struggle to conceive, and now, like a ship landed at harbour, this beautiful daughter, kind husband, girl number two on the way.

On Nina, she thought, you are the harbour. Little girl, I was the ship, storm-tossed. You were the place I berthed. The place I arrived after so much tumult. Oh, Nina, my darling. My precious girl, my safe home, my life.

A sense of doom enveloped Andrea as she closed the bedroom door behind her and looked up the narrow stairs to the conversion on the top floor.

Nina was in bed with the most peaceful expression on her face. She woke to her mother's touch, and with a gappy smile said: 'Mum!' Such a British word. Andrea looked at her daughter's hands, the ones she had seen in the dream. She picked up the left, and was shocked to find it cold and clammy.

'Honey, are you poorly?'
The child smiled. 'Your hands are hot, Mummy.'
'Yours are cold, my darling. Do you have a chill?'
A shudder seemed to pass over Nina. Andrea carried her past the bedroom door where Gabriel was probably back asleep, and into the tiny kitchen. She sat her at the table, in the wooden chair with the booster cushion attached, but the child's body slumped a little.
'Are you okay, darling?' Andrea called, 'Gabriel! Gabriel, come down!'
Nina was a talkative child, with many friends at her new primary school, although – teachers had occasionally noted – 'a tendency to be a little bossy with the boys.' This, Andrea had thought, was a good sign, though she wondered if they would use the same adjective for an assertive male child. Her child liked a pretty dress but had once taken a toy car apart with a screwdriver: the perfect meld of twentieth- and twenty-first-century female. Andrea knew she was getting ahead of herself, but you did that when you had longed and longed for a baby.
Now she looked anxiously at her wilting child, who blinked back up at her. 'Are you okay, Mummy?'
'Can you sit up? Maybe I'm being silly, worrying about you.'
'I think I need another one of my sweeties,' said Nina, apparently recovered.
Gabriel arrived, his pyjama fly hanging open. Andrea pointed at their daughter. 'Right as rain. Just exhausted by . . . yesterday.' She would not mention the bike crash, because she feared the return of Nina's terrors.
It was then that Andrea saw her daughter's hands.
They were clasped – unusual for a child of four. When Andrea separated them, they were trembling with such energy she felt a current might be running through them.
'What sweeties, darling?'

'The man came off the bike and I found them.' The child was sitting at the table, rocking left and right as if to a musical rhythm only she could hear. She spread her arms wide like an old-school preacher, and the hands vibrated as she held them out. Now Gabriel was alert too.

'Sweeties, darling?'

'Daddy, when the bike crashed, I saw them on the floor. They tasted nice. I just had one yesterday. I saved the other two. Or, no, maybe I had one in the middle of the night.'

Surely this was meaningless, thought Andrea. *She is groggy because yesterday was horrible for us all.* She remembered the noise, the shock, the flames, the panic . . . yes, there was a minute where everyone had been moving everywhere . . . Had there been a few seconds when she thought Gabriel had Nina safely, and Gabriel thought she did? Yes, for sure there had. And Nina had used that tiny sliver of time to pick something unknown off the floor and eat it.

Andrea shuddered even as Gabriel shot upstairs. He came back down with two tiny gelatin capsules which he held between the finger and thumb of each hand. 'Found them! What are they? Vitamins?'

Gabriel was staring at his daughter. Andrea turned to him and then back to Nina.

Nina had slumped left in the high chair and there was a thin line of white froth on her lips.

'Darling,' said Andrea, 'what have you done?'

CHAPTER THIRTEEN

When Edward approached his own house, almost skidding off the road in his haste, he saw, to his surprise, three people waiting.

Flanking Wendy were two kindly looking men who had the beseeching look of priests at confession. They must be twins. Both wore jeans and trainers, and both sported navy blue jackets, as if they had rushed into work at the weekend. They had thinning hair, but the one on the right evidently dyed his, while the other had let his go prematurely white. It was one of few features which separated them. The lack of fat on them made their movements angular, suggesting marionettes mirroring each other, controlled from above by a left hand and a right. The twin on the left with the white hair was smiling warmly, but with an air of worry.

It was the brother to Wendy Wrigley's right who stepped forward first.

'I'm Charlie Hurst – this is Hubert.'

'Hi,' said Hubert, with the white hair. 'A double-H, Hubert Hurst.'

'Don't ask about his middle name,' said Charlie.

'It's Roger. So the initials are HRH,' said Wendy, with an affectionate smile. 'Somewhat regal.'

'At school his nickname was Prince, of course,' laughed Charlie. 'Johnny was partly responsible for that.' At the mention of their departed friend, all three of them became suddenly downcast and a fog of worry settled on the Hurst brothers again.

'I am sorry for your loss,' said Edward, even though the murder had been nearly two years earlier. 'I didn't know you were at school together,' Edward continued. 'I thought Wendy said university.'

'Well, that was when we set up our gang, university medics.' Hubert looked into the middle distance. He took half a step forward, as if he was stumbling and about to fall. 'Our gang—'

'Us, Pippa, Zirch, Johnny, a couple of others. It was the four of us who ended up in Devon,' said Charlie.

Wendy put in: 'And then disaster struck. I came here to find my tribe again.'

'And we feel,' continued Charlie, 'so desperate to find out who or what or why. I mean, why would he be *murdered*?'

Wendy said sharply, 'Charlie, please!'

He gulped. 'I know you hate the word.'

'Hate is strong, but I do.'

'Did Wendy say you were both medical consultants?'

'I'm cancer, he's dementia,' said Hubert. 'We work virtually next door to each other at Exeter General.' He hopped left and right on his feet, a sign of nervousness.

Edward said, 'Now I feel even worse about keeping you waiting.'

'We wondered if you wanted us with you in the forest today,' said Hubert. He and Charlie were both like priests, simultaneously elevated and humble. How keenly they were feeling the pain of this, the loss of their friend. If Wendy had been responsible, or even just a genuine suspect, the twins would not want anything to do with her. It reinforced Edward's absolute conviction – her alibi was watertight because she was innocent.

The pain from the fatal shooting of Dr Jonathan Wrigley was

spreading like a stain. A mystery that would never be solved, unless he could untangle it for them.

He would try.

Wendy drove. The Hurst twins were persuaded she could handle the day without them.

'I'm so sorry I forgot my commitment,' Edward said when they were in the car. 'Yesterday was chaos.'

'Why?'

'You didn't hear about the accident at the pizza place?'

'Oh, of course. Yes.'

He could see her mind was elsewhere. As she took the country roads at speed, cornering faster than he would have wanted, he googled 'Dr J Wrigley murder'. He wasn't much of an investigator, forgetting the appointment and doing his research this late. All the printouts he had made from online articles were in his kitchen. Phone signal was patchy on this road.

'They're decent men,' she said suddenly.

'The twins?'

'They are so, so decent. They spend their lives just trying to help. They see a lot of people nearing the end. I think it gets to you.'

'I couldn't do it. When my listeners die, I feel it.'

'Found anything on your phone?'

'It's all the stuff I've seen before. About the location.'

'I brought an Ordnance Survey map,' she said.

On YouTube he saw a thumbnail with Andrew Coombs, followed by a pop-up advert. He clicked the screen to close the pop-up, but suddenly the amateur pilot appeared, full screen, speaking out loud into the car: 'The poor man was on the forest floor near the airfield. Spread out like a star in a white linen suit, right up against a tree, and we will never forget it. Naturally our thoughts are with the family.'

'I'm so sorry, Mrs Wrigley, I didn't mean to play that.'

'Wendy, please. And leave it on.'

Coombs was asked about his daughter. 'Still in shock from me turning the aircraft.' His tone was clipped, as if he was protecting her. Maybe they had nearly crashed. An accompanying photo, captioned ANDREW AND CLARA COMBS IN HAPPIER TIMES, showed father and daughter standing beside a tiny plane, both figures blasted by bright sunlight, him grinning, her face pixelated. The report cut to a Google image of the airfield which jerked to the forested area two hundred yards to the north. A red cross appeared alongside the words BODY FOUND HERE. Edward took a screenshot before the signal went.

The journey from Sidmouth to Chittlehamholt was more than an hour, even though she broke the speed limit most of the way.

They used a route that passed close to the north side of the airstrip, then took a right fork. After five minutes bumping along a track with hedgerows on both sides, they saw the entrance to the airfield itself. 'Shall we?' asked Wendy Wrigley, pointing. It seemed cheeky to park within it when they had no business there, but they did.

Sure enough, they had not been stopped for more than a minute on the edge of the pristine strip before a man in a gold hairpiece approached, jogging as if it was urgent.

He wore shorts and a pilot's blazer, double-breasted with epaulettes and five gold buttons. He introduced himself as Gracey, the 'manager-gardener-receptionist' of the place, and said – as telegraphed by his rapid approach – that this was not a car park for casual walkers.

Before Edward could speak, Wendy had disarmed Gracey completely. She locked the car and asked Edward to show him the screenshot. 'We need a man who knows his way around a map. It's personal to me.'

Gracey took the page as Edward unfolded it. There were ominous clouds overhead, and it was starting to spit.

'Where that poor doctor was found?'

Edward held his breath. Would Wendy be recognized by this man? Would he judge her like Coombs and everyone else?

'He was my husband.'

Gracey stared at Wendy as if hypnotized. 'Well. Thoughts with. God. That's thrown me . . . We had a new flyer up in the air that day, brought his young daughter, some sort of London banker' – the word, as he said it, loaded with negativity – 'and I watched him coming in to land, and the lunatic tried to buzz the body! . . . Excuse me, ma'am.' It was a distasteful phrase to use. He started pointing at a distant spot in the air. 'So I feel I know the vertical position because I can visualize his plane up there, dropping like a bloody stone.'

'Where were you when it happened?' asked Edward.

Ignoring him, Gracey turned Edward's phone landscape-portrait-landscape. 'Agh, I need to lock this display. It keeps turning. I don't know how helpful this map is, except yes, it's definitely over there, past the four planes, into the wood. Oh, Christ. Gosh. I don't know.' A gust of wind blew the lapel of his overcoat across his face, and he pulled it away quickly, like a highwayman unmasking himself. 'Walk between planes three and four, the Ikarus and the Cirrhus. The Cirrhus is grounded, in case you're alarmed there's a hole where the engine should be. Proceed around two hundred yards once you're in amongst the trees. Two hundred, three hundred? Stay in a straight line between this point and the gap between the planes. The red cross could even be accurate.'

'Where were you when you saw the plane buzz the site?' Edward asked again.

Gracey folded the map, handed it to Wendy and, without looking away from her, said: 'In ATC over there.'

'That shed?' asked Edward.

'We call it ATC. Good luck. And while you're in the mood for searching, please search yourselves for tick bites later, the bullseye mark on the skin. Lyme Disease is an absolute motorhome.'

It gave Wendy and Edward a bonding moment as they walked. She said, 'Where is that phrase from, "an absolute motorhome"? I mean . . .' and, as she laughed, he replied: 'Something to do with Scottish politics? Wasn't there a motorhome scandal?'

The two walked across the expanse of mown grass as instructed and passed between the last two light aircraft.

Soon they were in the forest, their trousers soaked by tall heather and brambles. There was no path. Wendy Wrigley had her phone out. Edward was trying to unfold the paper map as he walked.

'Would my phone help?' she asked, a little impatiently. 'With this I can tell north, south, east, et cetera. I have signal. Good old Chittlehamholt.'

'I guess airfields have masts. I don't need a mast for this.' He spread the map across his knee and marked the point at which they had entered the forest and then, after looking over his shoulder, the location of the ATC shed. There was a cross on it already – he had marked the location of the X in the TV report.

'You never came here?' he asked as they picked their way among the debris on the forest floor.

'No, never. Not before, not much of a walker, you know. And after . . .' She trailed off.

'Did he used to walk here on his own?'

'Yes. Especially if he felt unwell.'

'Unwell?'

'I thought I'd told you. He just had bad fatigue, a sense that he was stumbling a bit, messing things up. Middle age, I thought.'

'He wasn't much older than me.' Edward stopped walking. 'We are now right at the middle of the cross they showed on the TV report. It's where we're standing.'

They were beside a stream fifteen feet wide. The water flowed at speed, jumping and bubbling at their feet. Set back from the stream, twenty yards to their right and in a state of disrepair so total its original function was barely recognizable, were the remains of a bandstand.

The pair looked around miserably. They were both in waterproof coats. The spit had turned to drizzle, so thin you almost could not feel it, but gradually making their clothes damper. In places where the trees parted, the sky was a miserable grey and the canopy offered virtually no light. Occasionally one of them had been hit by what felt like a cupful of rainwater dislodged from the thick leaves and branches above them.

He looked at the screenshot on his phone again, shook his head and pushed it deep into the pocket of his raincoat. 'Someone doing the graphics just found a map with an existing cross on it. Probably an intern at the TV station. They had no more clue where it happened than us. The cross was probably for the bandstand over there.'

They trudged on. Now he was dependent on the Ordnance Survey map alone, criss-crossed with erratic lines drawn with a biro (thank God he had a pen on him, just sheer good fortune), while it rested on his thigh or a fallen tree. Eventually they came to the stump of an oak, cleanly cut. 'Wendy, I'm going to struggle finding the place.' He unfolded the map and spread it across the smooth surface. 'Could you—'

She knew instinctively what he wanted, and produced her brolly as she stood above him. Edward sank to his knees, immediately feeling damp seep through his jeans. He was conscious of her silence as the rain pattered on the surface of the small umbrella.

He spoke to the map. 'The first black line is the direction we were pointed by the chap with that yellow croissant on his head.'

'My husband struggled with his own hair loss; quite sudden it was too.'

'Apologies. That is the sightline from the shed he works in.' Edward put his thumb on a second line, finding the paper damp. 'Although he didn't realize it, the angle changes the end point.'

'A clearing?' she suggested. 'They all said a clearing.'

'That doesn't help, does it?'

'Wait,' she said. 'His body was found below a tree in a clearing.'

Now Edward stood, leaving the map spread across the tree stump. 'I don't see what you mean.'

'A clearing is a place without trees.' She looked at the canopy, thick with leaves and branches. 'But this was a clearing *with* a tree. It had a tree. He was underneath the tree, and they could see him. How do you see a guy from the air if he's underneath a tree?' She looked at the ground, tugged at the knot in her scarf and shook her head, as if the thought had taken off and left her behind.

He said: 'I work in a garden centre once or twice a week. I have friends there who helped me when my son died. A clearing,' he repeated. He was back on his knees, staring at the map, spreading his hands across it until the damp from the tree stump threatened to tear the thick paper. 'When did your husband die?'

'October the twelfth, the year before last,' she said bitterly.

He produced his phone again. A fleck of rainwater hit the screen. He checked the exact location of the cross on the screenshot against the Ordnance Survey map. Then he stood and looked around them, chose a tree with large, low branches and started to climb it. When he was fifteen feet up, he spent five minutes looking in all directions. By the time he descended she was walking in circles, staring at her feet.

'You've had an idea?' she asked.

'I know where it happened. I'm certain actually. This way.' And he led her through the forest.

*

He had worked it out. She had not understood the clue she had given him. But he knew. The doctor was found beneath a tree which had shed by October.

He explained as they walked. 'I don't know that I'm right.' Yet he felt some pride. He had brutally applied logic. 'A clearing. Tree leaves not in the way. An ash. We're heading for the tallest ash, because it needs to have stopped competitor trees from growing near it. This time of year it won't look like a clearing at all.'

They came to the foot of an ash that reached high into the sky.

'Good God. Could be fifty feet,' said Edward.

'I'm a bit overwhelmed and I think I need to sit this out,' said Wendy. She tore the scarf off her head, and the crimped hair beneath it sprang out as if an illustrator had created it with a sudden slash of fountain pen. She retreated to a fallen tree and put her head in her hands. He started walking over to her, desperate to say or do something that might make this less painful, but she spoke without looking up from the forest floor. 'Please just examine the scene if you need to. Take your time. Anything you can find might help me. It's not easy for me, being here, but I need your help, or this will always be the place that ended two lives. Jonathan's and mine.'

Edward paused. A chill wind blew, and the leaves around them shivered. What if the real killer of Dr Wrigley was here, hidden in the trees, watching them? The killer had successfully stitched up the widow. Whoever did the crime would surely not allow him to prove her innocence.

'May I ask a question? Was he insured, your husband?'

She was too far away to hear. He asked again, more loudly.

'Oh yes. Not that I'll ever see a payout.'

'Why not?'

'Long story,' she called. 'Small print.'

Of course. No policy would pay out if there was even the smallest suspicion she was the killer.

He stepped closer to her. 'But you haven't been convicted. How can they say that?'

'They'll say anything to avoid paying,' she said. 'I don't think about it much. True, if we find out he was murdered by a passing crazy person, and they get done for it, then they might just pay.'

Edward asked: 'And would they pay out for suicide?'

'Yes. But he wouldn't want to end his life. Why would he do that? And dispose of the crossbow after his death? Come on.'

She spoke bitterly. Almost too quietly for him to hear. They were fifty yards apart now. It was drizzling. Wendy was sitting on a huge fallen tree, innards opened like a patient in theatre, and he was staring up at the massive ash, thinking: *It must have been here.*

And then he saw it.

A hole in the trunk of the ash, cleanly drilled, not even a centimetre wide.

In the car, she was silent. Until, just as they approached the edge of Sidmouth, she said: 'You took a lot of photos.'

'I found something. But I don't know what it means.'

'Do you want to tell me?'

'Do you mind if I keep it close to my chest just for a few days?' he asked. 'Because I don't want you thinking I've solved something if I haven't. I won't know the meaning until I've checked.'

'Checked what?'

'The spot. I just need to be a hundred per cent that we were at the right location. I know how to find out.'

'Okay, but . . .' She tailed off. 'I thought you were eating the tree bark at one point.'

'I had to get close.'

'Whatever comes of it, Edward, you've listened and you've given me a little hope.' They were on Station Road, heading towards the centre of Sidmouth, and she stopped by the Woodlands Hotel where the lane narrowed and a sign with a red arrow told drivers arriving in the town they must give way. 'You do know I would pay you for this?'

'I don't want you to pay me anything,' said Edward. 'I just like finding out the truth of things, that's all. I'm not a professional detective. I'm just a . . .'

'Sleuth.'

'Yes, maybe. Along with my friends Kim and Stevie. And I need to meet them before I say any more. They'll have ideas.'

'I'll pay you five thousand pounds if you can solve it.'

'What?? But I . . .' *Five thousand?* He hesitated. He knew what he'd do with the money, even if taking it wouldn't be right. 'If we get the new inquest, which I guess is what you want, and you're happy with my work, there are a group of listeners to my radio show who would welcome a payment. I would hand it over to them.'

'Wow. Okay.'

As they came into Sidmouth and the phone signal reconnected, his mobile beeped so much it almost jumped out of his hand.

'We have to slow down, I think,' she said. 'Look – bad traffic.'

'Bad traffic in Sidmouth?' he said thoughtfully. In high summer, or during the folk festival, maybe. But not now, not at the start of the season.

They crawled along, past the entrance to Thirdfield Terrace. Edward ducked forward to see the apartment Kim was so attached to. It sat at the top of the white-painted block, looking down onto the cricket green. It would be, he thought, a lovely location.

He remembered the couple's conversation he had overheard from underneath the car. The odd use of 'parachute' – what was that, a code?

Wendy said, 'Look.'

When he took his eyes off Thirdfield Terrace and sat back up, he saw the police cordon. 'They've closed the promenade,' he said. 'They never do that.'

'Maybe that's why my phone keeps vibrating.'

He looked at his. Twenty-one text messages had suddenly arrived in his inbox. 'I have to go left,' he said. 'Can you drop me off?'

'At least tell me what you found.'

She was desperate to know. But he was focused on the chaos being caused by the cordon. For a moment, the line of traffic was completely stationary. 'I can't get closer to the radio station in the car. I'll have to go around the back on foot. I need to see what's happening. I'll call you, I promise.'

'You found something? Something helpful?'

'I think so, Wendy,' he said, wondering if this was the first time he had called her by her first name. Edward stretched his legs and straightened his back. He bent again, just as the car moved forwards slightly, and when he saw Wendy he wondered if she was about to cry. Her gaze was fixed ahead, and he saw her jaw was clenched and her lower lip trembled.

'One more thing.' He was leaning through the passenger window, going with the fractional forwards movement of the car by performing a kind of grapevine.

'Anything.'

'Did your husband's mother or father suffer from Motor Neurone Disease?'

She looked at him, dumbstruck, and then looked back at the road. Her mouth opened but no words came out.

CHAPTER FOURTEEN

By the time they got to the hospital, Nina just looked like an exhausted child asleep in her father's arms. They had driven themselves – they could not wait for an ambulance. The choice had been between the A&E at Exeter, a half-hour drive, and the Victoria, only ten minutes away, which had a Minor Injury Unit. They rushed to the Victoria. Gabriel broke every speed limit and every red light. A weekend morning gave them the chance to avoid traffic. At the hospital the reception area was clear, but it was so quiet they waited five minutes for the duty nurse to return from what seemed to be a tea break.

Gabriel was holding his daughter tightly, as if he might squeeze the life into her. Andrea had sat in the back of the car with their daughter lying across the back seat. She had been too limp to go into the booster chair. 'Gabriel, her forehead is burning,' she kept saying.

The nurse took one look at the child from behind her desk and ran around it to see more closely. 'You need Exeter.'

'Please,' said Gabriel, and Andrea burst into tears. 'You must have someone. She collapsed!'

The nurse was close to the child now. 'Foam at the mouth?'

'Yes!' said Andrea and Gabriel at the same time. There was only a thin line of white on Nina's lips now.

'We are worried she ate something she shouldn't have,' said Gabriel. From her handbag Andrea produced the sealed freezer bag with the two tiny ampoules.

The nurse, short and strong, with red eye make-up, took the bag and held it to the light. 'These just look like vitamin gels. Did she pick them up somewhere?'

'The pizza parlour yesterday. The one on the seafront where—'

The nurse interrupted Gabriel. 'The crash?' He saw her name badge now: MERCY AKUA. 'Poor thing, poor all of you.'

Andrea asked: 'Could they have come from the motorbike?'

Having no answer, the nurse said, 'I worry about meningitis with a floppy child like this. No mark on the skin?'

'I looked, but we rushed here,' said Andrea.

'A mark on the leg here . . .'

'A dog bite two years ago.'

'The legs, the arms, the bottom?'

'We didn't—'

'Could you take her to Exeter?'

Both parents shouted, wild-eyed. 'No! No, please, there must be someone here . . .'

A minute later, the child was in front of a consultant orthopaedic surgeon who gave his name so fast neither Gabriel nor Andrea heard it. 'I normally do broken things, so you have slightly landed me in the soup, young lady,' he said, sitting her heavily on the edge of the bed in his consulting room and now trying to hold her upright. He was a lean man in his sixties with a high forehead and kind eyes. Andrea sat next to Nina on the green coverlet.

'She'll fall if we don't hold her,' said the consultant. As he said the words he pointed a penlight into Nina's right eye, then the left, holding the lids open each time. 'Dad,' he said to

Gabriel, 'I think you might need to keep her head upright for me. Foaming, you said? At the mouth?'

'A little,' said Andrea, starting to sob, panic rising again.

Gabriel was fishing in his pocket for the freezer bag but gave up, his other hand steadying Nina's head. 'There was a crash yesterday in Sidmouth. On the promenade. We were there, he spilt some little capsules on the floor apparently. From his pannier, I don't know. Nina ate one of the capsules.'

'Two,' said Andrea.

'One at the restaurant, and then she said she ate one in the night, thinking they were sweets.'

The doctor exclaimed, 'What?' He stared at the small bag.

'I kept two. They were in her room.'

'Support her weight if you can,' said the consultant urgently, carefully easing his grip on the little girl and slowly standing up. 'It's not meningitis. No temperature. If anything she has a lower temperature than I'd expect. She may simply be in shock. I saw the news. It was an inferno by the end in that place and it's a miracle no one died.'

'The poor man on the bike did,' said Andrea, suddenly weeping, her daughter's tiny hand trembling slightly within her own. She squeezed it, her throat tight. 'That poor man. And my poor daughter. Will she die?'

The consultant breathed in quickly. He was pointing the penlight into the child's mouth, holding the jaw open, but he kept glancing down at the capsules in the bag being held by Gabriel.

'There is some red at the back of the mouth. We should rule out anything poisonous in those capsules, just to be safe.'

Gabriel pushed them towards the doctor, who took the freezer bag and held it away from him, towards the window, as if fascinated by what it might contain. The light flooded in and illuminated the capsules.

'Little bullets,' said the consultant, stepping closer, taking off his glasses and bringing his face right up to the bag. 'Might be nothing.' He twisted his mouth. 'Then again.' The morning sunlight shone through the ampoules and put two yellow dots on the right side of his face, just below his eye, dancing like sniper's marks. 'Right. You need to go to Exeter. We need to be sure of what we're dealing with here.'

'Okay,' said Gabriel, standing and gathering their things as fast as he could. 'Okay, I will drive us.'

'No, young man.' The doctor stood, his movements now filled with intent. 'There's no time for that. We're going to blue-light you in an ambulance.'

CHAPTER FIFTEEN

When Edward Temmis looked at his phone, he wondered how he had seen only the text messages. There were a dozen emails, all sent in the last two hours, and fifteen missed calls.

He rang Aspinall first.

'Where . . . the hell . . . have you been?'

'I was in the north, away with a—' Edward did not want to spell it out. Aspinall might not react well to the name Wendy Wrigley.

'With a what? A polar bear, a prostitute, an orchestra? Were you underground with a team of coal miners? A pot-holing club? Is that why your phone didn't work? You are walking on thin ice, sir!'

'I had to look at something in North Devon. It doesn't matter.'

'But—'

'I know, I know.' Edward heard a note of desperation in his voice. A *please-don't-sack-me* note he had never deployed before.

'This pizza thing has kicked off big-time. Are you back in Sidmouth?'

'Walking along the . . . well, not the promenade, it's closed. Walking The Backs, to the radio station.'

'Jesus. Who are you? What are you? You make a . . . a shifty promise to those old dears, you say we'll pay them scam damages when we can't . . . and now your show isn't even present when a bonkers story breaks on your doorstep. I'm aghast!' He seemed to be doing deep breaths to calm himself. 'Come in now, if you like. But we definitely need you later. I know it's the weekend, but I want you to do your show tonight.'

A sliver of hesitation. He had wanted to see Kim. 'Of course.'

'Melody has some info from the police.'

'Did someone die? I thought just the biker. I thought everyone inside got out okay? My friend Stevie Mason was—'

Aspinall exploded. 'If you hadn't been MIA, we might know what was going on!' He sounded as if he was trying to get control of himself. 'I know you have police contacts—'

'Not really, I—'

'You have more of them than any of the flibbertigibbets.' Aspinall's word for the under-thirties, the new generation who were supposed to be in the wings ready to take over when the ashes of older careers were finally scattered across the sea, usually made Edward smile.

Edward's only contact with the police was Callintree. He could try the officer, but he needed to use the connection sparingly. They barely knew each other. And – goddammit – he wanted to ring Callintree about the forest area he had just visited with Wendy Wrigley, because before he told Wendy what he thought he had discovered there, he must at least check they had been at the right location. The police would have photos.

He told Aspinall firmly, 'Okay, I can call him.' Wendy would have to wait a little.

'Let me make this clear. We have a story on our patch that's big enough for them to close off the seaside. You are the news guy on the station. If you can't lead this, I'll bring in Tessa K and we'll put you on weather.'

'I'm on it, I'm on it.'

'When is your contract up?'

There it was – the most definite threat a presenter could ever hear, not even disguised.

'I think next February.'

'Okay. This is how maths works. I want some better figures on your show to bring in more ads to raise the money you promised all those scam victims. Can you make sense of that?'

'Perfect sense.'

'So ask your cop why they aren't just clearing up the mess in Toppings. They removed the body, very sad and all that, and then you'd expect men in white suits to crawl through the place for an hour and reopen the promenade. Instead they've locked down half the seafront like we're in Covid or something.'

'The plates on the bike were false.' As soon as Edward said it, he wished he hadn't.

'How do you know that?'

'Can't say.'

'But why don't we know that – why haven't you put that out?'

'I was told to keep it under my hat.'

'*What?*' screamed Aspinall. 'No one has the right to hide this stuff from our audience. I run a radio station, not a railway station! This is the biggest story in Sidmouth since the fatberg and I need you on it, not disappearing upcountry with things under your hat.'

The Sidmouth fatberg had been international news. A lump of congealed fat, wet wipes and assorted non-flushables had got caught in the sewers, increasing in volume until it was the size of six double-decker buses. The sewage operative who found the fatberg was treated like David Attenborough. A team of engineers had to suck it out using what was described as a reverse hosing system. It was considered to be such an embarrassment to the town, the mayor had made a public statement saying, without foundation, that the engineers had evidence that much of the waste had originated in Exmouth.

'I'm sure it's not as big as that,' said Edward. 'It's a very sad motorbike crash where only the rider died. People who live on corners on fast roads are constantly finding someone in a Fiat Panda arriving next to them on the sofa while they're watching TV. We do that story a lot. In Honiton there's—'

'Look, I'm not arguing about this. The key point is that – apart from it being bloody funny – you can go from being the presenter with the tiny cog to a really big-swinging-whatever if you sit on this story and ride it like a fucking racehorse.'

Edward was literally struck dumb. How coarse was this man? If he used any of this language with Melody or any number of the Gen Z crowd, he would be bundled into the elevator with a one-way ticket to the ground floor. But still, the words had the intended effect.

'I'm on my way in.'

'I don't want a Tessa K stealing your lunch and dinner,' said Aspinall, just to drive it home. Tessa K was on breakfast now, but she had done a long spell sitting in for Edward while he took compassionate leave after Matty's death. She had been a little too good. He certainly did not want 'a Tessa K' moving in on his patch . . .

Moving in on his story.

Yes, he decided. The Pizza Parlour Crash would be his story.

'I will ring . . . the person at the police who I get along with.'

'Good man. And come in for a special Saturday edition of your show tonight. Did I mention that?'

'You—'

'I'm kidding.' He laughed cruelly. 'Come in or be fired.'

On opposite sides of town, Kim and Stevie both saw they had been added to a three-person WhatsApp group called CROSS-BOW. The first message came from Edward, who had set himself as admin.

> Meet at the back of RTR and I'll bring you up. We can chat in canteen, need to ask about Wrigley. Can't leave office at mo. The security guard at rear (Backs) is expecting you. Trevor.

The first to get there was Kim. She waited at the rear door, not wanting to ring the reception bell until Stevie had arrived too.

After ten minutes, wondering if she should just go in on her own, Kim saw a bright red Ford Cortina stop in the road with thick smoke pouring from its exhaust. At first she thought the vehicle had broken down – the model was forty years old, at least, with gleaming chrome wheel hubs – but then the driver got out and she recognized Stevie's fiancé Roddy.

He did not so much walk as stalk to the nearside of the car. Roddy waved his arms at another driver, as if about to jump on the man's bonnet and pummel the windscreen. Now he was at the passenger side door of the Cortina, he grabbed the handle and threw it open.

The car was a hundred yards away, but Kim made out Stevie in the passenger seat, the view partly blocked by Roddy's frame. She could not quite see what was happening, but it looked as if Roddy had grabbed Stevie's hair and was pulling her out of the car with a handful of it in his hand. Kim said 'No!' quietly, almost in a whisper. But then Stevie was out of the car and out of his grip, straightening up, and Kim waved, and Stevie saw her. As she waved back, Roddy turned to her.

Roddy was wearing sunglasses as he had been the first time they met, aviator shades. His tracksuit was blue today and Kim saw him grin in the distance. She thought she must have imagined the moment of violence, but as Stevie walked towards her, Kim allowed a look of concern to pass her face. She mouthed

'Are you okay?' to her friend, who behaved as if she had not seen or understood.

Then she saw that Roddy was still there, watching like a hawk, and an inner voice told Kim not to show any sign of concern. So, as Stevie reached her, she smiled.

'Nice to see Roddy. He's looking out for you.'

Stevie turned, smiled and waved.

'It's lovely, isn't it?'

Roddy shouted something – a word.

'What was that?' Kim asked.

'He shouted "Next Saturday", our wedding day.'

Stevie was unreadable. There was a chance for Kim to say something as Roddy stomped back to the driver's side of the badly parked car, but the moment was gone as soon as it arrived.

They went into the radio station and took the lift to the canteen. In the lift Stevie said only three words: 'Wendy bloody Wrigley.'

The fifth floor of RTR-92 had the best view of the sea. The studios were on the fourth; the fifth had been sublet as shared space with the hotel next door. The hotel called the space their restaurant. The radio staff called it their canteen. Friction was avoided through regular reminders of the restrictions – no staff meetings, don't use a table to work at for hours, don't do interviews, don't bring your own Thermos. Edward had been waiting for Kim and Stevie for nearly an hour.

He still could not believe Stevie had plunged into the burning building. Evidently she was more capable of physical bravery than anyone else, maybe because she had already suffered enough injury for a lifetime. Stevie was special; special to him and to Kim. She had had a tricky upbringing and now, despite each and every disaster, she made her way in the world without complaining. Wrong – she made her way in the world with constant complaint, a beautiful barrage of expletives thrown ahead of her advance, like smoke and shells laid down by troops in World War One.

When he saw Kim and Stevie walking towards him, Kim looked unsettled, trapped in her own thoughts. He waited until she sat down.

'You okay?'

'Life,' said Kim.

Stevie, apparently unbothered, said: 'I asked your security guy what's going on and he doesn't know. No one does.'

'I forgot how nice the view was from here,' Kim said wistfully.

Had he imagined her unease? 'The studios are the floor below,' said Edward. 'So they have their priorities right. Food then programmes.'

'Then donkeys,' said Stevie.

'There aren't any donkeys in the building at this point.'

'She's joking, Edward, although I know it's a sore point,' said Kim. 'So tell us what you found.'

'In the forest? I need you guys to make sense of this.'

Stevie tapped her knife and fork on the table. *Right-left-right-right, left-right-left-left.* A drummer's paradiddle. 'You might have to stop, Stevie,' said Edward. 'Hotel snooty about drumming.'

'Isn't this your place?'

'Long story but we share it with the hotel. For example, those six guys over there' – he pointed at a family in the plusher dining area, two elderly, two middle-aged, two children – 'are nothing to do with the radio station. About to walk the coastal path, I guess.'

'So go on,' said Kim impatiently.

'I just have this,' said Edward. Carefully, he reached into the backpack on the bench beside him. As he did, Stevie said: 'By the way, can you two come to my wedding?'

This was not on the menu. Edward looked up from the bag. Kim looked across at Edward. Classic Stevie, derailing them.

He could hardly blame her for it. His head was so full of thoughts about the forest and what he had found – what he thought he had found – that he was forgetting everything else.

Kim said, 'Your wedding to Roddy?'

'There aren't any others I'm planning! I know you don't like him, Kim—'

'I saw him pull your hair.'

The three of them went silent. The contents of Edward's bag would have to wait.

'Just now?' asked Stevie, her voice quieter.

Kim addressed Edward. 'I waited for Stevie outside. Maybe I got it wrong. He came around the car, grabbed your hair and pulled you out, and you were snatching at his hands, or so I thought.'

'So you thought.'

Edward said, 'He didn't, did he?'

They were at a crossroads. Kim wasn't sure. Only Stevie could confirm it. She seemed to think for a moment, and make a decision.

'Show us what's in the bloody bag, Edward. My hair isn't important.'

'He pulled it!' Kim raised her voice.

'He was just helping me out of the car! He put his hand under my arm is all!'

Kim put her head in her hands. 'I'm messing everything up.'

'We'll be at the wedding, Stevie, and we can't wait,' said Edward, for some reason feeling cross with Kim.

The two women were silent. Edward pulled from his bag a delicate piece of white silk with something wrapped inside it. The object suddenly caught the attention of Kim and Stevie, as if they had transferred all their upset into a moment of acute focus. 'A classy hankie,' said Stevie. 'It looks nice.'

'It's Wendy's,' said Edward.

'The killer's cloth,' said Stevie.

'Stop it,' Kim hissed.

Edward said, 'I have to be careful.' He unfolded the material. Folded within was a tiny brush on a plastic stem, surrounded by black streaks like charcoal. Now he laid it out on the table. 'Don't touch. What do you call that thing?'

'It's one of those mascara brushes,' said Kim. 'I can't remember what they're called.'

'Mate of mine was a make-up artist and that's a spoolie,' said Stevie.

'Right. So anyway, I went to the site of Dr Wrigley's death. Wendy had a fit of the vapours and sat it out. She was about a hundred yards away doing panic breathing. I found . . .' He stopped. 'Wait, let me show you.'

He pulled out his mobile but the battery was flat.

'Bollocks. The boss took all my charge, ringing me and shouting,' said Edward.

A quizzical look crossed Kim's face.

'I'll tell you about that later,' he said. 'For now – okay, look at this spoolie and the soot marks. I photographed the tree where – I'm sure it was the tree – where Dr Wrigley's body was found. He was dead with his legs around it. Shot through the chest. I found, at chest height, a hole in the tree. I'm thinking, did someone miss him first time and fire the bolt into the tree? So I went to Wendy to see if she had a pen or something I could push into the hole. She gave me the spoolie and the silk hankie.'

'She's just the type to have the tool you need,' said Stevie. 'So primped and organized.'

'I like her myself,' said Kim.

'I wrap the brush in the silk and push it into the hole. It comes out streaked with soot. What does that mean?'

'Soot?' Kim repeated, touching the material.

'Isn't that just tree shite?' asked Stevie.

'Smell it,' Edward said.

Kim asked, 'What was the hole for?'

'I thought I was going to find a broken bolt in there. The killer shot one, missed, hit the tree, shot Dr Wrigley with the second? But it's not that. A crossbow bolt wouldn't blast a hole in a tree and go so deep you can't see it. This was drilled out.'

Stevie held the handkerchief up to her face. She lifted her eyepatch, offering a brief glimpse of the milky pupil and the scarring on the lid. But she said, 'I know it might sound mad, but I have a bit more close-up sight with this eye now, you know. It seems to operate like a magnifying glass. Let me smell this.' She held the silk over her face. 'Powder.' Her voice was muffled. 'It's a smell like caps, do you remember caps?'

Kim put in, 'Of course. From toy guns.'

'I thought the same,' said Edward.

'I'm remembering something Wendy told me. The doctor's hobby was making fireworks.'

Edward looked at Kim. 'Oh! So he would have had some of that powder, surely?'

Stevie now had the whole of the handkerchief over her face. 'I love the smell of napalm in the morning,' she said, making the others laugh. She removed the silk quickly. The soot now streaked her cheeks, making her look like a Victorian urchin.

Edward said, 'I still have no idea what happened here.'

Stevie snapped her eyepatch back into place. Before she could open her mouth, Kim said: 'Wait. I think I know.'

The others both turned to her. Gingerly, he passed her the soot-marked silk and she took it by a corner. When she held it up against the light from the window – the big glass panes were reflective, or the seats and metal tables in the hotel's canteen area would melt on a hot day – the black marks seemed to form a shape like a silhouette, the ghost of a man's face.

Finally, Kim said: 'My mum has a new boyfriend. I think we should go and see him.'

Stevie said, 'What the hell would he know about sooty handkerchiefs?'

Edward cocked his head. 'He has some weird kind of hobby, right?'

'They don't think it's weird. He's one of these historical re-enactment fellas. Putting on medieval battles,' said Kim. 'My mum has started getting into the whole scene. She's even been trying to source an iron helmet. He has an injury in his throat from an accident.'

'Okay, frankly I'm baffled,' began Stevie, 'but I can't go today because I have a hospital appointment this afternoon.' The other two looked at her enquiringly. 'Routine, folks.'

'On a weekend?'

'That's what the card said. It's just—'

She was interrupted by a man who approached carrying a lunch tray. It was William Scott, the newsreader, posh-sounding, broad and with a lantern jaw that sprouted stray hairs the shaver had missed.

'Is it Pirate Day?' he laughed.

'Sorry what?' said Kim.

'The day when everyone dresses like a pirate and goes "aye aye me hearties". The eyepatch on this lady . . .'

Edward was on his feet in a fraction of a second, the sound of his chair shooting backwards on the lino making everyone else stare. 'You wouldn't laugh about that if you knew what had happened to her,' he said, shoving his own face into Scott's. 'You public school weirdo. Go and read the news in a silly voice.'

Kim flinched and Edward realized she had probably not seen anger like that in him before. She had been married to a violent man who could catch fire in an instant, and his own flash of temper may have upset her. He felt a pricking of his skin, his guilt appearing as goosebumps. He sat back down immediately. She said, 'Ed, Ed, he didn't mean it—'

'Oh I think he fucking did,' said Stevie, not helping. The newsreader turned and exited. 'But I like "Go and read the news in a silly voice". That's God-tier stuff. I'm having that line.'

Kim was silent as Scott slunk away. Then she asked, 'Do you need the newsreaders to like you?'

'To do my show? Not really. But he's the sort who'll complain. I didn't hit him, did I?'

'We can say he hit you,' said Stevie, making Edward laugh. 'Oh God,' he murmured. The meeting had lost its focus. Then Kim's phone beeped with a text.

'Everything okay?' Edward asked.

'It's Colin,' she said, reading the message. 'My office deputy, or near as. He wants advice on the couple who want to buy the penthouse. Although . . .'

'Although?'

'It's that strange duo. They may be a lot of things, but they aren't boring.'

'Use his line, "Go and read the news in a silly voice" – that'll sort it in a second,' said Stevie. 'Fucking genius that. Go on, Kim, type it before we forget it.'

CHAPTER SIXTEEN

The fifteen-mile trip to Exeter General, with blue lights and sirens all the way, took twenty-one minutes. Andrea counted every single one of them, her eyes glued to Nina's tiny figure.

They sat in the rear of the ambulance, two paramedics separating her and Gabriel from Nina, wires and machines attached to her every extremity. As Andrea stood for a moment to look over the paramedics' shoulders, her daughter's eyes rolled back in her head and her lips once again foamed with froth.

Andrea wept, her grip on Gabriel's hands like a vice, his own tears falling on their locked fingers.

At the hospital, the vehicle shut off its siren, gunned left, right and then reversed into position as the rear doors were flung open. Andrea scrambled forward to grasp for Nina's hand but, before she could touch it, Nina was lifted out of the vehicle on a gurney and propelled inside through double doors. Andrea and Gabriel climbed out of the rear of the vehicle and were told to wait by the driver.

They stood in the car park, hesitating before following the circus of noise and movement and terror that surrounded their daughter. Had they heard someone say 'meningitis'? Hadn't the consultant ruled that out?

Gabriel felt in his pocket for the bag with the yellow ampoules in and remembered the doctor had taken it with growing urgency.

'I'm wearing the wrong clothes,' said Andrea blankly. They both looked down at her dressing gown and slippers, claw-footed monster ones that made Nina chortle with glee.

'It's OK,' croaked Gabriel eventually. 'Nina loves those slippers.'

And then Andrea's knees gave way and together they huddled, sobbing, on the cold concrete of the loading bay, until a kind nurse ushered them inside once more – back into their living hell.

CHAPTER SEVENTEEN

Stevie was irate – and only with herself for a change. She'd been in reception in Exeter's main hospital, in a long queue, waiting to tell the person working solo at the counter that she had an appointment with the burns specialist, when she thought again about Edward's puzzlement – 'on a weekend?' – and checked the appointment card. She had misread the date somehow, and the actual appointment was on a weekday in July. God, really? Why did she have to be so disorganized? Her check-ups were constantly being rescheduled, but this mistake was on her. She opened her mobile phone, found the calendar app and changed the date.

When she stood up and looked around, huffing, wondering how often the Saturday bus ran back to Sidmouth, Stevie saw a familiar figure beyond the doors of the hospital. DS Callintree, from the pizza parlour. He looked neither on duty nor off, climbing out quickly of a police car, wearing jeans and a T-shirt. Her first thought was a selfish one. Might he be heading back to Sidmouth soon?

She started to move slowly towards him when he jerked his head up, attention caught elsewhere. She followed his gaze left and saw an obviously pregnant woman rushing towards him, waving in a way that suggested extreme distress. Stevie could not help herself. She started to walk towards them.

When the hospital doors slid open, she began to hear the single word the woman was repeating. Her skin was Mediterranean, her hair was dark, and she spoke with an Italian or Spanish accent. The same word was being said again and again: 'Nothing. Nothing. Nothing!' Jordan Callintree was raising his hands defensively.

Other people might have thought to avoid an exchange so obviously fraught, but not Stevie. When she appeared beside the woman, the policeman looked at Stevie and blinked rapidly several times, as if his brain was shuttering on a sequence of photos to find a match.

'Do you even know about the capsules?' asked the woman frantically.

'It's why I'm here,' said the police officer. 'The hospital are on watch to report anything that—'

The angry lady cut in, waving her smartphone at Stevie. 'The police have done nothing! You see? This is all I can do to tell people.' Stevie leant in closer – it was a post on Instagram with a picture of a very small, pale child, hooked up to wires and monitors in a hospital bed. The writing underneath said, 'PRAY FOR MY DAUGHTER. SHE WAS IN THE PIZZA PARLOUR ATTACK.'

Stevie felt it like a punch to the gut. She hadn't thought anyone else had been seriously injured! How had she missed this when she was at the scene? And *attack*? Wasn't it an accident?

A post like this might cause panic – no one had said the word 'attack' before – but this woman was so distressed, her whole arm shook as she held the smartphone.

'Mrs Lopez—' Jordan started.

'Nothing!' she shrieked again, turning back to the officer and waving the phone.

'Mrs Lopez,' interjected Stevie, trying to take some heat out of the exchange, 'I was in the pizza place too. This officer will tell you. I ran in the back to help him. What makes you think it was an attack? It wasn't, was it, Jordan?'

Rather than reassuring this poor woman, Stevie's blood ran cold when he shook his head.

'While I wouldn't say it's an attack, since last night I've been trying to trace the people in the restaurant, and so far you are the only ones we've found.' Jordan Callintree added stiffly: 'I'm not sure this is a conversation you can help with, Miss Mason.'

'Not help! She tried to help *you!*' Mrs Lopez looked astounded. She addressed Stevie. 'My daughter is in there with my husband in a terrible condition because of something she picked off the floor at the pizza place, and we get told nothing!' She turned back to Callintree. '*Nothing!* When were you going to come find us?'

'Mrs Lopez, I was called by the hospital, I *was* coming to find you. Please, take this post down,' he said gently. 'Look, we know who the driver was now, we moved very fast to locate his property, and I promise we will find out what has happened to your daughter. We do not yet know what's in those damned ampoules.'

'Have you found who he was then?' demanded Mrs Lopez.

'I'm a police officer. I can't start a press conference here with you.'

'She's a mother!' implored Stevie. 'Not the general public.'

'I know,' said Callintree. 'But it's a press conference if everything I say gets posted.'

Andrea Lopez waved her phone at Jordan and then stalked to the police car. She flung open the driver's door and threw the phone into the vehicle.

She returned, breathless, the pregnancy bump heaving. 'There. You have my phone. I can't tell my one hundred and twenty followers what you tell me, officer. Are you happy? Put the phone in a river for all I care. But please, I beg you, I beg you on the body and blood of Christ, tell me. *Tell me.* Say what I am dealing with as a mother.'

Jordan Callintree stared at his squad car, and for a moment Stevie thought he was about to fetch the phone. But as he looked away from them he spoke in a monotone. 'This truly mustn't go any further, Ms Lopez. But yes, we were able to trace the chassis number on his bike—'

'I am not interested in no chassis number!'

He pressed on. 'When we got to the flat, there was nothing in it. He seemed to live with absolutely nothing. His passport was hidden in the lining of a chair which is how we know his name.' He paused. 'There was also drugs paraphernalia. We think he may have been a user, or a dealer, or both.'

'Oh my God,' Andrea gasped. She looked like she was about to faint. 'My daughter took street drugs?'

'I can't tell yet but it's possible.' He pulled his phone from his pocket. 'I shouldn't be showing you this, but it's all we found.'

'What am I looking at?'

Stevie drew very slightly closer.

Two narrow, light blue plastic tubes filled the screen; one had a tiny red plastic disc attached and the other a blue disc. They looked to be about thirty centimetres long, with needles at one end, the other ends widening a little. There was what looked like a little dried blood on each.

'They were hidden under the sofa.'

'What does it mean?' asked Stevie.

'For drugs into the vein, we think.'

'Not that,' said Andrea Lopez, with a brisk shake of her head. 'Please, find out what is in those capsules!'

Callintree seemed to wake with a start from this strange situation he had got himself into. He swiped the screen clear and pocketed his phone. 'I've told you all we know. Please respect my confidence.' He went on slowly, 'Mrs Lopez, after the crash, everyone fled pretty quickly. We lost our witnesses. So we are just following up, and there's an alert out to the hospitals on anyone who has any sort of problem connected with the crash – they called me to come speak to you, though you found me first.'

Andrea Lopez's smartwatch buzzed on her wrist, and she touched it to read an alert.

'I must get your phone,' said Callintree.

'I don't need a phone. I need the truth,' said Andrea through gritted teeth, tears falling onto the face of the watch. 'Ah, my husband says the doctor wants to speak to us, I must go.' Her whole body seemed to be trembling, and she placed a protective arm around her swollen stomach. Without looking back she was gone, whisking through the doors, desperate to return to her daughter's side.

When Stevie looked back at Jordan, he was staring at his shoes, a deep frown across his forehead.

'What capsules, Jordan?' Stevie asked.

He seemed to be shaking his head, resolving something in his own mind. Without looking up or turning his shoulders, he spoke.

'His name is Lev Malnyk, a Russian name. He dropped or threw something into the pizza place and now we have a very sick child. We are an inch away from Salisbury here.'

'What do you mean by Salisbury?'

'You really want me to spell it out? I'm not going to.'

'You think the biker was trying to kill people?'

'Stop asking questions, Miss Mason. I've said enough.'

CHAPTER EIGHTEEN

Exhausted, Kim fell asleep on the sofa as soon as she got home. She dreamed of freshly hung wallpaper suddenly catching fire, the flames licking up the walls and melting the pattern: tiny red hearts becoming hot tears. When she woke after a couple of hours, she realized Edward would be on the radio. They wanted him to broadcast until midnight. God, how annoying, she had missed some of it. She touched the TV remote and changed to one of the radio channels. The screen said RTR-92 EAST DEVON in big letters. Below them, the size of a postage stamp, was a thumbnail photo of Edward and the words: SCHEDULE CHANGE.

She hit 'Start Again' to go back to the show's nine p.m. start and was surprised to hear a quiver in Edward's voice as he told his listeners: 'Tonight we're asking questions about the motorbike crash on Sidmouth Promenade. The first one is "who". Who did it? As we now know from the latest official police statement, the man who sadly died was Ukrainian. But from the Donbas, the part that leans towards Russia. And the bike he was riding had false plates. So we do need to ask who this man was, and why we seem to know so little about him.'

There was some programme music, and then Edward came

back in. 'The second question is "why". Why would he do that? What if it wasn't an accident? What if it was an attack? We don't want to speculate recklessly, but as long as there are no official answers, I feel we need to. False plates?'

Kim felt herself waking rapidly as she listened.

'The third question is "what". What was the motorbike rider doing there? Why have the police not only kept the barriers up but extended them further? What is going on in that pizza parlour that we don't know about?'

Edward repeated: 'Who, why, what?'

She snapped herself fully awake. There was an urgent pitch in Edward's voice. He was a relaxed broadcaster normally, but this did not sound relaxed. This police statement was new information, and Edward was clearly drawing connections between the identity of the rider and the extended police perimeter.

He brought callers into the conversation on the radio. And then he made what sounded like an official appeal – 'The police have again stated they need to make contact with everyone who was in the pizza parlour when the bike crashed there. Please don't worry, but do call Devon Police in Sidmouth or Exeter tomorrow at the latest if you were there.'

She went to bed after an hour and woke again with Edward's body beside her. It was four in the morning. She had almost forgotten he was staying tonight. Agitated, she went downstairs in the dark and put the kettle on. Edward's offer still made her smile: 'Come and live with me in a condemned house.' 'Why would I live in a dangerous wreck like that?' 'Because you sold it to me.' Maybe she was the dangerous wreck.

At least she had divorced Anthony. But the arrival of Roddy in Stevie's life was like nature rebalancing, an ancient law proven – vicious men would always find partners. She hated the idea of having to watch Stevie get hitched. She made weak tea and drank it, thinking: *Down with Roddies*.

CHAPTER NINETEEN

Sunday, 5 a.m. The police had moved the cordon around the pizza parlour three times during the past twenty-four hours. It had started at fifty metres, then moved inwards until it only covered the restaurant itself and two properties either side, with a space for cars to pass single file. That was overnight, but gradually, as if responding to the unseen activities and knowledge of the authorities, the cordon extended again as dawn came. By first light, police tape once again obstructed the whole of the promenade outside the burnt-out husk of the pizza parlour, forcing lone early walkers to take the stone steps down to the narrow strip of beach and walk below the sea wall. Everyone had seen the post by Andrea Lopez with the terrifying six words: PRAY FOR NINA ... PIZZA PARLOUR ATTACK.

Fifteen miles away, on the third floor of Exeter Hospital, Andrea Lopez sat by the side of her daughter's bed. Gabriel was asleep on Nina's other side, scrunched into a chair which couldn't contain his long limbs. In repose, his face was still grey, the tension that had aged him two decades overnight never leaving his expression.

Turn the Dial for Death

Please, Andrea prayed. *Please God, save Nina. Save my Nina for me, I cannot live without her.*

The machines beeped and whirred, and Nina lay as still as the dead.

CHAPTER TWENTY

Later that morning, Kim drove Edward in the Porsche to her mother's house. As the crow flew it was barely three miles west, but the River Otter stood in the way with precious few crossings. So she took the road to Bulverton and then up to the Bowd junction, turning onto Four Elms Hill. From there the road led to Newton Poppleford, over the river and then south to Colaton Raleigh.

'Should we pick up Stevie? Could you call her? She's close by.'

'Good idea, if she's around. The wedding is days away, gulp.'

As if trying to escape the fact of the wedding, Kim put her foot down at that moment and took a left turn a little too fast. Edward ended up leaning right, into her arm. 'Sorry – hang on—' She freed herself. 'Changing gear.'

He did not react, so she said: 'You really are deep in thought.'

'This bloody biker story. It's getting in the way of everything. The false plates are out there now, thanks to last night's police statement. But they are so bloody cagey on the rest. Ukrainian with a Russian name?'

'I heard your show. You think there's more to it, don't you?'

'Yes, there must be. The cordon yoyo-ing in and out just

doesn't make sense if it was just a crash.' Edward gazed out of the window again. Kim stole another glance at him.

'But the Russian thing, is that just nonsense?'

'Probably. "Man with slightly Russian name crashes", I mean . . .'

'With false plates.'

'True. False plates, Russian name. But still, no one hurt except him, and that poor little girl in Exeter General.'

They parked outside the vicarage. Stevie emerged almost instantly. 'I'll go in the back,' she said. 'I'm glad I haven't got child-bearing hips.' The Porsche was tight. 'So are we going to meet your mother's boyfriend, Kim?'

'All set up for us.'

In the back seat, Stevie groaned. 'We're going to have to get a different car if this is for us to do adventures in. My legs have gone to sleep back here.'

'Unexpected item in the bagging area,' said Kim.

'Well exactly.'

Ten minutes later, the car slowed outside Barbara's. 'So here we are.' And there Barbara was, as if by magic, standing at the front door. Kim approached on the garden path, Edward and Stevie following. As Barbara hugged her daughter, Kim heard Stevie say to Edward: 'I've got to tell you about something that happened at the hospital yesterday.'

'Oh?' replied Edward, but his mind was clearly elsewhere. 'Can it wait?'

'Now, Mum,' Kim began. 'This is my best friend. Well, both of them.' The older woman was obviously delighted to see Edward alongside Kim, and had been ever since she had discovered the relationship was serious. Edward Temmis had been, still was, her radio presenter of choice.

The four sat in the living room. Edward made a show of admiring Barbara's little wooden models, as he called them – it was Kim who corrected the phrase to 'automata', which she knew her mum would insist on. While Barbara was pouring tea in the kitchen, Kim whispered: 'And don't mention Fiona Bruce. *Antiques Roadshow* came to Honiton, and Mum couldn't get her bits seen.'

'Automata, please, not bits.'

'One-all.'

Barbara returned. 'The cameramen spent the whole time focusing on her bottom.'

'Who, Mum?'

'Fiona Bruce.'

Edward had lost track. The front doorbell went, saving them. 'At last!' said Barbara. 'Oh, I think he's staying by the van. Do you need me? Will you come back?'

'We'll come back,' promised Kim. And they all stood and peered through the front door at the man who had arrived in a van painted with the words OLD BATTLES FULL SCALE LIMITED.

David Marner appeared to breathe through a hole in his throat. That was the first thing Edward saw. A clear plastic vent, shaped like the barrel-stopper on a toy gun, protruded from the skin to the left of his Adam's apple.

He was broad, with enormous thighs which seemed to be wrapped in velvet, a pock-marked face and a small goatee which could easily have been part of a costume. His appearance was confusing, as if he had come half in character, half in his regular clothes.

'You wanted me?' His voice was a growl and a hiss combined, the sound of several different dangerous animals. 'We spoke on the phone, Kim. Mr Temmis, I like your programme.' He looked at Stevie. 'Who is this pocket rocket?'

Behind them, Barbara said: 'He calls a spade a spade.'

'Shut up woman.'

Kim snapped her head to the right. 'I hope that's just banter.'

'Oh it is,' laughed Barbara. 'He is funny as well as being unusually succinct.'

'Medieval battles tended to be rapid,' said David Marner, evidently thinking the statement followed logically. 'Miss Sinker, you asked me about using a bolt and a charge. I have set it up for you.'

'A bolt and a what?' asked Stevie. 'They haven't kept me in the bloody loop.'

'You said you didn't want to know,' said Edward with a wink. 'So now we're going to give you a little surprise.'

'I never get told anything,' said Barbara.

They drove behind Marner's van.

'This is to do with the sooted hankie, right?' asked Stevie from the back seat of the Porsche.

'And the hole in the tree trunk.'

'Edward,' said Kim, 'let me tell her!'

'No, don't,' retorted Stevie. 'If I can't work it out then I don't deserve to know.'

Marner had a field north of Sidmouth with a small area for car parking and a shed carrying an enormous sign: NO LANCES, SHIELDS, SPIKED MACES etc KEPT IN THIS SHED OVERNIGHT.

'We use this as an assembly point only. I get my customers here, we dress and practise, see how comfortable we are in chain mail or full armour. Then off it comes and off we go, sometimes out of the county.'

Kim, Stevie and Edward stood listening. Feeling that Marner needed a question, Edward asked: 'Is business good?'

'The Health and Safety is out of this world. I have to risk-assess every single weapon. They told me I needed plastic swords and I said fuck off and that was it. No further trouble.'

Edward heard Stevie whisper to Kim, 'I like this guy a lot. But don't let me forget: I need to speak to you and Edward about something.'

'Later?' Kim responded vaguely.

'Fair play to them,' said Marner, his voice like the hiss of steam from a kettle. 'Ever since this' – he pointed at the vent in his neck – 'they've been onto me like flies on shit. Ramrod injury. Very common. I was a fool.'

Kim frowned at Edward who grimaced at Stevie. No one seemed to want to ask what a ramrod injury was.

'I wouldn't normally do this for a customer, but Kim's no customer, she is the daughter of my queen.' At the mention of Barbara, David Marner suddenly seemed to bloom. His cheeks spread in a ruddy smile and he tossed his fringe away from his eyes. A kind of medieval bow followed, almost a curtsey, where he put his right foot behind his left ankle and dropped his head as low as it would go. 'What Queen B wants, Queen B gets.'

'Very nice,' said Kim. 'You can stay.'

'We have a bit of a walk, I'm afraid.'

He went to the shed door, took what seemed an age to release two padlocks and then grabbed a holdall from inside. 'Come with me.'

They walked in silence across the field. Edward was conscious, for a moment, of their steps in the mud falling perfectly into time, like soldiers.

At the far end, Marner showed them a solid oak. 'Not an ash. I know you asked for an ash, but it makes no difference.'

Stevie stepped forwards. 'I see the hole.'

'I drilled it earlier from the photo sent to me by Kim. I estimate this opening at three-eighths of an inch. That's the drill bit I used.' He dropped to his haunches and picked up a battery drill half-covered by leaves on the forest floor. 'Bit embarrassing, leaving it out like this, but it's been so dry.'

Stevie said, 'I think I know what you're going to do.'

'Haven't you been briefed by the others?'

'They wanted it to be a surprise.'

'Well,' said Marner, evidently warming to her, 'it may well

be that. This was a surprise,' he said, 'touching the vent on his neck. You do know what a ramrod injury is?'

Edward looked at his feet, embarrassed that they had all let the first reference go.

David Marner said, 'It was eight years ago. I was using what they called a ramrod, or sometimes a "scouring stick" because it's also used for cleaning. With muzzle-loading guns you push the gunpowder in and then the projectile. The projectile, the bullet, needs packing tight. There's always the danger of a spark, and that's what happened. Ram the projectile, compress the powder, create the spark and wham. I was stumbling around with a ramrod sticking in one side of my neck and coming out the other, like Lurch in the Addams family. Hence my trach vent, because there was so much trauma to the upper airways, they never worked properly again. Hence my voice. But I'm here.'

He turned to the tree. 'So, the same hole you had in the photos. An oak not an ash. Same height. Young lady,' he addressed Stevie, 'you still don't know what this is for?'

Stevie said, 'We were looking at a murder in a forest, so no, I have no idea what the hole in the tree was for.'

'A murder?' said Marner. 'How interesting.'

He opened the holdall by his feet and removed what looked like a black stick. He held it in front of him without speaking. 'Old one, flights torn.' His fist closed around the centre point of the crossbow bolt. 'No barb at the front, instead just a snub point. Hold this, Temmis.'

Edward took the bolt. The three were silent. The wind picked up and the leaves above them shivered as if in expectation.

Marner said, 'Black powder is what we use. These days, "gunpowder" tends to refer to the modern smokeless sort. For a re-enactment we muzzle-load rifles and pistols with powder first, then thick paper wadding. Nice effect, big bang and lots of smoke, no bullet, no danger, unless you manage to launch the damned ramrod like I did. I'll be careful now. Stand away from the exit.'

By 'exit' he meant the small hole he had drilled in the tree trunk. 'A gun you turn barrel-up, and you just funnel the powder in. A hole like this is harder. So we use pellets. You've seen them?'

The other three shook their heads. Marner drew a pair of plastic goggles from his holdall. Then another three pairs. They put them on without speaking. 'Stand clear. I don't want to lose my hand. One muzzle-loading accident, it's the muzzle's fault. Two, it starts to look like mine.'

He pulled a tight leather glove onto his right hand. 'Can I check, no one is wearing a wool jumper? Static I worry about.'

Edward looked around. All three said no. From the holdall, Marner produced a small black tin with a red-lettered WARNING on the front and carefully opened it, holding it away from his face. He pulled off a layer of cotton wool. 'Hodgdon Pyrodex pellets,' he said.

They were tiny, the shape of disposable ear defenders: smooth grey cylinders with a hole through the centre.

'No one light a cigarette, no one strike a match, no one move a muscle. One spark and my fingers are gone.'

He placed a pellet inside the hole with a fingertip. Carefully, he took a second and used his fingers to push the pellet deeper. 'Imagine doing this with fingers every time, how many must have been blown off.' He straightened up gingerly, as if worried about a spark from his clothes. 'Now, the ramrod. This is where it went wrong for me before, so I've learnt to stand away. Back off a little more, would you?'

He pushed the ramrod into the hole in the tree trunk like a surgeon carefully placing a syringe needle. Kim put her fingers in her ears. 'Shouldn't go off,' he said. 'No spark, you see.'

He stood back, stumbling a little on the uneven ground.

The three took a few paces to the right behind him, watching the tree as if they expected it to suddenly blow up.

'At this point I do something very unsafe and very silly,' he said. 'Just let me tick off my checklist.' He went back to the bag. 'Lid back on the black powder tin. Glove carefully removed so no trace remains on myself. Edward, do you have the bolt? The next part is quick. Here . . .'

He had backed away from the holdall with a thick magazine in his hand. 'Christmas edition of *Vogue*, gift of Barbara who has apparently now read it twice. Kim, hold it.'

They were now a good distance from the tree, perhaps twenty yards.

'Holding it,' said Kim, the surgeon's assistant.

'Edward, the crossbow bolt.'

'Here,' said Edward.

'You want to be part of our display, little madam?' He pulled a pistol-shaped metal object from the deepest pocket of his tunic and held it out towards Stevie. 'I tend to employ this for melting marshmallows and the odd crème brûlée. Useless for welding. Butane torch.'

She glared at him. 'What do you want me to do with this?'

'The holdall is over there, the tree is over there, we're safe. I want you to flick off the flame guard and click the trigger.'

She did. As the torch sparked into a blue flame, Edward winced. The flame made a soft whooshing sound. 'Okay, Mr Temmis – you hold the flight end of the bolt in the flame for at least a minute until it starts to glow, please.'

They stood there. Edward holding the bolt, Stevie holding the gas torch, Kim with the heavy magazine.

'The bolt's heating up too,' said Edward.

'Here.' Marner took it. 'Ouch. I see what you mean.' He pulled an oily rag from his pocket, and wrapped it around the centre of the shaft. 'Should be okay now. Give it another thirty seconds.'

As they watched, he said: 'I'll have to be careful with the next bit because it may happen very quickly. When I say "Go", Kim, you hand me the glossy magazine, Edward, you hand me the bolt, and Stevie, you shut down the burner.'

'How do I do that?'

'Knock off the flame guard and release the trigger.'

'It's glowing,' said Edward.

'Go,' said David Marner. He grabbed the bolt in his left hand – 'Shit, that's hot' – and took the copy of *Vogue* in his right. The bolt was facing outwards, with the smoking tail to Marner's left as he walked. He stood beside the tree, almost sheltering himself, and placed the bolt rear inside the hole so that most of the shaft was still exposed. Then he took the magazine and, with two rapid strokes, smashed the crossbow point so it was driven into the tree. There was silence. He held the magazine across the hole with the bolt in. Nothing. He kept the magazine in place and moved around the tree, embracing it from the opposite side, now holding an edge of the magazine in each hand so it fully covered the hole.

They stood and waited.

Still nothing.

'Sodding waste of time that was,' he said finally, dropping the magazine to the ground. 'Better stay back all the same.'

'What happened?' asked Edward.

'Lack of oxygen I reckon,' said Kim, to his left.

'Yeah, that's probably right,' said Marner, making heavy work of climbing over a log that blocked his route back to them. 'I think the pellets—'

There was suddenly a powerful blast, so loud that Kim screamed. Marner ducked, then spun to look back over his left shoulder. 'Christ alive, what just happened?'

Smoke was pouring from the tree trunk. They approached. 'Do not go near the exit hole until we've worked it out,' said Marner.

They came indirectly, from the right. Heavy smoke tumbled from the hole in the tree trunk. 'Let me get the ramrod,' said Marner. He pulled it from the holdall. 'This is how accidents happen.' He used the ramrod like a cotton bud in an ear, searching for a blockage.

'Where's the bolt?' he asked.

'Over here.'

It was Stevie, who had moved at an angle from the oak tree to another, thirty feet away. The bolt was stuck into the trunk at the same height as the hole it had exited from. 'It must have come out with unbelievable power,' she said. 'I can't even get the thing out. And it's hot.'

Kim and Edward looked at each other.

'Well,' said David Marner, 'you've proved something, though I'm not sure exactly what.'

'Oh God.' Stevie looked stricken. 'I think I was wrong about Wendy. The doctor did it, didn't he? He killed himself.'

'Search me if I know what the hell you're talking about,' said David Marner.

Edward stared at Stevie, who was shaking and stamping her feet. 'I can't believe how badly I got it wrong.'

'We've proved a crossbow bolt can be fired without a crossbow,' said Edward.

'Which means—' Kim began.

'It was suicide,' said Stevie. 'It was suicide, and we got the whole thing wrong. Everyone got everything wrong. Wendy Wrigley—'

'Is innocent,' said Edward.

CHAPTER TWENTY-ONE

Barbara was at the front door before they knocked. 'You must come and see the TV. Something terrible has happened.'

Stevie, Kim and Edward had come back without David Marner, who had said he would be along later. Barbara sat them down.

The broadcast had a live feel about it, unusual for a Sunday, with a grid of reporters in different locations, including one at Exeter General and another by the promenade. Edward had the sudden feeling he would have to go into the radio station without delay. The TV flashed the caption *APOLOGIES THAT YOUR NORMAL PROGRAMMES ARE DELAYED*, and showed press gathering outside the hospital. Nina Lopez's photo was in one corner of the screen.

As they watched, the rolling headline appeared.
TOPPINGS CRASH: LITTLE GIRL DEAD.

Everyone in the room gasped. Even Barbara put her hand over her mouth, despite having evidently seen the broadcast earlier. 'That poor little scrap of a thing.'

'Oh no, no, no,' Stevie cried. 'I saw the mother yesterday. This will break her. Oh God, this is so awful.' She fell back onto the sofa, shoulders heaving.

The presenter handed over to a reporter on the promenade, who explained. After Andrea Lopez had posted about the 'attack' yesterday, the vicar at the couple's church had circulated a WhatsApp message asking the congregation to pray for Nina. But about an hour ago, Gabriel had called him again: it was too late. Nina had died, with her parents by her side, holding her hands.

The vicar put five words on the church WhatsApp group:

> NINA DEAD. PRAY FOR THEM

News of the tragedy spread like wildfire. One of the parishioners was a journalist with the website *Coast Live*, and the devastating development was public before the police could offer any information to stop people panicking.

On the TV, Jordan Callintree introduced himself. Edward noted Kim giving him a sidelong glance. There were three television cameras, a photographer and two reporters with phones or pads. It was a hot day, and they had found a spot of shade outside the hospital. They bristled, moving as a single organism.

Callintree had nothing to say about the circumstances of the child's death, he told them, because the news had come from the parents and not the police and he was not authorized to add to it. There would need to be a full investigation.

It did not stop the questions. Stevie's weeping almost drowned out the television. Barbara turned up the volume. The reporters were off-mic but could just about be heard.

'Did the girl die as a result of the crash on Friday?'
'Did the little girl get burned or was she hit by the motorbike?'
He could reply to that. 'Neither.'
'So what was she actually taken into hospital for?'
'How are the parents?'
'I can't even imagine her pain,' gulped Stevie from the sofa.

Then came a stream of words from a reedy young man on the screen who held his phone with a wrist so relaxed it looked as if it was about to slide out of his hand. 'If it's connected to the Friday crash, what is your message? Was the crash deliberate? Why did Andrea Lopez refer to an "attack" on the pizza place? What is your message?'

The policeman said: 'I haven't got the latest medical details. There is no evidence as yet that anything happened to Nina Lopez as a result of her presence in the pizza parlour. She was taken ill yesterday and sadly that led to her demise.'

'That sounds like a cover-up,' said Barbara.

Callintree added: 'It will be up to the parents and the hospital whether anything is said publicly about the little girl's condition when she passed.'

The reporters were all about to ask questions, and Callintree held up a hand as the live camera nosed closer to his face. 'We do need to check on the welfare of others who were at the pizza parlour. There may have been as many as five families in there, along with one or two individual customers. We need to speak to them all, and I urge anyone watching who was there or knows anyone who was there to contact the police right away.'

'Why?'

The question turned out not to be from a reporter, but a patient who had come out of the hospital attached to a drip and was smoking. The camera found him and panned quickly away.

'He hasn't got any more to say,' Edward murmured. Barbara shut the TV down. Kim shot her mother a reproachful glance as if to say, *Edward didn't mean he wanted you to turn it off completely.*

Stevie suddenly said, 'I know a lot about this.'

They all turned to her.

'I was at the hospital yesterday. I saw Jordan, went to speak to him, up comes the mum. Just furious. She'd just put out the "pray for Nina" post. He said it could be terrorism by Russia.'

Edward jumped up, head spinning. 'Why didn't you mention this sooner? Anything else?'

'She ate a capsule that she picked up at the scene,' said Stevie.

'Who?' asked Barbara.

'The dead girl. She ate a capsule of some sort, something that had fallen out of the motorbike's pannier. That's all I know. Her mum was proper raging, shouting "Do you know what was in those capsules?" to Jordan.'

'Did she now?' Barbara was fascinated.

'Mum . . .' Kim started, but desisted. She could hardly tell Barbara to be less involved.

'You didn't think of telling me this earlier?' asked Edward.

'"Can it wait?"'

'Sorry?'

'That's what you said when I tried to tell you, mister. And Kim, you just said "Later" when I mentioned it.'

'Oops,' said Kim.

'Anyway, Jordan wanted it secret, so I respected that.' Stevie went on: 'He was there because of the capsules, the hospital had called him in, and it was right before they made the statement about the biker being Russian, so he must have made some kind of connection there because the last thing he said to me was about the Salisbury poisoning. Like he was worried it was another similar attack. He looked as if the life had gone out of him, poor fucking sausage.'

Barbara put in, 'We'll have less effing sausages in this house, please.'

Edward gripped his hair and pulled in frustration. The biggest scoop yet and he'd brushed Stevie off hours ago! 'Come with me to the radio station now, Stevie.'

'In whose car?' Kim asked Edward.

'Oh God, Kim, do you mind driving?' Edward asked. But then he stopped. 'I need to ring Callintree.'

He punched the contact into his smartphone. They all fell silent.

'Voicemail?' asked Kim, hearing the merest squeak of the taped message.

'Stands to reason,' said Edward. 'What a bloody day he's having. Okay, then I have to ring Aspinall.'

They all fell silent again. This time the phone rang out.

'Nobody's in,' said Barbara unnecessarily. 'Except me. I'm always in.'

'To the radio station now?' Stevie said.

'No, wait,' said Edward, lifting a hand like a traffic policeman, his mind going a million miles a minute. 'I've got an idea of someone we need to see who might be able to help us.'

'Who?' asked Barbara. 'There's no one interesting around here.'

'I can say, can't I?' Edward asked Kim.

'You haven't told me yet.'

'Of course you can say,' said Stevie, who was crying again. 'I'm sorry, I don't cry often, I'm just gutted for the mum. That poor, wee girl.'

'Tell us.' Barbara directed the words at Edward. Her tone was flat. She, too, appeared teary.

'The biker spilled something that Nina then ate. Or maybe the "something" was part of a deliberate attack. Whatever it was, they have to test it – the obvious place is the government labs. We can't get anywhere near that. But there's an old scientist who might just be in the loop. She's in Sidmouth, pretty much retired, but does overflow forensic services for the police, low-key stuff, prints and blood testing when they need it done fast and they can't do it themselves. I've interviewed Flo a couple of times for my show. I'm pretty sure we passed her house on the way here. Let's go.'

CHAPTER TWENTY-TWO

'Name is Florence Veitch.' Edward spoke as Kim drove the three of them. 'Mature lady, let's say, at least seventy, wants to be called Flo, glamorous like Mary Beard. Bushy eyebrows are all I really remember. She's super-smart and she set something up called "Forensics Incorporated" or "Forensics Limited", one or the other, which she basically runs out of her house. And she came on my show because there was a bit of a hoo-ha at the time about whether you could have a private firm doing drink-drive evidence. And also, by the way, she came over as a little . . . on the spectrum.'

Edward's description was interrupted by Stevie in the back seat. 'You can't say that. That's me you're talking about.'

'Okay, Stevie, sorry, eccentric. But she's made a living because the official service is so backed up. And that got privatized too so it's just a free market. She won't get this case, most likely, but she might have some ideas I can put on my show.'

'Her address?'

'I know it's around here . . .'

'You don't even have an address?' asked Stevie. 'Hey, I'm a bit jammed in here. If I don't get out soon I'll have to hang a leg out of the window.'

'Kim can use it for signalling.'

'I need an address,' said Kim.

'Turn down Dotton Lane, here.' Edward heard a slight impatience in his voice. He wanted to get to the radio station because there was so much to say. 'I think we'll see the house on Dotton. I went here about five years ago. She'd been on my show and invited me for Christmas drinks. Her wife had recently passed, I think.'

Kim looked doubtful at the idea that you could find a place without an address, but in Devon following hedgerows often worked better than following satnav. A jogger from out of town had died tragically ten years ago, holding a phone to find their way in the fog and failing to see that the narrow line between land and sea was a hundred-metre drop.

As if to prove Edward's intuition, a house appeared exactly where he said it would. White chimney, thatched roof that looked in need of restoration, the rest hidden behind the high hedges that lined the narrow road.

They turned into the drive. The gravel welcomed them. 'If she's in, she'll hear us,' said Edward. 'Having gravel is the same as having a burglar alarm fitted.'

The three of them went to the front door and rang the bell. There were two garden gnomes on the doorstep. One of them held a diploma and wore glasses. 'That's her,' said Edward, pointing at it.

'Oh! I thought she'd be taller,' said Stevie.

'Ssh,' said Kim.

'I'm thinking about that kid,' said Edward, the wait stretching on. His eyes pricked and he blinked them rapidly. 'What the actual fuck? What happened in that pizza house?'

'We're going to find out,' said Stevie. 'This place is isolated, isn't it? Absolute burglary target. High hedges, lives alone. You could be in here for a day and no one would notice.'

'Well,' said a voice, 'the dogs would.'

The three were silent on the doorstep.

Kim pointed at a small camera and microphone by the doorbell, not a known make like Ring or Blink, but more of a lash-up by the homeowner. The DIY doorbell-camera was as much a clue to the person inside the house as the academic gnome. She was already filling in all the blanks.

'On a Sunday? Must be urgent,' crackled the voice. 'Do I know you? Stand in the light.'

That required the three of them to step back from the doorstep, onto the gravel, where the sun lit them up. Edward raised his voice to make up for their distance from the microphone. 'This is Edward Temmis. You and I have spoken on the radio.'

'My God! So we have! The Tennis chap!'

'He's just a guy in need of a bit of expertise,' said Stevie. 'We're not invading, I promise.' And now, almost as if they were approaching a wild animal without wanting to scare it, they drew closer to the microphone on the contraption by the front door.

'Well,' said the voice, 'someone needs to know the truth of this damn matter. These bloody people. I don't want to be alone in this.'

Silence. Kim, Stevie and Edward, back on the doorstep, looked at each other. After a minute Edward said, 'Hello?'

This time the reply came from somewhere to their right. 'Over here!'

They moved back onto the gravel, the stones underfoot whispering their every movement. To the right was a small garage, the door painted white long ago, the paint flaking, dead grey aluminium underneath. Around the edge of the roof of the garage was wooden latticing, sketching out a terrace. They heard a hissing sound before they saw the professor.

'I just need to check it's you. Very good interview we did.'

'It was a while ago,' said Edward, looking up, as a barely human shape that was more sphere than rectangle appeared on the garage roof. The professor was in some kind of protective suit, a light blue veneer of thin material that had a hose line attached where her right thigh would be. The hissing sound was air. When she moved she pulled with her an object which must be generating the air, inflating the suit into a giant balloon shape. Behind a pane of glass in the hood, Edward saw wild eyes in a face with a smudge of lipstick on the mouth.

'You can't come any further,' said the professor, her words muffled behind the protective glass. 'Quite to my disgust, astonishment and surprise, and whatever other words you want to attribute to me, I'm dealing with a radioactive substance.'

CHAPTER TWENTY-THREE

At the words 'radioactive substance', Edward, Kim and Stevie all took a long step backwards. The professor cackled, the sound undeniably clear even over the hissing of the air supply.

Stunned, Edward called out, 'Is this a leak? A *radioactive* leak? Do you want me to call the police?'

The word 'police' made Florence Veitch almost scream with laughter. 'Someone needs to call the police, yes, but on them! Enough clowns for twice a circus!'

Kim murmured to Edward, 'Just tell her why you're here.'

'I have a show tonight. I was looking for information about the . . . problem at the pizza place. As you'll know, a child died. Something was spilled or thrown in there. I don't know. The police can't say or won't—'

'They don't *know!*' It was a smoker's rasp, coming from inside the hood like air from broken fireplace bellows.

Unusually polite, Stevie said: 'He just wanted your insight into whatever it might have been, ma'am. Just your expertise. Didn't want to get in the way of your work.'

'Don't "ma'am" me. "Professor" was earned.' She tried to move the glass visor, then said: 'No. Shouldn't do that.' Kim glanced at Edward. Every time the professor moved on the garage roof, the corrugated metal squealed below her. Either the metal would give way and she would crash through the roof, or she would suddenly float like a helium balloon into the sky.

Edward must have thought the same at that moment, because he said, 'I'm worried you might do yourself an injury up there. You don't need to worry about us invading. I just wanted to ask—'

The professor shifted position, tipping slightly as the metal bowed beneath her feet.

'I'm not worried about you invading. If I look like an astronaut then I'm sorry. I need to protect the three of you and the one of me. They have completely stitched me up, giving me a substance that is . . .'

She paused. As if she knew how heavily the next word would land, how the sound of it would be heard around the country.

In the silence, Edward spoke. 'Professor, I'm here for the radio station.'

'I'm here for the radiation,' she snapped back.

Flinching, Edward continued, 'I'm here because we've spoken before and I know your expertise. I know you're trusted by the police. I don't want to betray your trust myself. If you want to say anything publicly for my radio show, please say it and I'll report it. If you want to say things off the record, tell me, and we'll keep the conversation on that basis.'

The professor stood there, on the roof, moving her weight from one foot to another, each shift in her bulk making a sound like an unoiled door opening.

'I can't be recorded.'

'Sure. Understood,' said Kim, thinking she was now talking like a reporter herself.

'But I'll speak publicly because you should know what's happened here. I want to show you, to actually *show* you the scene in my garden, but I can't bring you any closer because of the—'

After a moment, Edward prompted: 'The?'

'For all I know I've had a dose myself. The radiation.'

They stood there in silence. Kim, Edward and Stevie gazed up at the doctor, who stared back through the glass visor as the suit inflated with a constant hiss. 'They landed me with this,' she said finally, 'and someone needs to tell the story.'

'I feel dizzy,' said Kim, 'and I'm not even standing on a tin roof.'

Edward had worked it out. 'You've been given the substance from the pizza parlour to test. We were only coming to ask some general—'

'Yes! Yes!' she exploded. 'With no warning about the danger at all! And the clown who runs Devon Police, that Thorne fool, passed this stuff to me using a pair of chopsticks. No care, no consideration. Wait there. No, I mean – go back to the front door. Give me a minute.'

It was more than five minutes before she reappeared. The door was unlatched and cracked open half an inch. The professor shouted from inside: 'Do not step forward yet.' When the door opened, she turned out to be pulling it from inside with a long length of nylon cord. 'When you walk forwards, stay away from me. Walk on the right and go up the stairs. Come to the upper-floor landing which is a safe distance. There should be an open window which looks onto the garden. Stand there and wait for me to appear. I've caged the dogs.'

As they entered the house, Veitch faded away. The three visitors did as they were told. From the upstairs open window, Edward saw the garden. To the right was a padlocked cage with two enormous dogs pressed so close to each other that they looked like a single beast with two heads. They growled a continuous rumble of complaint, as if they were not supposed to be locked away simultaneously. Edward was realizing he had blundered into something incredible here – his 'expert' was actually the person with whom the police had entrusted the motorbike rider's material for analysis, but whatever it was had taken Veitch by surprise and now the professor wanted to complain. Should he warn the scientist – attack the police now, you'll never work for them again?

Before he could answer the question in his own mind, the professor appeared below them. The dogs went so crazy in the cage that the entire structure jumped up and down on the lawn.

'I can't release you with this here, my darlings,' said the professor. 'Stay while we sort it and then, I promise, meat and drink all night.' She turned to see Edward, Kim and Stevie in the window. 'Dobermen. I don't think one should say "Dobermans".'

'Mad as a box of frogs,' whispered Kim.

The air seemed to be going out of her suit, because it now hung off her like a popped balloon, showing her slim frame.

'Let's listen. Can you record?'

'Okay.' She pulled out her phone.

'Wait,' said Edward. 'I think she said not to. Make a note, though.'

'Look behind me!' the professor called. The garden was sizeable, with rockeries on either side of an overgrown lawn. In the middle of the lawn, about twenty feet from the dogs, was a concrete paving slab with a large bust on it. The bust looked like a Roman emperor but could have been anyone.

'This is on the record!' the professor shouted from below them. 'Because I have standards and the police should not, repeat *not* treat a specialist like this.'

She might have been in a lecture theatre. She turned her body left. 'Behind me, at least a stone's throw, thank God, there in the middle of my lawn, you see a paving slab which nearly cricked my back when I carried it over. Above the paving slab is a bust of Edward Elgar. Under the paving slab is a layer of tin foil and every single baking tray I could lay my hands on. Under them is a hole, dug to five inches with garden tools I've not used in years.'

She paused for a moment, perhaps considering the wisdom of what she was about to do.

It was strange, to have this whole encounter without properly seeing her face. She conveyed her agitation by hopping from one foot to the other. Edward whispered to the other two, 'Boy, she is so angry.'

'You came to me for a chat, I gather,' the professor continued at last. 'Well, I would like to talk about the simply horrendous way I have been treated. Below that slab and all the other protective materials are two ampoules handed to me by the police. Passed directly to me using a pair of chopsticks by a woman I know to be the acting chief constable.'

Stevie called, 'Did you say chopsticks? I'm making a note if that's okay.'

The professor let out an outraged snort.

'I arrive at Police HQ, I'm brought into Acting Chief Constable Thorne's office. She's got two small ampoules on her desk. Imagine vitamin gels or similar. Very small. Thorne says, "I'm going to be careful not to touch these," and she lifts them using a pair of *chopsticks* that came with some sort of takeaway lunchbox.' The professor seemed to be gasping the words as she relived the moment. 'The inspector was with her, what was his name, Jordan something.'

Edward said nothing, wanting to keep his only police contact out of the story if he could.

Stevie put in: 'Jordan Callintree.'

Edward let his breath go. He had been dreading hearing Jordan Callintree's name, which would present him with the ultimate conflict of interest.

'Yes, well. He played no part, just stood there looking like a dried leaf. At the time we didn't know the child had died. But I am a cautious woman, young lady, and I insisted she put it into my hard-shell Kevlar sheath, a safety sleeve I made for exactly the eventuality where I'm handed something I don't bloody well want to touch!'

The professor was speaking so loudly that Edward wondered if she wanted the world to hear.

'They passed me these two ampoules and asked me to go away and examine them. They told me the government forensic service is backed up and loses things – well, of course it is and of course it does. I would describe her mood as very slightly angry. She didn't say it, but I had the impression she wanted to use her regular forensic muppets. It was Callintree who had told me to come to the station.'

Edward winced. This was getting worse for Jordan.

'They gave me no warning whatsoever about the possible contents. On arriving home, I sought to examine one under a microscope. I punctured the skin. It did not respond to any conventional chemical testing until I brought out this—'

She started struggling to free an object from the deep pocket of her lab coat. 'This is a very old Geiger counter. It measures radiation and I can tell you it went totally batshit-haywire when I tried it on a whim. Those chumps had presented me, with no warning whatsoever, with a radioactive substance. My counter is simply not sophisticated enough to measure the half-life or contamination, but it gave me enough to know there are major safety issues for anyone near these things. I immediately donned this inflata-suit and then buried them. You're safe there. Is my suit not inflating?'

'Not now,' said Stevie.

'Jesus Christ alive, I must move.' The professor stared at them, locked in position, as if expecting a question at least.

'Have you told them?' Edward asked. 'The police will want to know what you've found.'

'Oh, they'll find out all right. No one answered the phone, so I've sent ACC Thorne-In-My-Side a bloody email. Let's see if she can break away from her busy schedule and open it. She couldn't find the time to keep me or her colleagues safe from a dose of the green glow, so I don't know if she'll manage that, but who knows?'

Another pause.

'Let yourselves out. Put it on the radio, I don't care. I'm that pissed off.'

Now Edward wished he had not stopped Stevie recording it.

CHAPTER TWENTY-FOUR

Edward rang Aspinall on the move. It had only just occurred to him that some people were still completely unaware that anything was happening today in Sidmouth, much less that the biggest news story in the town's history was about to slam into this quiet spot on the seaside like a sixty-foot freak wave.

'I need the news studio and I need to broadcast into all the afternoon programmes,' Edward said as soon as Aspinall picked up.

'What the hell, why? No!' was Aspinall's immediate reaction.

Edward put his phone on speaker. 'I've got information on the child's death.'

'What bloody child's bloody death?' swore Aspinall. 'I'm off-base today.'

'I don't have time for this,' said Edward.

'You have time for the controller of the radio station or you won't work another day there.'

Edward hesitated.

Aspinall came back in. 'Remember you're on a warning. Remember I'm having to find half a million quid to underwrite those ridiculous promises you made.'

As she stopped at lights, Kim mouthed: 'Don't fall out with him.'

Edward said: 'A child died this morning. She was in the pizza restaurant after the motorbike rider attacked it. I think we can call it an attack now. I have a source. He was carrying a radioactive substance.'

'Jesus wept! And the radiation killed her? Like a nuclear device?' Aspinall, at the other end, was aghast. Edward could hear movement, as if he was exiting a building.

'I think she put something in her mouth.'

Kim roared away as the lights went green.

Aspinall said, 'Get yourself into the station now. I'll meet you there. We're about to do the biggest day's work of our lives.'

When he hung up, Edward said: 'Dammit. Wendy Wrigley.'

'What about her?' Kim asked.

'She's getting lost in all this.'

'Can't we just tell her what you found in the forest?' Stevie asked. 'Suicide by bolt.'

'Well, I was going to check something first with Jordan Callintree. He'll have crime scene photos on file. I just wanted to be sure we chose the right bit of forest,' said Edward, 'but after this I don't think he'll ever speak to me again.' He added, almost to himself: 'This is the biggest scoop of my life.'

Kim dropped him at the radio station and left to take Stevie back to the vicarage. Edward ran into the building, with its Sunday security, and found Aspinall waiting in reception. Edward remembered that moment before the meeting with the listeners, at Harpford Hall, when both their hands were wrapped around the same door handle and his boss was refusing to let him through to the stage. This was different.

'I just want to avoid a fuck-up here. I need you to tell me your source.'

'Actually I can. She was literally shouting information at us so it's not a secret. It's a professor who does forensic work. I went to see her to sound her out, and she turns out to be doing the job on Toppings.'

'How did I miss the kid's death? . . . No,' continued Aspinall, talking to himself, 'I can explain that. I was with family upcountry. I—'

'It's a Sunday,' Edward cut in. 'You're allowed not to have signal.'

'I'm not! Okay, I'm going to announce the news flash. I'll go in to see Crispin.'

Crispin Desmith (pronounced: der-*smith*) was the old actor who presented 'Sunday Delight'. The two-hour programme, an orgy of Fifties music and musical theatre, was a concession to listeners who were angry about the younger presenters. People joked that Crispin Desmith had been born Del Smith and adjusted his name to become more interesting. He wouldn't like the intrusion.

'Let me deal with it gently,' Aspinall said. 'I can't tell Crispin it doesn't matter what he thinks. He wears a cravat and drinks port on the weekend and he has contacts in Arts Council England who, whisper it, fund fifty per cent of DJ Satan because he's diverse. Crispin needs to be tiptoed around. Leave it to me. We ask his permission.'

'Really?' Edward thought he was paying Crispin too much respect. For once, the out-of-controller was treading carefully.

'If we ask, he says yes. If we tell, he says no. Now run me through what you're going to say.'

'The motorbike rider is Russian or certainly from the Russian-controlled area of Ukraine. He released a radioactive substance when he crashed. A child swallowed some of it. She is dead.'

'God Almighty. I was with my grandchild.'

'It all broke quite suddenly.' This was wasting time. 'The thing is, I don't know if the police even know what I've found out yet.'

'Can you call your source at the station and at least tell them?'

'I think this is going to burn my source.'

'Why?'

'He won't want me to know what I've been told. Let's wait until five minutes before we broadcast. Then I call him – them.'

'Five minutes is now. Call him, him or her,' said Aspinall. 'Tell him what you know and ask for his comment. Meanwhile I'm going to talk to Crispin.'

Aspinall went into the studio next door during a track from *Carousel*, using his body to barge the door, stiffly, all the motion in the hip, as if he was a faulty clockwork toy. Edward surreptitiously pressed the reverse-talkback button – something he would normally never do, because it was snooping. It allowed him to hear the conversation.

'Crispin, could you give way to a newsflash please?'

'Who from?'

'Read by Edward himself.'

'Hmm, *Edward*,' repeated Crispin, as if weighing up the value of his colleague's contribution. Edward feared he was about to hear some awful side remark: *That useless idiot*. But it did not come. Crispin said he would make space in twenty minutes, after three o'clock.

'No, Crispin, that's too late,' said Aspinall.

Crispin harrumphed. 'Fine, I'll do it after playing the *Porgy and Bess Overture*.'

'Well, how long is that?' asked Aspinall as Edward listened.

'Just under eleven minutes,' said Crispin, leaning back in his chair and showing a square of hairy stomach where a button on his shirt had popped open. Plaid shirt, green paisley cravat.

'Crispin,' said Douglas Aspinall, voice trembling with anger that was barely suppressed, 'we'll do it straight after this, what is it?'

'How can you not know? "If I Loved You" from *Carousel*, containing the famous line—'

Edward clicked the talkback off, just as Douglas turned and beckoned him, evidently unaware he had been listening in. Edward said, 'I need five minutes.'

'Hello Edward,' said Crispin, as Edward pushed his way into the studio. 'This finishes in three.'

'Perfect,' said Douglas Aspinall. 'Now you go call your man,' he directed.

Edward moved back out and stood in the narrow gap next to a huge jackboard which had been left from the station's pre-digital days. Here he could speak without anyone hearing. But would Jordan Callintree even pick up?

To his surprise, the police officer was at the other end after one ring.

'Jordan, it's Edward.'

'I know. I'm sorry I've been—'

'You've been busy. You don't ever have to give me the time. I understand. You were incredibly helpful at the start.'

'We have a real crisis now, Edward.'

'I saw you on TV, outside the hospital. That poor girl.'

'I know, what an absolute tragedy. The family vicar broke the news, basically, and we've been running to catch up.'

Edward momentarily lost his nerve. 'I, um, I need your help with Wendy Wrigley, the crossbow killing case. It's a big ask. She's been onto me to help her. I just need you to help me with the crime scene photos.'

'You're calling about that now?' Jordan's voice was incredulous.

Edward took a breath. There must be less than a minute left on the *Carousel* song. 'No. No, I'm not. I'm about to go to air with some information about the Toppings crash. You need to know.'

'What?' asked Jordan Callintree.

'I'm going to protect my source, because the person seemed very agitated, but here is what we're about to broadcast. The capsules the motorbike rider dropped were radioactive.'

'*What?*'

'Yes.'

'How . . . no, I would know!'

'I'm sorry, that's what happened.' Without mentioning the professor, Edward ran through some of the other details that would be in her report. When he had finished, Jordan Callintree said, 'And am I mentioned?'

'I won't mention you.'

'But the chopsticks?'

'Can you confirm she used them?'

'It's that bloody professor, isn't it? She hasn't been in touch with *us* yet!'

'Do I take that as a confirmation?'

He was silent.

Edward said, 'I can't tell you who I spoke to. I guess it will be obvious. Jordan, I have to go—'

'The professor. Bastard. I can't stop you, can I? Putting this out?'

'No.'

'The bloody chopsticks.' That really was confirmation. Silence, then: 'I want to thank you for telling me and for keeping my name out of it.'

It was the slightest pressure, but Edward felt it like a vice. Ten seconds later he was in the studio, ignoring the red light. He took the chair opposite Crispin, conscious that the old actor had been forced to fill for a full minute and was fuming.

Crispin said: 'Opposite me is Edward Temmis, presenter of the evening phone-in. You have rushed in with a newsflash about the horrible events on Friday.'

Voice wavering with nerves, aware that this was the most significant moment of his career, Edward said: 'The crash at Sidmouth pizza parlour two days ago may not have been an accident. A child has died, and police are investigating whether the biker, who had links to Russia, deliberately attacked the pizza parlour with a . . .' Here he paused. 'A radioactive substance.'

Crispin reached both his hands sideways, like a man on the roiling deck of a ship seeking a solid object to cling to – his programme was now at the centre of a national incident, maybe even a global event. Crispin asked a question into the microphone.

'You say radiation. But how was that delivered? Did he spray something, or what?'

Sitting next to Edward, Douglas Aspinall did a furious cutting motion against his throat: *No questions, Crispin, please.*

'I have all this from a very reliable source, and we suspect there is a direct link between the radiation and the child who died. The radiation was delivered in small ampoules – there may have been a large number, but the fire took them and the child' – his voice wavered – 'the child swallowed one. Nina Lopez.'

'She was radiated by something nuclear?'

Again, Douglas made the throat-cutting motion with his forefinger, and now leant forwards and hissed: 'Porgy! Porgy!'

Edward said, 'The police will face criticism because they had two radioactive ampoules to analyse. They did not take precautions with them, and indeed, there is a report that Acting Chief Constable Jane Thorne used chopsticks to move the substance around.'

Douglas's head snapped up. Crispin's eyes widened. '*What?*'

'Yes, chopsticks. The capsules were handed over for analysis to a local forensics expert without any precautions, and as a result there are questions about how far and wide the radiation may have spread, and whether anyone else was endangered.'

Douglas hissed, 'Porgy!'

'We'll play some more music for a break in these incredible revelations,' said Crispin. '*The Overture.* To misquote the great Elaine Paige, you know it so well.'

The music started. A crash of cymbals, a swirl of strings and then a lone bassoon, the xylophone, and the strings again.

Crispin muted the speaker.

Aspinall said, 'You weren't supposed to go Paxman on him. Are you okay, Edward?'

'Yes. Fine.' Edward stood. His phone was already bouncing with incoming calls, and now he saw Aspinall's was too.

'Right,' said Aspinall, muting the calls on his handset. He ignored Crispin completely. 'I want to get you in the news studio and you'll basically hold the fort.'

'Great scoop, Edward,' said Crispin. The two broadcasters bared their teeth in presenter-smiles. They had total understanding of each other. They had not needed a manager to barge in and force agreement.

There was one caller Edward could not ignore. He had changed Jordan Callintree's name in his phone so no one who saw a call from him flash up could identify the source. Now it said STARSKY. And Starsky was ringing.

'You didn't mind the chopsticks?' Edward asked his caller.

'I know that came from Veitch. It must have done. She's hung up all her phones. I'm blue-lighting to her home now.'

'You're not going to arrest her?'

'I need to help her,' said Callintree.

Edward was in the news booth, a much smaller space than the main studios. He was unable to shake the idea that someone might remotely open the large microphone suspended from the ceiling and listen to his end of the conversation, as he had done with Crispin. So he detached the cable from the end of the microphone. To be sure, he pushed his chair into the corner of the room, leant back against the black acoustic padding and covered his mouth as he spoke. 'Hey,' Edward hissed, 'don't rush inside when you get there, there may be radiation. And don't blame Veitch for this. She's been treated shockingly.'

'Thorne had a bad attitude with her. I wanted to use Flo Veitch because she gets stuff done fast. Anyway,' said Callintree, 'the chopsticks line is devastating. Um, I'll look into that Wendy Wrigley thing for you if you quietly keep me posted . . . the crime scene pics you wanted?'

'Oh yes. Thank you.'

'I can't send you any of the doctor's body.'

'God, I don't need that.' Edward could not believe how amenable Callintree was being. 'I'm at the radio station. Do you want me to do another appeal in a few minutes? Are you still looking for some of the families?'

'There is about to be a panic, so yes. Radiation takes us straight to Litvinenko, Salisbury, all that. That's World War Three.'

A sudden thought struck Edward. 'Is everyone in the pizza parlour in danger? My friend Stevie Mason was there.'

'I don't know. I am still taking this in. Maybe we'll have to get everyone tested. Me as well.'

The musicals show would end an hour early, at four p.m., despite Crispin Desmith threatening to resign over the schedule change. Aspinall told Edward he would be on the air for fifteen minutes at a time – from four till quarter past, from half past till quarter to, etc. During each period of downtime, he would try to get more information on what was going on.

'Speak to your source, get the latest. Who's your researcher?'

'Melody.'

'I'll get her in. You have a police source too, right?'

'Yes. But he's cheesed off with me.'

'Why?'

'The entirety of that broadcast was news to him.'

'Okay. Then do your show as questions. The whole show as questions. "What do you want the police to do?" "Why would someone spray nuclears around a café?" "If it was an attack, why did the motorbike rider die?" "Was Toppings the target?" All of that. Lots of questions, lots of calls.' Douglas looked at his phone. 'I had an alert on, and . . . hmm.' He swished at the screen. 'Well, events are moving.'

Andrea Lopez had posted on Instagram again. Her profile was now just a black rectangle and said MOTHER OF NINA, all in capitals.

Thank you for your prayers and love. Gabriel and myself gone in hospital because radiation. Being tested now. Can't see darling Nina and hold her body. LOVE YOU NINA DARLING YOU ARE WITH GRANNY GRANDPA NOW. She thought they were sweeties.

'She thought her granny and grandpa were sweeties,' Douglas repeated. 'It breaks your heart.'

'No,' said Edward, staring at the words. 'No, the sweetie reference is something else. She ate some items she thought were sweeties. So not just one of them.'

'Good God!' Aspinall exploded. 'How vicious are these Russians, doing that to a child?'

Edward sat for five minutes and thought about how to move things on. On the TV broadcast that they'd watched at Barbara's house, Callintree had said only: 'There is no evidence as yet that anything happened to Nina Lopez as a result of her presence in the pizza parlour.' He texted Callintree:

> How many ampoules did Nina eat?

The reply came straight back.

> Two. Kept another two.

So four had been removed from the pizza parlour? It was incredible. Edward began his broadcast. Melody came in. They took calls. He now had a lot of information, most of it not officially released, and the station was being bombarded by enquiries from media in London: BBC Radio 5 Live, Sky News, newspapers like the *Sun* and *Mirror*. Douglas came in with a scribbled note telling Edward to STAY IN THE STUDIO. Melody would act as producer/reporter. Edward got into a rhythm of facts, where he became familiar not just with the substance of what he was saying but with every syllable:

1. The accident at Sidmouth Pizza Parlour may have been a terrorist attack.
2. It is not clear if the pizza house was the intended target.
3. The motorbike rider, who had Russian/Ukrainian connections, was killed at the scene but his bike spilled a radioactive substance.
4. The police need to speak to every single person who was in the pizza parlour and it is urgent, urgent, urgent that if you or your family members were present when the crash happened that you get in touch with Devon Police immediately on the special hotline number which you'll hear in a moment.
5. The radioactive substance was contained in small ampoules. They spilled on the floor. Nina Lopez ate two and died. She kept another two which are being tested. Ampoules left in the restaurant were destroyed by fire.
6. The Home Secretary will make a statement. Please stay away from the promenade in Sidmouth.

Turn the Dial for Death

Edward's moment of exposure lasted ninety minutes. Longer than he might have expected. He spoke almost continually. Occasionally Melody would rush in with an update. They had also got a freelancer, Alfie Burton, who sounded like a child when he spoke on the phone, to get as close as possible to the burnt-out pizza parlour and give updates. He did it very well, even if he tended towards melodrama – 'You sense even the seagulls are aware, coming in low over the cliffs, squawking with their usual merriment but turning abruptly, silently, as they see the yellow and black of the police tape below them.'

The exclusion zone was now a hundred yards in all directions.

Listeners rang in tears. The vicar at Nina Lopez's church rang to urge prayer and said he was fasting in support of the Lopez family. 'The child not even five, it is so wicked, so wicked!' Then he was crying too. 'And in pursuit of what, victory in a foreign war?' People were jumping to all kinds of conclusions about why Russia might have launched the attack. The most obvious was that there had been a different target, but the motorbike rider had slipped on oil and crashed early. 'I am fasting,' said the vicar, as if that could stop a war or bring back a child.

Edward knew his moment of exclusivity was ending when Alfie, speaking live on his mobile, was suddenly drowned out by a helicopter in the air above him. Edward looked out of the window and saw a second chopper pass so close to the building that he stepped back. Alfie had stopped speaking in the racket. Edward could not hear himself think. The livery on the helicopter looked military. Now Alfie was shouting. 'The police, the police in the air above me – two of them. No, more.'

Edward texted Jordan Callintree.

> Helicopters?

The detective replied immediately.

> London have arrived. MI5, army, even the Met. Expect hundreds literally. Police chief in trouble.

Edward resisted asking any follow-up. Douglas had appeared in the control suite next door and was visible through the thickened panes of glass. He was making a circle shape with his hands which Melody and Edward stared at in puzzlement. Alfie was talking from the site, describing the arrival of soldiers. In Edward's headphones, Douglas Aspinall's voice came: 'Vinyl. Record. I'm making a record shape. Have put one in for you.'

Certain songs did not run the risk of being inappropriate, whatever the context. 'Fields of Gold' by Sting. 'Angel' by Sarah McLachlan. 'Dreams' by Fleetwood Mac. Douglas had loaded Sting. Alfie was talking about people in hazmat suits coming out of a van on the promenade.

'How can you see all this?' Edward asked, knowing the young reporter was at least a hundred yards back.

Alfie's voice was permanently high-volume, but a monotone, as if he was a bagpipe with a leak. Edward imagined the young man reading a bus timetable with the same urgency – 'THE NUMBER 38 IS DUE IN EIGHT MINUTES BUT WON'T STOP OPPOSITE THE CHURCH' – but it was far better to be engaged with a story than stupefied.

Alfie said loudly: 'I brought my binoculars and I found a flat roof,' and Edward was immediately filled with admiration. He had been like this once, insatiable for airtime.

'Keep us posted. We play Sting now and will return to our normal programming after this. News on the hour . . .' A loud, angry crackling in his headset made him correct. 'News on the half-hour as well as we all come to terms with this. And thank you, Melody, for the last, what—'

'Two hours,' she helped, showing her teeth at the other microphone. 'I pray for everyone and especially for the Lopez family and law enforcement who have to enter the building as everyone else runs out.'

The song came on. To Edward's surprise, Douglas came in with a smile. The short man threw his arms out, which Melody mistook for an attempt to hug her. As she moved towards him to return the apparent hug, he backed off in horror. He turned to Edward and said, 'Good job, boss.'

Boss! 'Were people listening?'

'Are you kidding? I think we had an hour where the whole world was listening. Our website crashed with people trying to access the live stream from the USA. And then,' he said sadly, 'well.'

'Well?' asked Melody.

'Not possible to be exclusive for long these days.' He held up a tablet, its screen glowing with a headline from Sky News. HOME SECRETARY PRESS CONFERENCE LIVE AT FOUR P.M.

The Sting record had only a minute to run. Douglas saw Edward glance at the timer on the digital player. 'Don't worry. Crispin has gone home – "I decided not to resign because I am proud of this station" – and Miriam Tamla is in. She'll pick up after this record from 3B. God knows we need some Motown.'

'I quite fancy a bath,' said Edward.

'Oh, you'll stay I think,' said Douglas. 'We'll need more from your police source.'

'I'm not sure I can trouble him again tonight.'

'They're panicking,' said Melody. She reached for her phone and read a story from Twitter. '"The police chief of Devon kept the nuclear material in her desk drawer and used chopsticks to move it around". That's literally the headline.'

'Crikey,' said Edward.

'She'll have to resign tomorrow, I should think, and that'll be another story for you.' Douglas looked utterly unmoved by his own brutal assessment. His mind must have made a logical jump, because he said to Edward: 'Don't start thinking your show is safe as houses. You've done a good day's work, but you still cost me hundreds of thousands with that damned Harpford Hall performance. But yes, that was a solid shift today. I want you both here till midnight. Can you do that for me? Broadcast live whenever you want. The rest of the time, aggregate the information that's coming in. Alfie will stay on his rooftop with the binoculars, assuming no one shoots him.'

CHAPTER TWENTY-FIVE

'We just heard a terrible howl.'

Kim was at Stevie's house. The sun was down. Her heart was in her mouth. She had listened to every second of the coverage on RTR-92. Her phone showed an alert from the *Sun*'s website: CHOP LOOKS LIKELY FOR CHOPSTICKS COP, and she had tutted at how brutal the media were, punishing the investigator before the criminal had even been caught.

Stevie lived with her parents, Moira and Theo. Kim wanted to say 'a vicar and his wife', but Moira was so dominant and Theo so shrunken that the more appropriate description would be 'a vicar's wife and her husband'. Drab and damp, grey at the gills, the vicarage was lumpen, like the deliberately inconspicuous concrete outpost of an East German police station. The colourless bricks were speckled black as if hot tar had been flicked at them. The church had long since sold the original vicarage as a second home. Still, Moira and Theo had been loving (almost obsessively so) to their adopted daughter.

It was the vicar who had opened the door and spoken, before Kim had said anything. 'She must have got a message upstairs.'

Moira and Theo were both grey-faced.

Moira said, 'After she howled, I knocked on the door and got a volley of—'

'Foul abuse,' the vicar put in. 'She shouted about her wedding. There were more f-words than I could count.' He grimaced. 'She shouted, "How can I get married on Saturday if they put me in isolation?" She was railing.' He pulled a strange expression, showing the overlapping greys of bad teeth, leaning at angles over his lower lip like seasick sailors in a rescue dinghy.

Moira also grimaced with eyebrows raised, tilting her head. The two of them stepped back from the front door.

'We've seen the news. They say radiation.'

Walking towards the living room, Theo, in his thin, reedy voice, a voice that sounded as if it was choked by the dog collar on his narrow neck, said over his shoulder: 'When will we find out exactly what happened in that pizza place? She shouldn't have run in, should she?'

Kim thought: *What I love about Stevie is that she is the one person who will always run in.*

'Why doesn't our daughter think?'

She doesn't think, she feels.

They put the TV on. Pictures showed an older woman, face streaked with rust-coloured trails from cigarettes or chemicals. Her hair was held tightly at the back with a yellow ribbon and she was captioned PROF FLO VEITCH. The huge inflated suit she had worn was now deflated and hung off her like a wrinkled prune. She was holding what looked like a lump of dark green metal and spoke in front of a small portico.

'This isn't up to the job, a Geiger counter from the Seventies, but thank God I had it.' When she lifted it towards the camera, they saw it had an L-shaped handle, like a Victorian clothes iron. A cutaway showed the top side, where a dial, a light and a circular meter with a needle were riveted into the metal surface. The reporter said something off-mic. 'Yes!' Flo Veitch answered. 'This thing went completely crazy.'

It was obviously a packaged report, because Flo Veitch's remarks were sliced short and the viewpoint now switched to the professor's garden, where six people in hazmat suits lifted a huge paving stone off the top of the hole and then used long pincers to access something inside it. The object was dropped into what looked like an enormous foil bin bag.

The shot cut back to Veitch. 'Are you aware that the head of police in Devon is having to answer questions about how you came to be asked to do this?'

'No comment,' said the professor. 'I do science not politics.' She shook her hair like a horse at pasture.

'What do you say about the report that the head of Devon Police used a set of chopsticks to move this material?'

'No comment.' A big gappy smile from the professor, showing yellowed teeth, one missing on the right-hand side.

Now the report cut to some archive footage of a short policewoman with a square face, walking along a passing-out parade of new recruits, all standing to attention. 'Devon Police Acting Chief Constable Jane Thorne is under pressure because—'

'Turn it off.'

Moira and Theo froze.

Kim turned. Stevie was in the doorway.

They all stood in silence for a moment. In her mind, Kim begged Theo and Moira not to say the obvious: *Should you be down here, darling, if you're isolating?* But it was Stevie who spoke first.

'I was sent a number to call.' She pushed her mobile towards them. 'It says "Urgent and Personal, from London Metropolitan Police." I rang and heard a message and I'm sorry, I didn't take it well. Can you listen again with me, Kim?'

'Let me see that,' said Kim.

'I don't see how looking at the message helps, considering I just read it out, you bell-end.'

Kim laughed – ah, a precious glimpse of the normal Stevie! – but her parents gasped in shock at the language.

'Don't worry,' said Kim, 'I love your daughter dearly. I probably don't get called a bell-end enough. Stevie, let's go upstairs.'

'Just keep a little distance. I'm serious.'

Kim followed several steps behind. The gap made the two women almost the same height. In her bedroom, Stevie opened the window, as if that would send any radiation out with the breeze. It was dark outside, a summer's night. Kim sat at the other side of the room in the only armchair, beginning to think that this might be a bad idea. She had no idea whether radiation on one person could move to another and stick, though they had spent enough time together squeezed into her little sports car that the point was probably moot. The room was small. Stevie sat cross-legged, at a diagonal. At least they were in the furthest corners.

'Am I glowing? Am I fucking glowing?'

'Put the light out and I'll take a look.'

To Kim's surprise, Stevie took the joke seriously and did it. They sat in darkness.

'You are not glowing.'

'Listen to this,' said Stevie. In the darkness she rang the number the police had sent her, and replayed the message on speaker.

This is an AI-recorded message for Stevie Mason. This is the Metropolitan Police. You may have been affected by the presence of radioactive material at Toppings Pizza Restaurant on 16 May. You are required to remain isolated pending further advice. You may not socialize, other than with individuals who are also isolating. It is better to remain at home. Do not use public spaces, shops or public transport. If you live alone, please call the number at the end of this message for help with daily necessities.

They listened to the number and sat in the dark. 'So that's it for the wedding,' Stevie said glumly.

'Is that so bad?' asked Kim gently. 'Maybe you could do with a bit more thinking time before jumping into this?'

Stevie spoke softly in return. 'When I told you about Roddy, I saw you hiding within yourself. I don't know you well, Kim. I hope one day we do become, I don't know, besties or whatever, at least mates. But I saw you hated him.'

'I didn't hate him!' Kim protested. 'But . . . I thought he was trying to change you, and I don't want you to change.' Stevie's steady gaze gave her permission to say more. 'Stevie, I was in a bad marriage. It was a shocker. I got black eyes and broken ribs and I learnt how to brace my shoulders so it hurt less when I got pushed into a wall. He always chose the same bit of wall, by the way. But that wasn't even the most hurtful thing. What hurt me was constantly being told I was a piece of shit. Boobs too small, feet too big, can't drive a car, having to tell him how I'm voting—'

'It sounds like living in Saudi Arabia.'

'That's it! That's what it was!'

'Although I don't think they have a problem with boob size over there.'

When they had finished laughing idiotically, laughing in the dark like naughty schoolgirls in a school dorm, Kim knew she had complete permission to speak.

'That marriage ended for reasons you may not know. It didn't end because I walked out. I'm a successful businesswoman, but I stayed because I couldn't see the bottom line in my own life – a guy was screwing me up bigtime.'

Outside, the Sidmouth wind picked up, rattling the open window as if heading for Stevie to hear the response Kim wanted.

'When we met at Nine Chairs and you told us you were marrying Roddy, he turned up and you became . . . someone who wasn't you. I saw a little bit of me in you. The quietened, married me. "Quietened" – such a good word for what happens to a victim.'

'Victim—?'

Kim was in full flow now, she was going all in, and Stevie's barked objection would not stop her. 'I wasn't myself in my marriage. I want you to be yourself! And I know this will sound, Stevie, well, you'd probably say "weird as fuck", but were you thinking you were lucky he fancied you?'

There was a long pause, so long that Kim wondered if she'd gone too far.

'Yes,' Stevie croaked at last. 'Yes, I did feel fucking lucky. I wear an eyepatch, I have these burns, there's my scoliosis that makes me five foot two with a spine like a letter "S". And I can't control my fucking gob. So yes, I'd say I'm lucky that I caught a di— a guy.'

'Well, you're wrong. He's the one who's "fucking lucky" – lucky to have a diamond like you. Lucky to have a princess who is going to be a queen one day. And if he can't see his luck, if you can't get married at the weekend—'

'I howled when they told me.'

'I know. Your mum said. But maybe this buys you some breathing space.'

'And maybe you should mind your own business.'

'And maybe I should go.'

A pause. In the darkness, Stevie began to cry.

'Don't go,' she said. 'You're my only friend.'

CHAPTER TWENTY-SIX

Edward took the road home at midnight, thinking: *That was the longest day of my life.* On his moped in the dark he saw two missed calls from Kim. He pulled over at Pinn Cove and cut the engine. But when he called Kim her number went to voicemail. He guessed she had called when she was with Stevie, where the signal was intermittent. He said, 'Been a long day. Let's chat tomorrow. Apparently the army are coming down. Or – are they here already? I'll be home in two mins.'

He slowed his bike at the approach to his house. The light from the moped swished left and right across the building like a prison camp beam, illuminating brickwork and leaning joists. Everywhere it fell revealed an imperfection – gaps in the brickwork, mildewed fascia boards, doors and windows that seemed to lean and tilt. In fact the whole house looked like a corkscrew, with six rooms downstairs, three above, two, then one at the top. The twist in the body of the building had been caused by the ground moving over years. The day had twisted like the house: Nina, Veitch, Jordan, the live show, the massive media pile-on. It was not his story any more, but he had been the first to break it.

Hadn't he left a light on? Perhaps the electrics had gone again? God, he was so tired. He could sleep for a week. Tomorrow, Monday, there would be more of it.

There was a small, solar-powered downlight that registered movement screwed to the side wall of the house, and when it lit up he saw the side return was open. He was starting to get annoyed at the version of himself that had left the house the previous day. He had not been hurried; he could not excuse himself by saying he knew what the weekend would bring. All lights off, side door open? His pushbike was visible, and that would probably get a drug addict thirty quid for his next fix. He was asking to be burgled, and he was lucky no one had tried.

He pushed the moped's kickstand downwards with his foot and left it on the drive, walking carefully forwards in the dark towards the downlight, as he removed his crash helmet. Now his ears were uncovered, he heard the distant whoosh of the sea. He had always told friends and family never to walk in the garden in darkness because you could easily go over the edge and kill yourself on the rocks below. He turned on his phone light to make sure he did not suffer that fate. The garden was supposed to last another hundred years, and then half of it had disappeared one afternoon, so he could not always be sure the lawn ended where he had left it in the morning.

His torch showed him solid ground, the grass he had mown only three days earlier. He saw his feet, brown lace-ups stained with dirt, push into the dark grass, the shadow shaking with every movement of his hand.

Edward reached the end of the garden and stopped a yard short of the cliff edge. He closed his eyes and felt the wind around him. Just the gentlest breeze, not cold, wrapping him, cupping him. He thought to himself, *Who throws radiation into a pizza restaurant in Sidmouth and kills a little girl?* And an answer came, as if on the wind: *No one. No one does that.*

If he had had the lawn chairs at the end of the garden, he would have sat down and fallen asleep outside, which he had done many times before in the warm season, his busy brain soothed by the sea. He turned to see where they were. They were by the house. His eyes seemed to catch movement near the back doors. Imagination was a powerful deceiver.

He turned back to the sea.

Now there was a noise. Unmistakable movement in the dark, by the side wall. He turned back again and – with a thrill of panic – saw shapes moving across the garden towards him.

There were two. Their movement had triggered the sensor in the side passage to come on again, so the figures became simultaneously more visible and impossible to see: tall black shapes like spirits.

'Hello?' he said, because they were only yards away now, close enough for him to hear a voice. They were dressed like police. 'Officers, what is it?'

But were they police? His heart banged like a drum. The outfits were ill-fitting, the trousers too short, and the two figures wearing them were huge. They wore peaked caps with visors. Was he asleep? Was he dreaming this?

No. He felt the grass underfoot. He raised his phone light to see their faces, but as he did so the phone was swept out of his hand.

A mask.

These were not human faces. He was looking at latex masks, pulled all the way over their heads. When they spoke or made noises, the mouths did not move.

'Stop the questions. Do you understand? No more questions.'

The voice was so muffled, he couldn't tell if it was a man or a woman.

'Stop the fucking questions,' said the second person, also sotto voce. This speaker held a walking stick. Knobbled wood, the outline distorted by the knuckles and knots all along the surface. They seemed to be in pain, groaning as they spoke. 'Do you understand? Fucking arrogant twat.'

The person raised the stick and swung it at his head, missing by inches.

He was so shocked by the confrontation, by losing his phone, that he took a step back . . . and then jerked forward as he remembered how close he was to the edge of the cliff.

The two intruders rushed him in that instant and grabbed him, shook him, shouted at him – always the same thing – 'Stop the QUESTIONS! No more fucking QUESTIONS!' – but one of them seemed to be causing themselves as much pain as they were doing to him, and screamed as they moved their body as if they were being struck by their own blows.

Edward tripped and fell. When he was on the ground, on his front, they delivered kicks to his ribs and kidneys that made him cry out in agony. One sank heavily onto his legs, their shins and knees grinding into his muscles, grinding to the bone until he screamed again. Meanwhile the second attacker remained standing, wheezing and moaning as if they were having a heart attack, pushing the walking stick into his back, searching for the line of his spine.

'No more questions, bonehead.'

And then they were gone. The one grinding their knees into Edward's body got up with a fleet movement, then seemed to help the other one escape. Leaning heavily on the stick, the second attacker yelped at every step they took. They shrank in Edward's line of sight like black spectres, heading towards the back of the house, into the side passage and escape.

Edward had no phone.

He lay in the garden, shaking like a leaf, panicking, shuddering, crying, murmuring to himself, dreading their return, until the first light of dawn came at four and he knew he was safe.

CHAPTER TWENTY-SEVEN

For her official briefing from Devon Police on Tuesday morning, Stevie Mason had set up her laptop to ensure her fiancé would not be visible. Her bed was against the wall and ran underneath the window. She sat on the bed, the computer on her lap, seeing the picture of herself with the slate-grey sky behind her; had summer been and gone? She watched the caption: THE HOST WILL LET YOU INTO THE MEETING SOON.

'Can't believe I take the week off before my wedding, and I have to spend it with someone who's radio-fucking-active. You look like a troll, sat there with your hair on end.'

Stevie said meekly, 'I'm sinking into the bed, aren't I? We can't get married at the weekend. And I'm not a troll.'

'What about the bloody refunds?' he said. 'I know your parents are paying, but still . . .' His voice was muffled. He was wearing a reflective red tracksuit, and had zipped the top half all the way to the neck and pulled it over his face, up to his nose. He also wore mirrored sunglasses.

'I can't hear you, darling. I need to watch this.'

'Are you in the waiting room? That clueless cop. What's he going to say?'

'An update, I hope. You'll hear. Just don't make a noise, Roddy, *please*. I had to sign something saying I wouldn't record it or have anyone else in here.'

'But I'm not "anyone else", am I?'

'No,' she said, 'you're bloody well not anyone else. No, you're not.'

'Say it again without swearing if you can.'

Stevie was tempted to unleash a volley of expletives, and normally she might not have been able to control her own response, but there was always something threatening about Roddy. He could sit there against the wall, coiled like a snake, half-asleep, and suddenly strike. Words were a weapon, all those comments about her looks, but – and she wished she'd had the courage to tell Kim this – he had been at her throat once, in a row over a burnt toastie. The movement of his hand on her neck had been excruciating with the scarring, so now, to be safe, she just said: 'You're not "anyone else", Roddy.'

'Say it without the sarcasm now.'

The stand-off was broken by a sound from the laptop. 'Hello everyone.'

Stevie muted her channel. 'Not a word, Roddy, please, darling.'

Roddy stretched the tracksuit collar even higher up his nose. She saw her face reflected in his lenses, saw her scarring, was grateful again that he had chosen her.

The policeman's face appeared. 'Acting Chief Constable, Devon Police, Jordan Callintree', it said.

Since the day she'd met him, she had wished a thousand times that she had not done it. The instruction to isolate made her wedding impossible. Roddy was only in her bedroom now because, as he put it, he 'did not believe in radiation, or wouldn't we all be dead from radiators?' He was anti-vaccine, very worried about chemtrails and 5G, and refused to believe in viruses 'because how can something exist if you can't see it?' She wished for his certainty.

She looked at the laptop screen as it populated with dozens of faces. She scanned them. Mainly men, some who had worked in the pizza parlour, some who were dads. Four or five women – she recognized Andrea Lopez, without make-up, face drawn, alone – and two couples, each trying to squish themselves into the same shot and failing.

'Excuse me one second,' said Jordan. 'I'm isolating too, so I have to do this on my own.'

He evidently had not meant all the callers to be visible to each other, because a moment after he reached for his computer screen, every face except his disappeared. The screen was now four lines of small grey squares, each with a name in the corner.

'Sorry, all,' he said. 'I've cut the video of you all for privacy reasons. Your microphones are open, but' – at that point there was a loud crashing sound from one of the callers – 'please mute yourselves now and then we can have questions at the end.'

'Fucking get on with it,' said Roddy.

Stevie was already on mute. She put her finger across her lips and shook her head at her fiancé.

Jordan Callintree had a window to the side of him so his features were in sharp relief. He wore a white police shirt open at the neck.

'You are all on this call because you were in the pizza parlour last Friday when the bike crashed. Thanks to the local radio station and to appeals on local TV, we've tracked you down and have asked you to isolate because we now know there was a leak of radiation as a result of the crash, and the terror squad are here from London on the basis that the biker had Russian connections. Or may have.'

'May,' hissed Roddy, pulling his sunglasses down for a second so he could visibly roll his eyes. 'March April May. He's just reciting months of the year now.' Stevie checked the mute icon nervously.

'Remember,' Callintree continued, 'I'm isolating too, so I very much feel your pain. I'm on the sixth floor of the Police HQ in Exeter and I have a camp bed here. The reason for us all isolating is that' – he seemed to be consulting notes – 'radiation can have a deleterious effect on a person's health, and that includes even small amounts of radiation from another person who has been exposed.' He looked up at the camera. 'I'm sure we've all been googling this like crazy. I have.' It was the wrong thing to say. He was supposed to be the expert, not another victim, and there was a growing hubbub of annoyance from those who were not muted. It swiftly turned to anger. Stevie saw the square with the name ANDREA LOPEZ disappear. There were more shouted questions from the other grey squares, the faceless names.

'What's the dose?' someone rasped.

'Why can't we get any medical advice?'

'Is there not some kind of state assistance we can draw on? I can't work!'

'Nor can I!'

Stevie tried to ask: 'Will there be more news later today?' but she forgot she was muted. There was a cacophony of angry questions. Someone seemed to be crying. Eventually the noise stopped – Jordan had muted everyone else.

'We can't all just shout. I've turned you all off for a second. Listen, I can't give you any information at this minute on the substance or the dose or the danger. What I want to say is that if anyone is at risk because of their isolation, for example because they can't get food, please message me on the dedicated number you've been given. If you and your family are all isolating, my information is that you are no danger to each other. But if you have young children, say, and they weren't at the pizza parlour but you were, you must stay away from them. We are talking separate rooms at the very least. Please, everyone. I know it's hard. If there are child welfare issues arising from that, please, again, tell me on the number provided.

'I know you all want more information. This next bit is vital. At six p.m. today, the Met will hold a press conference at St Giles and St Nic's and they will have a lot to say. Please don't ask me for details, as I am out of the loop. I'm going to unmute you now, if you have any questions.'

'If you're out of the loop, with respect, what is the point of you?' a voice barked as soon as the mic icons went on.

For a moment the police officer breathed in as if winded. 'Does anyone have any other questions?'

Stevie expected a racket, but gradually the grey squares started to disappear. There had been five rows of four, and a couple extra – soon there was only Jordan, herself, and two others.

'Looks like I cleared the room,' said Jordan.

Stevie unmuted herself. 'They just want the facts.'

'The Met will have them. Oh, hello!' he said, suddenly recognizing her. 'I bet you regret helping me now.'

'No,' she said.

'YES SHE FUCKING DOES!' shouted Roddy.

'Sorry,' said Stevie. 'That's my fiancé.'

Jordan pretended not to have heard. Another voice piped up. 'Do you know how difficult it is to run my business when I can't meet any customers? I'm at the newsagent's on Borough Road.'

'I hope,' said Callintree, 'that when the Met tell us exactly what's going on, there'll be a way of measuring your exposure and treating it, and we can get a timetable for our release.'

The other grey square fired up now. A young woman with a strong Indian or Pakistani accent. 'Is it cancer? Is that what we have to be fearing?'

'I honestly don't know,' Jordan said.

'Because that would be a life sentence,' said the woman. 'The fear itself is the sentence, even if the person doesn't get sick.' Her square suddenly disappeared, as did the other one, leaving only Stevie and Jordan on the call.

'Apologies for the shouting on my line,' said Stevie, staring at Roddy, who pulled a face.

'I assumed it was someone passing your window,' said the policeman insouciantly.

'So we find out more later. I was getting married on Saturday.'

'I-I don't think you are now,' said Callintree.

'That sounded bad though. What you said.'

'I mustn't speculate. I don't know the details.'

That sounded *really* bad, thought Stevie. She muted her end of the call and asked Roddy, 'Now it's just me and him, do you have a question you want me to ask?'

'Cancer and radiation,' Roddy said casually. 'Classic state control tactic. Control through fear. Don't accept any injections if they offer you them, Stevie, okay? Turn it off now. That muppet knows nothing. Fucking Covid needle dance puppet.'

But Stevie felt sorry for Jordan Callintree. If he knew more than he was saying, he was being very discreet. She was about to ask another question when Roddy jumped from the bed and slapped the laptop shut. 'Fuck him and his larks.'

She looked down, a sudden anger kindling inside her. The jibes, the casual authority – Kim's words ringing in her ears: '*He's* the one who's fucking lucky.'

'Now I want you to make *me* glow,' said Roddy.

Stevie looked up. The mirrored glasses stopped her seeing the eyes. She was staring into her own face – he must know she avoided mirrors at home. 'Take them off.'

He loosened the drawstring on his tracksuit bottoms.

'Not those. The glasses.'

He cocked his head to the side, smirked, obeyed. Removed them, folded the arms, passed them to her.

She held the glasses thoughtfully.

'I wonder why you wear these, when I stay away from mirrors?'

'Didn't give it a thought.'

'Expensive?'

'A ton, a ton ten.'

'Let me show you what you're doing to me.' She held the sunglasses by the furthest point of each arm. Slowly she pulled the end tips apart. At the instant one of the hinges broke, Roddy's hand shot out with a vicious slap. Sitting below him, she ducked slightly, and his open hand struck the top of her head.

'Hang on,' said Stevie, scooting backwards, trying to get out of range. 'I only broke one of them. You're doing more than that to me.'

As she began to bend the other arm, he snatched at the glasses. The frame broke completely when she pulled back, and he was left with a single mirrored lens in his hand.

'You're in trouble now,' he said.

She could have scooted further away from him, back across the bed where she would have been able to kick out if he came closer, but instead she moved closer, until her feet found the floor and she was standing.

He grabbed her shoulders and shook her.

'A hundred and ten, those glasses!' He was incandescent with anger, ten inches taller, almost dribbling the words. He grabbed the hair at the back of her head and yanked it, jerking her chin up. He span her ninety degrees, and pushed her.

In that moment, Kim's words came back to Stevie: *I learnt how to brace my shoulders so it hurt less when I got pushed into a wall.*

The wall hurt. Stevie's scoliosis passed the impact in a zigzag from her shoulder blades to her hips, but she had braced, just like Kim said, and the impact of the wall on her head went mainly to flesh not bone; her head struck the wall but she was not knocked out.

'I will smash sense into you,' said Roddy. 'You smash my glasses and I will smash you.'

'You've already broken me,' said Stevie.

He relaxed his grip for a fraction of a second, allowing her to fall back against the wall. She felt warm blood ooze from her head and drip down her neck. Now she was dizzy; maybe he had hurt her more than she knew.

'Hit me again and my parents will go to the police,' she gulped. 'You'll be the guy who beat up the woman who got radiated in Toppings trying to help the cops. So go ahead. You have one punch left in this relationship, and then we're through.'

Roddy stood opposite her. He kept glancing at the single mirrored lens in the palm of his hand, as if he needed reminding why he had every right to beat her.

'We're getting married, darling,' he said suddenly. 'All couples have issues like this.'

'One punch, one push, you choose,' Stevie said. 'Last chance.'

'We can get counselling.'

'The only counselling you need is to work out why you're so shit in bed.'

'I'm shit in bed because you're such an ugly fucking gnome.'

'That was it,' said Stevie, ghosting sideways and past him. 'Your last hit. Hope you enjoyed it.' She brushed past him to the door, expecting to be grabbed or struck, or even lifted and thrown. To her surprise, a shocked Roddy took a step back to let her past.

Stevie opened her bedroom door and saw her parents outside. Moira began applauding. Theo laid his hands across hers to stop her, then set off downstairs, saying over his shoulder, 'This way, Roddy. I'd say it's been jolly nice meeting you, but vicars don't lie. I'll help you find the front door.'

CHAPTER TWENTY-EIGHT

Edward's ribs ached. He could not twist. He could not laugh – not that there was anything to laugh about. He had taken a day off work after the attack in his garden, and ordered a new phone. The old one was still connected to the network – it must be on the rocks below the cliff, and it was tempting to climb down to try to locate it. Because it was still registered, he had to get a new number and he'd lost all his contacts.

His stomach growled, as if a depression was taking root there, and he looked for anti-inflammatories to settle it. When he took two, he shut the bathroom mirror and saw the face of an old man. *A beaten-up old man*, he thought. Hurting all over, sad inside. That was him.

His body was bruised from the beating. He was sure at least one rib was broken. He wandered about the house disconsolately. He saw how his two assailants – real police, fake police? – had got in. The side passage door had been prised open and they'd been lying in wait for him in the garden, which would not have been difficult. And what were they telling him? Not to ask questions? How the hell was he supposed to comply with that and keep working?

He was about to take his moped to Kim's flat when she arrived at the end of his driveway in her Porsche.

She looked angry, but the frown dissolved from her face when he burst into tears.

'What – honey, what?'

'Oh dear, oh dear,' he said, shaking his head.

'Where've you been? I tried to ring, you've been completely missing in action. You weren't even on the radio last night – what's going on?'

'I got beaten up.'

'*What?*'

He had to repeat it. She asked to see the injuries, as if she didn't believe him. 'Not out here,' he said. They went inside and he stripped off to his boxers.

She put her hand over her mouth.

'Literally black and blue.'

'In Sidmouth?' she exclaimed. 'What did the hospital say?'

'I haven't been.'

'Police?'

He had not even rung them, but he lied. 'They just gave me a crime number.'

'They need to see these bruises, honey! Go there in person! I should photograph you!'

'Kim, they were dressed as – or they were – police officers. What if this pair were actual cops? I don't want to make it worse. Jordan's been sabotaged by his own officers – what if they're all in on it? And the police are deep into their radiation investigation, and this is nothing by comparison.'

'But it's connected, right? It must be. They don't want you asking questions. Why not?'

'I thought everything was out there already,' he said, embarrassed to still be crying.

'They could have killed you.'

'They were literally enormous. And ferocious. One of them screamed every time she hit me.'

'She?'

'He, she, I don't know why I said that. I couldn't tell. I thought they were trying to push me over.'

'Over the cliff?'

'We were right at the far end of the garden, where it's crumbling away.'

'Hey – stand by for a crazy thought – what if it was those two weirdos who are trying to buy the penthouse flat?'

'The Asian woman is too slight,' he said. 'And wasn't he short? This pair were seriously big and chunky. Both six foot. Their outfits were weird. Why would it be them?'

'Bad people in pairs,' she said. 'Nothing more than that.'

'That's not quite the threshold required by a court,' said Edward. They laughed. He was surprised to hear his own laughter. 'Have you not thrown them off the trail, the penthouse pair?'

'We're on a go-slow with them, which I hope works. They do keep ringing though. Mad about the flat. They're not getting it, the weird bastards.' She looked tenderly at him. 'You'll be okay. So do you think "Stop asking questions" was about the radiation and your radio show?'

'Maybe,' Edward hedged. 'But you know what? It also made me think of Wendy Wrigley. I asked questions because she wanted me to. I need to speak to her. It kind of got washed away, all that crossbow stuff. I left it hanging. I wanted something from Jordan Callintree, but I can't face chasing him.'

'He did well out of that professor outburst.'

'Did he? The guy has to lead an investigation from a locked room somewhere, and the Met are taking charge of everything.'

'Mate,' she said tenderly, 'you need to take it easy.'

'I can't. I'm in today, and I saw that the Met have a big press conference at six p.m. Aspinall will want me to cover it; not that he can get in touch with me to tell me so.'

'Those bruises are absolutely horrible.'

'They wore latex masks,' he said.

'You never got a crime number, did you? You didn't go to the police at all, did you?'

His silence was as good as a yes.

'Edward. Why not?'

'I want us to solve it,' he said. 'I want you, me and Stevie to work out what the hell happened at the pizza parlour.'

'Oh my love,' Kim sighed. 'It might just be a question we never find the answer to.'

He immediately remembered the giants in his garden: *Stop the fucking questions*. 'Hey, that note I got. The same wording. "Stop your questions". The same people?'

'God, you're right, it must be,' said Kim, and her hand trembled as it slipped within his own.

When he got into work, Kim's concealer covering the marks on his face, he made sure to arrive early so he could watch the press conference and then go straight on air.

Aspinall was surprisingly cordial.

'You okay? A bug?'

'I was laid out,' said Edward, truthfully. 'But just a one-day thing.'

'Have you got anything for us from your sources? What are they going to say at this press conference then?'

Edward could have given a long answer to cover his lost phone, something about the difficulty of ringing someone who didn't want to be rung, the physical impossibility of extracting a reply from a man who was isolating on the top floor of police headquarters, but instead he just said: 'Nope.'

Aspinall had an unsmoked cigar protruding from the top

pocket of his jacket, the brown of the tobacco leaf camouflaged by the material of the jacket, the exact same shade, and he wondered if the cigar was there for a celebration.

Douglas saw him staring and withdrew the cigar. 'I have my own scoop today, and this is my reward.'

'Go on.'

'Prime minister's coming down. Sometime after the Met do their presser in the church.'

'Can I interview him?'

'I have a contact at Number Ten. I'm trying, believe me. The PM hasn't heard of you, obviously, but we've sold it on the basis that it would go live on the entire RTR network, all sixteen stations. Waiting to hear.' He put the unlit cigar in his mouth, thought better of it, replaced it in his jacket pocket.

'What do you want from me today?' asked Edward.

'Get down to the church for the presser, be in the actual building, okay? We are taking the whole thing live. Afterwards you can give us the post-match.'

'What, like analysis?'

'The full Gary Neville. What are we expecting?'

Edward was embarrassed to admit his absolute lack of intel; Jordan Callintree's private number had been on his missing phone. 'Worst-case scenario, they say yes, this was a nuclear attack on Sidmouth and they give some sort of read-out. They've made a great play of announcing developments.'

Melody came in. 'Someone is calling you. Stevie Mason? The office phone.'

To Aspinall's questioning glance, Edward replied: 'My mobile died.'

The controller said, 'Melody – can you fix him up with a new one? It's vital. He needs to keep asking questions. Meantime, give him yours.'

Melody looked like Aspinall had asked her to give him one of her legs or an arm. The 'ask questions' exhortation made

Edward shiver, and the sea of bruises across his body lit up in response. Melody put Stevie's call through to the tiny news booth and Aspinall waited outside to give Edward privacy. Again, Edward pulled the cable from the bottom of the microphone to be sure.

'Stevie?'

At the other end he heard a dramatic clearing of throat. 'Where've you been? I couldn't reach you! It's just so fucking shite, and excuse my French.'

'I'm so sorry Stevie, I know how much you wanted the wedding to happen this Saturday.'

She sniffed again. 'I kicked Roddy out. Kim showed me the truth of it. Anyways, I'm calling 'cause the victims had a briefing from the police but it was fucking useless. Can you tell me anything?'

'God. I'm sorry for Roddy.'

'Why would you feel sorry for him?' she said, misunderstanding.

'I'm sorry for you is what I mean.'

She did not rebuff the offer of sympathy, suggesting hurt she was hiding. 'Have you got any news, Edward?'

'I thought you might tell me.'

'Fucking bastard Russians if it's them. It's all doom and gloom. Are you going to be in the church for the press thing? Can you ask them how long everyone has to isolate for? Just ask for me, as a mate? Don't name me, obviously. It might be bloody years at this rate.'

'I'll ask, I promise.' He wondered whether he could go to air simply with the phrase 'doom and gloom', but as his mind turned she sighed, long and loud. She sounded like a broken version of herself. 'I'm so sorry, Stevie. My heart is breaking for you and I know Kim's is too. The presser will be on the radio in full, you know?'

'I've got the TV on and they're just showing shots of the empty church.'

'I've got to get down there. Hey,' he said, 'give me your number and Callintree's if you can. My phone died.'

He wrote them down, and then she said: 'I'm glad to help. Thanks, Edward, thanks for being my fucking friend.'

CHAPTER TWENTY-NINE

The Metropolitan Police Commissioner herself was at St Giles and St Nic's. The church hushed when she tapped her microphone. A camera light fired up directly in front of her and she winced. Six officers sat either side of her. 'It is six p.m. on Tuesday. The attack . . .' She paused. 'The *incident* in Sidmouth happened at two p.m. last Friday the sixteenth of May. A lot has happened in four days.'

Edward had arrived late, blaming Aspinall for holding him up. He walked in with the record function already running on Melody's phone. A friendly face at the back of the church – one of the vergers, no less – had recognized him and whisked him fifty yards to a space at the left end of the front pew. Next to him was a bald man wearing thick-rimmed spectacles, with a forest of A4 paper spilling from his lap. The man kept turning his left hand as if operating an invisible dial, an annoying tic. He acknowledged Edward with a distant smile.

Facing forwards, Edward saw a flickering television screen with Jordan Callintree on it. The Devon policeman sat upright and attentive, as if he was part of the powerful panel the Met had deployed, but the TV monitor was small, the connection was patchy, and the set was propped against the front leg of the trestle table. Most members of the audience would not even be able to see it.

The commissioner was the oldest person at the table, pushing sixty. Her face had the rough-hewn look of a woman who had fought her way to the top in a man's world. She was unsmiling, motionless, her face set like cement, hair concrete blonde. A hat held everything in place. The only part of her that moved as she spoke was her lips.

'My force have played out of their socks,' she said. 'When we were eventually alerted . . .' The pause was silent condemnation of Devon's farting around. 'When we heard, we came running. We deployed for a terrorist attack on our homeland.' Edward raised his eyebrows at the Americanism. 'We were right to.'

A pause. Still the woman moved nothing, not even blinking, staring straight ahead. There were more than two hundred people in the church, and you could hear a pin drop.

'I commend the investigations of our colleagues here in Devon and their . . . professionalism. They traced the bike licence to an address, giving us a name and a connection to Ukraine and possibly to Russia. We had a little more about the biker, but not much. After the work of a local scientist' – 'work' sounding like another word for vandalism – 'we had just the single intact ampoule left from the incident, and we then had the tragic death of Nina Lopez. May I ask that we now stand for a minute's silence in memory of Nina?'

Edward stood in the pew, more slowly than the people around him because he was holding the phone, a notepad and a pen. For a minute he thought of his only child, his beloved Matty, who had died at eleven.

When they sat back down, the commissioner of the Met continued, 'We now have a readout from the last remaining ampoule. If I may, I now bring in Dr Timothy Gregson, who is with the science and forensics branch of the Met and who has been liaising with our friends at Porton Down.'

Edward looked at the other twelve members of the panel for a clue as to who would be the scientist. But then the bald, bespectacled man in the space directly beside him got to his feet. 'Hello everyone.'

He turned awkwardly in the narrow pew to face the congregation. All being well, RTR-92 would now be patching through the line they had run from the sound desk at the back of the church. The man's left hand was still moving – the wrist rocking anti-clockwise and back again. He held the disorderly sheaf of A4 documents in his right hand, pinning them to his body with his right forearm, which was trembling slightly. For balance he placed a knee on the wooden pew.

'To the science,' he began. 'I am a specialist in poisons, chemical devices, and, more broadly, forensics. Myself and my team have spent thirty-six hours analysing what was a tiny sample. I can confirm it was substantially radioactive. An isotope called Actinium-224.'

Dr Gregson paused as a gasp echoed around the church, reaching into his jacket and withdrawing a banana.

'This is a banana.' He waved it. 'I appreciate people at the back can't see it. But it certainly is. I use this in schools. A banana emits radiation – no need to worry! Every banana does. It is pulsing fifteen becquerels, a measure of radiation, virtually nothing. But nuclear substances vary in power. When Putin poisoned one of his enemies in London, Mr Litvinenko, he used polonium-210 which contained *two billion becquerels* of radiation. This is why we had to identify the substance used at Toppings as a priority.

'Regarding our measurement – there is alpha and beta radiation, but' – he read the shifting bums in the crowd – 'I won't get into that. There are other units. Grays and sieverts, for example, measure human exposure. Grays measure the actual radiation taken in by a body.

'I'm afraid, with the child Nina, she was exposed to a

colossal number of grays because of ingestion. She swallowed two capsules. And children have a smaller cellular structure. I will return to that poor girl in a moment.

'Let me show you how this formula works in the Toppings case. Screen please.'

He gestured to a projector screen hanging directly above Edward, at the opposite end of the nave to the pulpit, that he had barely noticed until now. It was presumably extended and retracted to display hymn lyrics and the like. Gregson turned in his pew and began to read the formula directly above him.

Actinium 224
$7 \times 10\text{-}10$ sieverts per becquerel
Lethal dose 10 sieverts
∴ Amount required
$10 \div 7 \times 10\text{-}10$ becquerels
= 14bn becquerels
= 77 nanograms

It might as well have been a foreign language. Edward winced as noise began to slowly build in the church. The audience were surrendering angrily to the detail, becoming impatient, needing to know what this all meant. A whispering had started, which spread from pew to pew, almost a hiss, like steam blowing through the spout of an old stove kettle in the moment before the whistle blew.

Someone shouted, 'Get to the point! What is a nanogram when it's at home? Speed up, man!'

'Are we all infected?' someone else shouted.

The scientist seemed thrown by the reaction, as if he was expecting a more positive crowd. But the hundreds of Sidmouthians in the audience just wanted the conclusion. How much of this substance was a fatal dose? Who else would die?

'One gram is about what a paperclip weighs. Imagine a paperclip cut into a million pieces. Each weighs one nanogram. A lethal dose of Ac-224 would be one third the size of one of the pieces. We recovered a sample the size of a pea. That alone could kill, realistically, a million people. But—'

It was too late: the audience descended into chaos.

Eventually someone blew a whistle. An old-fashioned police whistle! It was not an officer – it was the old man who looked after Sidmouth Museum most weekdays; he must have locked up and come next door to watch the show. He blew and blew and blew on the whistle until the room was calm.

The commissioner pushed her mouth into the microphone and the volume when she spoke quelled the tumult. 'Wait, everyone. This is not supposed to be a bad news speech. Doctor, please get to the point.'

The scientist continued. 'I know I scared you by saying the sample had enough radiation to kill everyone in Exeter, but most of the radiation from Ac-224 is extremely short-range. Yes, it would kill someone who swallowed it, but not someone who touched it for less than, say, an hour or two. The motorbike rider with his lead panier would be safe, the pizza parlour customers are not irradiated, not one of you is irradiated, but poor Nina, who ate two of the capsules, is dead.'

There was a long silence as Gregson finished speaking, then a flurry of conversation, though with the heat taken out of it now. At that moment Edward saw that a television monitor showing the face of Jordan Callintree, which had been propped unobtrusively against a leg of the trestle table, had now fallen onto its back. One of the vergers had noticed and pulled it upright again. Callintree was evidently speaking, not realizing he had been on mute for the last thirty minutes.

'Stay where you are, everyone. That's not the end of it. Doctor, please give us the – I could almost call it "the punchline." Go on, quickly please.'

Turn the Dial for Death

'If this was a terrorist attack, it was pretty hopeless – like a terrorist trying to blow up a tower block with an indoor firework. It was certainly not delivered in the way any true terrorist would have planned,' he concluded. 'For that reason, I see no cause for the people isolating to hide themselves away any longer. My judgement is that not one of them will be irradiated.'

CHAPTER THIRTY

The revelation that there was no threat in the attack, no danger from the radioactive substance unless some poor soul actually swallowed it, was almost as dramatic as the equivalent bad news would have been. One minute this had been a dose that could 'kill a million', the next it was perfectly safe unless you ate it.

On saying his last word – appropriately, 'irradiated' – Dr Gregson had sat back down, his bottom landing on Melody's mobile. Before the scientist could be moved, he turned to Edward and said: 'I think that went rather well, don't you?'

Edward responded: 'In news we call that "burying the lead". Would you mind if I reached for my phone?'

People were moving around the church now, talking excitedly, and before the scientist could shift, or even realize what he had been asked to do, he was collared by an eager young couple in matching teal scarves who appeared in front of him with big, white-toothed grins. 'What wonderful news! We were on the seafront at the time of the attack and we were wondering about testing ourselves. You can get a cheap Geiger counter on Amazon,' the woman said.

Dr Gregson put in: 'Ah. That won't work, I'm afraid. A

Geiger counter measures becquerels not grays. You would need a blood test for that.'

The eager man said, 'Thank God that's not necessary!'

Beside Edward, the scientist suddenly yelled, 'Yowsers!' and jumped up, exposing the mobile phone on the wooden pew seat below him. It was buzzing against the dark wood. Edward took the phone and saw a messge:

> CALL WENDY WRIGLEY ON THIS NUMBER.

Edward pressed 'escape' to remove the alert. Could she not wait a few more days? This was the busiest period of his professional life. Surely she would understand? The attack on Toppings was overwhelming. His brain snagged on that single word again – could they call it 'an attack' now that the science said it was not? And if what happened at the pizza parlour was not an attack, then what the hell was it?

What possible reason would any man have, sane or insane, to travel with those capsules? If the pizza parlour was not the target, and the crash a genuine accident, what was he doing moving around a quiet Devon seaside town with enough radioactive material to kill – *No, wait*, he thought. If the remaining ampoule had the capacity to kill a million people, and his bike had shed twenty of them, that could have taken out half the country. What the hell could be the reason?

Edward shook his head: how would they ever find the answers to these questions?

The phone rang again. Around him was a throng of locals wanting to ask the scientist questions. Dr Gregson was retreating. Edward wanted to reach out and grab the man's brown jacket to get his attention – wasn't he at the front of the queue for follow-up questions? – but the phone vibrated insistently.

He answered.

'Edward, it's Wendy. I got this number from your friend Kim. I'm so sorry, but you didn't reply to my text.'

'Which one?'

'A minute ago, the one saying call me.' Her voice had a strange quality, almost an absence of any telephonic hiss or purr, as if it was coming through on an internet-quality connection.

'I didn't see it.'

She was, as always, polite. But for once her voice was insistent. 'You looked down at your phone and shook your head and deleted it.'

'You saw?'

'I was five rows behind you. I could hardly miss you, arriving late like that.'

'Where are you now?'

'Can you feel a person touching your elbow? That's me.'

CHAPTER THIRTY-ONE

Kim had turned the radio on to hear the Metropolitan Police press conference in Sidmouth parish church. She had to admit, although Edward had very little good to say about the Aspinall fellow, the station controller had organized the coverage excellently. The young reporter, Alfie Burton, was outside the church with two or three locals who helped him fill the time by talking about the dread they had felt in the past few days, and the fear that there was some motivation for the incident they were not being told about. Alfie and his guests spoke up to the moment at which the press conference started, at which point he said in his booming voice: 'We will now TAKE THE NEWS CONFERENCE LIVE, and afterwards Edward Temmis, who is INSIDE, will emerge from THE CHURCH to give us his assessment.'

At the estate agency, Kim said to the half-dozen employees in the office, 'Guys, gather around, we'll want to hear this.'

'This feels like the olden days,' said one of her Gen Z estate agents, 'listening to the wireless.' Kim did not want to explain. They were listening because she wanted to hear Edward.

After the scientist finished, there was only hustle and bustle from inside the church. The line clicked back to Alfie Burton, waiting for Edward Temmis. Alfie filled the space to the best of his ability, bringing in some of the Sidmouth residents who were now pouring out of the building – 'Great news, I think, but a very complicated presentation' . . . 'It still sounds nuclear and therefore it's still dangerous, isn't it?' . . . 'I feel we need to know more' – but when Alfie was left alone it became clear he had not taken a note of the more detailed science and just kept coming back to the conclusion: 'No threat to anyone unless you eat it, and that means no one has to isolate.' He added, 'I wrote down "Crippled Actinium twenty-four".'

'What good news!' said another of Kim's younger staff as they drifted back to their places in the open-plan office. 'Kim, I need to talk to you about the penthouse couple when you've a moment. They keep pushing.'

'The penthouse pair?'

'Yes. They know I'm fobbing them off.'

Kim managed, just, to avoid rolling her eyes at the mention. She would be dragged back into work within seconds, when she really wanted to hear Edward's take on the press conference. What a puzzle this was! She knew, because she knew Edward back to front, that he would immediately be trying to work out what had happened. She wanted to help. Just as she had wanted to help with Wendy Wrigley.

She was feeling a little guilty about Mrs Wrigley. She liked the doctor's wife a lot, and had plans for the two of them when things calmed down. If Wendy was being shunned, Kim would take her out for a drink and introduce her to some of her own friends. Maybe she and Wendy would buddy up and do stuff together. Kim always felt she was too private and yes, she could see them becoming friends. Wendy had been gently messaging her about Edward for the past few days, asking why he was not responding. Today Kim had been able to reply that his phone had fallen off a cliff – a step beyond 'dog ate my homework'. Then Kim had made the mistake of telling her, 'I think Edward has made some progress. We all went out to test his theory.'

The sentences seemed to electrify Wendy, who replied, 'I must talk to him then. I know there's a lot going on but he must have a minute for me.'

'I'm so sorry. Ever since the Toppings—'

'Oh, I know,' said Mrs Wrigley. 'How awful it is, and such a mystery as to why Russia would do that to this little town.'

Feeling terrible, Kim had passed on Melody's number, which Edward had shared with her earlier.

Perhaps that was why Edward had not, as planned, emerged immediately from the church to give his on-the-spot analysis to Alfie Burton: Wendy Wrigley had gone there for answers and found him.

Resigning herself to speaking to Edward later, she knew she should turn to the business of the Penthouse Pair, as she called them. She had asked her mother, 'Can I refuse to sell a house because the two of them were weird and nasty?'

'Yes!' Barbara had cried. 'You're the boss! Of course you can!'

'What if they start throwing money at me?'

'No! Of course you can't refuse that.'

She smiled. Because today was a good day. The Penthouse Pair could wait for a reply. Sidmouth already had its answer. There was no mass leak of radiation, and it sounded as if it had not even been a deliberate attack. Whatever the biker was doing was not terrorism, right? Unless he wanted to put all those dangerous ampoules into the water supply. There *was* that. She wished she could get Edward's view.

Stevie drifted into Kim's thoughts. She would be so thrilled to be out of isolation. Was that a happy picture in her mind's eye, of Stevie putting her wedding dress into storage for another day? The wedding was due to have been in four days' time . . . Kim hoped it would stay cancelled.

Kim took her mobile out of the office because she did not want her young staff to hear. She took the stairs at a clip and emerged from the front door, where there was a bench by a quiet stretch of road that caught the sun at this time of day.

'Stevie?'

'Who goes there?'

'You sound – wait.' The volume on her smartphone was quiet, and she turned it up. 'You sound fine.'

'Just fine? Well, apparently I'm not in prison no more.'

There was a voice in the background. Stevie spoke to someone else. 'It's Kim, Mum. Okay, I'll tell her it's not a prison.' Then back to the phone: 'It's not a prison, Kim. Officially not a prison. It's my bedroom at home and I'm now allowed downstairs. Bye, Mum.' A door closed in the background. 'Well, it *was* a prison. Fucking shite bollocks fuck, and excuse my French.'

'But you're out! Out of Isolation Station! You must be excited . . . the wedding?' Kim dared the question.

Silence.

'Stevie?'

'I put Roddy in the bin.'

Kim's heart lurched. 'Oh Stevie,' she gulped. 'I'm so sorry.'

'I thought you wanted me to!'

'No, I mean, I'm just sorry you've had to go through all that.'

'I broke his sunglasses.'

Kim snorted, tears in her eyes. 'Accidents happen.'

'Because I feel he was breaking me. I'm a little scared now.'

'You'll find someone else in a second!'

'Not scared of being on my own. Scared he'll come back at night and hurt me. He knows where my bedroom windows are, and I only have one eye left to lose.'

'Then come and stay at mine,' said Kim without hesitating, brushing the tears away.

'What if he attacks the vicarage with Mum and Dad there?'

'Why don't you all stay at mine?'

'All three of us? How big is your house?'

'It's a two-bedroom flat.'

'What, so I have to sleep in bed with them like *Charlie and the Chocolate Factory*?'

'Okay – I have to be honest. The spare room only has a single bed.'

'I don't even want to picture that. They wouldn't come anyway. Vicars can't leave their vicarages or they shrivel up. Mind you, Dad already looks like a guy who left his vicarage.'

'Would you come, though? Just to feel safe? You deserve to feel safe, Stevie.'

'I'm probably getting too cranked up. And there's good news – now I'm not radioactive, at least I can go ahead and get married.'

A knot of puzzlement and fear tightened in Kim's stomach. 'Sorry? Wait – you're still going ahead with the wedding?'

'Kim, I know this will surprise the knickers off you, assuming you are wearing some – yes, you probably are – but would you say we was friends, the two of us?'

Her 'of us' sounded like 'oz'. Kim pictured Stevie, talking quietly into the phone at her end so her parents would not hear. Short but mighty, with a face full of acid scars but a spirit unbroken. The single gleaming undamaged eye, the shock of brown-blonde curls. The foster child who stayed small but became a kind of giant. She remembered a particular moment when there had been forty people in a pub and Stevie had walked in wearing a pink cowboy hat and bellowed, 'NO PARTY TILL STEVIE GETS HERE, AND HERE I FUCKING WELL AM.' Her language was appalling, and it did not surprise her that Stevie's IT job at the council seemed to have been designed to keep her well away from the public. But that was, Edward had told her, some kind of Tourette's. And the Tourette's, she was fairly sure, had been exacerbated by her troubled life as a little girl in Glasgow. It probably had not helped that her parents' existence revolved around a little Anglican parish, their horizon too narrow to encompass all the wrongs done to their daughter.

'Absolutely we're friends, Stevie.'

'Okay. Truth now. I'm getting married, but not to Roddy.'

Kim felt the sun on her face and a gorgeous inner warmth as the knot inside her untied itself. 'You're not getting married to him on Saturday, but there's still going to be a wedding?'

'No flies on you,' said Stevie. 'Since it was too late to cancel anything, even the church, I decided to marry myself. We'll be thin on the ground, but I was hoping you'd still come.'

'Marry yourself?' Kim laughed. 'Stevie, my love, I'm sorry, I'm not getting it.'

'I mean I'll get married to myself instead of getting married to him. I saw on the BBC a story once, someone in Felixstowe did it. She got to forty-two, no one wanted her, so she had her big day on her own. Obviously we'll have a lot of gaps, because Roddy's family and friends won't be there. But I figured, why cancel everything just because he's a wart on the arse of the world?'

'Ha! I wouldn't miss it for the world.'

'Oh, good.'

'I'm sure Edward will feel the same, if he's not busy. He's still invited?'

'He's the team leader, of course he is. He's been all over the radio with this bloody thing.'

'Yes. Thank God it's over.' Kim had a sudden jolt of memory, of conscience. *It is not over for the family of Nina Lopez, and it never will be.* 'I don't mean "over", that's wrong, I mean at least it's not as bad as we feared.'

They took a breath, as if not sure where the conversation went now.

After a beat Stevie said, 'I can't remember if I told you, but I went part-time at the council. I know the IT job back to front but it's fifty per cent "I forgot my password" and the other fifty is getting AI alerts that someone's accessed porn. Half of all the porn accessed in the past year was on one computer, and of course it was the guy responsible for council standards. He went on a website called DANISH WOMEN GARDENING more than a thousand times.'

'That's porn now?'

'Apparently the word "gardening" means something else in Denmark. Roddy kept saying it was his dream job, checking other people's computers.'

'What are you doing with your extra time then, if you've got fewer hours at the council?'

Stevie hummed at the other end of the phone. 'Er . . . I'll tell you sometime. I think you'll like it.'

Kim volunteered a confidence of her own. 'If this is our first girly chat — Edward asked me to move in. He was gutted when I said a flat no.'

'Just tell him the truth.'

'What is the truth?'

'You're asking me?'

'I guess I am,' said Kim.

'Tell him you're like the girl who got mugged in a dark alley, and now you're scared of all alleys, even light ones.'

'Meaning?'

'Come on, Kim! Fucking *analogies*! Meaning that husband of yours left you in trauma and now you're avoiding anything that looks like a husband, even a brightly lit one.'

'That's the way the brain works, I guess.'

'I only know this because of my screwed-up childhood, and it's taken me a hundred years to sort through that bloody mess.'

'I'm so sorry.'

'But it had the reverse effect on me, where I tried to make a hopeless thing work. That faecal tracksuit Roddy was excited because I was a virgin when I met him, I think.'

This information was so left-field that Kim stifled a gasp. The sun was on her face, but she felt something in the depths of her like a diver's light, a beam that showed how deep her inner self went, and how much of her could suddenly turn to anger or love.

She took a deep breath. 'You're such a wonderful girl, Stevie.'

'That was a long sigh. Are you okay? You sound like someone tried to run off with your earrings.'

Kim replied, 'When someone hurts you, I think I feel it.'

'But I'm not hurt.'

'That's kind of what I mean. You get hit, I get hurt.'

'Sisters?'

'Maybe. In a different life.'

'That's no good to me. It needs to be in this one.'

'Okay. Sisters in this one.'

CHAPTER THIRTY-TWO

When he finally got to Alfie Burton's microphone thirty minutes after the press conference in the church had ended, Edward was dishevelled. The young reporter set eyes on the senior presenter and his face fell. He was dutifully standing by the radio station's van, parked at the church gates, one side almost touching the wall of Sidmouth Museum. He covered the head of his microphone to speak only to Edward.

'Grumpy Gordon,' whispered Burton, moving his eyes upwards. It was a way of directing Edward to what was happening directly above him. On the roof of the van, the three-metre telescopic mast was retracting. So the vehicle's broadcast systems had been shut down in preparation for its exit.

'GG just said "I'm not waiting any longer", and started turning things off,' said Alfie. 'Insisted on packing up because you weren't here.'

At that moment, Gordon moved around the bonnet of the van, shirt untucked, a traveller's money pouch hanging from his waist. He was Edward's age and wore flannel trousers even on the hottest days. His bulbous nose and ears were cabbaged, as if he had just withdrawn his head from a rugby scrum after twenty years.

His angry frown melted away as he saw Edward.

'Boss! I gave up on you! What happened?'

What had happened to Edward was that, just as Wendy had collared him in the church, the crowd folded in towards the radio host as if everyone had recognized him at once. Edward was offering yet more embarrassed excuses to the widow – sorry, he was on air, he had to get out to the broadcast van – but then got waylaid a matter of yards from her by dozens of people wanting information he did not have.

'Got stuck in there,' Edward told GG.

'Mate! How do you always look so slim?'

Alfie Burton looked astonished at Gordon's lighter tone, but Edward knew there would be no grumping when the engineer saw him. They had both lost a child in the same year. They were both, in a way, cross at everyone and everything – except each other.

'Did you think I'd gone missing in there?' asked Edward.

'Boss,' said GG, 'I have to confess, I'm on overtime here and I promised to see the wife in an hour.'

'You pack up if you've started.'

'Wouldn't dream of it!' said the man, transformed from cloud to sun, and clicked a control in his hand that was wired direct to the dashboard. The mast squeaked, juddered, and began to extend again. There was still a queue of people coming from the church, and some stopped to watch when they heard the radio van hum.

Edward had little to say that was new. He heard the on-duty presenter as he clipped on his headphones. It was one of the old guard, Brian Channon. Standing on the street, staring at his shoes to concentrate, Edward felt his heart sink. Channon, aged seventy-two, was now an occasional weekend fill-in after being dropped from his daily show. Giving the so-called 'Farmers' the occasional shift was Aspinall's way of keeping a lid on their fury – what was the phrase, 'Better to have them inside the tent pissing out . . .'? – but it felt strange, hearing a dusty Bobby Vee song fade and then Channon's voice, full of loathing for the presenter who had survived every cull and change of management: 'Well, Edward Temmis on the line, from the church – well, well, did you get stuck in there?'

Alfie Burton was supposed to be introducing Edward and asking the questions, but of course Channon had completely bypassed the young man.

'Met a lot of our listeners, all with questions,' bluffed Edward.

'And you, a qualified scientist, could answer them.'

'I'm not even a qualified presenter, Brian, same as you.' Edward kept the tone light.

Alfie Burton cut in bravely. 'Brian, I can tell you the church was packed. People are still coming out. We brought every word of the news conference to our listeners so you've heard what was said. Do you have a question you want me to put to Edward?'

'Why? Are his headphones broken?' Channon laughed cruelly. Edward was sensing this might be the old stager's last shift.

Edward tried to bring it back to the matter in hand, but as he did so his heart sank. Wendy Wrigley had emerged from the church and was standing by the wall, letting the crowds pass. She was wearing earphones. Was she listening to the radio station? He could not read her expression.

'Today,' he said, 'we are all thinking of that poor child. Nina Lopez. Even if it turns out there was no wider risk to human life with the contents of the motorbike, even if we are left with an absolute mystery, even if the so-called Russian connection makes no sense and it was not, as the newspapers call it, "The Pizza Parlour Attack", even if there was no Ukraine and no explosive, no radiation and no poisonous vapour, even if there was nothing, nothing to trouble us here in Sidmouth, a child died on our seafront. A family took their child to our promenade and a child with a future, who might have become a great writer or great scientist or great-grandmother, will be in a casket at a funeral this Saturday. We think of her. We think of the size of that casket, so small, so many years ungrown, so much life unlived. We all think of Nina. And of course, of Gabriel, the father, and her mum Andrea.'

Edward had accidentally eulogized the little girl, and to his surprise, when Channon's voice came back on the line, the older sounded too choked to speak. 'I have a – a great-great-grand-child on the way.'

Was that two greats, or one? It hardly mattered. 'That brings it home, Brian, I know.' Edward stared at his shoes, not wanting to think of his own lost son.

'And it's all such a mystery,' concluded a tearful Channon. 'Thanks mate. Edward Temmis there, outside St Giles and Nic's, with reporter Alfie Brunton.'

So Alfie even got a namecheck? His surname had been scrambled, but perhaps the old man had a soul after all. Edward continued to gaze at his feet, headphones on, the thick hair on the back of his head heating up in the May sun. He was like a dog, always needing a haircut. The rhythm and power of his own words had caught Edward by surprise and made him realize that, however much of a let-off the scientist had given the town, they must never forget Nina. At the other end of the line, Channon was playing Simon and Garfunkel, 'The Boxer'. Something tapped Edward's arm. Still holding the microphone in his right hand, he pulled off the headphones with his left. Alfie Burton was pointing at Wendy Wrigley. Now his ears were not covered, he heard her clearly.

'I need you to tell me what you know. I beg you. Whatever it is, however bad it is, I can take it.'

CHAPTER THIRTY-THREE

Ten minutes later, they were installed in the café nearest the church. The manager of the Sidmouth Museum had been at the press conference with his whistle, and now he was back on duty, he was making the most of the precious extra footfall by keeping the coffee shop open.

'Don't be angry with me, Mr Temmis.'

'Edward. How could I be?'

'I hijacked your broadcast.'

'It was over. You had every right to.'

Through the window, he saw people walking quickly, like figures in a speeded-up film, as if the news conference itself had been a kind of radiation spill.

Poor Wendy Wrigley. Evidently she believed Edward had the solution. And he was sure he did; he had just wanted to check the location with Jordan Callintree, but Callintree was drowning in his pizza mess. The Toppings crash – already Edward's mind had edited the word 'attack' from the description – had got in the way of him helping Wendy promptly. A waitress brought tea. He picked up the teaspoon and saw a fairground-mirror reflection of his guilty face.

He had asked for just one further, small delay. Kim would join them before he explained what he had discovered.

'You know I mentioned five thousand pounds?' Wendy prompted.

'I don't feel good about taking that, even for my listeners.'

'Edward, it's there if you want it.'

'Thank you, Wendy,' he said.

He glanced casually out of the window again at the thinning crowd around the church. He could just make out gold letters on a wooden board:

SACRED PARISH OF
SAINT GILES AND SAINT NICHOLAS.
HERE WE WORSHIP CHRIST,
THOUGH CHRIST IS EVERYWHERE.

His eye was caught by a couple moving with difficulty through the wrought-iron gate beside the sign. It was sheltered from the rain by a small thatched roof, propped up by four warped beams. Through the narrow lychgate, huge feet first, came a very large woman, tipped back on a wheelchair, being moved by a similarly enormous man. The woman's feet were so big they might both have been in clip-on hospital casts. They were in their sixties, and the man pushing the wheelchair was also gigantic in height and width. The wheelchair got stuck in the lychgate and, to Edward's surprise, the woman heaved herself out of it and hobbled sideways to draw a long, knobbled walking stick from the side of the chair. As the man pushed the back of the chair, she jammed the stick between the wheel and the side of the lychgate. She pushed and pulled it like the lever on railway points. The chair came free and she dropped back into it.

It could almost have been a comic scene. Except that Edward recognized the walking stick.

His mind took him with a whipcrack back to the violence he had suffered in his garden. He felt his sight blur and a wave of nausea. What was going on?

'What have you seen? You've gone pale,' Wendy said, her voice sounding as though it came from a great distance, but he had stood up instinctively and darted to the door of the café, where he nearly knocked Kim flat.

'Trying to escape me? You're sweating.'

'No, I—'

Looking over her shoulder, he lost sight of the couple within seconds. What was his mind doing to him?

He shook his head, like a dog shaking off water. Wendy Wrigley had been endlessly patient. Now was not the time to charge out of the café without a word of explanation. He led Kim back to the table.

With real tenderness she said, 'Nice to see you again, Wendy.'

'Edward was very keen that you should be here. You've found out something, I gather?'

'Kim worked it out,' Edward said, trying to regain his composure.

'Hardly,' said Kim.

'I'm all ears.'

'It was a thought I had,' Kim started. 'It was something Edward said about the height of the hole in the tree' – she held her hand up at chest height – 'then the smell of the gunpowder that he found in the hole. It made me think, well . . .' She reached over and took Wendy's hand. 'Wendy, it made me wonder if he could have done it himself.'

Wendy gave a choked sob. 'Really?'

'Yes. I'm so sorry. We got a friend to help test the theory.' Kim described the experiment they had done with David Marner. They had shown how a person could pack gunpowder into the hole, heat the bolt and have it fire with explosive force – without a crossbow.

Wendy cried as she listened.

'That must be it, that must be it,' she said, 'but why, why?'

Edward took up the story. 'Do you remember I asked you about whether his father had Motor Neurone Disease? You looked upset and said no.'

'It was a shock to be asked that.'

'I'm sorry I sprang it on you.'

'Full disclosure,' said Wendy. 'His mum had a thing called Huntington's.'

'Ah,' said Edward, 'I was sure of it.'

Kim said, 'Sure of what?'

'Wait,' said Wendy, 'you think Jonathan had Huntington's? He can't have, he took a test!'

'And did you see the results yourself?' Edward asked gently. Turning to Kim, he explained, 'Huntington's is always inherited, always deadly, but only goes to fifty per cent of the offspring. If you watched the Bob Dylan movie, it's what Woody Guthrie has from the first minute to the last.'

'That's what my Jonathan dreaded,' Wendy said, tears running down her face again. 'Going from sewing, fireworks and Airfix models to . . . well, I don't need to spell it out. You lose control of all movement, even your lungs. Oh God.'

'Wendy had mentioned so many things we should have picked up on,' said Edward. 'Jonathan had bad fatigue, a sense that he was stumbling a bit, messing things up. Fine motor skills – couldn't sew at the surgery. Memory getting worse. He was only in his fifties.'

'You told me half of that, Wendy, and I didn't realize,' said Kim. 'I'm so sorry.'

'But I didn't either,' said Wendy, trying to stem her tears with a crumpled tissue. 'That's the tragedy of it. And it makes such sense.' Her eyes welled again. 'Of course I knew how his mother had died. But he told me he had had a gene test and was clear. It was a lie, I see that now, but it made our lives so much simpler.

No explanations to the children, nothing to tell insurers. He carried that lie and he must always have been on the lookout for any change in his body. He must have felt that, if symptoms hit, he needed to be gone before they went full-blown. He would have lied on so many official forms.' She blew her nose. 'He must have known, poor man, and he didn't tell me. My poor Jonathan.'

She tugged absent-mindedly at an earring as she mopped away her tears, a diamond glinting with the movement. Edward had been led astray by her money to start with, thinking she had every reason to be a killer. But insurers would not pay out on a suspicious death, would they?

'The first thing that happened was when he made a firework. Just a little Catherine wheel for a friend with small kids. There was a bang in the garage and he'd lost a fingernail and taken the skin off his knuckles. That was the very first sign. So, as for blowing a bolt out of a tree with a charge, he would know exactly how to do that. Poor, poor Jon. Poor Jon.'

'Ah, so that's how he had the powder,' said Edward.

'How was she to know it meant anything? "He used to make homemade fireworks but then stopped". It doesn't exactly sound like a clue,' said Kim in Wendy's defence.

'But it's all in that sentence. He realized he had Huntington's disease—'

'Huntington's Chorea is the official name,' Wendy put in vaguely. Edward thought how different she was from the composed woman he had met at Harpford Hall. She said, 'Now you describe it like this, I understand.' She blew her nose loudly. 'He didn't want the crossbow there so no one would say "The man who killed himself". He dropped it in the river days earlier, I guess. He left a suspicious scene and he wanted the mystery. The mystery would hide the sad truth. He had to protect me, so he bought the cinema ticket. But because I had never seen a Marvel film before, everyone took it as a sign of guilt.' She shook her head with a sardonic laugh. 'Ridiculous. He was a Catholic. He'd rather be remembered as a murder victim than a suicide.'

'I wonder why he wore a white suit.'

'And took his life by an airfield like that,' Edward added. 'He must have wanted to be found quickly. That way, Wendy was protected.'

'He probably waited until he heard the plane,' said Kim, reaching over to touch Wendy's narrow hand. 'Oh God, Wendy, I'm sorry.'

'This will sound nuts,' said Wendy, 'but insurers pay out less on suicide. I think that might have been a factor. Unfortunately, they also don't pay out if the surviving spouse is a suspect. The money doesn't matter to me anyway.'

Edward sipped at his tea.

'Where does it leave you?' asked Kim.

'I can apply for the inquest to be reopened,' said Wendy, holding a finger below each eye and looking up, blinking. 'And when it is, I can hold my head up. I only need one or two friends with me, and I can let everyone else keep their hating and their vicious tongues.' She smiled weakly. 'Will you be my friends after all this?'

'I'll even ask you out for lunch,' quipped Kim, and Wendy wordlessly reached across the table and grasped her hand.

After a beat, Wendy straightened her back, folded her handkerchief and pushed it into the sleeve of her jumper. 'By the way, what did you make of the police press conference? The scientist was pretty cool, I thought.'

'I never understood it being a terrorist attack on a pizza parlour,' said Edward. 'What about you, Kim?'

'I just feel so sorry for the parents of that poor girl,' she said. 'I've no idea what the motorbike rider was doing.'

'Perhaps he just slipped,' said Wendy. 'A terrible accident.'

'The Nina Lopez funeral is on Saturday,' said Edward. 'I guess the police might even release the body now. The parents sent a message to the radio station saying they had been helped by my radio show and would like me to be at the church.'

'Oh Edward,' Kim said, 'you can't though. You're not free.'

Kim was not able to explain, because at that moment a tall man with a shock of white hair arrived at the table. Edward, recognizing one of the Hurst twins, could not immediately remember if this was Hubert or Charlie.

'Hi,' he said.

'Hube!' Wendy said, lurching to her feet to embrace him. 'Hubert is – was – a friend of Jonathan's. Hubert, this is Kim and you've met Edward of course, and they've been incredible. They've worked out exactly what happened—'

As if the enormity of the revelation had descended on her like a swarm of bees, Wendy swished her hand left and right in front of her reddening face and her eyes welled with tears.

'My dear,' said Hubert Hurst, 'are you okay?'

As she cried, Edward said to Kim: 'Mr Hurst was a friend of Wendy's husband. He had a lot of doctor friends.'

'Oh, you have a brother,' said Kim, who had been told about the Hursts when she met Wendy at the Clock Tower Café. Hubert didn't hear her. He had drawn closer to Wendy Wrigley. As he squatted beside her, she clutched his upper arm. 'They've explained what happened. No one killed Jonathan. But it's just so sad.'

'How did they work it out? You must tell me everything,' said Hubert, his face shining with compassion.

'I will,' said Wendy.

'Not now,' Hubert reassured. 'Not if it's too much.'

It was a tender moment. But Edward's mind was elsewhere. Almost as soon as Wendy was gone, head down, leaving the place quietly with Hubert, he said to Kim, 'This is nuts.'

She was still worrying about his double commitment on Saturday. 'What are you going to do?'

'Talk to the church.'

'How will that help?'

'You don't know what I'm talking about, do you? I saw them. I'm sure I saw them.'

'Who?'

'Those two beasts who beat me up in my garden. He just wheeled her past me. Then she was up out of her chair and I saw the stick. They both look like the Honey Monster. It was them.'

'Wait, I thought it was two men. You said "her" – so one of them's a woman, and in a wheelchair?'

'Yes.'

'How could that be?'

'When they beat me up, one of them kept screaming. Maybe she was in pain herself.'

Kim looked doubtful, almost amused.

'It's not funny, Kim.'

'It just sounds unlikely.'

'They were wearing latex masks and they were both six foot six. That's got to narrow it down. Come on, I want to ask inside the church if anyone knows them.'

The church was empty when they walked back into it, except for two or three helpers who were buzzing around with lengths of cable and chairs. The long trestle table used for the press conference under the nave had been split into two pieces and the legs folded below it. The halves were leaning against the narrow spiral steps that led up to the pulpit.

'Is the vicar in?' asked Edward when a volunteer approached. He was a young man with a thin polo-neck jumper.

'I think he left straight after the press conference. How can I help?'

Kim said, 'We saw a couple leave earlier and we think they dropped something.' She pulled a fountain pen from her handbag.

The volunteer looked. 'That's nice. Do you want me to take it?'

'I'd be happy to drop it off if you know them,' said Edward.

An older woman arrived, dressed as if she had just left a tennis court, with a sleeveless yellow jumper, white shirt and jogging bottoms. 'Who are we talking about?'

'Two people, one in a wheelchair.'

'Oh yes?'

'We saw them emerge from the church,' said Edward, suddenly feeling the pain of his lie, all the more serious for being in a house of God, 'and the man was helping the lady manoeuvre her wheelchair and he didn't see the pen drop.'

'Was this . . . quite a large couple?'

'Yes,' said Edward.

'I think I saw them,' said the young man. 'But I don't know who they were.'

'Shall we keep the pen?' asked the woman, unaware that Edward and Kim had already declined.

'We said we'd return it. But we don't know where they live.'

'Well,' said the woman, 'my name is Beatrice. We obviously don't do data protection here in Sidmouth, so it wouldn't be a problem to tell you if we knew. But I'm not sure. Give me your number, one of you, and I'll ask around.'

Edward handed Melody's number over to Beatrice, less and less convinced that he was right about what he had seen. They had been dressed in badly fitting police uniforms and had worn masks. Surely he could not swear they were the same pair who'd attacked him?

But he could.

They were.

He knew it.

Kim and Edward left the church silently, the job undone.

CHAPTER THIRTY-FOUR

For many in the town, the days that followed were a rebirth. The sun shone, as if confident enough to finally lift its head from behind the sofa-shaped clouds. The Metropolitan Police cordon had been completely removed by the following morning – there were rumours of an intervention by the mayor of Sidmouth, who owned one of the smaller seafront hotels and was furious at having had to swap all his regulars for big-booted London cops – and the only restriction in place as day broke was a two-man police guard outside the burnt-out shell of the pizza parlour. Devon Police had supplied the cover, which was symbolic. They were reasserting control over their patch. Jordan Callintree had insisted his men wore dark blue uniforms, not hi-vis.

Every clue had been extracted from Sidmouth Pizza Parlour. Geiger counters had been poked and swept across every inch of floor and wall. There was only the expected trace level of background radiation. Not even a blip of anything that should not be there. The fire had burnt the ampoules to nothing. The locals were no less interested in the story – why on earth would a Ukrainian motorbike rider slam his bike into that restaurant in particular, and if it was an accident, what exactly was he carrying the dangerous ampoules for? But in truth, once the tourists returned, the hysteria calmed to a hum of interest. People were busy, after all. So the place snapped back to normality in a morning.

With one exception. One livid scar; one gaping wound. The death of a four-year-old child might not have been caused by terrorism, but it was still a tragedy almost unimaginable to those used to the soft tidal rhythm of this Devon town. There was not a single person who had not expressed their hurt and anger. Many had wept.

The funeral service for Nina Lopez that Saturday was, as the family had requested, compact. Edward checked his watch. He was grateful to be there. He was also hurt by the argument with Kim earlier in the week.

He'd been choosing his suit for the funeral when Kim explained that they were still on Stevie's guest list.

'I thought you said she had dumped Roddy.'

'She's marrying herself. Her monobrow man is out of the picture, thank God, but she's going ahead with the event and we are all going to celebrate her.' She saw his hesitation. 'Don't wobble on this, Edward. It's eleven thirty.'

'Oh, but . . . eleven is the Nina Lopez funeral. Marrying *herself?*'

'She's a girl with a burnt face who only ever respected and admired you!'

'Oh, please don't guilt me. I love Stevie! It's just that—'

Kim calmed. 'I know. Nina.'

'I'll come to both.'

'You can't. I can't believe you even need to think about it.'

'I can't believe how guilty you're making me feel,' he replied, genuinely upset.

There had been no happy conclusion. Had Stevie been marrying her fiancé as planned, he would probably have attended. Kim pointed out the contradiction – 'You'll attend if she's getting manacled to her abuser, but not if she wants to celebrate freedom as a young woman?' He had resisted the pressure, because he was determined to attend the Lopez funeral.

So here he was. The church was a small modern one, with a sign outside that said DEVON PENTECOASTAL, a misspelling which had to be deliberate. The church was bright with frosted windows and red-brick walls inside and out. He looked down at the light wood floor and half-expected to see basketball court markings; the space could easily double as a gym. The chairs were plastic. The vicar was a woman in a suit. Edward sank into his seat and had been watching for a few minutes before he realized the empty chair next to him had been taken by a familiar figure.

Jordan Callintree wore his chief constable uniform. He sat upright and acknowledged Edward with a tight nod. They sang a hymn, 'How Great Thou Art'. Edward became conscious of the weeping of relatives and whispered to Callintree, 'A privilege to be here.'

The police officer did not reply. But a few minutes later, as the vicar delivered a long and heartfelt prayer ('We cannot know, O Lord, your mysteries, your ways, but we know you love us and you know we must trust you with the course of history, the course of our lives, and of course, we trust, that of our child Nina, so cruelly taken'), Edward heard the whisper:

'We must speak. Not now.'

Head bowed as if still in prayer, Edward folded the order of service, a thin piece of A5 that had obviously come out of a black-and-white printer, and wrote on it: 'Have to leave quickly – late for wedding. Talk on phone?'

Callintree took the paper. Perhaps he was conscious that, with his uniform on, he was entirely recognizable and did not want to be The Policeman Who Chatted in a Funeral Service. He did not reply for a few minutes. Then, as the prayer ended and the congregation resettled, he said: 'I am so angry I'm about to explode.'

Edward stared at him in surprise. He remembered how a younger Callintree had been the first cop to take seriously the death of his son and promise a real investigation. He would always be grateful. There must have been something personal in his expression, because the policeman was prompted to say more. He bent low and close to Edward's ear as the sermon began.

'Met stiffed me. Took advantage of me isolating. Did it all without me, cut me out, humiliating. Before that presser in the church, they even gave me wrong info to check I wasn't leaking. Never been so angry.'

Edward whispered, 'Looks like London has gone, though.'

Callintree said quietly into his ear, 'London has gone so fast they left skid marks. Now it's not terrorism . . .' He made a cutting motion with his hand. 'Basically "Goodbye and good luck". I get out of isolation and I have to motivate my people to investigate. I don't even know what I'm investigating.'

'This,' said Edward, gesturing towards the front of the church where the little girl's coffin had now appeared.

Callintree sat up stiffly as if stung. They watched the progress of the coffin. Edward wondered if he had heard right. He had filed reports on the church press conference, and he had seen the strange way Callintree had attended – on a remote TV link, with the monitor almost buried out of sight – but he never imagined there had been this level of anger within Devon Police. He wondered if part of the reason for Callintree's anger was because his rapid promotion had caused resentment among his colleagues, so they wanted him to fail; and he had no cover in a wider row. He wondered if he and Callintree were actually more friendly than Edward realized. The policeman's tone was of a mate sharing a desperate confidence, not a police officer briefing a reporter.

'We are both here in our official roles,' whispered Edward. 'Let's talk outside.'

Callintree moved his shoulders and, as if remembering his peaked cap was still on his head, removed it. The funeral continued. The conversation had meant Edward missed much of the sermon, but he found his eyes drawn constantly to Andrea Lopez. She was pregnant and drawn, her cheeks gaunt and dark smudges beneath both eyes, as though she hadn't slept since she'd last held Nina. Edward remembered that hollowed-gut feeling so well, and he bowed his head in a shared grief.

The service ended. Edward was glad to have come. He was honoured to have been asked personally. Afterwards the close family withdrew. They would follow the coffin to a crematorium.

The vicar recognized him on the steps of the church. He spoke softly. 'It was a private ceremony, Mr Temmis, but the Lopezes wanted you to know how grateful they have been for your work. I see the chief of police came too. An important gesture.'

It struck him that Gabriel and Andrea Lopez, and their entire family, had probably listened to his every broadcast because the police had been so sparing with their information. Shaking the vicar's hand, and seeing the man's eyes blaze green in the bright daylight drenching the church entrance, Edward said: 'I know this is private, but may I use a few of your words on the radio this afternoon?'

The vicar seemed almost to enlarge, like a pumped tyre. 'You may. You may. They understand this part of the day cannot be completely private. If I may suggest—'

Luckily he was interrupted by the person behind Edward. He walked briskly to his moped, conscious he was now running late for Stevie. His bike was hidden between two SUVs in the church car park. But as he turned the key in it, Jordan Callintree arrived in the space between the SUVs as if borne on a sharp gust of wind. 'This is mine,' he said, pointing at the car nearest Edward. 'Leave your bike here and we can talk on the way.' Callintree, now hatless and tieless, opened the side door for Edward. 'Where to?'

'You know Stevie Mason? She's getting married. But there's a twist.' Edward thought Callintree would be interested in the strangeness of the occasion – 'marrying herself' – yet the police officer seemed barely to listen as he drove them away from the church. When the explanation was over, Callintree immediately changed the subject.

'I may need your help, Mr Temmis.'

Edward looked over at Jordan Callintree and felt the tension and misery radiate. The clean-cut young officer looked beaten.

'What can I do?' Edward was struck by his disarray. 'You don't seem yourself.'

'I'm broken, mate, to be frank.' Callintree was indicating at a busy intersection, where the single-track road opened into a 50-mph carriageway with a bend. 'If I can . . . whoooar!'

He had pulled out, seeing the road clear to his right, but in the instant he nosed past the hedgerow and engaged the clutch, a van shot past the front of his car, horn blaring.

'Bloody weekend drivers.' Callintree suddenly pulled the car in. 'Can I just ask you for something?'

Edward looked at his watch. Kim would not be impressed. Jordan Callintree cut the car engine.

'It's been a nightmare,' said the officer, 'and my wife is sick of hearing me go on about it. The crime happens, my force messes up, Thorne goes, I get elevated – which is just a joke, a bloody *joke*, just a way of putting me in the firing line – and then London arrive with the army and choppers and dogs and all sorts in tow. At which point I'm literally isolated and I can't even get someone to bring me a cup of tea. My officers blame me for everything, even the leak.'

'The leak?' Edward's mind had gone to radiation, but he soon realized they were at cross-purposes.

'All the stuff about chopsticks and the professor being given dangerous nuclear material without any warning. They think I'm a careerist shit and I put that stuff out. Someone tweeted "The new Thief Constable" with a photo of me, and I'm sure it's internal.'

'You didn't put the stuff out. I did. I only found it because I went to Veitch's house.'

'Thorne got the blame. I got promoted. Then London arrive and my officers blame me for that as well.'

'I worry this is on me.'

The remark seemed to hang in the vehicle interior. They stared out of the windscreen. Edward was stunned.

'Mr Temmis. I don't have the patience for bullshit. So take this' – Callintree moved his hips and fished a small USB fob from his trouser pocket – 'sign of my goodwill. Not as easy to get hold of these as you might imagine.'

'What's on it?' Edward took the memory stick, white plastic with a lime trim.

'The crime scene photos from the Jonathan Wrigley murder, minus the gore. Don't ever say where you got them from.' He reached across and took the fob back for a second, as if having second thoughts. 'Do you want to tell me why you need them first?'

'Oh, sure. No secret. His widow is getting accused of murder but she's innocent. She wanted me to look at the crime scene with her. I think I found the spot in the forest and I found out what happened. I just needed to confirm I was in the right place.' Edward coughed, not sure how to phrase the next part. 'The moment may have passed, because now I've told her what I know and I think she can move on.' Something stopped him going into details with Jordan Callintree. 'I'm still grateful for this, though, thank you.'

Again, the police officer barely managed to look interested. 'It's out of my area, thank God, so not another of our fuck-ups.'

He gripped the steering wheel. 'Where are you going? Where is this wedding?'

Edward told him the name of the church. Callintree started the engine with a roar and tore away from the layby. 'I'll tell you what I want. I need your eyes on this Toppings case. My officers have lost interest. If I was an ordinary copper, I'd be out doing it, but being acting chief means I can't leave the building for a second.'

'You want me to investigate it for you?'

The policeman did not reply. But he did not need to. He gunned the car. Edward felt a bloom of excitement in his stomach. He had solved one case, and now he had another. But then he remembered the two enormous assailants in his garden who beat him black and blue, and his excitement was engulfed by fear.

Stevie stood at the front of the church. She had found the dress online and made adjustments, but she was still self-conscious in it. Above the waist it was pure rockabilly. The boned bodice was a quilt of musical notes, mainly black and red, and the neckline crumpled lace in the shape of a heart. The material was cinched brutally at the waist, but where a classic rockabilly dress would have sprung a skirt from below the belt, the lower half of Stevie's looked like traditional white silk. She felt strange, doing this – any girl would have wanted the real thing, the ceremony plus the sweetheart, the spoken contract and the signing, the confetti, the photos (my God! she had forgotten to cancel the photographer), the big lunch after. Friends, speeches, dancing, glitterballs and motorized party lights. It was not to be, although she would have a solo version of some of it.

Her parents would have to pay for the lot, but it was too late to retrieve the deposits anyway. She was feeling a little more self-conscious than she had hoped, sensing the congregation in the church had never seen anyone marry themselves. There was not even a Google result for 'self-marry'. The church was only a quarter full, but she'd spotted Kim and Barbara (bought along to bump up the numbers? Stevie didn't mind, someone had to eat one of those spare salmon en croûtes later), though she couldn't see Edward.

Her parents, in prime position on the front row, had been quietly ecstatic at Roddy's exit, but her father baulked at the 'irreligious nature' of her plan to marry herself. He handed the job to his curate, which was actually perfect: the youthful Reverend Noah Dobson, still in training and a part-time retail worker in Exeter, totally understood what this ceremony needed to be.

Once the ceremony was under way, it all seemed to pass in a blur. Stevie sensed her mother and father's discomfort, a slight creaking from their seats, as Dobson went as close as he could to, 'Do you take this woman to be your lawful wedded wife?'

Her father, to his credit, had walked her up the aisle, although withdrew quickly once she had arrived at her destination, as if he had suddenly come under fire. The vows made people smile. 'I, Stevie Jane Mason, take me, Stevie Jane Mason, to be my lawful wedded wife . . .

'To have and to hold, from this day forward, for better, for worse, for richer, for poorer, in sickness and in health, to love and to cherish, till death us do bring together . . .'

And best of all: 'With this ring, I me wed.'

Then, as Revd Dobson began to preach, a sweet sermon on the theme of loving oneself as God loved us, Edward Temmis arrived alongside a dishevelled Jordan Callintree. She felt a flutter of annoyance at Edward (how could he miss the start, leaving her on her own?) and then excitement that Devon's top policeman had found time to mark her special day. So that made the number thirty. Half the bridal dinners would be eaten. She wondered if there was a way of summoning another thirty from the surrounding villages.

No, she would keep her mind on the words of the young curate who was – she suddenly realized – praising her.

'A beautiful, steady, polite young woman.'

Stevie heard someone laugh. She was trying not to. *Polite?* At least he had not called her tall or sweet. In her mind she was the exact opposite of all the listed qualities. She was impulsive and explosive. The preacher was evidently ahead of others in his training, expertly dispensing little lies in a house of God.

When it came to presenting the married, ahem, bride, to the congregation, Stevie turned to face her friends and family, a delighted smile on her face. She'd done it! But then her expression changed.

Roddy was framed in the church doorway with a wine bottle dangling from his hand and a cigarette hanging from his mouth. The sharp light behind him made the cleanest silhouette, his head in a cloud of smoke. He brought the bottle upwards and put it to his lips, tipping it vertically as if polishing off the final drops. Then he brought the bottle across his chest and smashed the glass backhand against the thick wooden frame of the church entrance.

The noise – and Stevie's horrified expression – made everyone turn around.

Roddy stumbled a little, back into the sun and then forward. There he was, her rejected lover, a blob of jet black cut out from the sun, one arm seeming longer than the other, ending not in a hand but a jagged bouquet of glass.

Jordan Callintree was the first to run towards him.

CHAPTER THIRTY-FIVE

Ten days later, Kim was in Spice Route, the Indian Restaurant in Budleigh Salterton famous for its car park. It was drenched in summer flowers, and the customer joke was always that if the cooks swapped places with the gardener, the place would win a Michelin star. She had a text from Edward's new number:

> Ten minutes sorry. Order me the Chicken Disaster.

> Disaster already ordered

She tutted and asked for more poppadoms. On her phone was an email notification: 'Thirdfield Terrace & Slater-Glynne'.

What was that thing men used in a marriage that kept appearing as a hashtag on Instagram: 'Weaponized incompetence'? Where the guy kept saying, 'Oh luv, I'm no good with the dishwasher, I've just broken another three plates', and the wife is forced to take over all the chores?

Well, it was working a treat with Tank and Fire, the suspect buyers. Kim had made up her mind, and she rarely changed her view when she did that. She did not want their dirty money or their filthy lies, and so she had got Emily, a crinkle-haired puffball of bespectacled McFlurry, who took at least four days a month off sick with anxiety, to do the sale 'as a priority'. Emily had many good qualities – she volunteered with rescue animals and had all the time in the world to listen to her colleagues' troubles – but she had no future as an estate agent. Every bank account number was transcribed wrong, every phone number in her notepad was missing a digit. She had once sold a couple the wrong house by making a mistake with the Land Registry filing. Emily's incompetence was as weaponized as a scrambled SAS unit. But the delays did not put off Tank and Fire, and no other offers had come in. Tank and Fire just kept pushing the price higher, as if bidding against themselves. The vendor was in no rush because the leasehold on the apartment block was owned by an investment syndicate.

'Hey, lovely.'

Stevie peered at Kim as she sat down at the table.

'Kim, you were a million bloody miles away.'

Without even thinking, Kim asked: 'How do I put off two dodgy buyers who want to buy the most beautiful flat in Sidmouth? I've tried assigning the slowest person in the office, and all that happens is that I get emails saying the sale is getting closer.'

'You should put me onto it.'

'That's not such a bad idea.' Kim put her phone back in her handbag, then had second thoughts. 'Might keep this visible. Hoping Edward will text us his ETA.'

'Why are they dodgy?' Stevie asked.

'Lots of cash, second home, pretending to be lovers when clearly they aren't. Plump guy, ravishing Indian lady, from Kerala if I remember rightly. Oh, and Edward heard them talking and it was weird.'

'Why? What did they say?'

Kim racked her brains. 'Damn. If only I could remember. He was underneath my car, looking for a spare tyre that wasn't there.'

'Innuendo much.'

'Stop it. It was the day we all met at Nine Chairs. Something about the parachutes. No – parachute singular. "Is the parachute through?" Something like that. Edward will remember.'

Stevie held her phone to her mouth. 'Ask ChatGPT what "parachute" is slang for.'

The phone responded a second later. 'Please explain the context of this question so I can answer you.'

'Useless twit. Okay. Ask ChatGPT what illegal thing parachute is slang for in Kerala.'

The phone thought about it for a moment, evidently not in the least offended by Stevie's bad language. The robotic voice returned. 'In Kerala, India, crystal meth is described as "parachute" because the drug is commonly crushed and wrapped into small paper bulbs which look like parachutes.'

Kim sat in silence for a minute. She shook her head occasionally, and once murmured, 'Shit.'

'I feel like I brought you bad news.'

'Your phone did, yes.'

'You don't use ChatGPT?'

'I should.'

'I'm sorry it gave you that info, don't want it to wreck the night. It does tend to blurt stuff out.'

'No filter.' Kim brightened. 'It's nothing I couldn't have guessed. Well, in a way you've helped me. I can't accept dirty money.' She looked at Stevie and put the Thirdfield Terrace sale out of her head. 'You seem happy, Stevie.'

'"Seem" is one of those rumbly words.'

Kim looked quizzical, but Stevie did not elaborate. It was the first time Kim had met her since the wedding. Kim and Edward had got into the habit of making inverted commas with their fingers whenever they talked about that day – 'the wedding' – and Kim felt suddenly guilty about that.

'I've left you alone,' she said. 'I thought you might be on honeymoon.'

'Ha!' said Stevie. 'With myself? No, right back at work.'

'Still part-time?'

'I told you I'm doing a criminology course, didn't I?' It came over as a challenge: *How could you have forgotten?* Kim shook her head. 'Oh, maybe I kept it quiet. Forensics sort of. No dead bodies yet so I'm thinking I should go missing during a module and see if they can trace me.'

Her last word coincided with Stevie karate-chopping a poppadom, then taking both halves.

'Why criminology?'

'Can't you guess, lady? Didn't we three investigate something and weren't we good at it?'

'Ha, I guess so. Funny seeing Jordan at your wedding,' said Kim.

'Edward brought him. Luckily he found some non-cop clothes in his car boot or I would have assumed we were being raided.'

'He came in handy.'

'I actually wrote a letter of whatdyacallit to the chief constable of Devon—'

'Commendation?'

'—yep, a letter of commendation about Jordan Callintree because I thought Jordan was bloody superb, protecting us, getting Roddy in a headlock and disarming the bottle.'

'I hate to disappoint you, but Jordan is now chief constable. So your letter about Jordan will have gone to Jordan himself.'

'What? Knock me down with a feather.'

'What sort of phrase is "Knock me down with a feather", Stevie?'

The young woman looked surprisingly cheerful. 'I've been having some counselling about my Tourette's because it lets me down in appraisals and suchlike. I don't even know if it is wanker fucking Tourette's, and pardon my French. It's just random filthy language that comes out as easily . . . as easily . . . I nearly did it there. "As easily as fucking breathing". The counsellor says I need to try something called "substitution", where I swap the swearword just as it travels along my tongue. It's helped me stop saying the word "cunt" quite a few times.'

'What do you say instead?'

'Anything. I try "lemon". That creates a problem ordering cocktails, I can tell you.'

'You really are in good form, Stevie. Happiest I've seen you for a good long while.'

'You were right. I'd rather be with myself than with any Roddy.'

'Down with Roddies.'

'Utter scumbag.'

'Are you talking about me again?' said Edward, arriving at the table and dropping a battered brown briefcase on the couch beside him. 'Sorry, I thought I heard my name.'

The women laughed.

'Did you get my message?' Edward asked Kim. 'I have something important for you both.'

'I replied!'

He looked at his new phone blankly.

'Oh,' said Kim, realizing. 'Maybe I replied to your old number.'

'Somewhere on the rocks at the bottom of the Ladram Bay cliffs, a mobile just beeped.'

'That sounds like the start of a novel,' said Stevie. 'Somewhere at the foot of the Ladram Bay cliffs, a mobile just sang to a seagull.'

'I wouldn't read any further if that was the first line,' said Kim.

Stevie asked, 'How come your old phone fell down a cliff?'

Kim glanced at Edward, and saw him deciding to avoid Stevie's question. 'Your wedding was lovely,' he said, the most blatant evasion.

'My "wedding",' repeated Stevie sarcastically, doing exactly the same as Kim and Edward had done privately, raising her hands and making rabbit's-ears with two pairs of fingers.

Kim gulped at her own hypocrisy as she chided: 'Hey, it was a real wedding! None of that, naughty.'

'I took myself as my "lawful wedded wife", according to that young curate chap, who did the whole bloody thing at a kind of lean, and who – by the way – I think may have an intimate relationship with the kind of gin that is odourless.'

'Thank God for Jordan Callintree,' said Edward, inadvertently taking the conversation back to where it had been five minutes earlier. 'He's the reason we're here, by the way.'

'Oh!' said Kim. 'I thought it was because you wanted the disaster.'

'Did you order it?'

'What's that?' asked Stevie.

'It's what he calls the jalfrezi.'

'The car park's nice though,' said Stevie.

The curry came in stages. Edward drank too much. Tongue loosened by the Kingfisher, he told Kim and Stevie: 'Pretty much everything I report is from Jordan. He would normally be discreet. But he can't get his officers motivated on the case. He's lost the dressing room.'

He could have listed the scoops. He had had chapter and verse on the speed of the Met's withdrawal. A little more was known about the isotope, Actinium-224, although it wasn't good news. Anyone could have made it: there were now centrifuge machines you could store in a garage, but it was a dangerous game.

'That's the first report I ever broadcast which I couldn't understand myself.'

The view being taken by Devon Police was that this was not terrorism. The motorbike rider was transporting dangerous material (yes, it was still very dangerous) for some illegal private purpose. They had found drugs paraphernalia in the flat (bloodstained tubes). But none of it led to any firm conclusions. They wondered if a farmer was using unconventional means to destroy a herd, but the carcasses would still have to go to an abattoir, surely?

'And those bloodstained tubes were for drugs?' repeated Stevie.

'They had some sort of taps on them, blue and red, to control the ... what, heroin going into the vein, I guess.'

'Wait, no,' said Stevie. 'You're bringing something back to me. When I was at the hospital, before Nina died, Jordan was speaking to the panicking mum. Andrea. He was trying to give her information because she was so upset. He showed her a picture of those tubes – which is why I knew about them – and he said they were for drug use and she said, "Not that". What did she mean, I wonder?'

'What do you think she meant?' asked Kim.

'At the time I thought it was just a way of saying, "Oh my God, not that as well".'

'What else could she have meant?' Edward asked.

'It's rattled around in my bloody head. "Not that". What if she said "Not that" to mean "No, you're wrong, it wasn't that"? Meaning the policeman was wrong about those tubes? They weren't for drugs but something else?'

'I wonder what she thought she was seeing,' Edward said.

'She's been through so much, she probably won't even remember herself,' Stevie said. 'Poor lass.'

They ate for a bit, and he said, 'OK, so this is probably a good moment to tell you why we're here.' He tore a corner off the naan bread, thought better of putting it in his mouth just before trying to speak, and placed it on the edge of his dinner plate. The orange jalfrezi sauce began to creep into it like a bloodstain on a carpet. He pulled a sheaf of papers from his briefcase. 'This is a rental agreement that Jordan sent me. Confidential. I printed it out. The landlord's name is Cammell-Curzon. See, on the front.'

'Can I touch it?' asked Stevie.

'Sure. Why on earth not?'

'I was thinking prints.'

'Fingerpr—?' Edward began, about to say, 'Don't be ridiculous, this came off my home printer,' but then he saw she was joking. They were playing detective, the other two. But this was not a game. This was about Nina Lopez.

'What sort of a name is that?' Stevie asked. 'Richard Cammell-Cordon?'

'Cammell-Curzon,' I think, said Kim, reading over her shoulder.

'This eye doesn't see too well.'

'Yes, Richard Cammell-Curzon is the landlord,' Edward confirmed.

'Should just be DICK TOSSER-PRAT.'

'I don't think we've got time for a class war, Stevie.'

'Some of them do loads for charity,' said Kim vaguely.

Edward had already looked at the document in Stevie's hands. She held it unnaturally close to her face, a reminder that her eyesight had been damaged by the acid. The front page said: ASSURED SHORTHOLD TENANCY AGREEMENT; there was an index showing seven different headings for seven sections. 1. Parties Involved, 2. Property Description, 3. Term of Tenancy, 4. Rules regarding smoking, pets, and guests, 5. Deposit Information, 6. Termination Procedures, 7. Signatures as to Agreement.

'It's all on the front page,' said Edward. 'I printed out the whole thing, ten pages. But the name of the tenant and the name of the landlord are on page one.'

'This is probably printed off ChatGPT or some other AI service,' Kim said, leaning over Stevie's shoulder. 'It's the most generic tenancy I've ever seen.'

'JC gave me the whole thing, but – as you say – it's standard.'

'Richard Cammell-Curzon,' Kim read, still on page one. The address was in Beer, a pretty spot ten miles east where young families went to a resort called Pecorama and rode a model train at the top of a cliff. On a good day a warm breeze blew in from the sea. 'So, a Londoner,' she said.

'How do you work that out?' asked Stevie.

'Look at the house name,' Kim said, holding up the agreement with her finger against the address: The Old Rectory. 'Londoners always call things "old this, old that" to show off.'

'Wanker,' said Stevie. 'That's why I'm living with my mum and dad.'

'I'm guessing he has a dozen properties,' said Kim, always the estate agent. 'He's never lived in any of them himself.'

'This sounds like a nice place.' Edward took the first page and looked at the text below the signature. 'Why does that trigger you, Stevie? You live in a rectory yourself.'

'A new one,' bristled Stevie.

'Wait. Show me the other pages,' said Kim when they had all calmed down. She took them from Stevie and leafed through them. 'These things are always a mess. Meaningless. Non-smoking clauses and anti-dog clauses when the tenant doesn't smoke and has a pet snake.'

'Are you seeing something I didn't see?' asked Edward. 'I skimmed the rest of it.'

'Here.' Kim slid the paper back across the table so they could all see it. Edward heard his hearing aid whistle and turned it down.

'What am I looking at?' asked Stevie, craning her neck.

'Page eight. You have to list referees. Those signatures, see? May not matter, but useful. The names – they're always such a mess – not printed, just handwritten. Can you make them out?'

Stevie tried. 'One is Mettles.'

Kim put in, 'Nettles. And I think the other one is Hearts.'

'Victor Nettles?' Edward peered at the page himself. 'I missed that. Isn't one of them supposed to be vouching for the tenant?'

Kim shrugged. 'The way it works normally is that the landlord does the contract, gets a couple of his mates to sign – Mr Hearts is supposedly signing for Lev, as you can see – but all the landlord wants is his deposit. So he'll get the whole form ready and he just wants cash, Lev's signature, and that's it.'

'So we have three people to find – Nettles, Hearts, and the landlord himself.' Edward gathered up the various pages and shuffled the document into an orderly block. His phone pinged with a text which he ignored. He was on the first page of the rental agreement again. 'Lev Malnyk, Ukrainian address. I thought "Lev" was short for something—'

'Wouldn't the Met go and visit his home address?' asked Kim.

Edward queried, 'On the eastern side of Ukraine?'

'Good point. They might not come back.' Kim continued, 'Regarding "Lev", theoretically you always sign your full name.'

Edward blew his nose loudly. The curry had been strong and his eyes were watering. 'Our Lev has caused total chaos, that's for sure. I had a call this week from the tourist office saying they'd had forty per cent cancellations on boat trips. That's the main measure for how busy we are in summer.'

Stevie took the document back. She went to page eight again. 'Hearts is a doctor. At least, that's a surgery address. What if he really was Lev's referee? Bloody shit, he'd be the only one who knew him in this country. Excuse my—'

'Lots of people have doctors who don't know them,' Kim cut in. 'I heard there was once an era where you could go to see your doctor in person, but I don't believe that's true.'

Edward was staring at his phone, eyebrows raised. 'Wow. I never expected that.'

The other two were silent, waiting for more. Stevie broke the last poppadom with a sound like a gunshot.

'Go on,' said Kim. 'We're tense here.'

Edward spoke to Stevie, because she didn't know the story. 'Late at night, in my garden, the night I did that hours-long broadcast and broke the news that Nina had been killed by a radioactive substance, I got attacked by two massive people. Enormous. Police uniforms, I think, but it was all weird and I couldn't see properly in the dark.'

'Cops?'

'They wore rubber masks. I thought two men, but now I think maybe a huge man and a huge woman. Both over six feet four and twenty stone.'

'Forty stone of anger. That's actually scary. A burglary?'

'Oh no. Something else. That's when my phone fell down the cliff.'

'Better the phone than you.'

'I thought they were trying to shove me over the edge.' He shivered, but then remembered something at odds from the description he had just given. When he tried to examine the thought, it vanished.

'Fuck. Me.' Stevie's mouth had frozen on the poppadom. Her jaw hung open.

'That's what I said,' Kim put in. 'And he didn't go to the police.'

'What if they *were* police? It was something to do with the Toppings case, because they kept shouting "Stop asking questions", even when they were kicking me on the ground.'

'So what does the text say?' asked Kim.

Edward handed her the phone without taking his eyes off Stevie.

'I thought I saw them in church on the day of the press

conference. Massive man and woman, enormous, enormous woman in a wheelchair. We asked in the church and they said they'd let me know. I expected nothing. But—'

Kim said, 'This text is actually from four days ago. I think you missed it.' She read from the screen.

> Hi, its Beatrice from Giles & Nics. I trust you as someone said youre off the radio. Please return fountain-pen to Les and Lily Boyd, 28 Hope Hill, Barton Ottery. They don't have phone so won't be expecting. Thank you. Praise God. Beatrice

'What's the pen?'

'She was clever,' said Edward, nodding at Kim. 'The old "I think you might have dropped something" routine.'

Kim stared at Edward. 'You can't go, obviously.'

'I am going. I am definitely going,' Edward said stoutly.

'You can't go alone. They're violent.'

'*If it's them!* When I saw them at the church, one of them was in a wheelchair!'

Stevie said, 'People use wheelchairs at airports. It doesn't mean they're in them all the time. Maybe she has good days and bad days.'

'What, bad days when she needs pushing around, and good days when she tries to throw me off a cliff?' Edward exclaimed. He changed tack. 'Okay, squad. To business. We are sleuthing for JC. We are going to make progress on the Toppings case because the police can't be bothered and a child died.' The mood at the table immediately shifted. 'Kim, can you look up the referees on this rental agreement? Especially Hearts. And Stevie, you go and speak to the landlord. I think I should go see Lev's flat.'

'Hey, why can't you go and see the Cammell-Curzon guy yourself?'

'Because I'm too famous,' Edward said, at which Kim and Stevie laughed so hard that Stevie nearly fell off her chair and Kim had to spit a mouthful of salted yoghurt into her napkin.

'I guess I'd need to be undercover,' said Stevie, clearly warming to the idea.

Kim replied with a sigh, 'I may not have time at the moment, (a) because I have a job, and (b) because I've got to stop my favourite property in Sidmouth being filled with crystal meth.'

'Sorry?' asked Edward: the words made no sense.

'That's what a parachute is,' said Stevie. 'Long story. She told me.'

'Okay, I'll do the two referees, it's not a problem,' said Edward. 'I'll go and see the flat. Might help.'

Kim said, 'Have you got the photo of those tubes? I had an idea of how to find out what they are.'

He pulled out his phone and WhatsApped it to her.

'If we find out anything, it'll be more than Devon Police have done,' said Edward. 'I don't think the local cops even spoke to the referees. JC never mentioned them.'

'And when I meet Lord Bufton-Bottomstead—'

'Richard Cammell-Curzon,' Edward corrected Stevie.

'—can I do a little class war at him?'

'No V-signs, no effing-and-blinding please. Just get him to give you anything he can on Lev.'

'You spoil all my fun, Edward.'

The other two swept their plates quietly. A minute later Edward said, 'Do you want to see my wall?'

'That sounds dodgy as hell,' said Stevie. 'Is that some sort of code between you two?'

'I've no idea,' said Kim. 'I've never seen his wall.'

'Let me show you.'

CHAPTER THIRTY-SIX

On the first floor of Edward's house was a long room with no furniture and a smell of damp. The windows faced the sea. The carpet was white-stained-grey. The setting sun made the interior glow orange.

'Beautiful view,' said Kim. 'You could do a lot with this.' The garden was visible below, thirty feet of lawn and then the cliff edge and the black sea.

'Ever the estate agent,' said Edward affectionately, and touched her hand with his. 'I love you.' Stevie rolled her eyes.

Edward dropped the Venetian blinds, pulled the slats vertical to close off the sun and turned on a big spotlight resting on the floor which illuminated the wall to their right.

'Where did you get that?' Kim asked.

'The antiques shop in Newton Poppleford,' he said. 'Old movie light. It's great with the slats closed, but look,' he bent down and moved the slider on the side. For a second the metal slats opened. The room was filled with blinding white light.

'Turn it down, you lemon!' shouted Stevie.

'Sorry.'

'Sensitive eyes.'

'Ah, sorry Stevie.'

He slid the slats almost closed and twisted the light to face the wall. The surface had been peeled back to plaster. It was covered with Post-it notes, thirty or more. The women moved left to see better. The shadows cast upwards by the spotlight elongated the corners of the notes, creating an optical illusion, as if a square wall had been pulled outwards into the shape of a trapezium.

On the floor opposite was a beanbag and a shoebox with notepads, biros and markers, and unused blocks of different-coloured sticky notes.

'What are these?' asked Stevie, fishing in the box. 'They look like laser pointers.'

'I bought a couple off Amazon to help me concentrate.'

'Concentrate?' Kim repeated. 'Do you shine them in your ears or something?'

'No. Watch,' he said. He shut down the spotlight so the room was almost dark. He went to a pile of boxes in the far corner, which turned out to be amps and speakers connected to an old portable CD player. He pulled the player, trailing wires, over to the beanbag, sat it on the floor and pressed play.

The speakers blared 'Big Balls' by AC/DC.

'Sorry, that's a bit random. I have heavy metal CDs.' He turned the volume down and skipped the track. Metallica came on. He took one of the laser pointers from Stevie.

'This is what I do sometimes.'

In the near dark, he pressed the button on the end of the laser pointer and plumped himself into the beanbag.

'You can focus like this.'

He picked out words on the Post-its from the other side of the room as a guitar solo screeched.

Kim and Stevie looked at each other and shook their heads. But he had their complete attention – each time the red laser dot fell onto a square of notepaper, Stevie read the word it highlighted.

'Nuclear. Nina. Actinium. Lev. Rental.'

Kim chimed in. 'Hurst, Hurst, Zircher.'

'Wendy Wrigley's mates, doctors,' Edward explained. 'You can forget that side of the wall.'

Stevie stepped back. 'Wait. Are you saying these two cases are connected?'

'Not at all!' Edward exclaimed. 'I only had one wall.'

'Forest. Doctor. Spoolie. Marvel. Crime Scene Pix.' Kim turned. 'What's a spoolie?'

It broke the spell. He turned off the music, dropped the laser pen and turned on the spotlight. At the top of the wall a marker pen had been used to write WRIGLEY. But it was crossed out. Feeling a little irritated at the confusion he had himself caused, Edward pointed. 'You can ignore the ones on the left – Marvel, Forest, Spoolie, Firework, Hurst, Hurst, et cetera. Zircher. They're for the Wendy Wrigley case, gone now.'

'I do actually love this,' said Stevie. 'Metal plus laser. Total concentration. Was that Metallica you just played?'

'Good spot.'

Kim put in, 'Can't believe I haven't seen it before.'

'It's my private place.'

'At least you're not watching porn in here.'

'We can't be sure of that,' said Stevie.

Edward barely heard the ribbing. 'It's a tangle. It helps, then it doesn't,' he said, absorbed in reading the square notes. He picked up a thick black marker from the floor and added an 'S' to the word TOPPING, also written on the upper edge of the wall. 'They're not the tidiest.'

'They don't have to be,' said Stevie. 'And what's the microphone for?'

'Oh, nothing.'

Kim laughed. 'That's not an ordinary stereo, is it?'

'Yes it is.'

'No it's not!' said Stevie, approaching it. 'You've got yourself a karaoke machine here.'

'Okay, it's a fair cop. Sometimes I might sing along to Black Sabbath.'

Kim and Stevie laughed, and then, as one, moved closer to the Post-its. Edward stood with his back to the blinds. He saw his shadow cast faintly across them, broad and tall with unkempt hair. There must be a foot of difference in the height of the two women. Stevie was on tiptoe. She read the words on the notes.

'Cammell-Curzon. Ukraine. Empty flat . . . Empty flat?'

'There was nothing in Lev Malnyk's flat except for the tubes, found under the sofa, and a hidden passport, like he'd never lived there, or stripped it bare just before the crash. I always thought it was weird. I'll have to write "Nettles and Hearts" up there.'

'It sounds like some sort of vegetarian moussaka,' said Kim, thumbing at one of the notes. 'Here we go – "Drug tubes".'

Stevie said, 'I like that you wrote down "Fat Cops". The pair who beat you up?'

'The very same.'

Kim added, 'Who you are *not* going to visit without at least one minder.'

'Fancy it?' Edward asked.

Ignoring him, Kim said, 'I also like the fact that the last ten Post-its down the bottom there just say the same thing,' said Kim.

'Why? Why, why, why, why, why?' Edward recited, almost as if the words were a poem.

'Why did Lev do it?' Kim asked.

'No,' said Edward. 'Why was the flat empty?'

CHAPTER THIRTY-SEVEN

Stevie had been on a horse only twice before, and it was the fibre-glass one outside Sainsbury's which her mother had let her ride soon after her adoption. She avoided mentioning this at the stables. She was surrounded by big men and stout women making loud jokes about her height and her lack of eyesight. Making her feel small. The red jacket almost made her walk out.

The Ash Hunt took off from Ash Tremington, a village twenty miles northeast of Sidmouth. Ash Tremington did not have a large local economy – if you left out the local farmers, the place was just a crossroads with a post office and a church. So the stables and kennels where the hunting dogs and horses lived were like Harland & Wolff to Belfast: the centre of almost every working life. Young teens would do work experience as stable hands. Six of the village men worked as groomers to the twenty-four horses, and there was a team of volunteers who gave the thirty-six foxhounds all the love in the world.

The members were mainly local people, but some joined the Saturday rides from as far away as London, and one was even a regular from Manchester. Hunting had changed since a ban came in under the Blair government. That had been twenty years ago, but it was still a traumatic memory for places like the Ash Tremington stables. Would anyone take part in fox hunting without the fox?

Stevie had not expected references to a fox – even planning a real-life chase might be illegal – but it became clear the hounds were not supposed to kill anything. A man was standing next to her, dressed to the nines. Her eyes caught his beige waistcoat and she could have sworn it was velvet.

Quietly, he said: 'Don't mention "drag", don't mention "trail", not even once. You can say "fox" but if there are hunt saboteurs around it's best not to speak at all. You're not a hunt saboteur, are you?'

Stevie pulled her clothes into place. She hated every one of them. They had dressed her up like a toyshop doll in what looked like a child's red tunic, jodhpurs and leather riding boots. She must look like a character from a horror film.

She had taken Edward's request to speak to Richard Cammell-Curzon seriously. She did not want to be the Gen Z stereotype – 'Sorry, he never rang me back.' She started with a simple google, and quite easily found he was the Master of the Hounds on the exclusive Ash Hunt. It was like being town mayor – they seemed to give a different person the chain every year. This year it was Richard Cammell-Curzon who wore the hunt regalia and led the forays. His bio was brief and had an almost schoolboy tone:

I'm a London VC Specialist and friends call me RCC. Or Richard! I also rent local properties in East Devon and love my time in the county. I'm committed to the environment and passionate about underprivileged, etc. Ash Hunt was introduced to me a decade ago by a pal in the City, and it's the honour of my life to be this year's Master. My wife is Ava, my children are at college. My youngest is supported (severe Duchennes), so yes I am committed to getting people with disabilities on horses. Not always easy!

PS – VC means venture capital but the least said about that the better. Onwards, with bugles!

Seeing the bio had given Stevie an idea. Could she join the hunt as a way of getting an 'in' with RCC? She might not consider herself disabled, but she would fail an army medical. Her scoliosis meant constant back pain. But she wanted to wear high heels and she did.

She was tempted to ask Edward Temmis for his advice on how to join a hunt, but wanted to try something herself first. There was a colleague in the council IT department who had spina bifida and used a wheelchair. She had not socialized much with the woman but knew they were roughly the same age, and the other girl had a loud voice and the surname Rimmer. *Claire Rimmer*, was it? Yes.

'Need you to do me a favour,' Stevie had typed into Messenger when she found Claire's account. The message came back quickly. The woman was campaign-minded, and a Labour voter, so was more amenable to the scheme than Stevie could ever have hoped. The result was an article taking up most of page four of the *East Devon Gazette* a week later, which even trended on X for a couple of hours. The headline: POSH FOX HUNTERS SAY THEY WANT DISABLED PEOPLE BUT I'M THE WRONG SHAPE. And a photo of Rimmer in her wheelchair, looking almost violently angry, with a devastating paragraph below it: 'The Ash Hunt have apologized to Ms Rimmer for any misunderstanding. They are trying to trace the person who told her this. They claim to have an "open door" policy for disabled riders, and to have six with disabilities on their hunts, but when challenged they admitted that they were included because they wore hearing aids.'

Rimmer had never called the hunt. But Stevie (who had not told her colleague the reason she needed help) contacted the Ash Tremington stables two days after the article came out. She feigned ignorance of the furore. 'I have disabilities and would love to join the next ride,' she said. Her call was passed higher and higher up the chain until she thought she might actually be put through to Cammell-Curzon himself. At the other end she could almost hear the hot potato hitting every hand. They fell over themselves to make her feel it was worth waiting on the line for a reply. 'Bear with us, just a minute more' – did they think she was a national newspaper reporter, following up the *Gazette* story? She ended up speaking to a county woman who sounded simultaneously well-off and rugged, the best sort. She was businesslike and diligent, her voice deep and certain, although she lacked a little in the manners department – when she noted Stevie's measurements, she told her, 'We have a child's kit for you. That's no problem.' She asked about Stevie's disabilities and sounded impressed. Stevie even invented a couple of extra conditions for good measure: anxiety and anal perforation. The woman seemed to panic, changing the subject. 'No chair, though?' No wheelchair, confirmed Stevie.

Only when she hung up did she realize she had not been asked if she could ride a horse. These people just assume everyone can, she thought wryly.

YouTube videos had showed her how to assemble the kit she was wearing – the necktie was pre-knotted and fixed around the back of her neck with elastic and a clip, to avoid a rider getting accidentally strangled on a fencepost or tree branch. She knew not to button the single-breasted tailored hunt jacket. The crisp white shirt was the only item of clothing she had brought herself. The waistcoat was a thin, shiny wool, with tiny pockets, one of which had an old betting slip in (had the child gambled?). The breeches were a shade she decided should be called 'beige ridiculous', because that summed up the entire effect, like a cartoon character, shrunk in the wash. The only item she enjoyed putting on was the pair of leather riding boots, stained mahogany brown. Whichever kid had worn them had even smaller feet than her, but she accepted the pain for the style. They clipped and clopped like horses' hooves on the wooden outhouse floor, the bronze spurs heavy and purposeful as a cowboy's.

'Only for decoration.'

The man standing beside her was rotund with a moustache that looked stick-on, a red nose as crowded with bumps and divots as a topographic map of the Cotswolds.

'The spurs,' he clarified. 'Toy-shop spurs, won't hurt him. You must be Stevie Masson, so I expected a chappie, ha.'

The man had the bluff manner that people take on when they've counted their money and find they have enough to last them the rest of their life, and now they can be as rude as they want to everyone. Stevie had decided to skip the money part, so she recognized a kindred spirit.

'My name isn't Masson, try again,' she said, instantly reminding herself: *You're here on a mission. Don't make yourself stand out by arguing.*

'Testing you,' said the moustache owner. 'Never employ a man who doesn't correct his surname.'

'And what's yours?' asked Stevie.

'Martin.'

'No, your surname.'

'That *is* my surname. Francis Martin.'

'Your surname is Francis-Martin? What's your first name?'

'Young lady . . .' Then he saw she was joking and smiled. 'Miss Mason, I'm here to look after you. I don't know if you saw but we got a smashing in the papers because we said we had lots of disabled people and they all turned out to be retired judges with one hearing aid. So along you come, bit of manna from heaven, if you know the phrase? Our chance to show we are open, in the vernacular, whatever they call it, diversity thingummy, not just sportsmen and horsey types. What's your disability anyway?'

The words landed with Stevie as just a noise, just a stream of POSH POSH POSH POSH POSH, but Mr Martin suddenly blushed.

'I'm terribly sorry. I shouldn't ask. You turned your head and I saw.'

'Oh,' said Stevie, 'the acid burn that took half my sight is nothing. The problem is mainly spinal. What they call orthopaedic.'

'I love the way you Scotch say words like "orthopaedic". Like "murder".'

Stevie peered at him. 'I didn't think my accent was that obvious.'

'So your disability is hidden?' he said eagerly. 'One of my daughters gets back pain.'

'It wouldn't be hidden if I took my clothes off. Scoliosis curve in the spine, but really a twist, like rope coiled, and mine's too bad to operate on.'

'We'll get you a lopsided horse,' he said with a guffaw, his distinctly un-PC remarks apparently running rogue now. Outside there was neighing and shouting. Hooves stamping on gravel. He opened the door and the nearest horse bucked under its rider. Martin whispered, 'If you've never ridden before, now's the time to tell me. We don't take prisoners.'

Now was the time to tell him the truth. She opened her mouth and heard the words: 'I've ridden since I was two. I've done nothing but ride. I had my own horse for ten years, Eager. We jumped. He died. But we were fast together.'

Francis Martin clapped his hands and puffed his chest out. The riders, at least twenty of them, turned towards him and Stevie. 'Our newest member – well, actually a visitor, Stevie Mason!' The hunters were too busy with their bridles to clap, so they cheered. 'She said she wants a big one!' The second cheer was almost deafening. A long man with no chin threw his hat in the air. She looked for female riders and saw no more than two. Stevie forced a smile.

If there was ever a vacancy for dictator, and she got the job, this lot would be the first to face the firing squad.

As the horses settled, a stable boy led one to her.

He was a gorgeous creature, and clearly not the largest, but with a pad under the saddle, leather bit and reins, and stirrups that shone as if they had been polished all night. She sensed the riders turning to face her, all the horses being repositioned.

Francis Martin was still at her shoulder, and spoke quietly. 'Hold the halter here and say hello.'

'Hello,' said Stevie, the horse's head seemingly miles above her own.

'To the horse, not this lot. Softer.'

'Hello, my gorgeous,' she whispered, heart racing.

'Don't be afraid to pull the head towards you, he won't buck. Name is Chestnut.'

'Chestnut, Chestnut,' she whispered, conscious that the stirrups were level with her shoulders and the horse's nostrils looked big enough to envelop the whole of her head.

Something in Francis's movement, something indefinable, a closeness, suggested he was giving her more help than he would a person who had done all the riding she claimed to have. As she kicked her left foot into the stirrup, he asked, 'Do you mind if I hold your arse?'

He pushed up as she pulled on the bridle. It was not dignified but it was enough. The other riders were looking at her inquisitively. Could they see the truth, that she had never before felt the sinewed power of an adult horse beneath her? For a moment she quailed, high off the ground with a very long way to fall.

But then she saw him through the forest of horses and riders: the one person who was wearing a black tunic not a red one; the single riding helmet with a flash of colour, a large blue feather adorning the left side of the hunt leader's grey hat. So this was RCC, the owner of the flat the biker lived in, the man she had been sent to find. She straightened her back and grasped the reins. By God, she'd see this through.

'Welcome all.' Richard Cammell-Curzon was holding an old-style grey megaphone that whistled as he spoke. Expertly he took both hands off the reins for a second to adjust the volume. The whistling quietened. He seemed to be controlling the horse just with his legs and heels, because the animal stood stock still as all the other horses shook their heads and fidgeted. He lifted the megaphone and now his voice crackled, but clearly, as if down an old phone line. 'It's hot, I know, but we have our trail.'

He was a tall, well-built man with an athlete's shoulders and muscular legs. She saw parts of him through the throng of riders, as if windows were opening and closing. He was forty, perhaps, chiselled, high-cheekboned, with a neat blond beard. His nose was large, sharp, square like a Roman emperor's.

'I have brought Grandpa's bugle, as before. So on the call, my lords, ladies and gentlemen – on the call of the bugle, we ride!'

He tossed the megaphone at a stable boy, who caught it. Then he blew on the bugle, the instrument tiny in his large hand, the note as high as a party whistle. His horse's ears shot up. The place was suddenly awash with sound, almost deafening Stevie. She felt the massive muscles of her mount's back twist and torque between her legs. She saw – with gratitude – that her own horse was not moving because Francis Martin, feet planted firmly on the ground, was discreetly holding the bridle. His other hand gripped the reins of his horse near the halter. Suddenly a gate opened, and what had been a low rumble of slavering and breathing became wild barking, a blur of coat, leg, teeth, tail. Hounds wild with excitement. In their enthusiasm, the dogs mounted each other to be at the front of the pack, which moved like a river of fur.

Stevie caught Martin's eye. He said loudly, 'I've got you, just wait,' although amid the barking the words were barely audible. The hounds were looking for the trail. Francis Martin shouted, 'Hold the reins tight!' and let go to mount his horse, but whatever he wanted Stevie to do she had not done, because now the animal was moving, driven to follow the herd, and she wanted to carry this off even though the height and bounce combined to make her want to scream.

'Chestnut, Chestnut, slow, slow, slow, Chestnut,' Stevie kept saying. She felt her back get sorer with every bump, every divot. The stables adjoined a long, sloping field, and the horses began to canter across it, spreading out. Martin was nowhere to be seen. It was not enough just to hang on. She had to sit upright, like she had seen the YouTube riders doing, holding themselves, shoulders back. Her bottom left the saddle every time the horse landed a hoof on the thick grass. She dreaded a sudden stop, and then remembered the reins – they were her controllers, of course, and she should hold them firmly. She had seen that online too. She pulled them until the slack fed past her gloves, and now the horse's head ticked up, as if she was annoying it. 'Not too tight,' said a man's voice beside her. Francis Martin was looking at her with interest. His bulbous nose had begun gleaming with sweat as soon as they broke from the tree-shaded stables and into direct June sunshine. Despite his portly figure, or maybe because of it, he looked like a medieval king in his riding outfit. Gold cuffs on his tunic. She read his lips rather than hearing him – they were in a pack of at least twenty riders, all shouting to each other, laughing or whooping, spreading out and then converging, as if their mounts were choosing occasional moments to consult on the direction of travel. The exhilaration of the other hunters only stirred a feeling of raw terror in Stevie.

It was like being on a motorcycle with no idea what would happen if she turned the handles to rev the motor. She could handle herself while the horse was at a trot, hemmed in by the herd, but she knew she would soon be in open countryside. The thought raised hackles all across her body, a welt of physical fear she could feel lifting her skin, even making the scars on her face buzz, as if they were about to break open. She would be alone in this crowd of experienced riders, the lone beginner, trying and failing to hide her utter lack of history with any horse at all. She had joined the hunt to meet Richard Cammell-Curzon and, being honest with herself, to impress Kim and Edward too – this was incredible, thinking back; her ingenuity and ability to morph into the sort of person who could mix with Devon's upper class without giving herself away with a volley of Tourette's-powered expletives. So far she had avoided saying 'fuck' even once, but who was she kidding? Stevie had already given up on the crazy idea that she might draw level with the leader of the Ash Hunt for a casual conversation. She would be lucky to escape this adventure with her life.

Francis Martin, the portly little king, had evidently decided he no longer needed to look after her. Sink or swim, was it? His horse seemed to ghost sideways through the throng, the knight on a chessboard – forward and then diagonal. The horses were all snorting and coughing; up ahead, the hounds were scattered in all four directions, picking up and losing the scent, then converging when they found it again, some inbuilt radar telling each of them where the centre of the pack would be in the next thirty seconds.

The gate to the next field would be the test. She was, what, seven feet in the air? Five feet of horse and two feet of her upper body. Her helmet bounced left and right like Stan Laurel's bowler hat, the visual gag in a silent movie. If she fell, she would hit her head. Would she hit it on a rock? She did not want any more injuries, any more pain. Her curved spine stabbed reminders: *This was the kind of thing a doctor told you never to do.* That warning had been forgotten in her zest to prove herself.

This field had kept the horses at a trot: the chase did not really start until the next one. Maybe she should dismount now, just jump off, take the hit, apologize for her lies or pretend, yes, she had ridden, but not on a horse as powerful as Chestnut?

Body bouncing on the saddle, even at this slow trot, Stevie had worked out how to steer Chestnut. If she pulled the reins tight in her hands, the gigantic animal seemed to become more responsive. Was that all there was to riding? A middle-aged man with a ginger beard was alongside her.

'You'll probably know this, but hold the reins tight as you can. When they hear the gate open, they're like bloody paratroopers, all jumping through the hatch.'

The gate clicked and Stevie felt Chestnut shiver with excitement. One rider shouted 'No!' as his horse got impatient and jumped the fence, the gorse almost tearing his tunic off. Stevie felt her stomach turn and her heart sink. She leant towards the horse's ear, holding its mane. 'Don't go too fast, Chestnut, please. I'm small and I haven't done this before.' She had the crazy thought – would her Glasgow accent stop the horse understanding? She kept it simple. 'Slow, lover, slow. For me. Please Chestnut, please. Slow—'

Then she was through the gate. The horse jumped, straining the reins. She worried they might break and loosened her grip. But as soon as she did, he was away.

Who had given her Chestnut? He was a racehorse. The field had a camber, the shoulders sloping away. The horse bounced her so high in the air she was not even sure she would return to the saddle. Whatever happened, she must not scream. They tore past the other horses. Chestnut had sensed the inexperience of his rider and bolted through the other horses to shouts of 'Hey!' and 'Watch out, girl!' He was catching the hounds. She begged and begged, 'Chestnut, lovely, please, Chestnut,' but the faster he went, the more she bounced, and the more she bounced in the saddle, the less control she could exert on the reins. Faster and faster and faster . . .

He roared towards a second gate. It was shut. Stevie squeezed her eyes closed and grabbed the horse's mane, expecting a sudden stop and a moment in the air. But when she was airborne, she realized she was still attached to the horse and almost weightless. The other riders must be half a mile behind. The horse landed, hooves kicking into farm mud, soil and stones thrown sideways. The shouts behind her were some way back now – were they calling her? Warning her? Whatever happened, she would not scream. She would not scream.

'Chestnut!' she shouted, 'I will not scream for you!'

Still the horse barrelled on. And gradually she realized she could control it, at least slow the animal a little with a strong tug on the reins. He was jerking the reins out of her grasp, so she wrapped them around her wrist. Wasn't it always 'sit up straight' when you got taught to ride a horse? Move through the hips and all that? She was close to a road and dreaded Chestnut opting for a smoother surface, deciding to make for the nearest motorway. So when she got to the corner of the field, she tugged the reins to the right to head uphill across a wheatfield.

For the first time her panic was ebbing, and she picked out extraneous sounds. The stalks crunching beneath the horse's hooves. The distant sound of the hounds, following the trail across a nearby field. And now, to her right, a gallop – not her horse but Richard Cammell-Curzon's, crashing towards her from fifty yards away.

Chestnut was panting. Now at a canter, he was at last tired enough to be controlled. Cammell-Curzon pulled his horse up, but it must have confused his tug on the reins for a different command: it jammed into a sudden halt and threw its rider into a hedge.

CHAPTER THIRTY-EIGHT

'Oh my God! Oh my flying God!' shouted an upper-crust voice from behind a curtain of white flowers and red berries. 'Bloody hawthorn! Shit! I'm okay! I'm okay!'

Stevie did not know what to do. She could not dismount Chestnut. She had finally got control of her horse and brought it to a halt. RCC's horse was skipping around the field as if it had perpetrated the best practical joke. She peered past the flowers and berries and saw only flashes of white shirt.

'That was *not* supposed to happen! For crying out loud, Miss Mason!'

'What can I do?'

'Can you ride over to my horse and call her? Her name is Gibby. I don't want her following the hounds without me. She'll take to heel in a trice, that one, and I'll be a laughing stock.'

'Yep.'

Stevie amazed herself by kicking Chestnut – just the lightest heel-tap with her stirruped shoes – and getting the horse to move at a trot, but this time, unlike the last, keeping the reins as tight as she could. The horse could not hit its lethal acceleration. 'Gibby! Gibby!' she shouted. 'Here, girl!' She even had the confidence to turn back to where RCC had entered the bush at a diagonal, a flash-frame in her mind's eye of him half in, half out of the bush as he shot off the horse like a tumbling bullet, neither up nor down. The hole he had made in the hawthorn had closed behind him, as if the bush had devoured its invader. But now she saw two arms emerging. 'Gibby!' She turned. 'That's it, Chestnut. Boy meets girl, lovely. Kiss away.' The two horses nuzzled each other. Her heart lifted. She felt joy for the first time since she had arrived at this hunt feeling like a foreigner. A stab of joy. Here, where the camber of the field lifted, she felt the blood and muscle of the horse below the saddle like a medieval queen taking power from nature.

The leader of the hunt was a hundred yards behind and below her. Could she — dare she — reach for the reins of his horse, lead it back to him? She leant a little, released Chestnut from one hand. But her horse felt the grip loosen instantly and kicked, bucking like a steed in a Wild West rodeo, raising his front legs, kicking at the back, as if intent on a sudden escape. She quickly grabbed the mane and pulled the horse's head back. 'Not hurting you, am I, you little menace?' she growled. The other horse turned, and suddenly she saw Richard Cammell-Curzon alongside his animal. His face was streaked with blood.

'Climb down, can you, for a minute?'

But she was the queen. She would climb down when she wished to. She answered to no one.

They stared at each other. She was so breathless she was almost unable to speak. Her outfit, she realized, was sopping wet with sweat. His tunic was studded with thorns and fragments of the bush he had fallen into, his neck splashed with mud.

'Dog rose,' he said. 'Cushioned me and stung me. Pink flowers, prickles. Dog rose and hawthorn. Broke my fall, hey.'

What was his accent — what was the 'hey' he had added? Was that South African, Australian? She could only guess. The primal howling of the hounds, which could carry for miles, had faded completely now. There was only a still breeze. For no reason she could put her finger on, Stevie felt fearful. She did not want to dismount. Chestnut might buck as soon as he felt one foot lift from the stirrup. She might then be carried at a racehorse lick, hanging by one leg, unable to bail.

'Step down, little girl.'

That was it. She gritted her teeth. 'I'm not a little girl.'

'Scottish?'

'Glasgow and some other places.'

'We welcomed you as a disabled rider and you've taken off like bloody Lester Piggott.'

His voice was aristocratic, but with a tremble that she thought might be the result of shock from the fall. She stared down at him.

'I've never seen anyone go off like that, almost as if you never rode a horse before.'

She would never admit it. 'I like a fast ride.'

'You stayed on. Ninety-nine per cent of first-timers fall when they lose the horse like that, and I'm the hunt leader, so I had to follow, understand? I'm liable.'

'I'm not a first-timer,' she lied, not wanting to blow her cover.

'Okay. Well. Right. We were told – I was told – you were experienced. Obviously someone got their wires crossed. Let's just say you've not been on too many hunts before, hey?' He would not accuse her of lying. His face softened. He touched his forehead. 'Oh God, am I bleeding? I thought it was sweat.'

She looked at him. By chance, she was in conversation with the owner of the flat Lev Malnyk had stayed in and she must take her chance while it was there, before he was summoned away or someone else joined them in this isolated field.

'Do you want to climb up, and we ride back?' she said. 'Or shall I get down and we take a minute?'

His face was blank. His eyes were not focusing. The wound in his forehead dripped fresh blood onto the line of an eyebrow, and now the red liquid had found a channel down his cheek.

He placed his legs further apart. 'Crikey, I feel light-headed. Dismount, can you?'

She had to try. She stole a foot from the stirrup, but held the reins tight. Quickly she stood, straightening her left leg, swung her right leg over, and jumped from the saddle. But her left foot was still in the stirrup, almost at the level of her head. RCC saw it happen and raced around the horse, taking the reins and pushing the toe of Stevie's leather boot so the foot was released. 'Take the reins. I need to stop mine bolting.'

A moment later they were at the edge of the field. He had lengthened the halters on both animals and tied them to a fence-post. 'Don't like to do this, they hate it, but I need half a tick in the shade. Felt faint there. Went into that bush like a cruise missile.'

Stevie reckoned she had no more than five minutes before someone came looking for them, and then her chance of finding out about his connection with the biker was gone. She was so close, but she must not blow it by being obvious.

'What was your name again?'

'Richard Cammell-Curzon.' He had lit a cigarette. 'And you're Stevie, yes?'

'Stevie Mason.'

'Short for Stephanie?'

'No, not short for anything. Like the poet, I keep being told.'

'Stevie Jones?' he asked.

'Stevie Smith.'

'Got you,' he joked. 'Of course I knew that.'

She looked sideways at his face. The thin blond beard had traces of red, not blood but ginger. So beneath the helmet he was a redhead? His scratched skin was fair. He felt his face. His fingers were almost feminine. He kept pursing his lips, as if trying to suck a fly from his front teeth.

'I'm so damn embarrassed, the leader of the hunt, doing the flying squirrel in front of our newest member.'

'I thought I'd get an instant ban for taking off.'

'It was hardly your fault, Stevie,' he said. 'Not that I don't go with your story that you've ridden racehorses for years, but no one shoots off like that from a hunt when the hounds are going in the other direction. I'm just pleased it was me who fell, not you.'

'Your name. It's a coincidence. I have a friend in the police who mentioned a Curzon-Cammell—'

'Other way around—'

'No, I think they mentioned Curzon-Cammell. They were talking about the person who owned the flat the Sidmouth biker stayed in, you know, the guy who . . .'

She stopped. He was staring at her.

'That was me.'

'You?' She did her best to feign surprise.

'There's hardly going to be a Cammell-Curzon and a Curzon-Cammell.'

'I saw the biker was from Russia.'

'Russia? I wasn't told that. I was told Ukraine. Thought I should help, so I cut the rate a little. But it's not my bag, meeting the tenants. I can't tell you, when the girl died, when the attack in Sidmouth happened – attack or accident or whatever the hell it was – how sick I felt. What had he been using my bloody place for?'

'It's so horrible. Did the police speak to you?'

'Of course! The Met. I told them exactly what I've just told you. Never met him, never interviewed him, all done through an agency.'

Stevie peered at him. She simply had no register for this kind of man. She saw the blood and scratches on his face and wondered if he was in shock, and the shock and embarrassment were making him so talkative. She wanted more.

'Even with an agency,' she said, 'wouldn't he need referees or whatever? Or would you supply them?'

'Some landlords do that. It's not strictly legal. The referee should know the person. Wasn't his a doctor? I can't remember. For all I know, he might have made a name up. A funny thing though – the police came back to me later, Devon Police. They'd found things in the flat but they couldn't say what they were. I guess I was being immature.'

'Meaning – sorry, I don't get you.'

'They were a bit bolshy. They wouldn't tell *me* stuff, so I didn't tell *them* stuff. I should have, I know, but a landlord isn't supposed to creep around a tenant's flat. So I kept my mouth shut. I rather regret it.'

'You kept your mouth shut about what?'

'To be brutally frank, there was a bit of concern among the other tenants before the crash happened. So I had watched the place and let myself in when he was gone. The flat had virtually nothing in it. But there was a big machine in the living room. At first I thought, "DJ equipment". It was a big boxy computer on a stand. I wasn't sure it was for music. I think it was a 3D printer. The name on the outside was BONNET. Yup, I actually think it was a 3D printer, had BONNET on it in massive letters. I wonder what he was printing?'

Stevie said: 'Maybe those ampoules. Or maybe he was making something radioactive?'

'They swept the flat for radiation and found nothing. Odd, isn't it!' Richard Cammell-Curzon exclaimed. 'Do you mind if I—?' He showed a packet of cigarettes which looked to have been secreted in his waistcoat. 'These two are in love, I reckon.' As he lit the cigarette, he nodded at the horses. 'Odd, very odd,' he murmured. 'Bonnet.'

CHAPTER THIRTY-NINE

The estate where Lev Malnyk had lived was typical of the housing policy in the county. Six brand-new houses on a field, accessible down a narrow track – would it ever be turned into a proper road? Would the families here have a doctor, a school, or even a streetlight?

As Edward turned his moped up the narrow lane, he thought of the horror stories of people moving into new-builds and finding the plumbing was not connected or the electricity went out every time number six turned on their tumble dryer. And, of course, there were the new-build vigilantes – people like Richard Cammell-Curzon, who had people spotting new houses for them, outbidding locals and immediately turning them into rentals or, worse still, holiday lets. No council, no government had yet found a way to rewire the housing market in places like Devon, where London money always came in bigger briefcases.

He stood at the gate, where the track became a smoother, more solid strip of tarmac. He bet these houses had looked wonderful in an estate agent's brochure. Had Kim sold them? He rang her.

'No, not me. I would have said! Where are you?' she asked.

'Standing staring at them, trying to work out which one Lev was in.'

'Ask anyone, they'll know.'

'There's no one here. It's ghostly.'

'I don't sell new-builds, honey,' she said. 'The developer does it direct these days. There's so much snagging they usually need a couple of years sorting out. The buyers go mad when they find out the locks don't work and the laundry room floods. I spoke to Nettles.'

'Did you?'

'We can rule him out of anything. He's Cammell-Curzon's accountant. If he's involved, then the landlord must be too. You heard about Stevie?'

'No.' He felt sudden dread. The fear of bad news.

'She only went hunting with the landlord.'

'You're joking.'

'She tried to reach you. She was very excited. Quite a lot of swearing. I think she's decided she likes posh people now. Apparently he fell off his horse and she didn't.'

'What did she find out?'

'She says she texted you.'

'This bloody phone, I'll look. What a star. By the way, Kim – the agency who handled Lev's rental – their name was on the form, but I didn't take it in.'

'I love it when you use my name. It means "Listen". Okay, yes, that was Southleighs in Exeter. Do you want me to call them?'

'Could you?' Were they making progress? Not yet. He hung up, sought out the messages app on his phone to find Stevie's text, but before he could open it an old man appeared directly in front of him.

'Not seen you around here before,' said the man. 'I recognize you from *Devon Life*.' There had been an article: HOW SIDMOUTH'S FAVOURITE TALK-SHOW HOST BOUNCED

BACK FROM TRAGEDY. 'Enjoy the show,' said the man. 'I'm Terry.'

The man was fair, thin, slightly stooped, with liver spots on his face that marked him out as someone who had spent a lifetime working outdoors. He wore beige cords and a grey checked shirt – 'care home camouflage', Kim once called it – although he looked to have his wits about him.

'I'm reporting on the tragedy in Sidmouth,' said Edward, using only the feeblest cover story. Stevie had put him to shame with her undercover jockey act. But outright lying to one of his own listeners felt wrong. 'I know the Ukrainian lived here.'

'The Russian, surely? Russian pretending to be Ukrainian. That's what we all think. He did indeed live here,' said the old man, staring glassily, eyes watering in the afternoon sun. 'Lev Malnyk at number four. Made no sense, did it? The Met came half a dozen times, once in riot gear. Then the local force came, much more friendly, mainly just checking our window locks.'

'I guess they got the CCTV, did they?' asked Edward, pointing at one of the houses. The properties were arranged in a line, curved like an archer's bow. The first one had a camera on the front of it.

'That's mine, as it happens!' said the man, looking pleased with himself. 'Son-in-law put it in because he's good with that stuff. But there was a spider on the lens that stopped the movement sensor working. So it got this and that, but nothing to help them. Met were swearing like troopers. But you can't train a spider.'

Edward almost laughed. 'Did you see him leaving that day?'

'Who, Lev? Nope.'

'Did you know him at all?'

'He was in the fourth house, like I say, or the second if you don't count the ones opposite – back there, on the shoulder. I think a speculator bought it and divided it into flats almost straightaway. So there were comings and goings, but comings and goings I don't mind. I have tinnitus. What I mind is silence.'

Edward reflected on this. 'No one saw or heard anyone leave the flat after Lev died?'

'Well . . .' the old man started, and stopped. His left eye was tearing up and he used his little finger to sluice the water away. 'Tinnitus and watery eyes and a few other things.'

'Someone saw something?'

'She's not the lady she was,' said the man. 'She and I were friends years back, and blow me down, she ends up at number three. Two back from mine. The downstairs only. Dementia. Just sits, looking out of the window.'

'Did the police speak to her?'

'Several times, but it was just mumbo-jumbo. "A man walked in twice then came out four times", sort of thing. "A man walked in then walked in again". I accompanied them because her sons are useless, frankly. Broke my heart. I don't think they even took a statement in the end. "Someone went in twice and came out with a microwave." I think she mentioned a boat as well.'

At this, Edward was suddenly alert. 'Someone came out with a boat and a microwave?'

'One minute it was a microwave, then a box, then it was a boat, then it was a man in a mirror. What does that mean? Do you want to speak to her?'

'I do,' said Edward. 'I want to know about the box and the boat. I wasn't expecting a boat.'

'Bear in mind, the Russian guy's house was divided into four, so you might have had comings and goings from other tenants, and some might even have been Airbnb, so that's a lot of different names and faces. I reckon the Met gave up trying to get her to remember anything that didn't sound like a bad dream.'

*

She did not look like a woman with dementia. She came to the front door alone. She walked heavily, and Edward saw her feet bulged in worn slippers and her ankles were swollen with fluid. She had her glasses on her head, resting in a crown of tightly curled grey hair. She peered at her neighbour.

'It's Terry.'

'I know you,' she said, her voice rich with Caribbean intonation.

Terry said, 'She has good days and bad days.'

'Billy!' she said to Edward.

'No, this isn't Billy,' said Terry.

'Who's Billy?'

'Her son.' Terry turned to her. 'Billy's not here today,' he said loudly. 'I'm your neighbour. We know each other. Can we come in, Gloria?' He whispered to Edward, 'Cancer finished him. Went back to Jamaica on holiday, family home, never returned, broke her heart, so sudden, best not to mention.'

'I can hear you,' said Gloria. 'Watch yourselves on the motorway.'

'She thinks it's a motorway out here. Two cars an hour,' murmured Terry.

But Edward was stuck on the awfulness of Gloria's loss. His mind flapped like loose celluloid, running back over the last few minutes. His brain felt full, the thoughts heavy in his head. Gloria must be far gone, he thought, if she misrecognized this pale stranger as her lost son. But he wanted to reach out and hug her. He had lost Matty, and he imagined himself at her age, eighty and burnt out with grief, misrecognizing everyone as his son, his son come back to him.

They were sitting in the living room now. 'She'll go out to make tea, come back without it, just watch.' Terry's smile was not cruel, just accepting of a reality he had somehow avoided. 'They say you avoid the Demondee by playing Sudoku, but who has the time for that many numbers? Thatcher had it.'

'Demondee?'

'The demon dementia. *Demon D.* Catch up, sonny.'

Sonny. That word always did it. Oh God, was it going to be one of those days, where everything led back to Matty? Edward remembered, years ago, on the weekends he had his child, when his ex-wife was busy with her new marriage and new kids, his constant warnings not to kick the football off the edge of the cliff. How many had they lost? At least four. You always saw the white dot bob on the waves hundreds of feet below, a full stop on a huge sheet of blue paper. 'The sailors will find it and play with it on the decks,' Edward said, never cross; buying an unstable ruin had been his choice. He always played with his back to the edge, just to stop any crazy moment where his son might run forwards, forget himself, go off the cliff. His ex, Tara, was furious when she turned up early one Sunday, came down the side passage and saw the arrangement. 'I didn't think you even came out the back, and now you're playing football here? Come on, Edward!'

But a smile had played around her lips, he was sure of it. Sudden death, when it took Matty, was never going to be the exotic – off a cliff – but the obvious. Under the wheels of a car.

'We should turn our chairs to face the window: that might jog her,' said Terry. The two men took three wooden chairs and parted the curtains completely. The house was in a perfect position for observing number 4, Prince Andrew's Close. 'What number are we?'

'Don't expect logic,' said Terry. 'I'm nine, this is six. They didn't do a simple parallel count. I think they drew up the plans and then forced a couple more in. Or the person who did the numbering was having a bad day.'

On another occasion Edward might have laughed, but he felt his head bang with a migraine, as if a single word was rattling around inside it. *Matty. Matty Matty Ma—*

'You okay, sonny?'

'Sure.'

'You look a bit tearful.'

'It's the light.'

It's Sonny.

Gloria came back without the tea. The three sat on their wooden chairs facing the window. The sun was behind Gloria's house and, low in the evening sky, hit the roof of number four. Edward felt his stomach heave – not so much with physical nausea as with anxiety. What was wrong with him?

'That's number one, I'm number two,' said Gloria.

'Close,' said Terry. 'My darling, Edward is going to ask you a couple of questions.'

He wanted to find the right question for Gloria. His head hurt and his stomach rumbled with anxiety. He asked, 'Did you see the Ukrainian man, Lev Malnyk, leave the house?'

'No. And—'

'Yes?'

'Not Prince Andrew.'

'Not him?'

'Prince Andrew and Mr Lev. Left separately.'

'It's not good today,' whispered Terry.

'What's not good?' asked Gloria.

'Please don't worry, my love,' said Terry, 'and just see if you can answer Edward's questions.'

'I couldn't give the police much, except the mirror.'

'The mirror?' Edward put in.

'A man in a mirror.'

'Went in?'

'This came up with the police, Gloria, didn't it?' That was Terry again, and Gloria asked: 'Did it?'

Edward had taken his phone out of his pocket to make notes, but was stopped by a light touch on his arm. Terry, between Gloria and Edward, whispered, 'She doesn't like screens. Finds them upsetting.'

'Well, she's right there,' said Edward.

'A man in a mirror, that made the police roll their eyes.'

'Did you see anyone on the day of the disaster, Gloria?'

'What disaster?'

'The crash at the pizza restaurant in Sidmouth,' said Edward, beginning to understand why the police had left the trail after this visit.

'You know what he is talking about, lovely,' said Terry, with real tenderness. 'The police came?'

'Why didn't they ask me? I would have told them—'

'They did ask you,' said Terry, but now it was Edward who put a hand on his arm.

'—told them about the box.'

'This again,' said Terry.

'A big thing like a microwave removed by the man in the mirror with four arms.'

'Where did he take it?' Edward asked.

'Down there, silly!' Gloria said, pointing left, which was the obvious direction, the end of the estate they had entered from. 'He couldn't exactly go into the field, could he?' The field was behind the house. A barbed-wire fence marked the rear boundary of the properties. Edward guessed it had been put there by an angry farmer.

The conversation chugged this way and that, like a steam train grinding across countryside and trying to find rails. They kept coming back to the men who left the house opposite with the box, and every description was different.

Terry was asking, 'How many men were there, Gloria, with the box?'

No answer. Why did this box keep coming up? Was the box the mirror? What was removed from Malnyk's flat on the day of the crash? What if she had got the day wrong? He asked Terry, 'All these comings and goings with the mirror et cetera, was that the same day as the crash?'

'I believe so,' said Terry. 'No point checking with . . .' – he rolled his eyes towards Gloria – 'but yes, the police were here the day after the incident, and she was talking about yesterday, so that we do know.'

'So he came straight here, the man in the mirror? Were they wearing costumes or something?'

'Fancy dress!' laughed Gloria. Edward stared, wondering if that was an answer or just some kind of word association she was playing in her head. They would get nowhere here.

When Gloria said, 'Billy, would you like another tea?' even Terry looked moved by how lost his neighbour was.

Edward could not leave fast enough, mounting his moped and almost forgetting the crash helmet he had left on the grass. As he tugged it onto his head and put the key into the ignition, there was a tap on his shoulder – of course. Terry.

'Are you okay to drive? You're looking pretty shell-shocked. Dementia can do that.'

'I wish I had it myself sometimes,' said Edward. This man was hanging on to him like a limpet. 'Tasteless, sorry,' he added, not sure what to say.

'You're crying.'

'It's the wind.'

'You're wearing a crash helmet, which is airtight.'

'There was some wind when I put it on. The visor was up. The wind caught my eyes, and I put the shield down.' This was silly. He opted for candour instead. 'I lost my son. A sudden death. Your lady did too. She thought I was her son. I wondered if that's me in thirty years, thinking I've got him back. All the good memories are bad now.'

'Every sunrise is a fire that burns you down.'

'Who said that?'

'A country singer, I think.'

'I had memories of it in there. Never gets any easier. Burns you out from the inside, like the firebox on a train.'

'It does that,' said the man elliptically. 'Chin up.' He slapped the motorbike seat as if releasing Edward. Revving the moped, Edward asked: 'Which way is Barton Ottery from here?'

The old man thought about it. 'A minute from Tipton St John, isn't it? Tipton, then left at the bend, up the hill. If you get to the Wildflower Retreat, you've gone too far.'

Nothing Edward had heard in the last hour had made any sense at all, like looking at a map scissored into small pieces, shuffled and glued into a collage. It was a fitting end to an outing where Edward had learnt precisely nothing of value.

Or so he thought.

CHAPTER FORTY

Edward's head cleared as he pushed the moped to forty. He felt a spark of sympathy for the officers under Jordan Callintree, who had come back from every interview more confused than when they set off. Why had the flat been cleared on the day of the crash? What was in it that needed removing? He remembered the unread text from Stevie and pulled in at the entrance to the Golf Centre by Trow Hill.

He checked he was not at risk from the fast cars on the main road, took his helmet off and found the app on his phone. There it was, the latest message:

> Have been on horse with landlord RCC don't think he's to blame for any of it BUT he said he went into Lev flat secretly (BEFORE crash) and found 3D printer (make was BONNET) did he use printer to make the capsules or a gun or even radiation? He fell off horse started talking Stevie

Edward read it twice, punctuating it mentally the second time. *A 3D printer?* He looked up 'Bonnet Printer' on his phone but only found 3D-printed car bonnet parts.

So someone rushed into the flat to remove a 3D printer? And then Gloria sees it being rapidly removed after Lev's death, calls it a microwave, a box, a boat?

Every turn took him into a cul-de-sac, but now he was heading for a real one. Perhaps it was foolhardy, but he was going to visit the address where the enormous man and woman lived, if only to be sure it was not them who had attacked him in his garden. He would hold on to his ignition key and keep his exit routes clear. He had a reminder of the attack – as he pulled the throttle back, there was a twinge in his wrist where one of them had stamped on it.

He was sure it would not be them – the wheelchair – but he was desperate not to have to go back to Jordan Callintree and admit defeat, so he was clutching at straws now. This would be his attempt to make progress.

Number 28 Hope Hill, Barton Ottery, looked as if it had been built as a temporary living place in the Sixties, and somehow survived. It sat on a spur from the chocolate-box pretty hamlet of Venn Ottery like an ugly sister, more a cabin than a home, part PVC and part decaying hardwood. The house had been extended, and Edward could not imagine any council planner agreeing to what he saw – attached to the cabin was a long static trailer which seemed to have been knocked through at one end. The door at the end of the trailer was open, and the front door was ajar, and he heard yelling from inside.

It was the sound of an animal in pain.

He went up to what he thought was the original front door and looked through the glass panels. He saw only darkness. It was a bright day, but he sensed that at the back of the property ('property' needed inverted commas), all light was shut out by curtains. He wondered about ringing but there was no bell. He was about to tap on a cracked pane of glass with a single knuckle when he heard another scream. Definitely a woman.

'Sick, she is, we're used to it.'

He turned and saw a lone figure with a humped back moving at a snail's pace along the grass verge. An older woman with a shawl and a headscarf who had spoken without even looking up at the house.

Edward felt his fear replaced by sadness. This could not be the right property. These could not be the pair who'd attacked him. Even if they were the right size – the couple at the church had both been well over six foot – one of them now sounded like she was dying. And he had thought two men, right?

He was about to turn and leave when he caught sight of a flash of jacket in the hallway, hanging underneath longer raincoats abandoned for summer. On the edge of the jacket sleeve was a line of gold trim.

He moved the door slowly. He heard nothing from inside the house now, as if the people deeper within it had stopped breathing to hear the intruder. Edward shifted his bodyweight in silence, cursing that he was holding his crash helmet. There was a panting noise and another exhalation – not a scream of pain this time, but a deep groan that could have been from a male or female but sounded more like a dog. He stopped. There was a narrow flight of wooden stairs up to his right. The hallway rug was threadbare. The wooden boards beneath it creaked. Without repositioning his feet, he reached left and lifted the raincoats to see the jacket underneath.

There were two. They were huge, deep blue oceans of thick material. They said NYPD on the upper sleeve. They had silver badges on the front with the word POLICE embossed. There were three lines of gold trim at the cuff, which looked more like the kind of embroidery a pilot would have.

They were fancy dress outfits. Bought on Amazon or eBay.

He put his hand underneath the raincoats and felt the material. What . . . the . . . fuck.

So it was them. 'Stop asking questions' – and the violence. The sheer desperate hatred. Why?

He put his hand across the cheap material, turning his body to face the walls. Again, the floorboards complained as his weight shifted. As he reached up behind the raincoats, he felt rubber.

Jesus, no.

He lifted the macs off their hooks carefully. There they were. Two latex masks.

He stared. And then saw the movement in the doorway to his right. A man, at least six foot six, moving towards him.

'YOU—!' the giant screamed.

His own scream was joined by another from within the house. Shit, was the wheelchair woman going to jump up and join in? Edward was frozen to the spot for an instant. Then he jumped across the narrow hallway to the lowest stair. As he did, a hand shot out and grabbed his arm, tearing at the skin, ripping his shirt, losing its grip. It clattered against the side of Edward's head. His hearing aid was knocked out.

Edward backed up on the stair as the man faced him. Tall himself, even one step above the floor, Edward still did not reach his adversary's height. The man had a huge oblong head, wingnut ears, and the most piercing stare Edward had ever seen. The eyes were milky white, the pupils shrunk to a spit of grey. Edward held his crash helmet across his chest so he would have a single chance to fire it out with both hands and hope to catch the giant on the chin. After that, he was done for. Where did the stairs lead? If he ran up them, he was trapped.

'You!' said the man again.

'You weren't police officers. I thought you were police officers,' said Edward breathlessly. 'You're Les and Lily Boyd.'

He hoped their names might stop the man in his tracks, but at that moment, a long breadknife appeared at Boyd's shoulder. Edward did not need to look to see who was around the corner of the wall. The breadknife extended to reveal the other Boyd, who was just as tall, just as heavy, and now standing wheezing beside her husband. She had taken one of the masks and pulled it over her face, but it was not pulled on straight. It gave the horror-movie effect of a person whose head had spun a quarter-revolution. The left eyehole was over her right eye and the mask was moving inwards each time she inhaled. The knobbled walking stick appeared, wedged in the door frame as if it was taking all her weight. The breadknife was now an inch from her husband's jugular.

And there they stood, the only sound the rattling lungs of the woman.

Then Les Boyd said, 'And now we kill you.'

CHAPTER FORTY-ONE

There was an aching pause while Edward faced off against the two giants.

He took a step back and, thank God, found the next stair instead of tripping. The second stair gave him a tiny height advantage over the two, who were struggling to move forwards in the narrow gap between the wall and the rickety wooden banister. It seemed as if the masked woman had no sense of where the breadknife was. She stabbed the air blindly. It could just as easily penetrate her husband as Edward. As she stabbed, she screamed, a guttural noise like a trapped animal.

Les Boyd moved sideways, conscious of the woman's looseness of aim. 'Watch that bloody knife, get back in your chair.'

Edward's vision become hooded, as when a car accident happens and everything tunnels. Les was shoving him, trying to make him fall backwards onto the stairs where presumably Edward would be smothered and stabbed by Lily. He pushed the crash helmet at the giant, hoping to catch him in the face. The woman yelped as if every movement in her body caused terrible pain. It was the sound Edward had heard in his garden, where she had clumped at him with the lock-legged march of a zombie.

The crash helmet had missed Les. It made a dent in the wall opposite. Edward felt his shoe catch on a ruck in the stair carpet and reached left to stop his fall, dropping the helmet. Now he was defenceless. Les moved back. Lily moved forward. She swung the breadknife left and right at him.

'Bloody well take him, Lily, bloody well gut him.' The man's voice. The breadknife swished within an inch of his stomach. Up another stair. She would have to follow him. She took the first stair and stabbed viciously downwards at Edward's feet. He jumped. The knife cracked against the wooden step and got stuck in it. He kicked at her hand as she tried to withdraw it. Les had now moved left and was trying to climb the staircase banister. Up another stair Edward went. He glanced behind him and saw a darkened hallway.

Suddenly there was a silhouette in the pale light. Another person, thin, younger. This was it. He was dead. He had nowhere to go. He half-turned, not wanting to take his eyes off Lily. Directly above him, a man at least thirty years younger than the two giants was wiping tired eyes as if he had just woken.

'Mum, Dad, what the fuck?'

Edward barely heard. The voice was quiet. The hearing aid was knocked out and his damaged ear was the one closest to the younger man. Edward was too panicked to speak.

'This is the fucker,' said Les. 'Questions Man.'

'Mum, what—' The young man seemed to go into shock, his whole body trembling. 'Mum, put down the knife, my God, my God.'

The woman on the stairs pulled her mask off. Edward saw her face, the same face he had seen in the church on the day of the Met's presser, puffy and red, bright ginger hair, freckles.

'This is *him!*' she screamed.

'Get back in your chair, Mum, or you'll faint with the pain.' His eyes flickered to Edward, sprawled on the stairs, and his face tightened.

'*But this cunt—*' she screamed.

'Never mind "*this cunt*", what are you thinking of, threatening him with a knife? What do you think's going to happen? Are you going to *stab* him, really, Mum? Really?' With each question, the young man had taken a step further down the stairs, until he stepped over Edward, and stood between him and the massive couple.

With the son between him and the knife, Edward realized he had to get out of this madhouse before the mood turned again. If the son changed his mind, Edward could not take on all three of them, even with a crash helmet in his hands. He slid down the stairs, along the banister and around the man, pushing past the massive hulk of Lily Boyd.

She yelped again in pain. 'I need to sit down!'

Their eyes met. She leant against the wall and used her walking stick to spear the crash helmet on the floor. She lifted it with the stick and pushed it at Edward.

'Cancer of the pancreas,' she snapped suddenly, fixing mad eyes on him, 'and you won't let me go!'

Edward looked up the stairs. Les might have been stopped by his son but he was deliberately grinding the dropped hearing aid into the stair carpet with the toe of his boot.

'No more questions from you,' hissed Les Boyd.

Regretting that he had not taken Kim's advice and stayed well clear, Edward raced outside and started his moped, as if leaving the scene of his own murder.. When he looked back at the house, the hulk of Lily Boyd was in the doorway, propped up by the gnarled walking stick; father and son behind her. He turned back to the road and jumped. The old lady was standing in front of the bike handlebars. It was the pedestrian he had seen briefly earlier, slowly passing the house, headscarfed, hunched in her shawl.

'We're used to it,' she said. 'The lady is sick.'

'You're telling me,' he said. He tore away, hearing the moped's motor burn with the strain.

CHAPTER FORTY-TWO

At Matty's headstone, he sank to his knees. There was no one around, and he wanted to cry out. The grave was in Topsham, at a spot where the River Exe widened as the sea drew the water towards the beaches at Exmouth. The church had a cemetery over the water.

Matty had been buried in one of the last plots, next to a petite gravestone which said only WTF 1740, presumably the initials of a long-gone Wallace Theodore Flux or Wilma Thea French, although the modern meaning of 'WTF' meant that sometimes Edward came upon people laughing at the stone and photographing it. He never knew whether to be angry or join in.

Today there was no one. Would Tara come? He had sent Matty's mother a message, knowing she was the only one who really understood, even if they had stopped understanding each other years ago. He had stopped the bike and, through tears, texted:

> Really hard at the mo. Thinking Matty. Will be at Topsham in 20 mins to cry

He looked at the words. The message was so incomplete and yet she would understand it. Tara had remarried and had children but neither of them could move on from the day a car ploughed into their son. They had been already divorced, but the joint loss was like a remarriage.

The words on the gravestone were: MATTHEW TEMMIS, LOVED HIS LIFE, LOST IT TOO SOON, BREATHED HIS LAST IN DEVON AIR. The stones around Matthew's plot were weathered by winter rain and wind, and some letters on them were faded to a trace. Edward disliked the way his son's inscription was so new and so bold, a black wound in grey marble.

'Matty, Matty, Matty,' he cried quietly. He remembered the football games on the clifftop, schoolwork that stumped him when he tried to help, the inaugural slice of cake in the Clock Tower Café (too big for an adult, let alone a child), changing nappies in his son's first years, the rush to hospital when they thought their four-year-old had swallowed a battery (it was stuck in his shoe). The images raced like old film which had shuddered off the sprocket wheel, the celluloid shooting out of the projector into a tangle. That's what it was, he thought, a tangle. A tangle of images. A tangle in his mind that any moment of happiness could snag itself on. How could he inflict that on Kim? He had wanted her to move in with him. No wonder she had swerved that.

He might have been crying for five minutes or fifteen. The violence in Barton Ottery had shaken him to his core. His phone stopped him for a moment – Stevie texting:

> RING ME

Normally he would have responded in a second. But he was in the wrong headspace. He walked among the other graves and saw a new headstone like Matty's.

NINA LOPEZ, it said, with the dates. CHILD OF GOD NOW.

So they were united, in a way, he and Andrea Lopez. He hadn't realized Nina was here. He stood staring at the tombstone for as long as he had stared at his own son's.

He was at a loss. He rang Jordan Callintree, who picked up straightaway. The officer's voice had a heaviness to it, a series of words that sounded like one long sigh. 'Are you about to tell me you've found all the stuff we didn't?'

Should he mention the madness at the Boyds' place? What had she said – 'He won't let me go!', when he was not even touching her? What if they only wanted to warn him, to scare him off, but they did not know their own strength?

'Are you there?' asked Callintree.

'Sorry,' said Edward. 'A lot going on at this end. I'm guessing you talked to the lady with dementia at the estate.'

'My officers have interviewed her, yes,' he said, 'and I'm pretty sure they got nowhere.'

'We're just looking at different things.'

'Progress?'

'Confusion.'

'Maybe I've been too hard on my officers.'

'Look, I wanted to speak to Andrea Lopez.'

'Ah. Now that really is tricky.'

'I don't think she'd mind if someone gave me her number. I was at the funeral. I've just discovered her daughter is buried near my son.'

Callintree was silent at the other end for a moment. 'That's heavy. Is it genuinely a call she'd want to get?'

'I can't answer that either way,' said Edward, never taking his eyes off Nina's tombstone.

'Um, let me think about it. I'll send you the number in five minutes if I decide it's okay.'

Edward stood in the graveyard, waiting. Eventually, there was a buzzing and he looked at his phone. There was a number, and the text:

Turn the Dial for Death

> This didn't come from me.

The phone rang several times, then was picked up. The receiver was fumbled for a moment.

'Hello?'

'Mrs Lopez?'

Silence.

'It's Edward Temmis, from the radio station.'

She sounded drunk when she spoke, but then he wondered if she was sedated. 'How nice of you . . . to call.'

'I lost a child too,' he said quietly. 'I'm at my son's grave, in Topsham. Nina is here.'

Silence.

'Please don't speak if it's too much.'

He pictured her in bed, adrift in grief, because he heard a rustling sound that could have been blankets. 'You were at Nina's funeral, Mr Temmis. You gave us more information through the radio than the police did. The police didn't. Even. Damn. Invest-ti-gate.' The staccato delivery was rage, controlled, but only just. 'They closed the case.'

'They haven't closed it, I promise. They just hit a dead end, and the Met left.'

'I have seen no activity. *Nada*. None.' More energy now. He pictured her sitting up, elbows on knees, edge of the bed, hissing into the phone.

'I want to ask you a strange question, Mrs Lopez. They found tubes in the apartment where Lev Malnyk stayed. The police said it showed Malnyk was using, dealing—'

'No, no, no.'

'My friend Stevie heard you didn't believe it.'

'Stevie? Who is that? No, but that's not what those tubes are for. Look, I don't care about Lev Malnyk, maybe he was using drugs, but those tubes were for dialysis. My sister has at-home dialysis for kidney disease. Blood in, blood out.

Machine cleans it when your kidney doesn't work. Saved my sister's life.'

'That's an expensive machine to have in your house.'

'Oh, thousands of dollars, sure. Health Service would lend it unless you are rich.'

'Thank you, Andrea.'

'I was a nurse once. Sorry if I sound dopey. I asked for tranquillizers. They make me sleep all the time. Nina . . .'

It was appropriate, he thought, as she clicked off the line, that her daughter's name was the last word in the conversation, almost as if she was reaching for the little girl as she fell back to sleep.

He opened his phone and googled KIDNEY DIALYSIS MACHINE BONNET.

The webpage returned with a question: *Did you mean Kidney Dialysis Machine Bonot?*

So that's what it was. In his haste to scout the flat, Cammell-Curzon had misread the brand name and misrecognized the machine, which was understandable, a great lump of complicated white goods like that. Lev Malnyk was not 3D printing, he was on dialysis, and the police had missed it because . . .

Because the machine had been removed from his apartment the instant the accident happened.

The call sank Edward into deep thought, and he walked back towards his son's resting place. As he approached the grave, he saw the willowy figure of Tara there.

'Who were you calling?'

There was no harm in telling her. 'The mother of Nina, the little girl who—'

'I know who Nina is. Right now, everyone in the country knows.'

'She's buried over there.' The phrase was so brutal he put his hand up to his chest and crossed himself.

'Poor sweet little innocent lamb.'

He regarded his ex-wife with tenderness. She was always well turned-out, with dark mascara and oxblood lipstick. Tara exuded a have-to-be-somewhere-else-in-a-minute vibe, always, but reached out her arms.

'Come here, old man.'

He sank into her body and cried.

'What's brought this on?'

No one else could ask that question. The death of a child didn't 'come on' – it was never absent. But Edward knew what Tara meant.

'Oh,' he wept, 'a number of things. Being misrecognized as someone's dead son didn't exactly help. Being called "sonny" by a randomer. And this Nina case.'

'You're not involved in that, though?'

'Just helping the police a little.'

'What? Did they ask you?'

'Actually, yes.' He felt proud at his answer, but when he pulled away a little and wiped his eyes, he saw her looking at him with something like pity. 'Every time the paper refers to you, they say "crime-busting Edward Temmis, known as Devon's Rockford", or something.'

'Rockford as in *The Rockford Files*?'

'I guess so?'

He hugged her again, more formally this time. 'I hope you get hugs like that at home.'

'Don't . . .' she began. 'Don't do that.'

'No, I mean, if the sadness strikes you.'

'Oh. Well, thank you. I do.' She stared at him, her big brown eyes piercing. 'I have to be somewhere. I want to catch up. I'll always come to his grave for you, always. I'm here all the time. I love that he can hear the water.'

'Thanks, Tara.'

'How's that lady of yours?'

'Eh?' He was not aware they had even discussed Kim.

'What's her name? Vim?'

'Don't do that,' he said, borrowing her phrase. Tara responded by curling her fingers and placing the heels of her hands together, making a heart.

'Two hearts,' he said.

'Don't do that either.' They smiled at each other. Losing a child could break two people apart. But it also bonded them for eternity.

He did not see her leave. He was looking down at Matty's headstone and his whole body shook with the agony of it. *She has other children now*, he reminded himself, feeling disloyal to Tara even by having the thought. His body pinged and cracked, as if a loose power cable was swinging left and right inside him. What was this, Matty trying to tell him something? Two hearts?

Two hearts.

He felt those words burst inside him. The letters enlarged and broke, became fragments, dispersed, gathered again and made the words: TWO HEARTS.

'What are you trying to tell me, Matty?'

He sank to his knees and, for the first time, reached out with his hands and held the top of the gravestone. But the sobs would not come. This time his mind, far from being overwhelmed with emotion, sharpened. He opened his eyes. He was six inches from the bevelled edge of the grey marble, and every tiny indent came into focus. And now, as he let his brain lead him, a single fact took its rightful place.

Hearts.

The referee on the tenancy was a doctor called Hearts.

Hearts did not exist.

But Hurst did.

And because Edward had written 'Hurst', he had missed the obviously alternative spelling . . .

Hearst.

Change one letter . . .

There was a real doctor somewhere here. He knew now that there *must* be a real doctor, because Lev Malnyk had thousands of pounds' worth of expensive medical equipment in his flat. So why had the doctor put his name down wrong on the tenancy agreement and why had he not come forward to the police after the crash?

Because he wanted to be untraceable.

Was it possible that Wendy's doctor friend was the elusive Dr Hearts?

He thought of Stevie: 'Are you saying these two cases are connected?'

The simplest question of all. And he had laughed at her.

CHAPTER FORTY-THREE

Kim stared at the parcel on the floor of her flat. She could not believe it. The cardboard flaps at the top of the box stood upright, where she had cut the tape and pulled them open. Now she was sitting at the other end of her hallway, bum on the hardwood floor, feeling the bones in her hips but unable to move.

The towel had fallen off her ten minutes earlier. She did not gather it. Naked, she stared and stared.

She fetched her phone and texted Edward:

> Ring me

Then texted Stevie to see if Edward was with her, then let the phone drop to the floor with a rattle, as if the strength had fled her. As if the contents of the parcel, even at the other end of the hallway, were draining her ability to move.

The delivery had come when she was at home, at half past six, which was a stroke of luck, and she tried to imagine what might have happened if the courier had left it outside the door of her flat or, even worse, on the communal steps at the front of the building. Fortunately, they had rung the bell. She braved the shared stairs, having broken off from washing her hair, a towel wrapped around her hair and a larger one hiding her body. Her feet made damp marks on the carpet. The courier was on a motorbike, and he gave her the parcel two-handed and was already wheeling away when she was asking, 'Do I sign?'

Back in her flat, Kim had dropped the parcel on the floor – it was too heavy to hold for long, and her first thought was a delivery of books. She boiled the kettle for tea. She got back into the shower and made sure all the shampoo was washed out. She sat on the loo and had a wee, then stood at the bathroom mirror naked and plucked out a few stray eyebrows. She must eat a little more or train a little less, the bones abrupt in her face, always her mother's greatest concern: 'And I can *see your cheekbones*!'

The parcel was almost forgotten. She wrapped the towel around herself, saw it in the hall, fetched the smallest knife from the block in the kitchenette. What could it be?

In marker pen the front of the box said KIM, just her first name. Underneath were her flat number and postcode. There was no return address. 'By hand' was written in the top corner in the same black marker. She suddenly thought – bomb. She had seen too many Bourne and Bond films. Bombs were heavier, right? The box was a foot square at the end, maybe a little longer crossways. She took the knife to the line of tape that held the flaps together and saw the money.

She stared and stared. Money? At first she thought there was too much to count. But the notes were in bundles, held tight with banknote straps. She pulled out twenties at first. She flicked through them to check every note was for the same amount.

Then Kim went to find her kitchen scales. She counted a bundle of twenties – fifty, so a thousand pounds. She weighed them: 47 grams. Then a bundle four times the size, a whisker under 185 g. Four thousand pounds. She pulled out at least ninety more bundles, some a grand, some four. She weighed a few. All were exact, either 52 g or 185 g. One wad weighed 198 g – she counted each note with fingertip and tongue, and found an extra fifteen notes. Her head spun. But the thicker wads made it easier. There were fifty, along with fifty of the lighter ones, all packed tightly in the box – she made that a quarter of a million in cash.

Her eye went to the layer of green crêpe paper separating the twenties from the rest of the box. She pulled it away gingerly. Now her heart slammed in her chest. The towel had fallen away and she was counting naked. There were wads of fifties. She thumbed through one: fifty notes. £2,500. She weighed it: 46 g. She found another bundle twice as big. The second bundle was £5,000. Then a bundle four times the size of the first. £10,000. Then another forty, another layer of crêpe paper, and fifty more. Then she saw the wads of hundred-pound notes.

On her phone she asked ChatGPT, 'How much does a UK banknote weigh?' The answer was instant: *UK banknotes, regardless of denomination, weigh approximately 0.9 grams each. This weight is consistent across all denominations, including £5, £10, £20, £50, and £100.*

She turned the box upside-down and separated the wads into different denominations. Fetching a mixing bowl from the kitchen, she placed it on the scales and weighed ten wads at a time. She used her phone to make the calculation: £250,000 in twenties; £500,000 in fifties; £260,000 in hundreds. She thought she was heading for a million, but the amount was a little over. The absence of a round total bothered her, until she found the scrap of paper at the bottom of the box.

Turn the Dial for Death

£1m for the flat, £10k for you.

That was when she messaged Edward. Hearing nothing back, she texted Stevie.

> He's not with me that's for sure

> I've messaged him for you. S

Which unsettled Kim. She wondered if the texts might be evidence of her having received this box, which she must tell the police about as soon as possible. But wait – if it was payment for the flat, it was payment for the flat. She hated the idea that those two, that dodgy pair, would be the owners of her perfect penthouse, but this took persistence to a new level. She could not simply send the money back. How did you move a million pounds anyway? She would be fearful even of walking to the car with it.

She had forgotten she was naked. She spooled through the events of the last half-hour to totally understand what had just happened. Doorbell, evening delivery; motorbike courier. (Did he know he was carrying more than a million pounds in banknotes? Had he ridden all the way from the City of London with them? What if he came back tonight, broke in, robbed her?). Carrying box up to flat; towel falls off; box opened, money. Now what?

She hated to be the damsel in distress – hated it more than she could ever say – but she must speak to Edward. Not text, not WhatsApp. Actually speak. He would focus on what had happened, assuming he was not distracted. She grabbed her dressing gown from the bedroom, put her phone in the pocket and dropped into an armchair in the living room where she could have the conversation. She did not put the lights on. The sun was down.

When she looked right along the hallway, she saw the box sitting there, wads of banknotes strewn around it. She chewed her lip, stood up and walked over to the box. She paused for a second, then went to the kitchen and carefully packed the money tightly into a casserole dish, opened the oven door and slid the heavy round dish inside. She closed the oven door. No one would find the money there.

She called Edward.

Edward did not hear the phone. He was on his moped, racing through Sidmouth, mind moving as fast as the bike. In a single instant, in the crash-zoom of pain and concentration that came to him at Matty's grave, he had moved the case forwards with a leap. If Wendy Wrigley's Dr Hearst was involved, then Wendy needed to know because she might be in danger. But why would the man have removed the dialysis machine the instant the accident happened?

Evidently the doctor wanted no connection with Malnyk. There might be innocent reasons for that, or there might not.

As he reached Sidmouth's promenade, the sun was now fully down, the summer sea as calm as a garden pond.

He was opposite the pizza parlour, the burnt-out shell like a broken tooth in a pretty mouth. Local businesses were fundraising for better hoarding, with suggestions including the old cartoon of the bellied man in the bathing costume with a knotted handkerchief springing across a beach: 'COME TO SIDMOUTH!' To Edward, the burned building spoke of the death of Nina. There was still a faint aroma of soot and carbonized plastic. He switched off his bike and leant it against the waist-high promenade wall. No one would mind it being on the pavement after sundown. In a town where there had been an explosive tragedy, an unlocked moped was still safe after dark.

He tried to call Wendy Wrigley but the phone went to messages. The signal was poor, and it was possible his new number was unrecognized by her phone, so she would treat him as an unknown caller and block him. Damn, that was annoying. Now he saw he had a missed call from Kim. He had that back-and-forth moment, as when you walk along a thoroughfare and try to avoid an oncoming pedestrian, who goes left when you go right, right when you go left; and after left–right, right–left, you both stop and regroup. Kim–Wendy, Wendy–Kim. Eventually:

'Kim?'

'Edward.' The signal was terrible.

'Jesus thank God.' All one word: *Jesusthankgod*.

He wanted to say, 'Wait. I'm the one with the news. I've worked something out I think, and—'

But she was away. 'That couple. Tank and Fire. Oh, sorry, you wouldn't know them that way. The parachutes. Crystal meth. The crims – I don't know if they are, but I think they are.'

'Slow down.'

'You're breaking up.'

'I said slow down.'

'They've sent me – come on,' Kim went on, almost gabbling the words, 'you must know. You overheard them.'

'Under your car? The strange duo.'

'Who asked about crystal meth.'

'I don't know about that.'

'Weren't you there when I . . . look, never mind,' she went on. 'The point is that they've sent me the [CRACKLE] for the flat in [HISS].'

Edward said: 'I can't hear you and I don't know if it's your phone or mine. Look, I've worked something important out!'

She was still speaking, every other word replaced by a snap, crackle or pop. At some point he swore she said 'one million pounds', but the rest was lost.

'I've worked something out!' he tried again, but the line was dead, the signal swept away across the sea. Had she turned her phone off?

He called Stevie. 'Can you meet me at my house?'

'Sure. When?'

'In half an hour?'

'It's late. I'll get my dad to bring me.'

He had forgotten she had no car, not even a bike.

'Get a taxi, I'll pay.'

'What's it for?'

'I've worked something out but I don't know what it means.'

He texted Kim.

> That call broke up. What's going on?

He got nothing back. Was her phone off?

He sent her a second message.

> You get on with Wendy Wrigley. Can you call her for me? She isn't replying to mine. Tell her that doc friend HEARST (not Hurst) may have something to do with Lev Malnyk and to STAY WELL CLEAR.

As the text sent, he reached his hand into the pocket of his jacket and found a small object. The memory fob Callintree had given him with the crime scene photos. He stared at it for a moment and dropped it back into his pocket.

At home he waited for Stevie. The house yawned and sighed around him, as if it wanted to help work the puzzle out. He walked upstairs to his Post-it wall. He found the square that said 'Hurst Hurst'. What if that should have been *Hearst Hearst?* Where would that get him? The dementia lady had seen some strange people – the man in the mirror – removing a boat or box or whatever she thought it was – boat, box? How on earth could she be a reliable source?

But it must have been the dialysis machine she saw. And it was removed rapidly, within hours of Malnyk's accident. Why? Because they did not want the police following the dialysis machine back to the doctor. But why? Why, why, why, why? Was one of Jonathan Wrigley's doctor friends involved with the ampoules somehow? Why? What could a doctor possibly want with radioactive capsules?

He fished the fob out of his pocket again, struck by a thought. Originally he had needed confirmation that he and Wendy Wrigley had located the spot where her husband had killed himself, and not been looking in the wrong place. By the time Callintree gave him the crime scene pictures, they were irrelevant – he had already been forced to tell Wendy what he had found, all the clues that led to her husband's suicide. It all added up; he had solved it. She was happy. They had been in the right place.

But now he stood in the darkened hallway of his home, staring at the fob.

He went to the PC and turned it on, slotting the fob into a USB socket that hung from the back of the tower. It showed up on the desktop with the warning, *DANGER: Think before opening outside sources like this.* He had spent enough time thinking. He clicked.

When he saw the crime scene photos arranged like a grid on the screen, he breathed a sigh of relief. That was the very spot. Well, he knew it must have been. He saw Callintree had not included any close-ups of the doctor's body – a serious crime if he had done, never mind sackable offence – so the most he saw of Dr Wrigley was a flash of white clothing in the corner of some shots. He killed himself in a white suit, in order, they assumed, to be found faster.

There were more than two hundred photos on the drive. They covered that patch of forest from all angles. Outward, looking from the tree; and then focused on the place where the body lay. He looked at the trunk of the ash and began to zoom in.

His jaw dropped open as he stared.

CHAPTER FORTY-FOUR

Edward needed to act fast. He jumped from the computer and grabbed his phone. The message to Kim! He opened WhatsApp and saw – thank God – the ticks against the message were still grey, so she had not seen it. He deleted the text as the doorbell rang.

Ah, Stevie would help. He could see the blonde frizz just above the line of the frosted panes in his front door. He threw the door open before she could ring the bell again, startling her.

'Did your dad bring you?'

'Yes, he's—'

The car engine revved on the road. Edward rushed past Stevie into the darkness, almost pushing her, trying to catch the car. 'We need him to take us . . . Hey! Hey, vicar!'

He sprinted towards the rear lights as they receded, hoping the man in the front seat might look at his rear-view mirror, see the shape in pursuit and stop the car. But he did not. Stevie was walking towards him down the street.

'"Hey Hey Vicar" was a Sixties song, wasn't it?'

'Wendy,' was all he could say.

'What? Get your breath back.'

'Wendy . . . the photos of the scene . . .'

'Man, you need a cup of tea and a sit-down. What the fuck is wrong with you? You look like Heart Attack Jack.' Then, with unusual softness, she asked: 'What's eating you, Edward?'

He barely heard the words, relying on the movement of her lips. 'Come upstairs to my wall,' he said. 'Quickly.'

She did as requested, the stairs creaking under their feet. Almost to herself, Stevie said: 'You know, when this place goes off the cliff, you may not get a warning? You'll just get creaking like this.'

'I lost my hearing aid if you're speaking,' said Edward in front of her. 'I need to face you. Apologies.'

'How does a person lose a hearing aid?' muttered Stevie.

In the Post-it room, Edward went through his routine. He switched on the spotlight and picked up a laser pen. 'Take a look at the words on the squares. Remember what you said?'

'No,' said Stevie a little bolshily. 'You'll have to be more specific.'

He turned on the laser pointer and a red dot appeared in the circle of the 'O' of TOPPINGS. 'I've focused on this side, because I thought we were done with the Wrigley case.'

'Um, I thought we were too.'

'Well, I took her to that spot in the forest and found the tree. I know it was the right tree, by the way, because I looked at the crime scene photos just now. In the forest I found the hole drilled into the tree and used Wendy's spoolie to get at what was inside.'

'You did. You told me.'

The laser dot had swept left to the word 'Spoolie' now.

'But what I hadn't thought of until now was she told me she was allergic to a lot of make-up on the day we met, and she specifically mentioned mascara.'

'It would explain why the brush wasn't like everyone else's,' said Stevie. 'When you showed us the silk handkerchief with the explosive on, I remember thinking it's the first time I've seen a mascara brush without loads of shite caked on it.' There was a pause. 'So why the hell did she have the brush then?'

'Because she bought it for the purpose. *She brought it for me, Stevie,*' said Edward. 'The neat white silk square, too, I've no doubt. She knew what we were going to find because she had put it there. Right down to the powder in that hole.'

'What?' said Stevie. 'No, no.'

'Yes! And she made sure I had the tools. I just looked at the crime scene photos. I didn't even bother before because we'd tied the whole thing up, or so I thought. I zoomed in on the tree; there was no hole in the trunk. She drilled it later. She drilled it for me.' He kicked the wall. 'And I thought I'd been so bloody clever,' said Edward, turning off the laser pen and dropping it into the shoebox on the floor. 'Thought we'd solved it. What an absolute plonker.' He pulled the sticky note marked 'Forest' off the wall. 'I went into the forest with Wendy, looking for the spot, and she said, "A clearing is a place without trees, but this was a clearing *with* a tree. How do you see a guy from the air if he's underneath a tree?" And like the mug I am, I thought I'd got the answer ahead of her. I thought she hadn't understood the clue she gave me, but she knew right enough. She might as well have directed me there.'

'It's sounds like you're dealing with a criminal brain here.'

'Oh, and the accidental remark which I didn't clock at the time – "I have a phone signal, good old Chittlehamholt." She wouldn't say that if, as she claimed, she hadn't been there before. Reliable, trusty Chittlehamholt. Wendy swore it was her first time.'

'But she can't have killed him. She was in the cinema.'

'Watching her first Marvel film, on an afternoon? But maybe someone else killed him and she was in on it.'

'But why?'

'Let me show you something.'

He pulled the Post-it note with the two doctors' names on. 'Hurst Hurst.' Those are Dr Jonathan Wrigley's university mates who still live in the area. I met them, just sweet cancer specialists, nothing to see there, as gentle as monks. But that's how I spelled the name – H.U.R.S.T.'

'How else would you spell it?'

'H.E.A.R.S.T. That's the other spelling.'

Stevie was rubbing her forehead. 'It's dark in here and I have a headache. How does the other spelling help?'

'Because Hearst is a scrambled version of "Hearts", the doctor who signed Lev Malnyk's rental agreement, the doctor who had Lev Malnyk as a patient, supplying him with a kidney dialysis machine that was then removed after Lev's death. He made his name untraceable when he signed that rental agreement, but he didn't want to write an entirely false name down. He writes "Hearts", and it leads everyone astray.'

'Dialysis?'

'I spoke to Andrea Lopez. You *are* genius, Stevie, getting that information from Cammell-Curzon. He saw a big machine in the flat. The police found those tubes. But they were nothing to do with drug use and the machine was not a 3D printer. It was a dialysis unit and those were the tubes you need to get the blood in and out. Oh,' exclaimed Edward, 'God alive, I've got it! I've got it! The lady with dementia—'

There was a banging at the front door.

'Wait here.'

'Who are you expecting?'

'Hopefully Kim. Then I can tell her what I've told you and we can work out what the hell Lev Malnyk was doing carrying radiation around Sidmouth on his motorbike, and why it got Dr Wrigley killed. Hang on up here, I'll bring her up.'

*

Edward felt a lightness of head he had never experienced before, as if clouds had parted in his mind. There was such a beauty to the solution, but the picture in his brain was like a painting with a circle cut out of the centre.

As he bounded down the stairs, he stopped for a second.

The stairs. That made him think of Les and Lily Boyd. Their attack on him was not random. At their house, their violence had redoubled. Lily was ill. She used a wheelchair when she wasn't trying to kill radio presenters. Unhinged, maybe dying. So why would a dying woman scream like that at him? Why would they be furious about his "questions"? Why, when he was not touching her, did she scream those five words—

You won't let me go.

Something else came to him. When they had beaten him up in his garden, he thought they had tried to push him over the cliff. But that grab of his arm – by Les Boyd, he was sure – was not to push him. It stopped him falling. They didn't want to go that far. It was something other than psychopathic hatred. *Stop asking questions.*

He froze on the staircase.

What was he missing?

The second knock at the front door jolted him back to reality. He opened it. Kim was standing there in the porch light. Her expression was odd: lips pursed and eyes narrowed a little, as if she had just been bitten by an insect.

'Thank God,' he said. 'I need to talk to you about Wendy.'

Kim's brow furrowed. Wendy Wrigley herself appeared. She had been standing to Kim's right, out of view of the front door. 'That sounds serious, Edward. Why am I in danger?'

He said nothing for a second, just processing.

'Your message to Kim said I was in danger. Why?'

'It's just a worry I have. Come in, both.' He was about to say, 'Stevie's upstairs,' and call her, but something stopped him.

'We raced here after Kim got your message,' said Wendy. 'It sounds really scary.'

Had he got this completely wrong? No. The crime scene photos . . . oh God, no. The police images were still on the screen on the PC in the lounge. A zoomed-in photo of the tree trunk without a hole in it. Would the screensaver have come on? Wrigley must be kept away from that room. He spoke as naturally as he could. 'I didn't think you saw my message, Kim.'

'I did—'

'But the blue ticks—'

'Oh. Well, yes, I saw it on my lock screen. I rang Wendy and she came straight to me and insisted we come over.'

'I'll always be grateful to both of you if you've saved me from something horrible. I do have money to make it up to you,' she said. 'Edward, you've already saved my reputation. A solicitor has the details of what you discovered vis-à-vis the death of Jonathan, and he was stunned by how brilliant you were. He believes we'll be able to reopen the inquest and get our suicide verdict.' She added, 'Tragically.'

And here we go, thought Edward. The child actor will now perform. Hadn't she been in a TV soap once? And she had flannelled him about not being any good as an actor 'because I'm just too truthful'. As if. Well, he needed to be at the same level and give nothing away.

'I was worried,' said Wendy. 'If you know something more—'

He would give her Hearst and see the reaction.

Edward said carefully, 'I think your husband's friends, the Hearsts, might have a connection to the pizza crash. The Ukrainian who smashed into Toppings had a doctor called Hearts; he was down as a referee on the flat rental. I thought Hearst was H.u.r.s.t. but then it came to me, Hearst and Hearts. So that was my worry. You need to be careful with those twins from now on.'

A strange look crossed Wendy's face, as if she was going through a dozen possible replies in a fraction of a second. 'Oh no. No. That makes no sense. I'm close to Hubert. He would have mentioned something so dramatic, surely? You're sounding very excited, if I may say so.'

She's ducking and diving, thought Edward. He would increase the pressure a little. 'Did Hubert or Charlie ever mention Lev Malnyk to you?'

'Shall we have a cup of tea before we talk? I'm parched.'

Kim was silent. She must have worked out that something was very wrong. He knew the tone of the conversation would sound starchy to her, and not at all collaborative, as if he and Wrigley were touching swords but not yet fencing. On another occasion Kim would have made herself part of the conversation, but not now.

He made three cups of tea in the kitchen as Wendy watched him like a hawk.

Finally Kim said, 'Why did you tell me Wendy was at risk, Edward?'

'Because of these Hearsts. If they're connected to the motorbiker, then—'

'Oh, this is so silly!' Wendy exclaimed. 'You've met the twins, you couldn't find a more gentle pair if you tried! Shall I call them and get them to come around?'

'That might not be a good idea,' said Edward, feeling his pulse quicken. *Please, no.*

'Oh, we must! If only for amusement. They are so kind; lovely friends to my husband since university and I feel certain that they will enjoy our little performance.'

The last word conveyed threat more than any other might. Before either of them could stop her, Wendy had put on her reading glasses and opened the contacts on her phone.

Kim and Edward stared at each other.

They heard Wendy's side of the conversation only.

'Ladram Bay.' She gave the address. 'The famous house that's falling off the cliff. Tonight. It's the radio presenter. Talking about Toppings *again* . . .' The last word emphasized with a roll of the eyes, as if they were the last people in town still droning on about the pizza parlour crash. Wendy laughed. 'Yes. Yes, I think so . . . Yes. No. Just Edward and his delightful girlfriend, Kim.' She hung up.

The three of them were silent.

Edward wished he could speak to Kim on her own, tell her the incredible level of danger he was feeling at this very moment under the veneer of this classy, tidy Devon lady, her searching gaze clear of any mascara or eyeshadow. It occurred to him that the whole story she had told him about Dr Jonathan Wrigley 'getting tired', changing his diet, 'being unable to do small tasks for patients like sewing', slowing down, losing focus . . . it had all been made up. All designed to lead Edward to the conclusion that a victim of murder had taken his own life.

Good God alive, did he look like the mug she must have thought he was? *'Mr Temmis, I want you to investigate me.'*

He was still struggling to understand the sequence of events. Say one of the Hearsts had gone out with Jonathan and the crossbow, ostensibly to shoot rabbits, and turned the weapon on him. But if he wanted to make it look like suicide, he would have left the crossbow at the scene, surely? By removing the crossbow, the unknown Hearst had created a crime scene. The lack of suspects had confused Devon Police utterly and led to an open verdict. Something must have gone wrong. Something that meant they had to remove the weapon.

'I need the loo if you don't mind,' said Wendy. 'While we wait for the boys.'

'Around the corner on the left,' said Edward.

When she left the kitchen, she pulled the door to. It gave Edward the chance to lean over to Kim. 'She's got something to do with it, the Toppings crash.'

'What?' asked Kim, jaw dropping. 'I saw she was behaving oddly; I didn't want to say or do anything to show her I'd noticed.'

'What do you mean, oddly?'

'Hyper. Blinking a lot. When we arrived, she said she'd hide by the front door to make it a surprise for you. I think she just wanted to hear what you said if you didn't know she was there.'

'Bastard. I can't explain yet.' He lowered his voice even further. 'Stevie's upstairs but say nothing about that. Hopefully she can hear what's going on.'

'She might have fallen asleep. Where's your hearing aid gone?'

'Pardon?'

'Don't bloody joke with me at this moment.'

'I'm not, I genuinely didn't hear you.'

The loo flushed. 'I said – oh, never mind.' The kitchen door opened. It was a different Wendy who stood in front of them. Her eyes blazed. The perception of increased height – her standing, the two of them sitting at the kitchen table – gave her presence added authority. She was the teacher. They were at her school. They would listen.

'Kim, could you come here for a moment? I want you to come here so I can show you something.'

Kim hesitated, but at an almost imperceptible nod from Edward, did as she was summoned to. What danger could there be with two against one? She was several inches taller than Wendy Wrigley, who now moved to her left, easing herself between Kim and the kitchen counter.

'What's going on?' asked Edward.

'Edward, dear, do you remember us meeting on the day of that Harpford Hall event, with everyone misunderstanding what you were saying because you had no voice? I thought, "Here he is. I've found my simpleton." But I think I misunderstood you too.'

She squeezed a hand into her skirt pocket, withdrew a key and threw it on the table.

'Take this, you'll need it in a minute.'

'What is it?' asked Edward.

Kim stood stock still. 'What is this about? Edward's trying to help you. *We're* trying to help you.'

'You know,' said Wendy, 'I might have believed that until I took the merest snoop into your lounge, and saw your computer. Tut-tut, Mr Temmis. Someone's not very good with their screen discipline, are they?'

'Edward?' Kim asked.

Wrigley rootled around in her handbag for a second. In a flash she had nail scissors against Kim's throat.

The sharp ends were pushing into the skin, and a drop of scarlet appeared where the vein was already punctured.

'Kim!' Edward shouted.

Wendy started to speak very quickly. 'I don't know how you got those police photos, Mr Radio Show, but I know you're in deep with that policeman, and I can see exactly what you've been looking at. No hole, right? That's me judged. Judge and jury you are, worse than all the sodding seaside chavs in this stinking town.'

Kim screamed as the scissors went further in.

'If you want to save your little lady here,' Wrigley began, 'you'll take this key now, *now*, and lock yourself in the toilet I've just been in. You won't get out of the window, either, because you'd need to be a midget and the lock is rusted shut. So, lock yourself in and push the key under the door.'

She jabbed the nail scissors further into Kim's neck. Now blood was running down her throat. Kim yelped again. Edward stood. He had to pass Wendy and Kim on his way out of the kitchen – could he take Wrigley? He bet he could. He was more than a foot taller and at least five stone heavier.

But as he weighed up the possibility, Wendy said: 'In the words of Clint Eastwood, before you decide to rush me, *honey*, ask yourself if you feel lucky. Well do ya? Because if you aren't, your sexy lover here will go to the floor with these scissors deep inside her jugular. And she will bleed out while the ambulance tries to find your ruin of a house in the dark. So think about it.'

At which Kim cried, 'Noooooo . . . no, Edward, don't try anything, please.'

So he did not. He shot Wendy Wrigley a baleful stare and picked the key off the table, scraping it into the wood as he did.

She said: 'And your mobile, please.'

He pulled his new smartphone out of his trousers and dropped it on the table. As he left the kitchen, hearing Kim's whimpering, Wendy shouted: 'Now! Don't delay! Lock that door!'

He saw Stevie's mobile on the window ledge by the front door. *Oh please*, he begged, *no one call it*. He shut himself in the loo. Could he just pretend to lock it? Too obvious. He turned the key and sealed himself in.

Then he did what he was told. Pushed the key back under the door.

CHAPTER FORTY-FIVE

Kim was going into shock – her legs trembled and spots danced at the corners of her eyes.

'I can't stand,' she whispered.

'Then walk,' said Wendy. She forced Kim into the hallway and towards the left, up to the toilet door. 'Pick up the loo key there. Don't try anything.' Kim bent, shaking, for a moment releasing the pressure of the scissors on her neck. Then she felt the point of metal in her side as she moved lower to pick up the key.

Kim squealed as the blade pierced the skin between her ribs.

From inside the loo, Edward said: 'Kim! Kim darling! Are you okay?'

She did not have the courage to answer. Wendy pulled at the door to check it was locked. 'Sit on the bottom stair,' she told Kim. 'Don't move from there, not even for a second.'

'You wouldn't kill me,' said Kim, hoping Stevie was listening but wondering if the total silence upstairs meant she had fled the house to get help. Did she have her phone? Would she be heard if she made a call?

'All I wanted was for Edward to clear my name after that

botched business in the forest. And he did. You're standing in the way of me and a lot of money, sweetheart, and that's not a safe place to be.'

'I don't understand,' said Kim. 'Was the motorbike crash your doing?'

'Nope. That was all Lev, a bloody freak accident that's nearly scuppered us. No reason for that to happen whatsoever.'

'Was he a terrorist?'

'The opposite! A quiet chap. You might almost say a peacefulist.'

'I don't understand,' said Kim.

'Can Edward hear me in there?' asked Wendy, a little more loudly than Kim was speaking. 'No. Okay. Well. We had a great scheme, and it nearly went wrong, and tonight we'll get it back on track.'

'What do you mean?'

'You're going to die. You and that disc-jockey idiot who's locked himself in the loo. But wait a while. All will become clear. Do you need another tea towel?'

Kim was pressing a handkerchief to her neck to mop the blood. She should stem the flow by pushing harder. 'No.'

'You mean, "No thank you, Wendy." Where have your manners gone?'

'Can I ask you something?'

'Sure.'

'Do you have anything to do with the people trying to buy the Thirdfield Terrace flat?'

Wendy looked genuinely confused.

'No.'

'I don't think I believe you.'

'We've always rented because of Jonathan's job.' It was strange, hearing her refer to her husband as if the marriage was normal and his death had been a natural end.

'Why did you kill him?'

'I didn't! I was in a cinema, watching Marvel, hadn't you heard?'

'Why did Dr Hearst kill his friend?'

'I'll give you two words to help you work it out. Ready?'

'Yes.'

'Assisted—'

There was a single loud bang on the front door. Kim suddenly worried that Stevie might have actually fallen asleep, might now be woken by the noise and come down without thinking. *Please Stevie, don't answer that knock*, she willed.

Wendy said, 'Ah, I only gave you the one word. It'll have to do. Our visitors are here. Don't move or it will not go well for you.'

Kim knew this was her only chance. As Wendy opened the front door, she lunged up the stairs. But she missed her footing immediately and heard an exhaled gasp from Wendy and a rush behind her. She was dragged back down the stairs by someone with impossible strength, her head bumping the threadbare carpet on the way down.

In the hallway, Kim lay face down, not wanting to rise and see who had come through the front door. It must be the Hearsts . . .

She felt Wendy sit on her back.

'Bitch,' said Wendy Wrigley. 'You're lucky I'm not taking these scissors to your skinny butt. I will in a second.'

Edward shouted, 'Kim?'

'Don't do that,' said a man's voice. 'No marks.'

'Hmpf,' said Wendy. 'Fine.'

Kim shuddered with sobs, tears streaming down her cheeks. Without any chink of doubt, she was going to die.

'Look at the computer,' Wendy instructed the new arrival.

Kim heard steps on the carpet – more than one person now – and then, from the lounge, where the computer was, loud cursing. 'How the fuck did he get these?'

'It's that policeman. It must be,' a second voice said.
'This is on you,' voice one said.
'I don't see why.'
'Because you took the crossbow away!'
'I've told you why a thousand times.'
'Roll her over.'
They took Kim's body, stiff with panic, and turned her over.

The toilet door opened inwards, and was quite heavy, which would make breaking it down nigh on impossible. Edward had heard the sound of others arriving in the house – and at least one man's voice – but it was impossible to make out details of the exchanges through the thick wood he pressed his ear to. After the horrible scream and then a sound on the stairs which could have been Kim escaping, falling or being dragged, it was too quiet to hear more. The keyhole was too near the door jamb to allow him space to press his good ear against that. He tried an eye against the keyhole, saw nothing but blurred shapes. Worried about Stevie's phone again: *Don't ring.* They would know she was in the house if it did.

He began to despair. No sound was bad news, he was sure of that. Was the new arrival the other Hearst twin? He put the lid down on the toilet seat and sat there, willing himself to concentrate. The loo window was tiny, and jammed shut. Still, he could hear the sea on the other side of the door. Wendy seeing the police photo of the undrilled tree trunk had been a disaster of the first order. But until he had seen it himself, he had not understood how completely the doctor's widow had suckered him. And for what? She needed to clear her name, but what was the connection to the Toppings crash? How the hell could she be involved in that?

At the loo door, he heard a voice.

'Temmis, I'm going to unlock the door and open it slowly.'

'Who is this?' he asked.

'Charlie Hearst.'

As the door inched open, Kim came into view. She was in the armchair at the other end of the hallway, gagged, eyes bulging. Beside her was Hubert Hearst, recognizable from his shock of white hair. He was holding a syringe.

'Kim?' asked Edward.

A movement to his left, his brain sparked and he was unconscious.

CHAPTER FORTY-SIX

When Edward came round, he was on a chair in his garden facing the sea. His head thumped and his temples burned. How long had he been out for? The ocean came into a kind of focus, though it was ten miles of blackest water beyond the cliff. The moon hid its face behind a long strip of grey cloud. He was tied thoroughly to the chair, but not gagged. He opened and closed his mouth, feeling the pain as his jaw worked. He moved his elbow and it touched something. Kim was beside him, similarly bound but gagged.

Charlie Hearst moved slowly around the front of the pair. The vague light of the moon framed him as he spoke. He had the unquestionable authority of the surgeon. His voice was calm.

'I feel we should give you an explanation before you die. And a choice.'

Hubert appeared at his side. Edward was staggered again at the incredible physical similarity, save the hair colour. 'We work together,' said Hubert. 'In everything.'

'And we believe in choice, don't we, Hub?' said Charlie. 'That's how all this started. Why don't you tell us, Edward?'

'Tell you what?'

'What you worked out. I want to know.'

He looked sideways at Kim. There was now a fresh plaster on her neck, as if the twins had treated her for the injuries Wendy had caused.

'I spoke to a lady with dementia opposite Lev Malnyk's house. I now understand what she told me. The day after the crash she saw people removing a box – Lev's dialysis machine. The man in the mirror. I'm looking at the man in the mirror now. That's you two.' His voice, he knew, sounded slurred. But he had to talk. He had just noticed, in Hubert's right hand, the syringe. Moonlight jumped in the plastic stem like a lanternfish. 'She said something like, "Four people went in and two came out." It was like a crossword clue. She was seeing double. Identical twins.'

'Okay, that's good. So she saw us both.'

'You gave Lev the dialysis machine,' Edward continued, head still spinning, 'because you wanted him to do something in exchange. My guess is that he was supposed to deliver those capsules for you. I just don't know why.'

Kim was trying to speak.

'For God's sake,' he snapped at last, 'let her say what she wants to say!'

There was a pause and then the twins nodded to a figure behind Edward and Kim. Wendy, out of view, put her fingers to the back of Kim's head. She loosened the gag until it hung around Kim's chin like a neckerchief.

'Assisted dying.'

Edward asked, 'What?'

'Wendy started telling me. That's what they were doing.'

'Assisted dying?' Edward's brain spun and he tried to grasp the threads. 'So . . . you were helping people die? With the capsules. You gave people radioactive capsules . . . so they could choose. You believe in choice and you wanted to let people choose when they died.'

The twins nudged each other, with a little smirk. *Look at the clever radio guy.* Edward flexed his fingers against his bonds, impotently furious.

'And Lev delivered the radioactive capsules for you, did he?'

Charlie Hearst said, 'Not for us to confirm or deny, but you have permission to feel the warmth of completeness as you put the story together.'

Smug git.

Hubert added: 'You will have a choice between syringe and cliff in just a moment, so we don't mind you narrating our little history here. We'd quite like to know what you think.'

From behind them, Wendy said: 'We don't have time for this. I'll get you quickly to the end. It began with fine intentions—'

'It still has the *finest!*' cried Charlie Hearst.

'It had, has, the finest intentions,' Wendy agreed. She was still not visible to Edward. 'They see cancer patients and others in the most hideous pain. No doctor is even allowed to administer fatal morphine—'

'The rules are bizarre. We were showing kindness,' said Hubert.

'—meanwhile the government makes promises and does nothing. My friends here found a way of repurposing some of the isotope used in radiography. I didn't follow the science like they do, but it will kill you in a week and leave no trace. The first patient they offered it to had bone cancer. Imagine the pain of the bone of your skull becoming perforated, looking like an Aero bar? He took a dose and was beautifully comatose within three days. No coroner found the cause because the isotope is so unstable it evaporates—'

'Isotopes don't evaporate, but I'll let you have that,' Charlie Hearst told Wendy. 'And that's all we did. Offer a service.

But you see, we needed funds, and so there had to be a charge. And let's leave it there.'

There was a moment of silence. The sea churned its infinite symphony below them.

'It's about money,' said Kim. 'Your husband died because of dirty, filthy money.'

'I need to explain,' said Wendy, still standing behind her.

'By explain you mean justify,' said Hubert.

Edward put in, 'If we're going to die, we should know. I want to know why Wendy killed her husband.'

'I was IN THE CINEMA,' she shouted behind him.

'So who did it?' asked Edward.

'Tell him, Hubert,' said Charlie.

'Why should I? Why does he need to know?'

'Because this is on you, Hubert. You were so efficient and so clever until you decided to remove the crossbow.'

'I told you a hundred times, I cut myself on it. Imagine the forensic trove for the police.'

'You cut yourself on it,' his brother repeated mockingly, as if to increase the humiliation.

Wendy said: 'And that left the mystery, and the suspicion on me, and there we are, Edward and Kim, you have your story.'

'So why did you bring me in?' asked Edward.

'You want to know?'

'Not really. I have a suspicion.'

'I'll explain,' Charlie broke in. 'We don't have time to go around the houses. My brother messed it all up, so the police were never going to go for suicide. The mystery left Wendy under suspicion. And although the police investigation had long since stalled, she just couldn't *bear* to live with the ostracization.' This last was said with such contempt that Edward and Kim both winced.

Behind them, Wendy gave a tut of outrage. 'It wasn't *just* the ostracization, Charlie. It was *everything*. My phone line might as well have been cut. Nobody called. No one said hello. The church group took me off the bloody volunteer email lists, I was oh-so-*very*-politely told not to bother coming back to whist club, and the school basically barred me from doing reading time with the children any more.' Her voice got higher and higher with each perceived insult. 'I was being cold-shouldered in the street. Ignored by former friends. And as for the lunches—'

'Oh my God,' Kim snorted suddenly. '*As for the lunches?* You were so piqued because no one would go for lunch with you any more? And there's me, such a fool, feeling sorry for you, thinking *I* would take you for lunch when all of this was over.' She was laughing now. 'You blew your life up, brought us in and blew this whole thing apart because of *whist and lunches?*' Kim's chair creaked under her as she bent forward, trying to catch her breath through gales of forced laughter, as Edward stared in amazement.

'You fucking *bitch*.' Wendy stormed around to stand beside Kim. 'It wasn't just the lunches – I used to be someone, and now thanks to bloody Hubert and the bloody crossbow, I'm a nobody. A NOBODY! Think how you'd like it if someone took away your flashy Porsche and your bloody business and wouldn't even sit down with you for a fucking sandwich any more – you wouldn't be so smug, you cow.' She gave Kim's chair a hard thrust and it wobbled on two legs before settling back, ending Kim's laughter abruptly.

Charlie stepped forward and warded Wendy away. 'Don't knock her over, Wendy, for God's sake. You've done enough harm with all of this already, she doesn't need some extra bruises before she takes the injection, does she? Go over there and calm down.' He nudged her away, back towards the house. 'Go on, go.' He turned back to Edward and Kim, both now sober once more.

'Ahem. So as you see . . . Wendy had had enough. She needed to find someone completely credulous to clear her name. She had you down as a mug, basically.'

'A mug?'

Kim said, 'Don't,' as if fearful that Edward's growing anger might attract some sort of retribution.

From behind them once more, Wendy said, 'Given that we've arrived here, and you found everything out, you can have the satisfaction of knowing that I was wrong. You are no mug, Mr Temmis.'

She started pulling Kim's gag back into place, but Kim shook her head.

'Wait. Can I just ask why your husband had to die?'

Charlie spoke. 'We work as one. Or we used to. He was going to go to the police. Whistle-blow. We couldn't allow it. Let's get on with it.'

Hubert Hearst stepped forward, syringe in hand once more.

His brother spoke. 'We have a choice for you both, which we thought you might enjoy. You've spent a lot of time following the trail of our Actinium-224, and now it's coming to find you. Safe to hold, lethal to swallow, and horrific for the human body if injected direct into the heart – you can have that. Or you two lovebirds can walk off the cliff, just miss your footing and go down together. It'll be a suicide pact and you'll be spoken of with reverence for—'

'Cut the guff, Charlie,' said Wendy. 'I know nobody can see us here, but I don't want to spin this out. Ask Kim.'

The Hearst twins were still between Edward and the sea. He swallowed. His body was shaking. 'If you inject us, the police will know.'

'Not if we throw you off the cliff,' said Hubert.

'Injection, or walk,' his brother repeated.

'Put the syringe down,' said Kim. 'Put the syringe down and we'll walk.'

'You'll have to untie us,' said Edward.

'You'll go singly,' said Charlie. Edward sensed he was the dominant twin; had he come out of the womb a second before his brother? Charlie Hearst was the brains. He was the business. There was no doubt about it, watching the way the others deferred to him.

'I think I met two of your customers,' said Edward suddenly. 'Les and Lily Boyd. She's in terrible pain. I understand now why she hates me. I stopped her dying. I didn't mean to. But my show meant you couldn't deliver any more ampoules.'

'Oh, don't worry,' said Hubert. 'We'll get back to business pretty soon. I'm sure the Boyds – did you say that was the name? – will be on our list.' Edward gaped. If Hubert didn't recognize the name of his own customers, how many did they have?

'You wouldn't believe how many people we've got paying fifteen grand for a capsule that costs tuppence-halfpenny to manufacture,' Hubert was saying, as if reading Edward's mind.

Charlie shouted: 'Stop running your mouth off!' and suddenly there was an explosion of bright light.

Somewhere in the house, a spotlight had been turned on at a window. The beam wobbled and found the group. Coming from behind Edward, it cast his shadow and Kim's across the two brothers. And then they heard the woman's voice through a megaphone:

'Do not move. This is the police. We are here in numbers. Look down and you will see you are targeted by snipers.'

Sure enough, two red dots danced on the twins' chests.

'Move backwards five paces.'

The twins did that, checking all the time that they were not about to step back over the edge of the cliff. 'Do not move a muscle or you will be shot.' The laser dots moved up their chests to their foreheads.

Edward recognized the voice. If he was wrong, a bullet would be his reward. He lurched up, still tied to the chair. But he could not move his feet because his ankles were tied together, or catch his fall with his bound hands. He fell sideways, smacking his head on the grass. There was a scream and a rush of movement at his feet. He could not see the twins. He saw a flash of Kim in her chair, and then, with a rumble and tremble and rush of noise, the earth began to move.

Kim screamed.

The cries of the Hearst twins echoed off the cliffs as the ground beneath them crumbled and they plunged over the edge.

CHAPTER FORTY-SEVEN

Jordan Callintree arrived before any of his officers. The spotlight Stevie had used was now dangling from the window of the Post-it room, throwing a beam down the side of the house.

Wendy Wrigley was long gone. Callintree had had to scramble the RNLI and a police helicopter to find the Hearsts' bodies, but the darkness – at high tide, at the foot of a sheer rockface – would make the search nigh-on impossible.

'They can't have survived that drop. How do you live here, Edward?'

Normally Edward would have responded with a joke about the sketchy estate agent who sold him the house, but right now he had no brain to form a sentence or voice to shape the words.

'Someone must have moved, the garden went.'

'What do you mean, "the garden went"?'

'I have sensors at the far end to pick up movement. Just cheap ones. Three of them have disappeared. I think I lost a yard of garden. And,' he added quickly, 'very sadly, those two.'

Kim looked at her feet and repeated: 'Sadly, did you say? Hey, I was tied up. I was gagged for a bit. Edward was hit on the head. At the end they must have moved back a little and put too much weight on the most unstable part.'

'How did you not go over yourself, Miss Sinker?'

'By a miracle,' said Edward.

Jordan Callintree asked, 'If they tied you up, who set you free?'

'Stevie did,' Kim murmured. As soon as the brothers had fallen, Wendy had shrieked, and then there'd been the sound of running. Stevie had been down in a flash but Wendy had already disappeared.

'I see,' Jordan said, looking stern. 'And you were stabbed, Ms Sinker?'

'It was Wendy Wrigley who did that.'

Edward said: 'Wrigley and the Hearsts. They're the ones you want.'

'I found a syringe at the end of the garden. I left it.'

'Stay well clear,' said Edward. 'Actinium-224.'

'Good God. Will do.' Callintree breathed in, shaking his head. 'It won't be hard to find Wrigley. Credit to your pal.'

'She took her time,' said Kim.

'Aye, time well spent,' said Stevie, approaching in the dark. 'It wasn't easy, getting the mic into that stereo and moving it to the window without anyone hearing. And then the spotlight—'

'The laser pointers too. Genius.'

'You can give me details later,' said Callintree. He looked up. A helicopter was moving in the distance. 'I hope that's ours.'

'I don't think the twins will have made it,' said Edward.

'I think that's an understatement,' said Jordan Callintree.

Kim started weeping. As Edward held her, he felt tears on his own face as well.

Callintree looked at Stevie. 'I have quite a lot of questions for you, Miss Mason, since you watched all this. Meanwhile, I have to find Wrigley and bring her in. Assisted dying, you say? We are going to need to reopen a lot of inquests. This lot might go down as Sidmouth's first serial killers.'

CHAPTER FORTY-EIGHT

Kim had been taken into hospital for checks and they said she needed forty-eight hours. The police guard at her bed was a novelty. She got back to her flat two days after the violence at Edward's house. Her mother rang as she opened the front door.
'I cleaned it top to toe.'
'Okay, Mum.'
'You can't just go missing.'
'Busy with the police.'
'Are they making progress with anything?'
'Some.'
'One step forwards, two steps back I suppose.' As she heard the phrase, Kim stepped towards the kitchen.
'You didn't use the oven, Mum?'
'Of course I did. There's some chilli on the hob.'
'Wait – you used the oven?'
'Of course I did.'

Heart in mouth, Kim saw the casserole on the hob. God alive, had she cooked the chilli inside the oven? She slowly opened the oven door. The other casserole dish was still there, but she thought she could smell ashes . . .

What does a million quid smell like when it's burnt?

She pulled out the pot. Placed it on the hob. *Please Mum,* she thought, *don't be the person who puts the oven on preheat even if you're just using the stove.* She lifted the lid.

The cash was intact. The smell of ashes was probably just her mum's cooking.

She was so dazed by what had happened in Edward's garden two nights earlier that she could do nothing but stare. She was now certain that those awful customers, Tank and Fire, had lied about their relationship (the slap was the clue) and lied about the source of their money (in a cashless age, who sends a box of banknotes?). The idea that they were both retiring to Devon having made enough to live off for the rest of their lives was crap. They were buying her beautiful penthouse – she really did think of it as hers – to hide the cash they had made with their crimes. Parachute meant drugs. A million pounds from drugs.

Kim knew what she had to do.

CHAPTER FORTY-NINE

The death of the Hearst twins at the bottom of Ladram Bay during what was described as a 'police operation' caught the imagination of the town. Edward's feet had barely touched the ground since the nightmare had played out at his house, and he had been desperate to see Kim. But the police had urged them not to be in touch with each other at all while their statements were taken, as defence barristers would seize on that in court. If there was a court case.

Since that evening, he had rung Kim only twice. Her reply simultaneously confused him and put his mind at rest:

> I'm gonna be a bit private for a few days. I know you'll understand.

It was strange, having the full story and being able to say so little on air. Jordan Callintree had got all the information and begged Edward to give out only the broadest details – not to say, for example, that the Hearst twins had fallen from his own garden or what the circumstances of their final hours were. No one anywhere connected the Hearst deaths with the Toppings crash or the Wrigley murder.

A huge memorial was planned for them in Exeter Cathedral, which made Edward nauseous. Wendy Wrigley was still missing. Edward understood that Jordan needed to be the one to solve it, and they agreed that Jordan would present the solution as a scoop on Edward's show. Aspinall was getting jumpy but Edward no longer cared.

He did his nightly programmes. The calls were on the vandalism of six 'Branscombe in Bloom' flowerbeds and the unlikely proposal to reopen Sidmouth Train Station, which had been closed in the Sixties and was now a tyre-fitting business. 'How can you have a train station without rails?' asked one listener, pointing out that the old railway line to Ottery St Mary and Tipton St John, laid in the 1880s, was now mainly a footpath.

There was only one public development in the pizza parlour case. The council, still considering the whole incident a mystery, proposed renaming a street in the centre of Sidmouth 'Nina Lopez Alley'. They faced a backlash because the cobbled alley in question was not an attractive route. It ran down the side of Boots to the swimming centre car park and smelled when it rained. A middle-aged man rang Edward's show to say, 'We knew our council couldn't run a tap. Now this.'

Edward found himself wondering how the Hearst/Wrigley network had operated. They could not advertise. Their daily work must have connected them with dozens of terminally ill patients. Perhaps Jonathan Wrigley went along with it – until money entered the equation. No wonder that enormous couple, the Boyds, were angry with Edward. Lily, in and out of her wheelchair, always in pain, had been promised release; and then the motorbike accident triggered so many questions that the operation was shelved. The Boyds blamed Edward for all the questions. Fair enough. Poor, lost souls. In a way they were victims of the gang too. And yes, they had definitely stopped him falling from the cliff. The crazed stamping he would have to forgive.

He had only one unanswered question now: why was Jonathan Wrigley in a white suit that day? He imagined his friend Hubert persuading him to walk in the forest, bring the crossbow, kill some rabbits or just use it for target practice. But surely he would not have worn a white suit at Hubert's request? It was an odd thing to go walking in. Yet it helped the Hearsts, because it meant Wrigley was seen from the air and his death timed almost to the minute.

Perhaps at the start Jonathan Wrigley and the Hearsts were motivated by compassion for those poor, hurting people, sick and lonely in big rural houses or rattling around in council flats, aware of their dementia or with tumours fit to burst. Bone cancer, Parkinson's, Motor Neurone Disease, Huntington's. Would this case ever get to court, if Wendy Wrigley was ever found? He imagined the expressions on the faces of twelve jurors being asked to understand what on earth it was the brothers had done with a centrifuge and Actinium from their radiotherapy unit to create the perfect murder weapon: like a disappearing dagger.

He booked himself an appointment at the audiologist to get a new hearing aid.

'What happened to the last one, sir?'

It was stamped on by a man with a New York City cop outfit who thought I'd stopped his wife dying. No, he wouldn't trouble them with that.

'Um, a cat ate it,' Edward lied.

'We can clean it if—'

'No, no thank you. I couldn't do that.' As the hearing tests got underway, he felt a text arrive and hoped it was Kim.

The audiologist, a kind woman called Sandy, said: 'That buzzing might mess up our readings. Do you want to look at the message and start the test again?'

'Could I? It's a friend I've been worried about.'

But it was not Kim. Just Stevie saying, 'Call me.'

'Do you mind?' asked Edward. 'I'm worried it might be urgent.'

The audiologist said, 'My mum and dad listen to your show every night so they'd be very upset if I got in the way.'

He asked Stevie: 'What's up?'

'Kim.'

'What?'

'Have you heard from her?'

'No.'

'I went around,' said Stevie. 'She behaved so weirdly. Sent me away.'

'What? You two are mates!'

'I wondered about trauma.'

'I'm at the hearing aid place. Let me come straight to you after that.'

An hour later, he was at the vicarage. Stevie's parents were out. He called Kim and put the phone on speaker as it rang.

'She won't pick up.'

Just as Stevie said it, Kim answered with a strained 'Hello?'

'A week! That's the longest time we haven't spoken for in recent history.'

'I'm sorry. Feel free to have a go.'

Steve chimed in. 'I'm here too.'

'Hi Stevie.'

'I wouldn't have a go, Kim. You sent me a text and so I knew you hadn't been abducted or, I don't know, exploded.'

'Exploded? Have you had a series of exploding girlfriends?'

'Not in that way, no.'

Stevie laughed. 'We were worried for you. That was traumatic.'

'For you too, Stevie, with your brilliant lasers. But it's not that. And I can't say what it is. I just can't tell you. Not on a phone. Not by text.'

Edward asked, 'In person?'

'Watch your TV in about ten minutes.'
'He's at my house,' said Stevie.
'Put the news on.'

The phone connection beeped and she was gone. Edward made a cup of tea and put the news channel on. It was bang on eleven in the morning. The graphics fired. The volume was low – or was that just the missing hearing aid? – and as Stevie turned it up, a newsreader with large earrings and eyebrows like charcoal strokes fixed her gaze on him and talked about Ukraine. Was this the item? He turned on his phone and noted the stories. Russia accused of moving further into Donbas. Then gambling: two biggest British firms report record profits. Cardiff Council refuses to change 20 mph limits. A London drugs gang smashed, suspects arrested. Mugshots of a thin Asian woman on the left, a well-groomed blond man with a needy expression on the right. Then sport, then weather. Edward and Stevie exchanged mystified glances. Edward texted Kim.

> Didn't see it.

She rang straight back. 'Don't text, okay?'
'But—'
'Don't text, don't ring. Come to mine.'

He took his moped. Stevie sat on the back. He had never had a pillion passenger before, and the bike sounded as if it was about to break in two. In the town centre, Stevie realized she would get prosecuted for not having a helmet and – before the bike collapsed – she got off. She said she had to buy some groceries, which to Edward sounded like an excuse.

At Kim's door, he rang the bell. She opened it with a warm smile. He was struck by her beauty and how much he had missed her, even just for this week. She stood in jeans and a bright white shirt, straightening her back as if she was trying to be as tall as him when she reached up to kiss him.

'If you're being held hostage,' he whispered, 'whisper the name of your favourite flavour crisps.'

'Cheese and onion.'

He affected the air of a man suddenly relaxing, mock-wiping his brow. 'Phew.'

'Where is Stevie?'

'In town. I tried to get her here but the bike wouldn't take it.'

'Our heroine. Our little crimefighter.'

'Oh yes,' said Edward. He made to move through the doorway, but Kim blocked him. She threw her arms around Edward and held her body up against his. She whispered, 'Don't speak too loudly. I'm not joking. Discreet please.' She detached herself and brought him inside.

'Did you see the news?' she whispered.

'Why are we speaking so quietly? I have trouble hearing.'

'I've done something I don't want anyone to know about. Did you see the news?'

'Yes I did.' He reached for his phone. 'I noted down the items.' His voice kept adjusting to its normal level; he kept lowering it again. 'Russia, gambling, speeding, drugs. Did I miss one?'

'Oh, I'm forgetting. You were under the car.'

Edward peered at Kim. She led him to her bedroom. He felt his heart beat a little quicker as if he was a teenager again. But it was not the double bed they were heading for. They passed it and she opened the French windows. 'Toss your phone like me.' She threw hers onto the bed cover. He did the same. 'I never know what they pick up.'

'Bloody hell,' he said, 'I feel like I'm presenting a radio programme where the headphones don't work. I can't understand what you're doing.'

'The drugs story. The couple.' The French windows led onto the tiniest of balconies, and she was leaning as far out as she could, her face close to his.

'Yes?'

'You didn't see their faces. You only saw their feet.'

It was starting to dawn on him. On the bed, her phone started to vibrate.

'You want to take that?'

'It's my mum.'

'How do you know?'

'You'll find out.'

'So your customers have been arrested?'

'Arrested two days ago, I think, and now charged.'

He looked at her, wondering if he was beginning to understand.

'Do you remember what you heard her say?'

'Something about parachutes.'

'And parachute is slang for . . .' She moved in so close to him that her lips touched his ear and he felt her breath as the wind. 'Crystal meth.'

'Crys—' She placed a forefinger across his lips. 'How did the police get them?'

'I wonder,' she asked. They withdrew back into the bedroom. She locked the French windows. 'I'll leave you thinking about that. Not another word, please.'

'Your mum's calling again.'

'She's calling you now, look.'

Their phones had gradually slid closer to each other on the duvet, and Kim was right. It was now Edward's phone that was flashing with Barbara's name. He moved to pick it up, then looked at Kim to check. But she made no objection.

'Hello?'

'Edward? I'm so sorry to call. You know I don't make a habit of it. I should probably call more often, ha. Look. I can't find Kimb—'

Kim took the phone, waved an apologetic hand to Edward, and said: 'I'm here Mum. What's happened?' She pressed the speaker button and the reply came out.

'Something strange.'

'Go on, tell me.'

'I've been sworn to secrecy.'

'Who swore you?' Kim asked.

'It's an anonymous note on the WhatsApp and it went to everybody. We don't know what to do.'

'Don't tell me about it, Mum.'

'Why not?'

'Just best to do what it says.'

'But you don't know what it says, darling.'

Edward was frowning.

'Gotta go, Mum. I guess best to keep it secret, eh?'

Edward opened his mouth to speak, but Kim stepped back slightly and held up her hand like a traffic warden. What on earth was going on?

At the other end of the line, Barbara began: 'It just says—'

Kim cut her off. 'Don't tell me what it says.'

'You think I should do it?'

'I think you should do it.'

She hit the red button. 'Sorry,' Kim said to Edward, 'I forgot it was yours.'

'I feel like I've gone through to another dimension. Something tells me your crystal meth couple are connected to that call from your mum. Am I getting warm?'

'It's best we don't talk about it in here. I'm just superconscious of not being involved with any of this.'

'Any of what? God, this is like doing *The Times* crossword upside-down.'

'I love you by the way. I'm sorry I went missing.'

'You were in hospital, partly.' A thought struck Edward. 'I wonder if that couple were arrested after a tip-off of some sort.' He looked at Kim piercingly, the faintest smile playing around his lips. 'A tip-off from an anonymous source, who is simultaneously exotic and practical.'

'Rules me out,' said Kim.

'By the way, the news on the pizza place – it'll be out soon.'

'So long as I'm not in it.'

'I think they have a plan to keep us out of it.'

'I keep listening, thinking you're going to reveal it on the radio.'

'Jordan and I did a deal. Nothing until he makes arrests, and then everything goes to me first.'

'What does Aspinall say about that? I bet he's thrilled.'

'He's angry at having to wait for something he can't be told about. He's always angry.'

'Is he still going to sack you?'

'Hope not.'

'Bloody hell,' she said, 'that really would be the icing on the cake.' Her eyes widened.

He forgot to tell the story. He was suddenly swimming in those pools of green, the smashed-gem green of her eyes, and he saw her lips part. 'Where did you go to, my lovely?' he said.

'Secret places,' she told him as he removed the belt from her jeans.

CHAPTER FIFTY

When Barbara arrived at Harpford Hall, the door was jammed. From inside, the voice of an older man barked: 'First name, surname.' She replied, 'Barbara Sinker.' He asked for her mobile number and she felt pleased with herself for remembering it.

The door cracked open. She slid through the gap and into the village hall. The last time she had been there was for that crazy presenters' meeting. Now she looked around. Even in daytime the place was gloomy, and she went to turn the lights on.

'So,' said the man. It was the red-sweater pensioner with the long neck who had shouted at Edward. Trust him to get there first. 'We've found it. It's real. I'm in charge. How much was your loss?'

Barbara was too embarrassed to say the real figure, so she went in lower. 'Thirty thousand. Thirty-two thousand,' she added, feeling the precision would make it more believable.

'I remember you from that meeting with Temmis,' said the long-necked man. 'I wonder if he knows about this.'

'I don't know what you mean by "this", I haven't a clue what's going on.'

He drew closer. The sweater looked newly washed and the red was almost fluorescent. Barbara could smell his breath.

'You won't talk?'

'No,' said Barbara.

'Not to son or daughter?'

'I only have a daughter. I'll keep shtum.'

'Someone left our compensation in a box here.' There was more knocking at the door. He went towards it, but said over his shoulder. 'There was even a note saying how we should divvy it up.'

He pointed at the hole in the front of the stage and Barbara realized there was a person in there. As she approached, a hand shot out.

'Count them.'

'Is this for me?'

'Yes. I heard you say thirty-two? We have enough for everyone.'

'It was forty-three, actually. I hate to say it out loud.'

There was a pause. Was this anonymous man angry with her? She peered into the space under the stage.

'What did the note say?'

A face appeared. He had the same rounded jaw as Red Sweater; his son, perhaps?

'Who's asking?'

'Barbara Sinker. I'm on the victims' WhatsApp group.'

As he manoeuvred himself in the crawl space, she caught sight of the hoard. Piles of twenties and fifties, arranged in a line, like tower blocks on a main road, stretching back into the shadows.

The man lifted a sheet of A4 paper and read. 'This money is donated to the victims of the scammer at the radio station, so each can have what they're owed. The rest to be donated anonymously to the station itself.'

'Oh goodness.' Barbara was nonplussed. Then: 'Does it have my amount on there?'

He checked the list. 'Sinker, yes, forty-three.' He handed her another pile and a reusable Sainsbury's bag. 'Here you go.

I think you should go now. We don't want this getting out. No reference on the WhatsApp group please.'

'I saw the message was deleted.'

'Went after an hour. Dad screenshotted it. We got here first. You're the . . .' He paused. 'The twelfth, I think.'

'I hope no one gets missed out.'

'We'll do our best.' Again, the hint of impatience.

The door to the hall opened again. The long-necked man was challenging everyone, it seemed.

'I hope we're not breaking the law if we take money like this.'

'There's a law against "theft by finding", but you can't steal a gift, can you? No one lost this, they gave it.'

'I suppose so,' said Barbara uncertainly. She moved away, pushing the notes deeper into her tote bag. Forty-three thousand pounds in cash . . . she felt very, very nervous. Would she keep it at home? She could make it last for years. She would store it in a vase. She knew which one.

Barbara straightened up. Suddenly, today was looking like a very good day indeed.

CHAPTER FIFTY-ONE

A month after the scene in his garden, Edward Temmis went on air with Jordan Callintree sitting opposite him in the studio.

Wendy Wrigley had been picked up in Scotland. She was facing a second investigation for her role in the death of her husband. But Devon Police were now making progress 'at pace' in the Toppings case.

'So Acting Chief Constable Callintree, what can you tell our listeners about that?'

'We believe lethal ampoules were being delivered to addresses around Devon to people desperate to end their lives. They were being charged more than ten thousand pounds to receive a single delivery. It is likely that Lev Malnyk had no idea what he was carrying or how dangerous it was.'

'Who was behind this?' asked Edward, the next in his list of agreed questions.

'Ms Wrigley is a key suspect. But there were also the twins who died in Ladram Bay – they were the link with Mr Malnyk, the motorbike rider, whom Hubert Hearst first met when Malnyk needed treatment for a long-standing kidney condition.'

'Has Wendy Wrigley been charged?'

'She has been charged with being an accomplice in the shooting of her husband. At the moment we are working on a file for the Crown Prosecution Service in the other matter.'

'Thank you for your time, Acting Chief Constable Callintree.'

Edward played some adverts. The two men stood up and shook hands.

'I can't thank you enough,' said Jordan Callintree. 'I seem to have a chance at the top job now.'

'You'll be brilliant at it.'

'But I'm going to say no,' said the young cop. 'I'd rather be investigating. I don't want to have to leave it to you three.'

Edward looked left towards the control room. Aspinall was standing, beaming, and started clapping when their eyes met.

Jordan Callintree said to Edward, 'One last thing. You were asking about the white suit. How would you get a guy to put a white suit on to go on a walk? I found this. Sad, really. Cheers, Edward.' He handed over a magazine cutting and turned for the studio door.

The article was scissored from an edition of *GP Quarterly*, printed eight years ago.

Underneath a photo of a young, fit-looking man in a bright white suit was a caption: DR JONATHAN WRIGLEY MOVES TO DEVON FOR QUALITY OF LIFE.

The text quoted him. 'Once a year I wear this suit in memory of my mum. She died giving birth to me, and it's what brought me into medicine. I wear white because she's with the angels.'

So there was no Huntington's in the family. And they had killed him on an anniversary of his mother's death. Perhaps they had even planned it that way.

His stomach churned: if he and Kim had gone over the cliff at the end of his garden, no one would ever have found out the truth of the Toppings crash at all. Much less the death of Dr Wrigley.

Oh, but they would, he realized, correcting himself. Stevie would have heard it all. Stevie would have been the witness.

He could not sleuth without Kim. Neither would have lived without Stevie. They would stand or fall as three.

And now he was certain.

They would investigate again.

ACKNOWLEDGEMENTS

Two brilliant scientists helped me with the nuclear end of this. Dr David Tsang (Dept of Physics, Bath University) and Dr Timothy Gregory (senior nuclear chemist at the National Nuclear Laboratory in Sellafield) were so kind with their time, giving me incredible amounts of information about the way certain radioactive substances degrade and the harm they can cause. In the end, their science gave way to a degree of fictionalising by me; if you're an expert and you want to object to any of the radiation in this story, please come to me, not David or Tim!

My two great writing workmates are Kerr MacRae, my book agent, and Martha Ashby, my publisher at HarperCollins who first gave me the idea to have a murder in Sidmouth (and then another, and then another . . .). I love the location because Rachel and I took our daughters there every summer for years. I have especial devotion to the Clock Tower Café and would like to thank Suzy, Lewis and all the crew for supporting my first, *Murder on Line One*, with such great humour. And cake.

HarperCollins have an outstanding team. Their marketeers are the supreme Vicky Joss and Alexandra Sequeira; the best PR person in London is Elizabeth Dawson; Holly Martin is always super-encouraging in the Sales dept and above all hilarious at work parties; my thanks to her colleagues Harriet Williams and Ruth Burrows for their hard work too.

Then there's H360 – Jean Marie Kelly. Design – Megan Smith. Editorial is Renée Lewis alongside the Queen Ashby. Copyeditor – the brilliantly-named Pen Isaac (I still need to find the keyboard shortcut for the en-dash, Pen). Proofreader – Rhian McKay. Audio – Fionnuala Barrett (we have such fun). Production – Deborah Wilton.

The new MD of Harper is Frankie Gray and it's great to be on her squad.

Oh: Libby Haddock is the best PR organiser in the world. If she books a train, it runs.

Sometimes someone reads your manuscript and it spurs you on. The first to read mine was my ITN colleague, Jenny Line. Her unbridled enthusiasm gave me so much energy. Thank you, Jenny!

I think I mentioned our Sidmouth family holidays, but of course this comes with thanks to my wife and daughters, Rachel, Martha and Anna, who have every right to think I'm an idiot but only ever say so when it's absolutely necessary. Love you.

This book is also for all the writers I've met while talking about Edward, Kim and Stevie at book festivals around the country. People like Lisa Jewell, Kelly Mullen, Cally Taylor, Vaseem Khan, Jane Casey, Tim Sullivan, Abir Mukherjee, Clare Mackintosh, AJ West. That's not even half the people I should name who inspired me to keep going and write something every day. They've all taught me something. Crime writers are a fabulous gang.

Lastly, my sincere thanks to you, especially if you've bought this because you enjoyed my first book. When I meet my readers I love the connection. Come and say hi.

If you enjoyed *Turn the Dial for Death*, you'll love the first book in Jeremy Vine's Sidmouth Murder Mysteries series, *Murder on Line One*.

Read on for an extract from the *Sunday Times* bestseller . . .

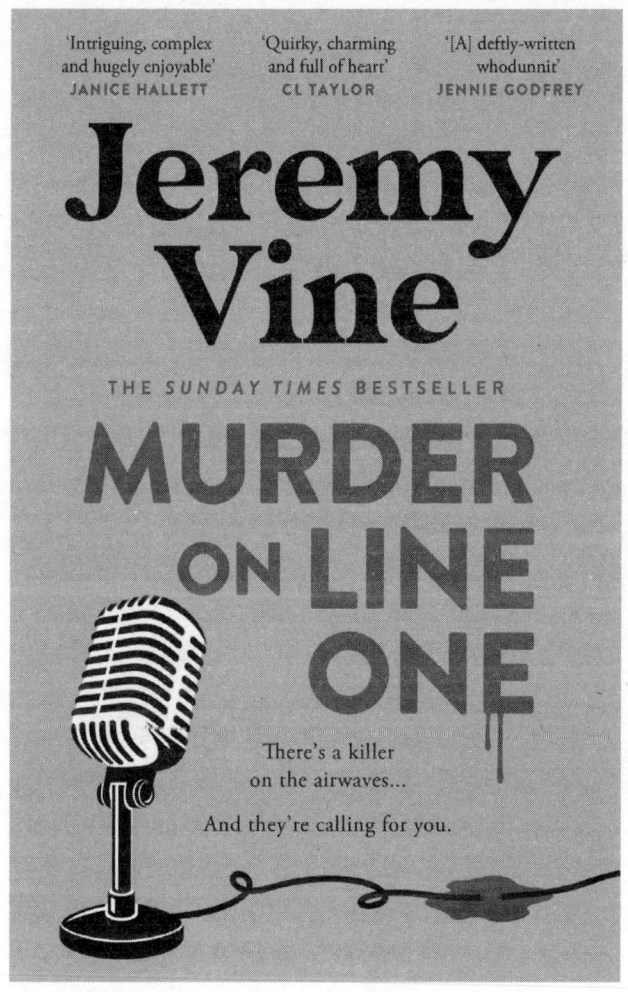

CHAPTER ONE

He could smell the lad. Smell his son on the field as he approached. The unquenchable, restless love of the parent, scanning the air like radar. The lion's nose – the wind always told you where your cub was. The February cold stung his cheeks as a slap would. In the distance he heard the teams shouting 'Pass! Here!' and strained for Matty's voice.

He could not wait to reach the touchline and call out his support. The mist rose from his mouth as thick as vaped cinnamon. Approaching the other parents, he felt a sudden cough leap in his chest and stifled it, hugging his overcoat. A cough at this moment might have sounded deliberate, a way of ensuring they turned and greeted him. He would rather be alone.

The sports field was on Pinn Lane, a former wheatfield halfway between the school in Cubitt St Clare and the coast at Sidmouth. The seaside was a four-mile drive from the school; the boys must have been disappointed when the coach stopped halfway, after the sharp left which put the River Otter behind them. A sign read SCHOOL SPORTS PRIVATE, suggesting a world shortage of colons. On the field, the occasional lopsided bounce of the football was a reminder of furrows here in years gone by, a memory of wheat grown. Some sheaves still sprouted behind the goalposts; once a wheatfield, always a wheatfield.

Edward Temmis hated that the kids did the trip from Cubitt by minibus even on the hottest summer days, all those youngsters seat-belted and cooped up behind toughened glass, but he guessed it was school insurance that made the protection of a vehicle necessary. Perhaps that could be an item for the show one day.

Avoiding the home supporters – the gaggle of parents on the far touchline who knew him – meant lifting his knees high to cut through the long grass and brambles at the back of the pavilion, which still showed the last cricket score of summer.

This was one of those days when you could not imagine going without an overcoat, much less wearing sunglasses or hearing the thwack of a cricket bat. He admired the boys for coming out in shorts on a day like this. They were twelve; some were thirteen already. At eleven, Matty was the youngest by a year. He admired his son for staying with the team; his boy was the best player by a country mile. No gloves on the pitch – which was, quite literally, 'old school'.

The shouting got louder. He felt the damp from the unkempt grass reach his shins, and cursed a bramble that caught the end of his trouser leg. No one heard his expletives. He could have been invisible.

Emerging from behind the pavilion, incognito, safely away from the other parents, he made for the left touchline and chose a spot where any action in the midfield would stop him being seen by the mothers and fathers on the line opposite. He began shouting for the team. Stupidly he had left the fixture list at home and had a sudden panic about where the visiting players had come from. This was the Devon and Cornwall Schools' League. Cubitt St Clare Boys were mid-table, punching above their weight, not least because of a couple of crackers Matty had scored from midfield. Matty's mother would have loved to hear about that.

An observer might have wondered about this tall, heavyset dad with a whiskery growth of beard and dark hair curling beyond his collar who joined the visiting team's parents and, rocking backwards and forwards in those big shoes, shouted for his child. They might have noticed the hearing aid when he reached behind his left ear once or twice. A boys' football game was not the sort where fans of opposing teams had to be kept separate, but the way he called his son's name and urged him to 'pass, Matty, double back, that's it!' or 'watch for the long ball, just run, it'll find you!' was a little hard on the ears. The parents around him – the away fans, visiting from Dittisham, he now remembered, forty-five miles distant – shot each other glances.

'Nice to have you with us,' said one of the mums eventually, as if she was the one the others insisted should speak. The woman was much shorter than Edward, with a smart, pea-green coat and matching driving gloves. He wondered if Dittisham was a private school.

'What's the score?' he asked. 'I was late.'

With that he adjusted the hearing aid. She might have thought he was trying to hear the answer, but Edward was actually trying to turn the world down. He was just here to shout for Matty. The woman turned and contemplated him. The calling of the boys on the pitch quietened, momentarily, for a throw-in. 'I know your voice,' she said. After a pause, as if she had tried and failed to place it, she turned to another woman next to her. 'The score, Chloe?'

'There isn't one,' said the woman. She was dressed all in muddy green, taller and altogether more imposing than her friend. Her jeans were streaked with oil. She kept her eyes on the pitch, as if refusing to be interested in the stranger.

Sensing that the two women desired some sort of acknowledgement, he wanted to say his name: 'I'm Edward Temmis,

Matty's father. Matty plays for Cubitt's.' He could have added in a raised voice, 'I don't have to explain why I didn't stand on the home line.' He was on the wrong side of the pitch because he did not want to stand with the parents from Matty's school, and there were good reasons for that, reasons he did not want to explain. So Edward sank into his overcoat, screwing up his eyes to find his son as he stared at the mob of boys around the ball.

There was a Dittisham lad who broke clear on the other side at that moment, trapping a loose ball that had been headed by one of the Cubitt's boys and, left toe killing the energy in the ball for a second, turned his body and completed a back-heeled pass to one of his team members.

'I know it now,' said the woman beside him. She tried again. 'I realize where I know your voice from.' Instead of turning to her left, where Edward stood, she angled her body right and spoke to the friend in the oil-encrusted jeans. 'The radio.'

That would have been the end of the conversation, which Edward had barely heard and had no desire to continue, except that the second taller woman suddenly said loudly, 'Oh! I know it too. I know it now. Oh goodness. Excuse me, Cheryl.'

And, while he focused on the pitch, she turned and walked off purposefully.

'I don't know what's got into her,' said Cheryl.

'Your friend?' he asked, sounding uninterested. He touched the hearing aid, realizing he was not going to be allowed to tune them out.

'We're Chloe and Cheryl,' said the shorter woman. 'So we sound like something halfway between a CBeebies cartoon and a porn movie.' She giggled at her joke, which he thought she must have made a dozen times before. He hadn't expected the words 'porn movie' from a woman in an immaculate coat with gold buttons, but his laughter caught in his throat and the cough he had stifled ten minutes ago emerged.

To counter it he raised his voice, spluttering: 'Matty! Matty! Pass here! East–west! This side! Now! Now!'

He had been too loud.

Something happened beside him, a fractal shift in the way the light curved. Cheryl shifted her weight from one foot to another and said softly, 'But aren't you . . .? Didn't you . . .? No, that can't be.'

The Dittisham boys had the ball again. They played in a mauve and white stripe. A fair-haired lad, about the same age as Matty but bigger and bulkier than Edward's son, tore down the left, and for a moment Edward worried that Matty would try to intercept him and get trampled. But he shouted anyway, 'Get over here, Matty!'

And then he felt the hand on his forearm.

'Oh, Edward,' said Cheryl. The tone was as far away as it was possible to be from her brisk and rather remote greeting not five minutes earlier. When he looked down at the woman, he could not take his eyes away from a dash of scarlet lipstick that had moved from her upper lip to one of her front teeth. It made him think of blood.

'Oh, Edward,' she said again, and he saw that she was crying. Her make-up ran. Her grip tightened.

At that point he could have hugged her and cried his eyes out, for reasons both of them would understand without speaking another word. But no, he was here to support his son and would not be distracted. A Dittisham beanpole with red hair brought the ball down. That must have been Matty who tackled him.

As he turned back to the pitch, his pride overcame him. Again and again, louder and louder, he called for Matty to pass it, bury it, lob it, lift it . . . *'Just walk it through to the goal!'*

Now he turned his hearing aid fully down so that, at least on his left side, there was no return path and no one could interrupt him with a clumsy question or the conversation he knew was coming. But he could no longer avoid the way the mums and dads on the opposite side of the pitch were huddled around Chloe, the denim-clad woman who must have walked two hundred yards of touchline to reach a group of perfect strangers.

He pulled his arm away from Cheryl by taking a step to the left. He was supporting Matty. That's what he was here for. He would not let Chloe or Cheryl or Clare or Carole or Chris or Clive or whoever these people were . . . No, he would not let them stop him. They had no right. He was here for his darling eleven-year-old, his Matty, who was so good at everything, so loving towards his father, so promising, so bright. And such a goal-scorer! Hey, was that him now, through on goal?

He grew hoarse as he called his son's name. But strangely, each time Edward shouted, his words seemed to stop a player on the pitch. One at a time, they halted their runs. They said something to each other. The ball went out of play and no one went to fetch it. Some of them stared at him. Two hugged each other.

Cheryl, the lady he had met less than half an hour before, put her arm around him and held him close. This time he did not resist. Chloe was walking back with some of the Cubitt's parents, at first hugging the touchline and then, with play apparently suspended, cutting across the pitch itself.

'What's happened?' he asked, the question directed at his shoes as the new arrivals gathered around him.

Cheryl pinched her nose. Her eyes narrowed. He turned on his hearing aid and it whistled.

'Lovely man, it doesn't help you if I mince my words.' She inhaled the winter air deeply, like a chain smoker drawing on her first cigarette after a long-haul flight. 'I am a business coach. Honesty is at the heart of what I do.'

Then she uttered three quick sentences.

'Edward, your son is not here. He is not on the pitch. Edward, your son is dead.'

'An intriguing, complex and hugely enjoyable small-town whodunnit, with vivid characters and a sophisticated plot'
Janice Hallett, *The Examiner*

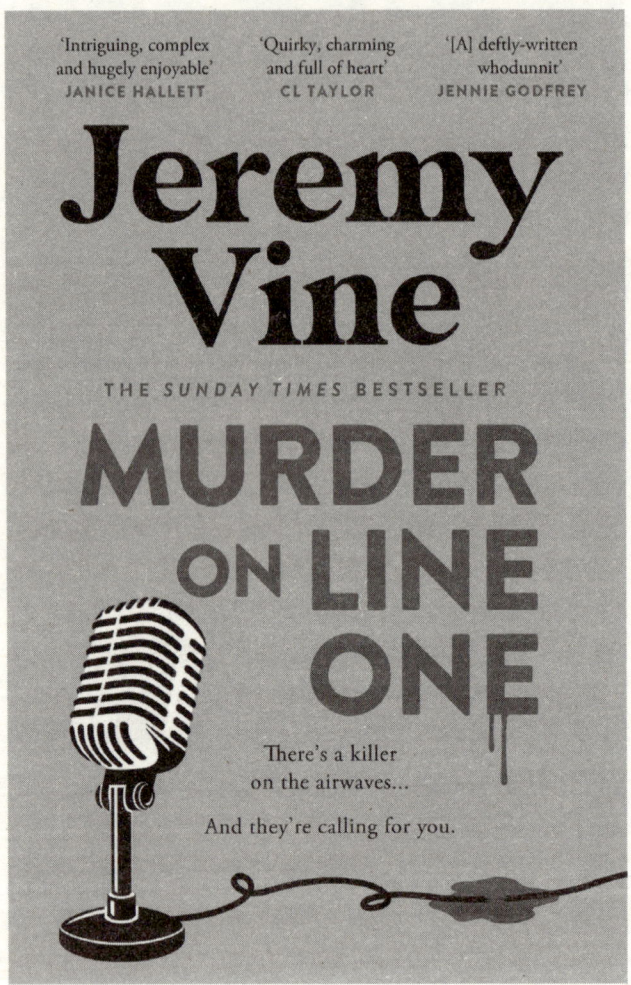

Murder on Line One is available now in paperback.